Luke Smitherd is a former musician time writer. He has had various jo stints as a radio copywriter, an u vacuum cleaner salesman (for four vacuum cleaner out of the box) dancer, during which he fell over and then smashed his legs into the podium railing trying to get up 'stylishly'. He is currently travelling all over the place while writing and can barely believe his luck.

ISBN-13: 978-1499399080
ISBN-10: 1499399081

First Published Worldwide 2014
Copyright © Luke Smitherd 2014

All rights reserved. No part of this publication may be reproduced, stored in a retrieval system or transmitted, in any form or by any means, without the prior written permission of the author, nor be otherwise circulated in any form of binding or cover other than that in which it is published and without a similar condition being imposed on the purchaser.

All characters in this publication are purely fictitious, and any resemblance to real people, living or dead, is purely coincidental.
Proofreading by www.novelproofreading.com

Books By Luke Smitherd:

Full-Length Novels:
The Physics Of The Dead
The Stone Man
A Head Full Of Knives

Novellas:
The Man On Table Ten

Serial Novellas:
The Black Room, Part One: In The Black Room
The Black Room, Part Two: The Woman In The Night
The Black Room, Part Three: The Other Places
The Black Room, Part Four: The End

Print Editions
The Stone Man
A Head Full Of Knives
In The Darkness, That's Where I'll Know You: The Complete Black Room Story

For an up-to-date list of Luke Smitherd's other books, his blog, YouTube clips and more—as well as to sign up for the Spam-Free Book Release Newsletter—visit www.lukesmitherd.com

Acknowledgements

Firstly, as ever, thanks to the wonderful Angela Barron for reading all of the initial draft parts as they were produced, and for her helpful comments and insights. Love you, kid.

Secondly, a BIG thankyou to Michelle McDonald for all of her very selfless and continuous social media help. Absolute superstar; it won't be forgotten. And thirdly, the people who went above and beyond by sending a kind financial donation to the cause. One word: WOW. That really is going the extra mile. Special thanks to Renee gaylor, Mark Venezky, Sherry Diehr, and Neil Charlton; your money helped pay to proofread this book!

And as ever, here's to the rest of you, the ones that took the time to leave a four-star-or-above review for The Black Room books by the time that *this* book was published. Now, there's a lot of you (Woo!) and some of you even left a review for each one (that's the stuff!) so it's entirely possible that your name might appear here twice. I'm sure that you won't mind if that happens though, right? ☺ By the way, any name in capitals are written that way purely because that's how they were written on Amazon

So big thanks to:

BigDog, Katrina, R. Gaylor, Barbara "In Honor Of Books", Brennan Johnson, Angela B, drac, Kelli Tristan, Jrussell424, Jazzy J, Amazon Customer (there's a lot of you called Amazon Customer, so change your names so I can give you a proper shout out! :-D), Pooly4, Matthew Smith, Daniel J Smith, Neil Novita, Mark D, Amazon Customer "reading addict" (see? That kind of thing will do ☺) John Steele, Michelle Kennedy, venfam, John Hurell, Terry M, J. Plock "painter", Christopher Roberts, Big Mike, Matty G, Daniel, Jeff, Joann Gardner, Marta M. Rawlings "Seans Mom", Kelly Jobes, L. Spaiser, Jacque Ledoux, Cynthia P, Kris Hinson "kmommy", Rocky, Jean, Susan C, Swebby, infrequent, mjoanne, EPadgett, Az, Tina Marie, Rogue, Beam, Urbananchorite, KC "KC", Steve Mattingly, wjmouse, Forever Amber "Irene", Leslie Young "Fuzzette", Pamela Williams, BSM, Tessa, Alastair Norcross, MT, TEChan, Susan McReynolds, Andrew Hatton-Ward, Sean Welch, Jennifer DeFiore, Lori Pleasure, Gail, Patty M, Blanchepadgett, Kindle Customer, Gary Johnayak, steve wucherer, Laura Lee, Allison, Brain Johnson, Don, Susan Baldwin, ck, Joslyn, Lady Andrea R, Kathy Heil, Kristi L. Smiley, JEFF PLETZKE, Ryan, MT, drake andross, Beam, Rogue, Iacwaron (possibly Lacwaron?), Jean, C.S. Wolfe, Melissa Quimby, Xraygirl81, Roger P. Halligan, Cinderrific, Sandra Drozda, William B. White, Patti LaValley, RJWREADER, Kate Kaplan "katekap", Daisy, BoneyD, Guy Beauchamp, D. Maccauley "Don", Russell Jones, Scrooby1, ChezIsMe, futureboy "Ian", Stacey Lewis, Pauline R, Jonesy2208 "jonesyuk", Dolittle666, C.S,. Wolfe, PaulineHB, Karenr, Andy P, Chaz Bronte "CHAZZA",

Maria Hale "Lucy", Emma Hopewell, Lyndsey, ossygobbin, Styubud, Brian J. Poole, Hazel Clifton, Ian Henry, simon lyon, Karl Smith, D. Medleycott, Christine Chapman "Chris", Dr. Andrew R. Glover, pandachris "pandachris", simon211175, Julian, o c ideson, Tracey, Bootaholic, Suzanne Foster, fergus67, Jonathan, P W R Wilcox, Mrs Jane McRobbie, infrequent, Deborah, Mr S. D. MacMaster, Victoria Willett, Mrs R K Lees, Jonnieboy, Allybally, Marmite, Tony Nichol, David, Kevin Gaskell, IJT, N. Hamblin "NH", Nicola c, Jam, Sue Phillips, Mrs Kindle, D. Plank, P. Fitt, john woodhouse, Trueblue "S. Row", Miss Frances Ashton, ALEX MARSDEN, Jacox, Celestine, Saul, Daniel Selby, P. Hughes "Pete H", Rebecca Sloane, Heather Art, Fingertrip, Shelly, Lesley Hattersley, Gordon Draper, Tia Claire 28, T. Selkirk, L. Miller, Chris Stothard, Miss Baldwin, Steve Gatehouse, Bloomers, Scott Sanders, Mark Pad, J. D. Wittering "lovealbatross", I. D. Ball "fastbutdim", Joan Campbell, B. Hawthorn, Danny P, Sharon22, InFESTation, get28, R.C. Mansfield, Steve Pettifer, The Fro, Neil Harris, karlos the jackel, Amazon Customer "UrchinGirl", Barry Causier, SARooke, jim stirling, VAN, Maria Hale "Lucy", MRS K. DYE, Chazwin "Chazwin", M. Burgess "StumpyBunker", Andy P, Danny P, Katie, Huwbat, Silversmith, Odette, wayne, Celestine, Zoe Reed, Benno, David Lambourne, Mr Ken B, Piskiechick, david barton, Taratiger, Colin Kebbell, Aingeal, Rowie, lgmichael, Becca, Mounty, Paul, Miss Baldwin, tazaxel, and L. Miller.

You guys made all the difference.

For Jeff and Lynne, who inspired this book.
Jeff, you get a new rope, and Lynne, all you ever want is a belly rub. I have plenty of those.

A Head Full Of Knives

By Luke Smitherd

We must all obey the great law of change. It is the most powerful law of nature, and the means perhaps of its conservation.
—Edmund Burke

We tremble with the violence of the conflict within us, — of the definite with the indefinite — of the substance with the shadow. But, if the contest have proceeded thus far, it is the shadow which prevails, — we struggle in vain. The clock strikes, and is the knell of our welfare.
—Edgar Allen Poe

Faust complained about having two souls in his breast, but I harbor a whole crowd of them and they quarrel. It is like being in a republic.
—Otto von Bismarck

Nothing is born into this world without labor.
—Rob Liano

Walk into a local pub and buy somebody a drink, they say I'm being flash. And if I walk in there and say hello and don't buy 'em a drink, they say I'm being tight. You can't win.
—Five time darts world champion Eric Bristow

*I must have had a million damn unlucky days
But there ain't no cloud that a bottle can't chase away.*
—Del Amitri, *Some Other Sucker's Parade*

Part One: "While They Are Saying, 'Peace and Safety!'"

Prologue
***

When the world began its biggest change, it started at the house of Duncan and Molly Nash.

It hadn't been theirs long, either; married two years before, they'd only recently scrimped enough for the vast deposit required through long, sweaty hours in an industrial printing warehouse (for him) and tense days filled with workplace politics at a marketing firm (for her, which had brought in the lion's share). The place had been worth it, though. Situated in exactly the right kind of new-money neighbourhood, the mock-Tudor house was big, imposing, and way outside of their actual means, topped off large with gardens front and back that cemented the illusion of opulent wealth. Both considered it to be their dream house, and it more than fulfilled their secret, undisclosed goals of showing the people they'd grown up with just how far they'd come. *It's for the kids,* they'd say, when they felt they had to justify it ... but they'd add a simpering little laugh so that people knew they were only half joking.

Not that there *were* any kids yet, and neither of them felt any need to change that status quo. In fact, Molly was pondering that exact same issue as she pulled up on the gravel drive in her glistening black Audi TT, and coming to the same conclusion yet again: life was just suiting them far too well right now. *At least another year*, she idly thought. She plucked her mobile out of its holder on the leather-effect dashboard, checked it for the umpteenth time, and then dropped it into her fake Gucci handbag as she stepped out of the car and headed for the house. Negotiating the deep gravel driveway in her heels was always difficult, but she was getting used to it. At least it had been dark out when she'd actually fallen over that one time.

"*Duuunc,*" she called, opening the front door and listening for movement from the living room, "come and give me a hand, will you? Sainsbury's was a *nightmare,* I've never seen it so busy outside of Christmas. Local mouth-breathing morons taking all day to choose between tins of *beans,* for God's sake." She bent down to fuss their dog—a permanently distressed-looking Pug called Sandy—who had trotted over with her stub of a tail frantically wagging at Molly's arrival. As ever, Sandy's breath came out in broken-sounding rasps when excited, accompanied by the odd high-pitched whimper of delight. Duncan called her the ugliest thing on the planet. Molly called her *darling*.

"Dunc?" Molly repeated, grinning as Sandy flopped onto her back with her chin held out, as if she were summoning her own personal belly-rubbing slave. "Come on, you lazy sod, that took me two hours. The least you can do is help me get it in from the bloody *car*." There was still no answer, but Molly was only half listening anyway, chuckling at Sandy's paws wiggling spastically in the air as she received the attention she permanently craved. After a moment or two, however, Molly remembered her husband's silence and stood up with a sigh, noting once again the distinct lack of immediate assistance from her other half. As she crossed the hallway and headed towards the lounge, she suddenly remembered all the other times he—

Molly stopped dead as she entered the room, mildly shocked at what she saw. Duncan was standing by the patio doors, as still as the grave, looking out through the glass with his hands clasped together behind his back. Thrown into silhouette by the grey winter light from outside, his large rugby player's frame looked unusually so, as if whatever he was watching had made him swell slightly. Molly could hear that he was breathing steadily and deeply, but despite the heavy-sounding inhalations coming from her husband, she still saw no movement in his body. Ordinarily, she would have asked what he was doing without a thought, assuming that he'd spotted an interesting bird actually using the ornamental birdbath, or that he'd caught his arch nemesis—next door's cat—taking another tiny shit in the rhododendrons. But there was something unusual here that made her pause, something different about the situation. It wasn't that the TV was off, she would later think, meaning that his attention hadn't been caught during a programme, nor was it that the stereo wasn't on (if he was in the living room and not watching TV then he would be reading *What Car?* to the sounds of his Ibiza Chillout CD) ... so what was it? The stillness? The complete lack of movement in his body? That was all a part of it, certainly, but this ... this was something else. She just couldn't say *what*. Concerned now, she found her voice.

"Dunc?" she asked quietly, stepping gingerly into the thickly carpeted room, slightly self-aware and embarrassed at her own inexplicable concern. She actually jumped slightly as his head snapped around quickly to face her, whiplike, at the sound of her voice. His eyes were wide, and they looked her up and down, as if he were scanning her for something. Molly's hand went unconsciously to her mouth, as if trying to stifle a tiny cry of fright that didn't quite come. Duncan's eyes looked haunted and sunken as if he'd had no sleep; Molly knew he'd slept like the dead last night, the same way he did every night. His still-thick blonde hair—he was only in his early thirties after all, still a young man—was as immaculately swept and held in place as it was when she'd left earlier that day, but his eyes were that of a man going cold turkey. She was so startled by his gaze that she said nothing, dimly aware of the now rapid thumping in her chest. She was suddenly very frightened, caught in the invisible beam of his glare like a small animal under a silently hovering hawk above.

He stared for another moment or two, then turned back to the window, freezing into position once more, a hulking statue of some obscure tribe's imagined deity. The removal of his eyes seemed to break the spell of Molly's paralysis, if not her fear. This was a very weird and worrying situation, for sure—had he had a stroke? Some kind of mental seizure? Had he had some kind of terrible, shocking news?—but this was her *home*, her *husband*, and what the hell was she thinking anyway? He clearly needed help; he'd been shaken up badly in one way or another, that much was obvious, and she was jumping like a teenager sneaking out after hours. She pushed her nervousness away as best as she could, trying to forget about her sudden and sharp awareness of the size difference between them, about the way she now noticed the breadth of his shoulders and the thickness of his neck as if seeing them for the first time, and began to cross the room towards her husband.

"Dunc?" she asked again, still in that quiet voice she'd found but in a more steady tone. "What the hell's happened? Are you all right?" *Shannon. The heart again.* "Oh God, is it your mother? Did something happen to her?" She reached him, placing her outstretched hand onto his thick back and feeling it begin to shake rapidly beneath her touch, a small whimpering sound emanating from his barrel chest.

"Oh, Jesus. Oh no. Is she all right?" Molly gasped, placing her other hand on Duncan's shoulder and squeezing. "Is ... what did they say? Is she ... what happened?"

Duncan began to turn again, slowly this time, his face already red from the torrent of tears tumbling down his cleanly shaven and moisturised cheeks. Duncan *never* had stubble. The stare was now gone, replaced by screwed up eyes that looked so piteous and tragic that Molly's heart ached for him. She loved her husband very much. Of *course* she did; she earned twice what he did, and married him despite everything her mother (and her friends) had said about *that*. His head was bowed slightly, which at their close proximity and very different heights meant that he would have been looking directly into her eyes, had his been open. Her hands left his shoulders and went to his cheeks, caressing them gently, and then her arms went wide— very wide—to draw him into an embrace. She moved chest to chest with him, and looked up again to tell him that she was so sorry to hear it. This brought her face up perfectly as he opened his weeping eyes, regarded her for a moment, and then dropped his forehead suddenly and viciously onto the bridge of her nose.

The impact felt like an explosion in the centre of her face. Immediately, as an indecipherable electric storm of immense thoughts jabbed at the inside of her mind—shock, confusion, betrayal, incomprehension, shock again, for her nose, her *face*, her face was *ruined*—her legs became empty and buckled, her body following them to the floor. Her hand went to her face and came away as a crimson mitt, and she looked up as she gasped and spat away flecks of blood from her lips. Duncan remained standing there, eyes wide again, his fists clenched by his sides, unmoving. The last tears remained stuck to his cheeks.

"Du ... du ... du ..." she babbled, her own eyes wide now too, tears flowing down her cheeks as her trembling head shook gently from side to side, trying and failing to register what had just happened. She sat up and held her blood-covered hand out to him, fingers spread wide, a gesture that showed him what he'd done, asked him why, pleaded for help. His face didn't change at all as he silently took a step forward and kicked her in the side of her head with his booted foot. The upper part of her torso collapsed like it was made of straw and her head bounced slightly on the well-cushioned carpet with a heavy thud. She blinked once, twice, seeing his hulking frame above her as an increasingly hazy blur, before the blur became blackness and she succumbed to it.

The room was silent again as Duncan stood still once more, staring blankly down at his wife's body. A small pool of dark red began to form and spread from under the left side of her face and stain irreparably into the expensive shag pile as blood continued to pump gently from her nose. The silence was broken as Sandy trotted into the room, stopping by Molly's unconscious body and sniffing at the dark growing circle on the carpet. She looked up at Duncan, whose eyes shifted to the dog and regarded her for a moment or two. Sandy cocked her head and sat, confused. Something was off here, but even the little dog—more in tune with mood and body language than her mistress, for along with smell and other methods unknown to the human mind, these were the social currencies of the canine world—couldn't tell what had changed in her master. It was bad, whatever it was. Sandy began to whine gently, but Duncan ignored this as he slowly made his lumbering way around Molly's sprawled frame. He reached her head and bent, holding his sausage-like index finger under her nose for a moment and allowing it to be drenched in crimson liquid. Once it was suitably covered, he raised it to Molly's forehead and drew a thick red line across her skin. Just like his dog, he cocked his head as he looked at it. He sat there for several minutes, as Sandy quietly urinated on the carpet a few feet away. She hadn't had an "accident" indoors since she was a puppy.

Eventually, Duncan got to his feet, his eyes not leaving Molly, and began to leave the room. As he passed Sandy, he reached down once more, and the dog yipped slightly and flinched away, prepared for a strike. It didn't come; Duncan's large hand covered the dog's entire head, and rubbed it absently as his now-vacant gaze looked at her fur. Sandy didn't stand up against his hand as she normally would have done, increasing the pressure, but instead she just continued to sit where she was, confused and trembling.

Duncan then stood and left the room, heading to the kitchen to fetch the landline handset and call an ambulance.

***

Chapter One: Chops and Change, A Very Lonely and Confused Hotel Room, More Early Signs, and An Interactive Play a Day Keeps the Doctor Away
***

Without really knowing why, Martin hoped that the other one would be there again today. Obviously, part of him hoped it would be because Scoffer seemed to enjoy it so much, but there was another part of him that wanted to see it for his own benefit. It made him feel just a little bit better, somehow. There was an ebullience and a delight there that was infectious.

As he pushed the annoyingly expensive stroller in front of him—Elizabeth's choice, not his, which of course meant that he could never sell it, and knew that he probably never would even when Callum was old enough to buy his own house—he breathed in the crisp early winter air through his nose and took pleasure in the sharp feeling against his nostrils. It was definitely good to be out of the house, even though he always needed a lot of self-talk to get himself outside. These internal lectures always ended the same way, so much so that he didn't even know why he bothered to argue with himself: *the boy needs a walk. And, for fuck's sake, so does Scoffer.*

While both of those thoughts were true, the last one made him feel particularly guilty. Scoffer had been majorly neglected by Martin since Elizabeth's death, if only in an emotional sense. While he'd taken up his sister Trish's very early offer to walk the dog every day and take care of his feeds, he'd been so very dead inside for such a long time that he couldn't bring himself to do any more than occasionally stroke the dog's head absently whenever he came over for attention. There had been no meaningful play, no real emotional contact between master and canine, for the best part of a year. And Scoffer was such a very *loyal* animal. Martin, to be fair, had always been an equally loyal owner. But while he was carrying round a blackened lead brick where a heart used to be, it had taken every ounce of his energy to get up in the morning and look after his son, even with Trish's help. Playing with Scoffer the way he and Elizabeth had used to play with him together ... seeing Elizabeth in Callum's face every time his son looked at him with those serious blue eyes ... if he let it all in, he'd felt like he would curl up and die. And so he'd done the bare minimum. It was all he had to give.

That had all changed the day the walks started. The first step on the road to recovery, that started with the worst guilt trip of his life.

The day he'd come back from therapy and found Trish in his house. And Bryan. How the hell she'd got Bryan's number, Martin didn't know; as far as he knew, they'd never even liked each other.

What's wrong? he'd said, noting the weird atmosphere in the room. He'd known that Trish would have let herself in with her spare key, the one she used to get Scoffer and feed him. She'd had Callum at her house for the day, while he himself was getting treatment. *And why the hell are* you *here?* he'd added, turning his attention to Bryan, who'd just smiled sheepishly and raised a hand. Bryan had then looked at Trish to rescue him, a kid caught holding the water balloon. Martin had known then that this wasn't his best friend's idea.

Do you know what today is? Trish had said, calmly but firmly. Trish always did calm but firm very well; she was one of life's *brisk* people. Martin had tried to get the date ... the 11th? The 12th? He hadn't been sure. Back then, the days had been rolling into one for a very long time. Just as well his publisher had extended his deadline indefinitely, given his loss. They'd always had a good relationship.

Martin had simply shrugged, giving up.

Thursday? What is this, an intervention?

It had been a deliberately rhetorical question. The situation was just odd, and annoying. He'd stopped drinking, even in the depths of his grief, as he knew he'd let it get out of control. It was the same reason he didn't take drugs. He just wasn't that kind of guy. Trish's face had softened then, and when she'd spoken next it had been without judgement, without aggression. She'd just wanted him to understand. She gestured at Callum's crib, where the boy lay sleeping.

It's Callum's birthday, Martin. Your son is one year old today.

It hadn't registered immediately, sounding like an odd thing to say, a flippant statement like *your electric bill is overdue* or *the neighbours are moving.* And then the room had started slanting sideways and he'd been collapsing, a human mess of saltwater and snot as it had all come bubbling through in a torrent, the inner mess that he'd been burying more and more every day under tons of emotional cement. Not just his son's birthday. The day Elizabeth had died. She'd held on long enough for Callum to live. How could he not have remembered *that?* Was he so far gone? He'd started hysterically apologising but Trish had already been holding him and telling him he didn't have to, as Bryan stood awkwardly by with his hand squeezing Martin's shoulder.

That had been the turning point, and afterwards Martin was intensely aware of just how much he'd been on autopilot. He began to engage with his son, or at least tried—Callum was not the most interactive baby—and after a while, once he'd gotten into a consistent routine, Trish dropped the other shoe and politely reminded him that he really should '*start walking his own fucking dog again*'. And of course, he'd done so; once he remembered to love his son, having enough to give to his dog as well was easy. If anything, he'd gone too far the other way. With the amount of treats and toys Scoffer now received, he was already the most spoilt dog in Coventry, and if it wasn't for the lengthy walks, he'd probably be the fattest.

Walking them both together seemed like such a beautifully simple solution. Callum in the stroller or his baby sling, Scoffer happily on the lead, constantly looking up at Martin as if he couldn't believe his luck to be out *again*. To Martin's happy surprise, the walks did him a power of good too, starting off as just half-hour affairs that took them around several blocks and back and then expanding over several months until a walk could last as much as an epic three hours. It was time out of their house, his and Elizabeth's house (it was still on the market, although he was already toying with keeping it) and that in itself was enough, but he also found himself thinking of story ideas again for the first time since the accident. Trish had poked her nose in again, worrying that the walks were just another retreat into solitude, but then she saw the faint glimmer of light returning to Martin's eyes and heard the way his voice was moving out of that dull monotone, and into the rising and falling inflections of his previously airy Midlands accent. Martin had never been the loudest guy, but he'd always had a very whimsical personality. He was slowly, very slowly, coming back to life, even if he wasn't anywhere near done yet.

They crested the gentle rise of the bottom end of Hearsall Common—they'd long left Cheylesmore behind and had circled Earlsdon—and Martin felt Scoffer stop dead. Without looking, he knew his pet had dropped into the intensely blank stare and body lock of the dog who has just spotted something *extremely* interesting. He looked ahead, trying to spy what Scoffer was seeing. Callum moved restlessly in his stroller—the walk was a particularly long one today, and he was beginning to wake up fully, a baby who never was any trouble when it came to sleeping—as Martin gazed across the medium length grass as it blew gently in the faintly chill October breeze.

"You see him, Scoff? Is he here?" Martin asked the dog, smiling slightly. He looked down at Scoffer, to see if he responded. The dog didn't, his attention on far more important things in that moment with his entire body snapped into position. He wasn't big for a Staffordshire bull terrier, and didn't really have the full, round barrel body that many of them did, but even so, the grass still didn't quite reach the bottom of Scoffer's belly.

Could it be hiding in the grass ahead? Is it long enough?

Martin looked for the giveaway of the long tail sticking up above the upper edge of the grass, and saw nothing. His smile widened for a moment.

Easy way to find out.

"Scoffer," he called musically, and while the dog still didn't move his head, he began to whine gently with excitement, gaze still locked on the horizon. Martin chuckled, enjoying the moment—he didn't laugh very often these days, and little moments of pleasure were tiny golden nuggets to be captured wherever they came—and bent to unclip Scoffer's lead. The dog's feet started to lift up and down, shuffling on the spot as he realised what was happening, and his breathing started to come in snorts and spurts. Martin then theatrically pulled the lead away from Scoffer's collar, and without a look back, Scoffer shot across the common to a spot in the green expanse that only he could see. Martin straightened up and watched, smiling broadly as he watched the stocky golden brown body streak across the grass, tail up, head straight. Martin waited. Scoffer kept running.

Got to be. Absolutely got to be.

As if his thoughts had been read, he was proved right. There was a tiny explosion of white about five feet ahead of Scoffer's charging path, and Martin actually laughed as he saw it; the other dog bursting out of its hiding place in the green carpet, tail wagging frantically with its paws in the air as it leapt upright onto its back legs. Scoffer jumped at it as he reached the end of his run, and the two collided hard in midair and fell to the floor in a mad tangle of flailing canine limbs. Immediately, they were back up on their feet, and propelling after one another in a series of tight zigging and zagging circles, mouths wide open, a moving picture of boundless joy given physical form. Occasionally, they would catch one another, roll around chaotically on the floor, and then pull apart, deciding telepathically who would be the chaser and who would be the chased.

Martin put one hand in his pocket and watched the mad spectacle unfold before him, his other hand gently rocking the stroller to send Callum back off to sleep. As ever, Callum effortlessly obliged. Martin tried to remember how many times they'd seen the white dog; was this the fifth? The sixth? And never any sign of an owner, or even a collar that Martin could see. His best guess was that it was either a stray or that it belonged to one of the houses that lined the left-hand side of the common, and had found a way out from the high fences that ran along the side of the path. It was certainly harmless as far as Martin could see, despite its slightly intimidating size and wolflike appearance. Only once had it come close enough, and been still enough, for Martin to get a really good look at it. It had remained standing dopily with its tongue hanging out after coming to a stop within touching distance of Martin, panting frantically as it tried to cool down after its last intense bout of chaos with Scoffer.

It was mainly malamute, Martin thought (he'd had to look up the breed, thinking husky at first but knowing that a husky wouldn't be big enough) and definitely crossed with some kind of bloodhound or basset hound or *something* like that. The giveaway was in the face; it cheeks were bigger, and hung lower, in a way that was completely at odds with its fuzzy, wolflike body. He'd already half-assigned it the name *Chops* as a result. It was big, that was for sure, but not huge; Martin stood around five feet ten, and he thought that the dog would come up to roughly the top of his thigh. It rarely acknowledged Martin, looking at him excitedly now and then, but far more interested in its playmate. Martin didn't know if it was male or female, as the huge layers of thick, fuzzy white fur—shot through with dark patches here and there—made it hard to see, as well as the breakneck speed with which it charged after Scoffer. Like many wolflike dogs, it had startling near-white pupils that Martin could see even at a distance.

He heard a noise from the stroller. Callum was already starting to stir again, even after going under just a few minutes ago.

Time to head back. How long have you been out today, anyway? Nearly four hours?

Definitely the longest yet, certainly. How many times had Callum been fed? He didn't remember. He'd been lost in thought, book ideas spilling freely again, and it had been so nice to get away. But this was bordering on neglect.

You sure this isn't another escape, Martin? And speaking of ideas, when are you actually going to get some actual writing done instead of just daydreaming?

He didn't choose to answer the question, and instead called Scoffer back. He had to do it twice, to his annoyance, but Scoffer did untangle himself reluctantly after the second time. He trotted back over to Martin and panted heavily as the big white dog stood and watched him go, its stare intense and uncertain on its big pleasant face as if to say *Wait ... are we done? Really?*

Scoffer began to whine quietly—as he always did—as the lead went back on, and he remained looking back at his playmate, but he came along easily enough when Martin began to push the stroller back towards the path, the wheels slowing slightly in the thick grass. Martin smiled as he listened to Scoffer's heavy panting, and turned to offer a wave to the big white dog where it sat quietly on a nest of green, ears up and head cocked forlornly.

"Bye, Chops," called Martin, wiggling his fingers at the now-distant dog. "Say bye-bye, Callum." Callum wasn't interested, chewing on his stubby fingers and drooling on his chin with his usual serious expression. They reached the concrete, and Martin fished out his phone to dial for a cab. It would take too long to walk back now.

The big white dog watched them leave and didn't move until they were out of sight, except to lie down heavily with its large head on its paws. It continued to lie there long after they were gone, facing the direction that they'd taken, until the grey sky above began to turn to black.

***

Duncan Nash sat on the end of his bed in the tiny room in the roadside hotel, squatting as it did like a giant grey shoebox next to a twenty-four-hour motorway service station. He'd paid using his credit card, knowing full well that the police would probably be turning up very soon as a result, but that didn't matter. He'd just needed a quiet room for a few hours to get things sorted out, and as it turned out he'd needed less than even that. He was done.

In his hands he held several sheets of previously blank paper that the lady on reception had kindly given him, along with a loaned pen. He'd used the lamp stand by the side of the bed to write on, cramping his large back up as he bent over it to write. It had been stiff, and uncomfortable, but necessary, and now he was finished. He reread the pages again for the eleventh time, still finding things to correct here and there as he wasn't at all sure that he was saying it right. He decided that it was as good as it was ever going to get, and slapped the pages down onto his right thigh. Resting on his left was his phone. He picked it up and dialled, his expression blank.

The line buzzed a few times, much longer than it normally did. Shannon usually picked up straight away, her phone immediately to hand. Just like her daughter. He knew why she wasn't doing so this time; he could picture her, possibly sat in a group of people gathered around Molly's hospital bed, people that she was now telling *It's him, I don't believe it. He's ringing. What do I say? What do I say?* Her husband demanding the phone, angrily holding out his hand and saying *Let me talk to that bastard, I know exactly what I'm going to say that fucking bastard.* Shannon would turn away from him, holding her own hand out like a shield to keep him away, her husband's advance spurring her into action and making her push the answer button—

"Duncan?" said a trembling voice on the phone. "Duncan, is that you?"

"Hi, Shannon," Duncan said. "Yes, it's me." *Is she all right* were the next words that wanted to leave his mouth, but they didn't come.

"*Duncan*," said Shannon again, her voice already crumbling into tears of sorrow and rage. Confusion. She'd always liked Duncan, he knew. She'd always been nice him. She'd approved. "Duncan. Dun ... where are you?"

"I'm at a hotel," he said, his voice surprisingly level. When he thought about it, he *felt* surprisingly level. All of the tension was finally gone. He heard her say *He's at a hotel* to someone. "Are you at the hospital?"

"*Of course we're at the fucking hospital!*" she barked, her voice grating. Duncan was surprised, but not by the sudden yelling. Shannon *never* swore. "Where ... do you think we'd ..." She fell quiet, and then the line was muffled slightly as he heard her talking to someone else and saying *I'm fine, get away or I'll smash this phone, I mean it.* There was a pause, and then she came back on the line. "Duncan ... Duncan ..." He waited for her to find the words. He owed it to her, at the very least, to have her say and ask her questions. "For the love of God, Duncan ... how could you *do this?* How could ... she loved you so much, Duncan, *we* love you. She has a *concussion*, Duncan. You broke her nose, you flattened her pretty nose ..." She struggled to keep her composure as Duncan took in what she'd just said.

A concussion, then. Bad, but not serious. That was all. That was good news, he knew.

"Is she awake?" he said.

"She's sleeping," said Shannon absently, as if she were confused by the question. "Duncan ... they said you called the ambulance. Did you call the ambulance?"

"I did."

There was a pause.

"Duncan ..." she said again. It was beginning to sound like a game of Simon Says. "Tom wants to kill you, do you know that? He wants to get the boys from the club and find you and kill you. I think I want to let him. I knitted you that jumper for Christmas."

"I remember."

"But *how* could ... aren't you even sorry? You haven't even tried to tell me that you're sorry."

"I'm sorry."

"You bastard. You complete bastard."

"I *am* sorry."

A voice in the background repeated something Duncan couldn't really hear for the tenth time, the loudest yet, and Shannon finally repeated it for them.

"Where's the hotel?"

Duncan thought about it. He couldn't think how to describe it. The place was the first one that he'd come across.

"I don't know."

Silence again, except for Shannon's heavy, wheezy breathing.

"Are ... are you ..." she babbled. Duncan could hear her having an idea, having found the possible way out that she'd been frantically searching for. "Have you been ... are you sick? Have you been having ... God, headaches or anything?" Her voice was cracking severely, and the tears were going to come again.

"I don't think so."

"Then *why*, for God's sake, *why* —"

The conversation was over. He'd already found out what he wanted to know, he'd given Shannon a chance to ask her questions, and now she was just repeating herself.

"I have to go, Shannon. I really am sorry. Honestly. I love Molly very, very much. Please tell her that when she wakes up, and that I am so very sorry." He *was* sorry, too, and he did love her as much as he said ... but at the same time, he was glad he had done it, even if it had to be her. It *had* to be done, and the relief he felt now was almost blissful. That was probably why he felt so flat but relaxed now. He did wish it didn't have to be her though. He wished that an awful lot.

"No, Duncan, you stay there, *you stay there*—"

He hung up, and switched his phone off.

Duncan sighed heavily, the very last of his nervous tension leaving him. He was utterly at peace. The knowledge of what he'd done saddened him greatly, but it was as if it were locked away, overpowered by the deeply soothing balm of satisfaction that came from knowing he had done a very, very good thing.

He stood, picking the papers up off his leg and dropping them onto the bed. Molly would read them eventually, and as mangled as his words usually were when written down, these would speak for him far better than if he had spoken them aloud himself. They would have to do.

Crossing into the bathroom, he looked into the mirror and noticed how tired he looked—how sunken his eyes were—as he picked up the scissors that he'd bought at the petrol station. They were part of a three-piece set of varying sizes, and he'd left the smaller two in their clear plastic packet in the other room. Four quid for three heavy-duty pairs of scissors sounded like a good deal. He'd always bought those petrol station offers: pocket torches, thermal gloves, heat reflectors for your windscreen.

He opened the thick blades, and they let out their light whisper of gently grinding metal as he gave another heavy sigh of his own. He wished there was a way back ... but he was surprised again how little fear he had. He *was* worried about the pain though. This was going to hurt. He was a big boy, he reminded himself.

Duncan gritted his teeth and gave a guttural grunt as he plunged the open scissors into his neck. He had just enough grit in himself to twist them savagely, ensuring the success of the job, before letting go of the handles jutting from his throat and then sitting down with a heavy thud on the cheap linoleum floor.

I hope you understand, Molly. I really do.

***

3000 BLACKBIRDS DROP DEAD IN ARKANSAS ON NEW YEAR'S EVE
By Arthur Maivia

TURRELL, Ark. — Thousands of dead blackbirds startled New Year's Eve partygoers as they dropped out of the sky over a small community in Arkansas.

All areas of the town, from buildings to agricultural land, were given a liberal carpeting of deceased red-winged blackbirds, to the point that some residents reported it being difficult to drive down the road.

"They were just strewn all over the place," said local police officer Charlie Bigelow, "I mean, they were everywhere. I've never seen anything like it in my life."

According to the Arkansas Game and Fish Commission, over 3,000 birds were discovered dead. The initial theory is that fireworks set off at midnight may have startled the blackbirds to such a degree that they crashed into buildings, vehicles, and one another, with some even flying directly into the ground.

The commission stated that "the blackbirds were driven down to a much lower level of flight in order to avoid the fireworks exploding higher up. Due to blackbirds having limited vision, collisions were inevitable once the birds were flying at the level of buildings."

The commission did say, however, that they still planned to analyse the bodies for toxins or disease, suggesting that the matter was not completely closed. Other theories abound, such meteorological conditions confusing the flock enough to lead them straight into terra firma.

"I got up in the morning, and there was just all these black shapes lying all over the yard," said Paul Kruger, whose roof was also damaged in the incident. "It took me hours to clear them all up."

Terry Droese was part of the impromptu cleanup team that assembled on New Year's Day. They filled several dumpsters with the bodies. "It was not a pleasant task," said Droese, a worker at the local construction plant. "They just seemed endless. You'd think you'd done a lot, then you'd look up the street and see how many were still lying there, waiting to be picked up." Even now, several blackbird carcasses lie on the streets of Turrell.

Many in the town see it as something of a blessing. The extensive population of blackbirds could leave collective droppings so large in places that they would be several inches or even feet deep, and the sky would often disappear behind clouds of them at dawn and dusk. A natural cull of their numbers has been welcomed.

"They'd eat 50 pounds of feed a day," he said. "You couldn't keep them full."

The Cornell Lab of Ornithology in Ithaca, NY, says that there is up to 200 million red-winged blackbirds in North America, and that they are one of the most common species in the country. Test results on the carcasses should be obtained within a few days, and several wildlife disease researchers at various universities have asked for a set of the bodies for study.

***

"The question is," said Dr. McMahon, "do *you* think you're ready to come off it?"

Martin thought about the question for a moment, listening to the soft sound of the grandfather clock in the corner and Callum's occasional sigh in his sleep. Martin's son was in his baby sling on Martin's chest, even though he was really getting too big for it. Martin liked McMahon's surgery, despite its purpose, and wished he could make his study at home feel just like it. The rich mahogany that seemed to cover every surface—he thought that McMahon would drive a car made of mahogany if he could—made it feel like a room that wouldn't have felt out of place fifty, a hundred years ago.

A car made out of mahogany. It'd have to have a clockwork engine, and instead of car *keys it'd have one of those* clockwork *mechanism keys, the ones shaped like a T that you put in and twist until you can't twist them anymore, and once you let it go it'd start winding down, turning the engine, and then you could drive it, and the gears would be just that,* clockwork *gears—*

"Martin?"

He'd gone again. What had he been thinking about?

The fluoxetine.

That was it. He didn't know if he was *ready*, exactly, but he felt that, somehow, he'd turned an important corner a short while back and stayed there. The landscape had—as it always did when it came to the way he saw the world—shifted so slowly under his feet that he hadn't even noticed it. It had been a sheer, jagged cliff face before him sixteen months ago. Now, if he looked a bit more closely, saw it for what it was ... he thought he could see a slight forward incline to it. One with handholds.

"I think," he said, raising his eyebrows and shifting in his chair, "that ... yes. I think I'd like to try. Maybe try a week or two without it, see how I do."

McMahon smiled, sitting back and picking something off his sleeve that Martin couldn't see.

"Well, it doesn't work that way, Martin, remember? I'm very glad to hear that you're feeling more capable now, and your score on the PHQ-9 reflects that, certainly. And if you want to start moving past the fluoxetine, that's good news. But you know you can't just stop dead on antidepressants. You have to come off gradually. First every other day, then with a two-day gap, and so on."

Martin knew. He'd been told all about it when he'd first been prescribed them. Of course, he'd started off on much stronger medication initially, and that had put him into a comfortable cloud of bouncy numbness that suited him just fine, thank you ... but they'd told him that he couldn't stay there forever. He'd resisted, not wanting to come back—the most will he'd shown since Elizabeth's accident—but he'd gone along with it in the end, sheeplike. On reflection, though, he knew that it had absolutely been the right thing to do. And he was grateful; he was over a year down the road, and progress always looked *so* much better with a year's perspective.

He gently squeezed his sleeping son's back, pressing the baby to his chest without knowing he was doing it, and nodded.

"Okay," he said. "Let's do that then."

"You know, given your previous score, I would have said you'd need two years on the fluoxetine before you came off, but given the improvements you seem to have made ..."

"I know. I just ... I'm doing okay, and I want to try." The pills, unlike common perception, didn't magically make everything better, but they *did* take the edge off the darkest lows and gave him just that extra ten percent needed to keep his legs moving, to keep himself breathing in and out and to actually care about his appearance, to watch what he ate, to decide that actually, maybe going to see a film wouldn't be so bad, to actually think it might be worth *trying* to believe that *possibly* tomorrow *might* be an option worth the *chance* of taking. And now, he felt like he'd made that mental process a habit; that he'd developed some small clockwork of his own. He wanted to go solo.

"All right then," said McMahon, nodding and turning to his ancient-looking computer, tapping at the keys and no doubt wondering if he could find somewhere that sold monitors made of wood. "Drop it to every other day for the next three weeks, then give me a call. And there was something else, wasn't there, something to do with Callum? Has he been ill?"

"No, no," said Martin quickly, putting a hand on the back of Callum's head and stopping himself from not quite covering his son's ears. His instinct was to do so, certainly; the inexplicable guilt he felt from saying what he was about to say, or the fact that he even thought it, immediately seized hold of his insides like a hot mechanical press. "I'm just ... I just wanted to check something. I know you're not a paediatrician, but while I was here ... and if you thought something was wrong, you'd refer me if I was right. Right?"

McMahon nodded once, slowly, eyes shut, eyebrows raised. *Of course.* With his balding head and impressive grey beard, the facial expression that he was pulling made him look more sage than ever. Martin was always amazed that the man was still working. Maybe he was younger than he looked. The doctor remained silent, letting Martin continue. He looked like a man who knew what was coming. Martin sighed.

Just say it. You're being a good dad. It's important to check these things. If he needs help, this is how you get it.

"It's just ..." Martin said, eyes trailing over the many medical books on McMahon's shelves, putting it off as usual, taking interest in anything but that which he had to deal with. He mumbled something, and looked down at Callum.

"Pardon?" asked McMahon, gently.

"He doesn't play," said Martin again, quietly.

There.

McMahon stayed silent. He knew when to do so. It was a key part of the job.

"He ... I don't ever really hear him laugh either, you know?" said Martin, looking up at McMahon, searching his face for any judgement or mockery. The age difference between the two of them—Martin in his early thirties, McMahon anywhere from fifty to eighty—felt very apparent, and Martin suddenly saw himself as a foolish child in the older man's presence. "He just seems to ... *sit,* or sleep, or feed. I mean, *we* play, but I wouldn't call it play, you know? I'll get the toy or whatever, and make it dance about, or get the squeaky thing and blow it at him you know, like *here* and *here,* and he'll look and he'll engage with it ... but it's not ..." He looked at his sleeping son, and his heart ached in a way that was like a physical blow. "He's not *playing.* It's like he's just curious. Like it's just something to figure out. He's just so ... serious."

But that's your Callum, isn't it? Your son? Can you imagine him not *being so serious all the time? Would that be the boy you love otherwise?*

True.

"I read that they should enjoy making noises from four to six months—"

You read it in Elizabeth's book, the one she bought—

"—and he's never really been one for noises. He *cries,* of course, when he wants feeding or if he's wet, but generally, he hardly cries at all and he's so easy to settle down. You can just give him something to distract him and he'll be away, just holding it and looking at it with this, this ... man, such a *serious* look on his face ..."

He fell silent, wanting some sort of encouragement to continue before he made more of a fool of himself. His face felt hot. He looked at McMahon, and saw the doctor gently moving back and forth on his swivel chair, relaxed and nodding, looking ambivalent. No judgement there.

"All right," he said. ""Does he respond to his own name?"

"Yes," replied Martin, uncertain if this was confirmation or denial of his concerns.

"And he recognises you."

"Oh yes." That felt good to say.

"And he's interested in you?" Martin thought about it.

"Very, I suppose. He's always touching my face. And he looks at me whenever he sees something he doesn't know."

McMahon smiled.

"Has he learned any words yet?"

"Several."

"To say himself, I mean."

"Oh. No, then."

"Does he use bricks?"

"Toy bricks?" Martin regretted the question immediately.

Of course fucking toy bricks. Idiot. He's not working down on the site.

McMahon smiled paternally, and Martin went redder.

"Yes, toy bricks."

"Uh, yes."

"And you don't think that's play?"

"Well ... I don't know." Callum never seemed to be playing at *anything*. More like he was just getting on with things. McMahon grinned and leaned forward, putting his forearms on his desk.

"Well then, for now, I really wouldn't worry, Martin," he said, warmly. "Some children are simply more curious than playful at that age. Just think about how fascinating every single thing in the world is for Callum right now. He's content, and safe, and looked after, and he knows that. Have you taken him to a sensory group?"

"A what?"

"It's a stimulus experience for infants. Introducing them to sounds and sensations. Very popular right now. Children and parents love it. I'll give you the name of a local class." He snatched up a Post-it note, jotted something down on it, and then passed it to Martin who barely looked at it. He wasn't sure if he was being brushed off, or if the doctor had actually listened and was simply saying what Martin secretly suspected; he was a paranoid parent. A parent who was going overboard with concern because he hadn't connected with his son when he first arrived.

"He should start talking soon, Martin," said McMahon. "And let me stress that it still doesn't mean anything if he doesn't, *but,* if you're still worried in a few months, give me a call and I'll arrange an appointment with a specialist. I can do that now if you really wish, but I certainly don't think it's necessary at this point."

Martin wanted to say what was on his mind—*so ... it's not autism then*—but as was so often the case with him, he felt that he couldn't. Here was the professional, the trained and vastly experienced medical man, and he was a writer with a half-baked notion in his head. Who was he to even put forward the possibility of contradicting this expert?

"Okay. Okay then. Thank you."

"Not a problem at all, Martin." He rose, and extended a hand. Martin copied the movement. "How's the house move going, by the way?" McMahon added, as they shook hands. Martin rolled his eyes, happy to be back in the realm of small talk. He felt the grip on his insides lessen.

Are you sure you still want to move though?

"Three viewings in what, two months? All going swimmingly," he said. McMahon chuckled dryly, and shrugged.

"Slow market. It'll pick up. Stick with it."

Martin curled his lip theatrically in a *yeah right* manner, and then suddenly realised just how close he was standing to the older man. They were about the same height, and Martin was suddenly seized by the mad notion of kissing the doctor right in the middle of his hair-lined mouth, purely to see what the hell the older man would do as a result. Martin thought it would be *fascinating* to find out, even if the idea of kissing a man—especially one who was possibly in his seventies with a beard and who hadn't long since eaten lunch—was not in the slightest bit appealing to him. Plus, it would be incredibly embarrassing for McMahon, and he was a good guy; Martin wouldn't want to do that to the doctor, plus it would mean never being able to go back to the surgery, but man, how interesting would his reaction be … Martin then realised that he'd gone off again, his mind taken off-track and disabled as it so easily was. He'd never been able to stop it, as he'd never realised that it was happening. He'd also been standing in silence in front of the doctor for a second too long. The other man's brow was just starting to show the first signs of furrowing.

"Well, see you later then, Doc!" Martin said, a touch too brightly, and then turned and walked out of the door much more quickly than he would have done normally.

You never learn, do you? You're your own worst enemy.

***

Chapter Two: Not So Much Déjà Vu But Sacre Bleu, Scoffer Just Can't Leaf Things Alone, Subterranean Homesick Blues, White and Red, and The Brotherhood of the Raid
***

Hours later, and several hundred miles away, a lone man suddenly spasmed, buckled, and then crashed to the floor of his opulent private quarters, spilling and smashing his glass of brandy. He was lucky. Had it been ten minutes earlier, he would have been smoking a cigarette at the same time, and the combination of flammable booze and burning tobacco could have been disastrous in the heavily silk-draped boudoir. No one would have known about it until it was too late, given that night had fallen some time ago and the rest of the compound was fast asleep. He'd even sent Charles away early, feeling restless and wishing for solitude.

This piece of good fortune was lost on him in that moment, however, as he was currently focused on trying to breathe. This one had hit him on a level that even he, after all his years of merely talking the talk, found hard to believe. He spasmed on his front like a freshly caught fish, as his hands clutched of their own accord only to find fistfuls of carpet, and his calf muscles ached from clenching. It was way beyond anything that had ever come before, even during the years in Lausanne. A calm, quiet voice in the middle of the hurricane wondered if this might be something new.

A heart attack? A seizure? You've been so good lately, really looked after yourself. Surely not?

Then—

Would it really be so bad if it was one of those?

Then, just like that, the moment passed. Instinctively, he gasped in a lungful of air, and flopped over onto his back with relief, needing to breathe, breathe, breathe, and savour the oxygen.

You're all right. You're all right.

Then—
Was that ... was that ...

He couldn't get excited. No. That's how he'd gotten in trouble before. The drugs. The downward flow, the landslide. It was dangerous to think like that. He knew how dangerous hope could be if it was false. Even so, as much as his shaking mind tried to tell him not to savour the oh so sweet taste of *thrill* all around him, the knowledge was coming, and it *was* knowledge, sweet God almighty *this was real and he knew it.*

He grabbed the seat of the nearby chaise loungue and pulled himself up on trembling limbs. His silk robe hung very loosely on his scrawny limbs, burying him, a body that just didn't seem to ever put on weight despite being subjected to the finest, richest foods and (until recently) booze on a daily basis. His mother had said it was because his racing mind burned off all the calories in his body. Now she was dead, and after all this time he was starting to believe that she might have had a point.

He staggered across the vast floor of a room dripping with splendour, an embarrassment of riches on display for any visitor to see. He had chosen the decor years ago at the height of his pomp and self-absorption. Now he was just plain bored of it, boredom that was turning into disgust, and that was something that he already had enough of. Reaching the ornate writing desk that he never used anymore, he yanked out a drawer and grabbed some paper, found a pen. Slumping into the antique desk chair, he gripped the gold-plated writing instrument in a shaking hand and waited. Would it come? Of course it would. He already knew it, and the delight and luxury of *certainty* hit almost as hard as his earlier collapse had and he began to laugh like madman. Knowledge shot down his arm and into the pen, which began to write as it were leading his hand and not the other way around. He watched, wide eyed and fascinated, laughing like an amused child.

Eventually, the pen finished its arthritic journey of achingly slow loops and dips around the page, and his hand spat out the pen from its grip like it had discarded something foul. And maybe it had; as he read what was written there, a feeling so powerful came with it that the laughter died in his throat with an actual whimper. It was only two words, but he couldn't stop reading and rereading them, as if by doing so he could discard the invisible blanket of deepening cold that had draped itself around his shoulders, clinging to him and then sinking deeper. He didn't know the words' meaning or relevance, but he felt it just the same. It was a name.

MARTIN HOGAN

His hand covered his mouth and was immediately wetted by his involuntary tears. He didn't even notice the warm, dripping dampness that was spreading at his crotch. First placing the paper back down on the desk with the same trembling care that he would take with unstable dynamite, he then frantically grabbed at the pocket of his robe for his phone.

***

"Martin? Hello?"

"Hm? Oh, sorry Trish. Just watching Scoffer. He hasn't done this in years, always used to crack Liz up."

It hurt to say it, but the feeling was surrounded in warmth, like a stinging nettle hidden in a thick duvet. Elizabeth *did* use to laugh her head off at this, and so did he. And it was funny now. Delightful.

He was standing in his kitchen, leaning on the wall and looking out into the garden through the window. The baby monitor on the counter fed through the gentle, steady sounds of Callum's contented breathing, and the only other noises to be heard were the crispy-sounding thrashings from outside and Trish's voice down the phone line.

"Done what? Oh, the leaves thing?" She chuckled at the mental image. "You should have raked them all in by now."

"Mm," murmured Martin, not wanting to say what he really felt which was *are you fucking kidding? A fairly recently widowed man looking after a baby and a dog and you think I should be concerned about leaves in the back garden?* He kept his mouth shut for good reason though; while he was right in principle, he knew that this was just Trish's way of trying to help get him back into a normal life, normal conversation, normal nags. What he did say was:

"Frankly, the leaves can kiss my ass, Trish."

"Charming," said Trish, good naturedly, and Martin knew the now-common question was coming next. "So, what are your plans for the day then? Writing?" Martin smiled, and shook his head.

I'm doing all right, Trish. For now, I'm okay. Just let me come to it without forcing it.

He watched Scoffer perform his latest diving run, and actually grinned.

It was a routine that was as daft as it would later be meticulous. The first autumn after they'd brought Scoffer home from the rescue centre, he'd seen the falling leaves for what was clearly the first time. He was still really only a puppy in those days. The centre said that he'd been kept indoors in a high-rise flat without ever being walked for the first year of his life, so the wonders of nature were still much a mystery to him. The falling leaves had been, as far as Scoffer was concerned, the greatest show on earth. He caught them, charged them, turned them over, ran away from them, all with that wide-eyed intensity that only a dog can bring. And it had left Elizabeth in hysterics on the floor, tears of laughter rolling down her face, and Scoffer's wired and confused expression as he looked at her and tried to figure out what was wrong only made it worse.

The next autumn was different though.

Not that it wasn't as funny. It was, and Elizabeth's shouts of *He's doing it again!* from the kitchen had brought Martin running every time. But there was some kind of method to Scoffer's actions on the second occasion, and on every occasion since, whether the leaves were in actual freefall or lying around on the ground. Scoffer was now seven, and while he was as playful as ever, he seemed to have less and less interest in that particular game with each year, until he stopped altogether. That was the other reason Martin hadn't raked them up; the first autumn since Elizabeth had died, whenever Scoffer had been out in the garden, he'd done very little except sit lifelessly and stare at the hedge (thinking about it now stung Martin's well-abused guilt muscles once again. Scoffer had loved Elizabeth as much as anyone, and worse, he couldn't fully understand where she had gone) and Martin very much wanted to see him romping around again. Maybe the leaves would remind him of a happier time, now Martin was engaging with him again as well?

Whatever the reason, Scoffer was very interested in the leaves once more, and the second routine was back. It was carried out in several stages.

First, Scoffer would find the biggest group of fallen leaves that he could. Then he would dive into them and flail around with every available part of his body, scattering them about as much as he could. He'd then immediately spring to his feet and race towards the nearest leaf, picking it up in his mouth and carrying it *here* or *there*, and then go and get another one and place it somewhere else, arranging them in no particular way, stopping dead now and then to regard his handiwork with laser focus. This would go on until he spotted another collection of leaves that caught his attention, upon which he would crash headlong into those and the whole process would begin again until he was a panting, exhausted mess. The whole thing was carried out at immense, breakneck speed.

It was the same again today ... but maybe, Martin noticed, a little more slowly, with a little more care. Extra time was being taken to stop and look at what he was doing, Martin saw, Scoffer's chunky head swinging back and forth between the various leaves that he'd already moved.

He's getting older, don't forget. Seven years old. What's that in dog years? Forty-nine?

He couldn't imagine Scoffer that old. He still had the personality of a puppy.

"Martin?"

"Sorry, Trish. Who knows? Maybe today's the day. Dust off the laptop. Maybe even a drink with it."

"Well, good. Good. Just, you know, take your time. Whenever you're ready."

Well if that's the case, stop bloody asking then.

He sighed. She was trying to help, as always. The trouble with Trish was that Martin was never sure how much of it was from pure good intentions and how much of it was from her own intolerance of things *not being right*.

Then he noticed Scoffer's tail, always so upright and vigorous when at play.

Why's his tail between his legs?

"Have you told Michael over at DiBiase that you, you know, you're thinking about starting something new? He'll be happy."

"Well, I don't wanna get his hopes up just yet. We'll see." The murmured noise at the other end of the phone made it clear that this wasn't the answer that she wanted, and that she *wanted* him to know that, but wasn't actually going to voice her opinion. *A standard Trish move,* as Elizabeth would have said.

They always liked each other though. You knew that.

"Ah, maybe I will," he added, just to get her off his case a little. "Throw him a bone. He's been pretty good about, well ... everything, after Elizabeth."

"Yeah. Yeah, that's true. Yeah, you should do that." He could hear her smiling, relaxing.

And doesn't the idea relax you too? The idea of getting your teeth into something? The knowledge that writing again is even a possibility?

It did. Martin just didn't know at that moment that he would never complete—or even begin—another novel for over a decade. *Change* was coming, with him at the heart of it, and the world would revolve around Martin Hogan even if no one would ever know it.

***

Meanwhile, thousands of miles away in Brooklyn, New York, Liam Horowitz was (as he would later put it in his statement to the police) "busy minding his own business" and waiting for the F train at York Street to take him into Manhattan. For the time of year, it had been surprisingly warm, and the platform was hot. Sweat lay on his back in a thin sheen, and made his shirt stick to his skin under his cheap suit as he tried to avoid to making contact with the many people crammed in around him. That would only make it all stick to him even worse.

It was ridiculous. Summer had been bad enough, feeling like he was living in some kind of crazy, sweltering urban swamp every time he descended into a subway station. He'd seen at least two people faint from the heat. He'd been looking forward to more bearable winter temperatures, but so far the difference hadn't been anywhere near as much as he'd hoped; this time last year, he'd been wearing a coat to work.

Even the skinny woman next to him seemed to be feeling it, and she was only dressed in a thin vest top and a light summer skirt. She was swaying gently on the spot, her eyes closed and her forehead creased, clearly trying to mentally cool off in the interminable remaining minutes until the next F arrived.

You and me both, honey, thought Liam, leaning out for the umpteenth time and gazing along the track into the darkness of the tunnel, hoping—*begging*—to see a set of headlights as sweat continued to bead on his forehead. *Fuck this city. Fuck this job. Dad was right. I was better off in Chicago.* He didn't mean it—he was all but guaranteed the branch manager's position in New York when Kenny left in a few months' time, which was the reason he'd transferred to the city in the first place—but he was hot, tired, and extremely irritable. All of which added to his confusion when he looked back at the woman and saw her gazing straight at him—in her heels, her eyes were almost level with his—with an incredibly concerned expression on her face, sorrowful even. Liam actually turned his head over his right shoulder, expecting to see her looking at someone else, but no; she was gazing directly at him.

Oh, for crying out loud, he thought, *score two for Dad. My first New York Crazy. Three months without one, that's got to be good going though. I really didn't need this today. I don't need this at all. Do I really want to be a bank manager this much? Is it really worth it?*

He didn't say anything, hoping she would eventually lose interest and go away, but she continued to stare, her bottom lip now actually quivering. She looked so crestfallen that Liam knew she would start crying any minute. He had a mental flash, and suddenly realised what she reminded him of; the penguin in that Bugs Bunny cartoon where Bugs is trying to get the little guy home to the North Pole. Once Bugs drops him off, he starts to walk cheerily away, but turns just in time to see the penguin's desperate, sorrowful eyes staring after him, full of tears. But why was the penguin crying—

He came back to the moment, felt desperately uncomfortable now, and decided to pretend that he hadn't seen her. It was impossible that he hadn't, of course, but he didn't know what else to do. He looked away, and took his phone out of his pocket for something to pretend to do. There wasn't really any space to move away without a major effort, and that thought made him realise what he was doing.

A six-foot black man being made nervous by a skinny white woman on a New York subway platform. Racial progress, of a kind.

He almost laughed, but he didn't want her to think he was laughing at her. She really *was* making him nervous. He looked up to see if she was still staring at him, and as he did so he heard a faint clinking sound. She was still staring at him, and had now taken her keys out of her pocket. The centre of the key ring was clenched inside her right fist, with the various keys sticking out between her whitened knuckles.

Wait, that's a bit—

She moved fast, and even though Liam instinctively brought his arm to protect his face, his laptop bag in his hand slowed the upward progress of his arm. She got there first, and her keys carved a long gouge into his cheek, narrowly missing his eye. She got her entire body behind the sudden strike, and as Liam cried out and backed away—she had remained silent, even when she swiped at him, that sorrowful expression never leaving her face—he took a stumbling step backward. Her left hand came around, fingers clawed, as people to Liam's left and right jumped away in surprise at the sudden commotion, seeing this slender woman inexplicably attacking a young business type. Liam turned his shoulder and got his other arm up this time, still too shocked to strike back, but his second backward step with his left foot became a slip, and he began to fall. Had the people around him not moved, they would have blocked his backward momentum, but as it was there was now no one between him and the edge of the subway platform.

He got his right foot back in time to catch himself briefly on the platform edge, his left foot now in the air, but as his arms pinwheeled desperately, he realised that his weight was suspended much too far into space to be able to swing himself forward. There was a long, horrible, frozen moment where he seemed to be able to take in every dumbly staring face on the platform, all stunned into inaction as he hung there. Two thoughts came to him at once through this captured moment of pure terror, terror that exploded as he saw the subway walls around him light up with the oncoming glare of subway train headlights, heard the seemingly deafening, dooming rumble of its wheels, the blare of its warning horn as it saw him far too late:

Man, you really were *right after all, Dad. You had no idea how much.*

And

Hoboken, it was crying because it was from Hoboken and didn't even want to go to the North Pole in the first place—

And then two scrawny hands were gripping his leg and pulling, and time smashed back into action as he felt himself being dragged forwards and it was the crazy woman, pulling him back onto the platform to save him as other people unfroze and grabbed his arms, his sweat-sodden shirt, his collar, and pulled him to safety. He heard the train pull to a halt just behind him and felt the gentle rush of air puff around it, from it, out of it as the doors slid open and the majority of the people around him carried on with their journey, stepping onto the train because this was New York and they had to keep moving, had to get past that particular day's craziness and on to work. His limbs turned to water and he flopped onto the concrete floor of the emptying platform, completely stunned and looking into the faces of two or three concerned people that were still holding him various places, asking if he was okay, was he all right, what happened, who was that woman—

The woman. Liam snapped his head back and forth, unable to see her, and then he could; she was blocked by a blonde-haired man in a blue T-shirt who was facing her, arms outstretched and marching forwards to ward her off, shouting at her and telling her to calm down, asking her what the fuck she was trying to do. She didn't look like she needed to be told to calm down now, though. Her expression was the same, and her hands hung by her sides as she looked sadly at Liam. As he locked eyes with her, she suddenly ducked under the arm of the man shooing her backwards and darted across the few feet between them, squirrel-like, and the man clutched at nothing but air as she rushed past him.

Liam tried to find the voice to warn the people around him, but their backs were to her, all their attention on him, and he was still too dazed, too stunned, too damn *hot*. Before anyone could react—or before the blonde-haired man reached her—her finger had lashed out and swiped itself through some of the running blood from the gouge on Liam cheek. Just as quickly, she'd smeared the blood in a line across Liam's forehead, but already the blonde-haired man had his arm around her neck and the people around him had let go of Liam and turned their backs to him, blocking her path.

Liam remained on his knees, gasping and unable to speak, as she was dragged backwards across the grey platform to the stairs in a bundle of shouting humanity.

She wasn't shouting though. She wasn't even resisting, allowing them to take her away effortlessly, the very picture of passive cooperation.

Her eyes never left his though, until they disappeared up the stairs.

Liam didn't move for a few more minutes, getting his breath back and trying to figure out what the hell had just happened. There were just a handful of people left on the platform now, and all of them were doing their very best to pretend that they couldn't see him. It almost felt like he'd imagined the whole manic episode, were it not for the gouge on his cheek and the line of still-wet blood that he could feel drawn on his forehead.

Later, Liam completed his trip into Manhattan, during which he handed in his resignation at the branch that afternoon.

***

Martin could tell that something was severely wrong with the white dog, even at a distance.

It wasn't hiding. Instead, it was standing in plain sight in the grass up ahead, although *standing* wasn't quite the correct word; it was slumped slightly, head down, moving painfully slowly then stopping every few feet to look around itself in a dazed fashion. Scoffer was already whimpering and hopping from foot to foot, anticipating being taken off the lead for another play session, but Martin didn't oblige.

"I don't think he wants to play, Scoff. Calm down, buddy," Martin said, stroking the Staffie's head and not taking his eyes off the forlorn-looking white shape in the distance. They were back at Hearsall Common, the sky above a cheerful blue that seemed to be in stark contrast to the large, miserable-looking animal before them.

Where the hell are the bloody owners? Look after your bloody dog, stop letting it get out!

He pushed the stroller ahead of him, Callum's upside-down eyes staring up at him as they went, and Scoffer trotted alongside. He continued to whimper with frustration with every step, starting to bolt now and then but catching himself every time as long-embedded training unconsciously kicked in. Martin had spent a long time training Scoffer not to bolt as a puppy, and he was grateful that he'd done so every time he took Scoffer for a walk. He half-expected the white dog to move away as he drew closer. It had never been close to him before, and Martin half-assumed that it might be nervous around strangers, but if it was, it was showing no sign of it today. It didn't even seem aware of Martin's presence.

As he came closer, Martin could see that its eyes were only half open, the eyelids drooping down and then opening halfway again, over and over, and the dog seemed to sway slightly after every step.

No, definitely not right. This guy is in a bad way.

Martin's temper rose slightly. He wasn't an aggressive man, or a loud one, but this kind of animal neglect brought out the worst in him. Yes, he hadn't played with Scoffer in the really dark times, whilst he wasn't himself—

not that he really was himself now, not yet anyway, but he was on the way—or hadn't given the animal much one-on-one time, but he *had been* grieving for a dead wife at the time and had still at least made sure the animal was walked and fed properly, and that he stayed clean and healthy. He'd never, even his darkest times, let Scoffer get in this kind of state. They hadn't seen the white dog for a week or so, and he'd wondered why, but now he thought maybe the animal had been punished for getting out.

He was within a few feet now, and could see that the white dog looked leaner, a fact that was clear even through the thick fur. Some bastard hadn't been feeding it.

Or it doesn't have an owner.

No way. It always looked too clean and healthy before today ... although right now its fur had muddy patches on it here and there.

Then maybe something happened *to its owner.*

It was certainly possible. Martin stopped right in front of it, and still the dog didn't acknowledge his presence. Instead, it continued to slowly move its head here and there, not really appearing to recognise anything. Scoffer continued to whine.

"Scoff. Sit."

Scoffer did, but with a reproachful sounding moan. He wanted to play, or possibly get closer to see what was wrong with his playmate. Martin squatted down, putting himself between the stroller and the white dog—better safe than sorry—and peered closely at it. It was a gorgeous animal, even in its current state, with startling white eyes peering dully out from its unusually shaped crossbred face. It hung its head and started to pant.

"Hey, Chops," cooed Martin, using the name he'd given it in his mind without realising that he was doing so. He extended a hand, slowly, and stroked the dog's thick fur on its right flank. The dog's head came up and turned towards Martin's arm, noticing his touch, and stared at the limb with hazy eyes for a moment before turning its head back to the ground. The dog was clearly away with the fairies, reaching the end of its endurance. Martin squeezed slightly with his hand, feeling prominent ribs. This dog had not eaten for many days.

It began to turn inwards now, hazily walking in a wavy, aimless circle, and as it exposed its left flank to him, Martin gasped, seeing the white fur so surprisingly tainted.

There was a long-dried bloody smear on the dog's fur, blood that had come from the deep bite mark on its left-hand side.

What ... the ...

The bite mark had to be the work of another dog, maybe a fox—Martin could clearly see the bite pattern—and even though it wasn't bleeding any more, it was deep enough to be concerning. The fur had come away around it, and the pink skin looked sore and enflamed.

Has to be infected.

It was obvious that whatever had happened, no one was looking after this dog now. It was clearly half-starved, dirty, wounded, and absolutely out of it.

It better not have an owner. If it does, I'll make sure they nail the son of a bitch to the wall.

He continued to stroke the dog, gently rubbing its dazed and weakened head as it tottered lightly on its paws. Martin took out his camera, wanting to get a photo of the wound for any potential legal matters that might come up in the future. He wanted to make sure that there was proof, should it be needed, that some serious shit had happened to this dog. Chops moved sharply though, spooked by the sudden roar of a car engine in the distance, and moved his left-hand side around and away from Martin.

You can get a photo later, Martin thought, and with that he realised that already knew what he was going to do, he was just making a halfhearted effort to talk himself out of it, one weak, going-through-the-motions voice in his head checking that he had loud responses to his token resistance.

It could be rabid.

DOES IT LOOK RABID?

Okay, but you have a baby in the house.

THERE'S A DOOR BETWEEN THE UPSTAIRS AND THE DOWNSTAIRS. ANYTIME CALLUM IS SLEEPING, HE'LL BE UPSTAIRS WITH TWO CLOSED DOORS IN THE WAY, FOR CRYING OUT LOUD, AND THE REST OF THE TIME I'LL BE WITH HIM.

But you know nothing about this dog.

LOOK AT IT. IT CAN'T BE OUT OF ADOLESCENCE, IT'S JUST A BIG PLAYFUL PUPPY! IT'S CLEARLY AS SOFT AS GREASE.

That was certainly true. Now that he was close to it, he could see that the dog, though large, couldn't have been more than two years old.

How is Scoffer going to like another dog being in the house?

ARE YOU KIDDING? SCOFFER LOVES THIS THING.

...

AND ARE YOU SERIOUSLY SUGGESTING THAT WE LEAVE IT HERE? LIKE THIS?

...

WE TAKE IT HOME, CALL THE RSPCA—

And let them take it!

WELL, WE LET THEM FIX HIM UP—

And then they can take it!

...

Well?

WELL ... WE'LL SEE, WON'T WE?

There was no answer. Both sides seemed to be in agreement that, at the very least, they had to get the dog home and seen to. There was no resolution, but at least there was a course of action to be taken. It was enough for Martin, as was usually the case. He continued to stroke Scoffer's head, as he began to pull the shoelace out of one of his trainers in order to use it as a makeshift lead.

***

"BROTHERHOOD OF THE RAID" ATTACKS CONTINUE WORLDWIDE, INTERNET MEME CULTURE" TO BLAME FOR RAPID SPREAD, SAYS ARCHBISHOP
By Stephanie Austin

The sudden explosion of copycat attacks around the globe—ones clearly inspired by the 23 separate worldwide incidents from Thursday of last week—are down to the "all-pervasive influence of Internet meme culture", and are a "perfect example of this generation of impressionable minds feeling a need to take part in whatever they see as exciting online" according to an open letter by the Archbishop of Canterbury.

The Archbishop called for parents to "take a greater interest in what their children and teenagers are doing online, to see which ideas and movements they're buying into, and to explain the importance of knowing that there is a human cost in everything."

23 separate attacks were carried out on unsuspecting members of the public last Thursday, all linked by the marking of the victim's forehead afterwards with their own blood, except in four cases where soil, water, a marker pen, and a lipstick were separately used (notably in instances where no blood had been let). More concerning is that in several cases, the attackers were people the victims knew, and in some instances were close family members or loved ones. So far, only Artyom Koslov, 29, remains the only suspect in custody, and he has still refused to make a statement or answer questions since assaulting Abram Volkoff on a public bus in Svetlograd last week. The other assailants remain at large, and police say that they are pursuing several leads.

Since then, however, over 300 similar attacks have been carried out across all continents, with the majority of the results being photographed and put online. Several Facebook groups have been set up, and have since been taken down by the company, who said in a statement that the groups violated their user agreement. The largest (now defunct) group's founder, Peter Regal, who is currently being investigated by the police, openly admitted that he had carried out one such assault himself after being "inspired by the people in the news ... it was their way of saying that they'd had enough, that they weren't going to be pushed around. It's a movement, a brotherhood, a sisterhood." While it has since been confirmed that Regal, a former salesman for an office supply company, is a recovering alcoholic with a history of workplace incidents, his beliefs seem to be shared by a growing number of copycat attackers worldwide. The name for his Facebook group—The Brotherhood of the Raid—seems to have been taken on as a banner term, with the hashtag #brotherhoodOTR trending on Twitter and cropping up all over social media.

UK police, while insisting that this is still a "minor issue", advise members of the public to remain vigilant when shopping, travelling, or commuting alone, and to remain aware of their surroundings when approached by people that they do not know.

***

The doorbell rang, and Martin opened it to see his neighbour, Mrs Kingston, standing there with an expression that seemed to switch constantly between polite tension and open hostility, as if her face were engaged in a battle of wills with itself. This was unusual, to say the least; Mrs Kingston was always a picture of benign grace and good-natured small talk.

"Hi … everything okay?" asked Martin, uncertain. It was late as well, or at least, rather late for an unannounced visit, well past eight o'clock with the winter sky having long turned from grey clouds to muffled stars. The older woman pursed her lips slightly, and wrapped her arms around herself gently, only wearing a turquoise woollen jumper and skirt. She'd clearly come straight round to the house quickly, having not bothered to put on a coat on a cold night.

"Hello, Martin," said Mrs Kingston, her voice trembling slightly from either the cold or from anger. Her plump, matronly face was already starting to redden from embarrassed, restrained fury, and when she spoke her eyes remained focused squarely on Martin's chest, never looking him in the face. What the hell had happened? This was the woman who'd offered to mow his lawn after Elizabeth had died, to babysit, to do his housekeeping. The woman who'd brought round extra lemon cakes that she'd made when Liz was still alive. A wonderful neighbour. "I'm sorry to disturb you so late, but I've just gotten back from the supermarket and I'm afraid I simply have to have a word with you about your dogs."

Dogs, plural. As he'd known he inevitably would, he had taken Chops in permanently. After looking up the correct procedure online, he'd called the dog warden, who'd come round pretty much straightaway. She'd been concerned, but not shocked by Chops's appearance—Martin guessed correctly that this sort of thing was common for her, and that she'd seen worse—and had then explained to him what would happen next. She would take Chops for seven days, during which time he would be tended to, of course, and they would also check to see if he was chipped—it was a he, as Martin had quickly found out—so that they could track down the owner and see if prosecution was necessary. After that, presuming the owner wasn't capable of looking after the dog, or that they were negligent—*We can't make any major assumptions though,* she'd said, *as the dog might have just been injured after running away during a walk or whatever*—she'd transfer him to the local shelter. Martin had then asked, calmly and without realising that he was going to, what would happen in that instance if he wanted to keep the dog. Throughout all of this, Chops remained asleep in front of the radiator, having passed out immediately after wolfing down some chicken and gulping down some water. Martin thought Chops would probably be sick later, and mentally kicked himself for giving him a full feed so quickly.

The warden had shrugged, again answering a question that was commonplace, and said that if the owner wasn't found, or if they were and it was found that they had been negligent, then the shelter would check that Martin was acceptable. If he was, then he could go through the normal adoption procedures.

If the owner isn't found and then turns up later, she'd said, *then they can legally reclaim the dog at any time, no matter how much you've spent on vet bills or whatever.*

Providing they hadn't been negligent or abusive, he'd said.

Yes, providing that.

All that had been several weeks ago, and after a mountain of cash in the form of expensive vet bills, medication, wound treatment, inoculations, and new dog paraphernalia (the second basket had turned out to be pointless as the two of them were immediately sharing the same bed willfully), Chops was now a resident of Martin's home. He'd forced himself to be extremely wary; he had Callum to think about, as well as Scoffer. Playing in the park was one thing, but dogs were territorial animals, and even a dog of Scoffer's easy going nature might turn resentful and aggressive at having another dog sharing his home. But it had all turned out to be effortless. Chops wasn't the slightest bit interested in Callum anyway, and neither was Callum interested in the new dog, having long become used to the presence of Scoffer and being far more keen to stare, fascinated, at his bricks. And as for Scoffer, Martin hadn't seen him this happy since Elizabeth died. Chops even joined in the leaf moving game, waiting until Scoffer finished shifting the leaves into their various piles and then smashing them up. The house felt fuller, happier, and Martin was immensely grateful for Chops's arrival.

Like the Waltons, only less annoying.

Elizabeth's line in his head brought the old dead feeling trickling back into his stomach—it'd been absent for most of that day—as he remembered her looking at a photo of him, Scoffer, and her with her heavily pregnant baby. Two months later, the passing car had swerved onto the street and hit her in the back outside the Post Office, shattering her spine and ribcage and puncturing her lung. She'd made it to the hospital, but by the time Martin had arrived, only the machines were keeping her alive.

We're trying to save the baby, Mr Hogan.

That was the cruellest thing about grief, Martin knew. How new, happy times brought back memories of similar ones from the past, and delight turned into a scrape on the brain. He composed himself—*progress*—and answered Mrs Kingston.

"Have a word? What have they done? They've been here all day, I've been with them."

"All day?" asked Mrs Kingston, immediately. Martin started to say *Yes* and then stopped. He hadn't actually been there all day, had he? He'd gone into town with Callum to buy a new battery pack for the laptop, as he knew the current one was useless and held no charge, and didn't want to be stuck to an outlet every time he wanted to write.

Anything to put off starting the actual *writing, eh?*
SHUT UP.

"Well actually, now I think of it, no, I left them in the back garden for an hour or so when I went out. Why, were they barking or something?"

Mrs Kingston let out a slight, bitter chuckle, and then her lips pursed tighter, eyes still kept fiercely away from Martin. This wasn't her style at all. She was, as everyone said, a very nice lady. Martin began to get a sinking feeling.

But they couldn't have done anything because they couldn't have gotten out, there's the—

"No, Martin, barking wouldn't have been a problem, especially not when I was *out* at the *supermarket*. It's my herb garden."

The sinking feeling became an elevator in freefall. The herb garden. The pride of Mrs Kingston's, well ... life. She was forever going from house to house, offering free, fresh herbs, partly out of pride, and partly out of kindness, and Elizabeth for one had always loved it, even though she'd made Martin do most of the cooking.

"You think my two have done something to it?"

She looked him in the eyes now, open hostility in hers.

"They've *destroyed* it, Martin. It's ruined. There's clearly two sets of paw prints left in the soil, and soil's all that's *left*, pretty much. They've chewed so many lines through it that it looks like someone's gone through it with a lawnmower!"

Lines?

"Lines?"

She looked confused at the question, and then answered anyway.

"Yes, lots of, lots of *trails* all through it, so many that there's practically nothing left. And there's soil *everywhere*. Martin, you know I never like to cause trouble or bother, and I can't imagine how things must have been for you after what happened to poor Elizabeth, but if you're going to keep dogs you've got to be *responsible and keep them under control!*"

Martin's own confusion came to the fore, annoyed greatly at the implication, but knowing that it had to be true. Lines? Patterns? Sounded like Scoffer's leaf game, all right.

But it CAN'T have been, because of the—

"Okay, let's just hold on a second here, Mrs Kingston. There's no way it could have been these two. They can't get out of the back garden."

"Well, they clearly have!"

"No, look, just listen," Martin said, snapping a little now. "Scoffer used to be able to get out when we first got him, but we put a stop to that years ago. Once he figured out how to open the gate as the catch was never great, we put wire around the thing to permanently close it. Wire's been there for the last, what, five years? We just don't use the gate anymore as a result, of course, but ..."

Not "we", Martin reminded himself, wincing internally. *Hasn't been "we" for some time.*

Callum. Me, Callum, Scoffer, and Chops. That's a "we", and that's my family. So dammit, we don't use that gate, and that's the right word to use.

"And you know how high the fence is around that garden," he continued, "you know that they couldn't have jumped that."

It was true. The cheap timber fence was over six feet high, and ever since he had tied the wire around the lock himself, Scoffer's afternoon excursions into the street had stopped happening. He was beginning to feel more assured now, and with that came a growing anger. She'd just assumed it was his dogs? Came round here to accuse first, and not ask? Who the hell did she think she was?

Easy. Take it easy. Don't get emotional. You've been getting way too emotional, overcompensating.

"Well, there's no one else on this street with *one* dog, let alone two," she said, raising two fingers to emphasise her point. "So where else did they come from?"

"I don't know, but I know these two *couldn't get out,*" said Martin, emphasising his own point and only just managing not to raise his voice. "So what can I say?"

Mrs Kingston fell silent, looking him in the eyes with her chest rising and falling heavily, her face red. They were at an impasse, both knowing their own individual truths that they found undeniable.

"Keep an eye on your dogs," she said finally, quiet and low and full of frustrated hurt. She turned before Martin could reply, and walked to the end of the short path to the street. Unable to help himself, Martin offered a parting shot of his own, knowing that it would cost him a friendly neighbour for good and deciding that in that moment he didn't give a shit.

"I do, *thank you very much,*" he called, and slammed the door.

He immediately regretted it, rubbing a shaking hand over his face. Why had he let that shake him up so quickly, and so much?

She mentioned Elizabeth. You have to keep an eye on that when there's other people involved. You can't crumble every time you hear her name. You're moving past that.

Correct ... but maybe he was having a hard time weaning off the fluoxetine?

We'll see. Now check that gate lock.

Good idea.

He headed through the kitchen and out of the back door, after letting a frantic Scoffer and Chops out of the living room. He'd shut them in there to stop them from harassing whoever was at the door, and now, freed from their prison, they went charging around the house to find whoever may have entered the building. For all of Scoffer's good behaviour, they'd never been able to stop him going bananas every time someone came to the house, and Chops was infected by his playmate's excitement. Martin left the pair to their hunt and stepped outside.

It was fully dark out now, and darker still in the small alleyway between his and Mrs Kingston's houses, so Martin couldn't see the gate lock until he was practically on top of the gate itself. He pulled his phone out of his pocket and switched on its torch function, which illuminated the lock so brightly that he might well have been looking at the small radius that it revealed in full daylight. Instantly, there was no denying it.

The wire around the lock had been chewed through.

"Shit ... "

He owed Kingston an apology. Martin rubbed at his face, and knew right away that the culprit had to be Chops. He was a bigger dog, with the literal chops to pull off that kind of chewing, as well as the fact that he'd probably already escaped from one home.

They didn't find the owner though, did they? No one came forward, and he wasn't chipped. He wouldn't be here otherwise.

So he might have always been a stray, or a puppy discarded from a litter for whatever reason. Regardless, he needed to find a way to fix that lock that was chew-proof. It'd have to be pretty hardcore; yes, the wire was old and maybe it had rusted enough to turn brittle, but even so ...

In a funny sort of way, finding out that he was wrong actually made him feel better. He could go and apologise to Mrs Kingston, and explain that while what he said was true, that the dogs had chewed through the wire and that he was sorry. She was a gracious enough woman that she would appreciate the apology and forget the whole thing, he was sure, and maybe even apologise back for coming on a bit strong.

He headed back inside, and caught sight of Chops sitting at the bottom of the stairs, chewing on Scoffer's rubber bone.

You little bugger, Martin thought, but he knew enough about dogs to know that telling him off now was absolutely pointless. Chops wouldn't even know what he was being scolded for. Even so, it was impressive that he'd figured out how to get out of the garden. A right little Houdini, that one. No more unsupervised time in the garden until the gate was fixed.

He couldn't stay angry at Chops anyway, not only because he knew that no matter how comfortable he seemed, this was a new way of life for Chops and his escape instincts were to be expected, but also because this large white ball of fuzz was so damn cute that Martin had little resistance. He was already bonding with the big lump.

Liz was right, Martin thought with a sad smile, *she always had to be the bad cop.*

It suddenly occurred to him that he had no photos of Chops yet. He was never really one for taking photos—that had usually been Elizabeth's job—but he was surprised that he hadn't gotten one of the new dog before now.

Well, it's not been official very long, has it? Him being part of the Motherless Family. Why would you take one anyway? You see him all day every day, and you certainly don't use Facebook these days, so why would you need it?

True. But he *should* take a photo, he knew. He should log this early time of Chops's days with him, capture an image of it.

"Cho-ops," Martin sang as he walked over, his phone still in his hand from when he was inspecting the gate. The dog ignored him. Chops had already been responding to his name, but when he was busy chewing, he sometimes needed a second call. "Chopsy," said Martin, crouching down on one knee as the dog looked up, tail starting to wag. The bone was still between his jaws. "Heh, yeah, keep that there for the photo, you big dope," chuckled Martin, the sound of his own laughter rare and pleasing to him. "That's how I'm used to seeing you anyway."

He held up the phone and pushed the camera logo, and waited until the app booted up and focused. Chops's big face was framed in the centre of the screen. The dog remained perfectly in place until, unsurprisingly, he moved at the last second, resuming chewing just as Martin pressed the shutter symbol, leaving him with a perfect snapshot of Chops's neck.

"Ah, bollocks," said Martin, sighing. "Chops? Here. Look here." The dog looked up again, and Martin again had the shot lined up perfectly, but this time the app took forever to focus, and by the time the shot was ready the dog had looked down again.

"Bloody hell," muttered Martin, half amused, half annoyed. "Come here, buddy." He very gently took the dog's muzzle in his hand and lifted slightly, holding Chops's mildly confused face up for the camera. "*That's* better," Martin said, smiling as he lined up the shot. He'd been uncertain at first of stroking Chops, once the dog was healed and back to being the energetic soul he clearly was; as a possible stray, Martin had zero idea of how Chops might be about human contact. The warden had even warned him of it. The shelter, however, after having Chops in their care, were emphatic about just how friendly and affectionate the big white walking carpet was, and they'd been right. It was already clear that Chops loved Martin, even after the few weeks he'd been there.

The dog pulled his face away from Martin's hand before he could take the photo, calmly moving his head out of Martin's gentle grip in a way that said *what are you doing? Not interested, thank you. I have a bone to chew.* Again the digital shutter closed on nothing but a wall of fur, and Martin laughed once more.

"Ah, come on, buddy!" Martin chuckled, reaching again for the dog's face, raising the camera and readying to take a quick photo this time, blurry or otherwise. "I just want to—"

Chops's head whipped towards Martin's hand—so quickly that he didn't have time to move it away or cry out—and the dog's teeth sank deep into the flesh between Martin's thumb and forefinger. *Then* Martin cried out, yelping in pain and pulling his hand away as Chops released his grip just as quickly as he had struck. Martin fell backwards from his kneeling position onto his bottom, hard, grabbing at his wrist and holding his hand up to his face. As he stared in shock at the puncture marks in his skin, already oozing blood, Chops darted off down the hallway, his tail between his legs.

Martin sat on the floor, breathing fast and hard, staring dumbly at his bleeding hand with his mouth open.

Son of a ... son of a ...

"Son of a *bitch!*" Martin gasped, the pain now reaching his brain as it tried to get a handle of his next, immediate option.

Infection, might get an infection. Rabid ...

NO, CAN'T BE RABID, THEY'D HAVE CHECKED HIM FOR THAT AT THE SHELTER.

He bit *you, he fucking* bit you!

YOU WERE GRABBING AT HIS FACE LIKE AN IDIOT AND HE DIDN'T LIKE IT, WHAT DID YOU EXPECT?

That was too much, way too much. That wasn't a nip, this was a full-bore bite, he didn't have to bite that hard, a dog that turns like that is dangerous. His fault? Your fault?

CALLUM.

Doors or no doors, this dog would be around his son, a son that would soon be all over the place, poking and prodding at a now seemingly volatile dog. He always watched his son, and he watched the dogs around his son, but if this could happen to a grown man then it only took one missed moment to create serious consequences. He thought of Callum upstairs, safe and sleeping, and the voices were off again.

But is it the dog's fault? He's been around Callum so much with no incident, the kid isn't even interested—

YOU'RE GOING TO RISK YOUR SON?

No, but I caused this, and Chops is a good dog, such a good dog—

YOU'RE GOING TO RISK YOUR SON?

No, but a dog less used to human contact than usual just got a hand around his face twice, he gave you a chance the first time—

YOU'RE GOING TO RISK YOUR SON?

No—

WASH YOUR HAND.

Yes, first things first, and again it was enough, it was good to leave the dilemma behind and focus on something practical, fixable. He shakily got to his feet, still pale with shock, and wandered to the downstairs toilet, wounded hand now throbbing. Where was Chops now? He'd run off down the corridor, towards the kitchen. The dining room/study door was next to the kitchen, and the toilet was next to that. Both doors were open, but there was no prize for guessing where Chops had bolted to; the two dogs' shared bed was in there, next to the computer. Martin had placed it there, imagining him writing while they slept at his feet. A lot of sleeping had happened, but no writing yet. Either way, that was sanctuary as far as the two dogs were concerned. That was where they would be. Was Scoffer in there too, wondering what on earth had happened? Martin didn't care just then. He had to clean his hand.

Wincing as the ice cold water hit his hand, water that had travelled through chill winter pipes, he felt the contradicting painful numbness spread over the wound and he gritted his teeth against it. Blood ran off in thin rivulets as it mixed with the clear liquid from the tap, and Martin could see the clear, ragged edges of the small holes in his hand. He pumped the antibacterial soap container and braced himself for the sting as he smeared it over the cluster of wounds, and that was when the house phone rang in the living room.

Of course, there was the following noise of Scoffer barking, another habit they'd not been able to train out of him. By the sounds of it, Scoffer was in the living room at the opposite end of the hallway, to Martin's surprise. The dogs weren't together. He rinsed off the soap quickly and gratefully, wrapped the hand towel around his fist, and stormed off to answer the call, anger now providing him strength but not dimming the shake in his limbs.

What a fucking ridiculous night. This better not be a sales call, or you are in for a hard time, asshole.

He was greeted at the living room door by an excited looking Scoffer, wearing a look that seemed to say *did you hear me? I was telling you about that noise again! There it is now!* Martin ignored his dog and picked the house phone up in the living room that he rarely used anymore. He pushed the green answer button and gripped the phone tightly, feeling too weary to give someone a verbal roasting yet relishing the prospect of doing so.

"Hello?" he said curtly, anger clear in his voice. A man's voice answered.

"Monsieur Hogan?"

Monsieur?

"Speaking."

There was a brief pause on the other end of the line, and Martin could hear the speaker's breathing clearly, as if he'd just finished running a race.

"Are you watching the news?"

What?

"I beg your pardon?"

"I know ... it is an odd question. Are you watching the news?"

What the fuck?

"Sorry, who exactly is this?"

A pause again. No audible breathing now, as if he was now under control.

"You need to turn on the news. BBC one."

Martin almost laughed as he realised that this conversation couldn't be any more perfect for tipping his anger over the edge.

"How's about fuck off, nobsack?" Martin said, furious now, and went to hang up, but realised that he couldn't. What the hell was this, after all? This was too out of the blue, too bizarre, and too terribly timed for him to get his head around it fast enough. "Actually, *who is this?*"

Kingston.

"Are you Kingston's son, or something? Seriously? Is this about her fucking *herbs*? Seriously? She only just left, and she's at it again already?"

The voice sounded confused for a moment as it responded.

"Uh ... no, Mister Hogan. I don't ... please, I am sorry, I know this is coming out of nowhere, but please trust me, it is better this way. Please turn on the news. It is important."

Please turn on the news? What? What? And what's with this guy's accent?

The speaker was continental European, clearly, although his English sounded excellent, refined. Martin's mouth worked silently, completely lost for words in his anger and confusion. Of *course* he wasn't going to turn the TV on. All he wanted to do was slam the phone down in a fury, smash it even, as this was so completely the opposite of what he needed after being bitten by his new dog, realising that he would probably have to send it away again, and that thought hurt far more than he expected, another loss. And now this *dick* on the phone, making weird requests that *of course* he wasn't going to carry out ... and yet even as he screwed his face up and shook his head, so outraged and confused that he couldn't find the right words to tell this guy *exactly how much and how far* he could fuck off, he was crossing the room to the TV, one-half of his brain working on its own agenda and being smart enough to know that he simply had to. How could he not? Did he really think that he wasn't going to find out?

"Are you kidding me? Are you fucking kidding me?" he lied, hitting mute the second the TV came on and waiting for the LCD screen to stop showing the manufacturer's logo and reveal the digital TV guide. There was no way he was going to give the guy the satisfaction of knowing that he'd done as he'd been told.

"Have you done it?" asked the voice.

"No," Martin lied again. "Who is this? Who is this?"

BBC One. He selected it and pushed the enter button. It was indeed the news, silently showing a series of images that would no doubt be accompanied by a reporter's voiceover had Martin not muted the speakers.

"I am actually a friend, Mr Hogan. I am trying to help. Are you seeing it?"

"Seeing what? The TV's *off.*" The feed cut back to the studio, with the middle-aged news anchor giving some follow-up comments to the story. The caption to the frozen image in the right-hand corner read BROTHERHOOD OF THE RAID.

The Internet thing? The copycat stuff that Barry was on about that time?

"Can you just look at it for a moment? Please? Just watch it, and give *me* a moment while you do."

Even though he wouldn't know an upper-class continental European accent from a working-class one, the speaker sounded educated. One used to speaking in well-to-do circles. For some reason, this just made Martin even angrier.

"Not until you tell me who this is. How did you get this number? This line is ex-directory."

"Please, Mr Hogan, just continue to watch and give me a moment."

"I told you, *I'm not watchi—*"

Continue to watch?

"Just a moment longer."

He knows. He can see you.

All of a sudden, what seemed like an infuriating, but still unsettling prank suddenly became something very frightening indeed. Martin's body immediately felt cold and stiff, and it was a major effort to get it to move over to the large living room window. He felt crudely exposed in front of all that glass, the protection of the house suddenly seeming paper thin and meaningless.

Someone ... someone's watching the house? Why would they ...?

He was a reasonably successful romance writer, a low-to-mid level success that left him comfortable enough to just about live off his royalties. His income was boosted by workshop bookings, true, but he was certainly far from being majorly famous, or someone who could be considered wealthy. He knew this. It was unlikely to be a money thing.

It could be another Janet Duggan.

Nine years before, just after the peak success of his career—*A Careless Slip*, which he'd somehow never really managed to capitalise on or creatively better—they had to take out a restraining order on a woman from Oxford who had become fixated on him, or more importantly, upon Liz. It had started with Janet Duggan waiting outside Liz's work, at first just sitting and watching until Liz passed—no one knew how long she'd been doing it before Elizabeth spotted her a few times—and progressing to turning up anywhere Liz went alone, always at a distance, of course. The police were no help until Janet Duggan had started sending increasingly bizarre and rambling letters to Liz, always in the same scratchy handwriting that escalated into a barely legible mess by the end. *He doesn't love you, he loves me, we were meant to be together, it's only a matter of time, his books were written for me, we wrote them together, they're all my ideas.* Excellent, wonderful Liz never believed any of it, and if anything, the letters helped assure her that Duggan was delusional. They were the rants of a lunatic.

Liz wouldn't leave the house after that; not necessarily frightened but wanting to avoid any unpleasant incidents. She wouldn't go anywhere unaccompanied, but somehow Duggan still managed to confront Liz between exiting the doctor's surgery—Martin had been waiting in the car to pick her up, having nipped to the bank while she was inside—and begin screaming hysterically in her face. Liz, to her credit, tried to simply walk around the yelling madwoman, but Duggan had kept making avoiding her impossible. Elizabeth had then immobilised Duggan with a wrist lock before placing her in a choke hold until she passed out. Duggan, for all of her constant surveillance of Elizabeth, had somehow failed to realise that the black belt Liz wore at ninjutsu class *wasn't just for show.* Liz had then calmly walked to the car, although clearly shaken up by the affair, and asked for Martin's phone so that she could call the police.

Duggan had been arrested and diagnosed as schizophrenic and a danger to the public health. She'd been sectioned, and Martin had heard later that she'd been badly wounded by another female inmate. She'd used a plastic board game piece that she'd somehow managed to sharpen. Duggan wasn't getting out any time soon. Even so ... was it happening again? A man, this time? Someone more physically threatening? Martin wasn't a weak man, and even though he'd become criminally guilty of neglecting the gym since Elizabeth died, he was still reasonably solid, and at his average height he weighed around a fairly trim one hundred eighty pounds. He wasn't a fighter, however.

Why do I need to train anyway, he'd joked to Liz, *when I'll just set my wife on 'em?*

"Monsieur Hogan? Are you there? You have stopped watching, I think?"

Martin didn't answer, and peered through the window, scanning the streetlight-lit—but still dark—road outside. His house was nestled in the bottom of the cul-de-sac's curve, so his view was good. He got his answer immediately.

There was black van parked one hundred feet away from the house, squatting just outside of a streetlight's beam like a fat black bug.

"Monsieur Hogan?"

"Fu ... " Martin couldn't breathe.

Callum, an urgent voice insisted in Martin's head, and only just made it through.

The voice spoke again on the phone, but it wasn't addressing Martin, the speaker clearly turning away from the mouthpiece to talk to someone else. Martin could just about make the words out, as ice ran through his veins and he staggered backwards slightly.

"Okay, we are safe. Obtain."

Obtain?

CALLUM.

Martin was already turning, about to bolt for the stairs on instinct alone to get to his son, when he heard the faint clicking sound coming from the back of the house, followed by an explosion of barking.

What's happening? WHAT'S HAPPENING?

Martin flung the living room door wide and charged out into the hallway. He saw the two dogs excitedly barking at the kitchen door, or more specifically at the three large balaclava wearing figures that they could see through the door's glass panel. The figures were clearly men, dressed in black, and carrying some kind of automatic-looking weaponry. The most frightening thing was that, apart from the clicking Martin had heard when they'd been doing whatever they'd done to get into the house—

They wouldn't have even needed to do anything, you left the back door unlocked, you asshole, what the hell is happening, what the HELL IS HAPPENING—

—they were completely silent, despite their intimidating size. Martin remained frozen where he was, locked in place by fear and the sheer lunacy that was occurring right now, *right in his home.* It was dreamlike, airy almost, in spite of the solid bulk of the intruders and the glistening black *realness* of their guns.

They saw him now, and straightened slightly, realising that stealth was out of the window. There was the briefest of pauses, and then the men burst through the door, the man in the lead pulling out some kind of unusual looking pistol and shooting something into both of the barking dogs at their feet. Neither of them whined—they didn't have time—and as the men charged down the hallway, Martin caught a glimpse of the dogs staggering slightly before dropping in a heap on the floor.

It wasn't the sight of his dogs being shot that broke the spell. Even in his fear Martin could quickly and detachedly process that the gun wasn't a normal gun, that the small coloured tag attached to whatever they had fired meant that they hadn't shot bullets into his pets, and it all led to the projecting of the word *tranquiliser* onto his brain in sixty-feet-high letters. That sent his concern crashing back onto more immediately pressing matters, and it was the thundering of the men's boots as they dashed the short length of the hall towards him that brought him leaping back to himself in a lightning bolt eureka moment. Another word was sent up, the same one he'd thought when he'd first realised the danger:

CALLUM

With only a second or two to move before they were upon him, Martin turned to his left and bolted towards the door that led to the bottom of the stairs. He was thinking wildly as he moved:

Inwards, the fucking thing opens inwards, *you're going to be delayed, you won't have time to close it*

His icy cold hand grasped the door handle and turned it, feeling insane as he pulled it inwards and *towards* the men that he was trying to get away from, knowing that the motion was costing him precious milliseconds as his back broke out in goose bumps, preparing to feel the heavy grasp of the first of several grabbing hands—

No tranq for you; they aren't tranq-ing you, why not

Then he was through the doorway, his feet biting into the first few steps and charging upstairs towards the room where his son was now crying, Martin realising that he could hear Callum's squalls that must have begun when he was startled awake by the barking and banging. Martin didn't have a plan, only instinct, operating on a certainty of action that came to him rarely if ever, knowing only that he had to get to his son, to get there and maybe barricade the door with the bookshelf; yes, the bookshelf might do it if he could get it turned over and sit on it in time—

Something hit the stairs between his ankles, expertly thrown and timed perfectly in order to trip both of his feet as they charged. Martin stumbled, knees hitting the thinly carpeted steps painfully, but he was already getting up before a hand grabbed first his ankle, then his opposite calf. He fell forward again, and felt himself gripped on both of his thighs by someone else as weight dropped onto his back, pushing his chest flat across the edges of two of the steps as his chin fell against the upstairs landing floor.

You almost made it—

He thrashed again and began to scream, fear and frustration and confusion coming out at once, Callum's room was right there, *right there*, feet away. A gloved hand went over his mouth and Martin bit down, hard, hearing a grunt from behind him, and he tried to scream again but the weight increased on his back and compressed his lungs.

"Don't scream, Mister Hogan!" a voice from behind him hissed, and it was a different person to the one that had been on the phone. "Calm down! Calm down! We have to do this, so calm down, calm down, calm down."

"Get ... out ... of ... eghhhh ..." Martin managed, the last part choked off.

"We don't want to hurt you, Mister Hogan," another voice said, coming from his left, several bodies now squeezed into the small space between the banister and the wall. "We've been told not to, and to avoid putting you under if possible. Just cooperate, and we'll get this done quickly." Both voices had been raised slightly, sounding as if they were under some effort to not shout but needing to be heard over Martin's grunts.

Callum, CALLUM—

"Get ... out ..."

There was silence from the assailants, the only sound being their strains and Martin's wheezes and moans.

"He's going under," said the first voice, not addressing Martin, sounding like he was talking to someone who wasn't there. There was a pause while a response was waited for, and then Martin thought that he might have heard one faintly along with a crackle of radio static. Then there was a sharp, punching sensation in his left shoulder, and Martin lost consciousness.

***

Chapter Three: I Can Never Take It Back, The Swiss Connection, The Power of the Written Word, and The Three Begin Their Journey
***

PROPERTY OF SUSSEX POLICE ITEM 117-WC24 NASH INCIDENT EVIDENCE 5A 3/10/2014

Dear Molly,
    And I mean that. You are the *dearest* thing to me that I have ever known in this world.
    It comes down to that fact. The fact that you will never, ever understand why I did the terrible, terrible thing that I did to you. I could blame it on a psychosis, a brain twist of some kind, I don't know, find *some* way to say that I wasn't of sound mind when it happened, and you might even believe me, might even forgive me. But you could never trust me again, and you would be *right* to never trust me again. You can never trust me again, *because I might do it again.* Do you understand? Why the fuck did I even write that, of course you don't. Anyway. I shouldn't be writing this letter, I know I shouldn't, but I *have* to. I need you to know how much I love you.
    That's the other thing. I wouldn't take it back, even though I wish I could so desperately. Why it had to be me, I don't know, but it did.
    And that's the third thing. The thought that I might have to do that to someone else. That wouldn't be anywhere near as bad—still bad, but not as bad—but I know that with every blow, I would see your face. I can never see that again.
    So I have to leave, and the thought is comforting, Molly. If you ever read this and feel some shred of forgiveness, pity even, please don't. I feel at peace as I go. Things are coming, Molly, changes all over the world, and I think that this planet isn't going to be a very nice place to be. I thought about taking it further, to save you experiencing any of that, and *please* understand that the

thought wasn't out of malice or anger. It was out of love. I don't know if I should even tell you that, as I know how that sounds. It sounds like the crazy lover who decided that he loves his wife so much that they need to die together to be protected from the world blah blah blah, and that's the exact reason why I *didn't*. I realised that would be exactly what I was doing. So I leave the choice up to you.

But I'm saying it now because when things start to change, and the *world* starts to change, and I'm not here, I don't want you to say *why didn't he tell me? Why didn't he take me with him, why didn't he save me from the burden?* I would have done—oh God, I would have done—but I didn't have that luxury, I didn't have that option. I had to do what I had to do the way it had to be done, and there was no time to sit and explain that bad things were coming. Just remember that I would have warned you before, and that I'm warning you now.

I would have taken you with me if I had the right. I love you. I love you so much. I'm so sorry. This is my punishment, but selfishly, it's also my blessing. Ah fuck. It's all such a terrible mess. My head is so, so

I love you
 I wish I could have
I'm sorry sorry sorry sorry sorry never enough
Duncan

***

There was faint road noise, and dim light reaching under his eyelids. These were the first things that Martin was aware of, immediately followed by a sharp headache. He tried to move his hands to his forehead, but couldn't. They were bound behind his back. The knowledge that he was abducted came quickly as he associated *bound hands* with *kidnap*, and then memory rushed in of big men, tranquilisers, barking dogs, and—

Callum.

His son. Alone.

Adrenaline flooded his brain and wrestled with the majority of the chemical fog still in there, and Martin opened his groggy eyes. His shoulder ached badly where it had been hit with whatever they'd fired into him. Martin's gaze was met by that of another man, an extremely tired-looking man at that, so much so that for one crazy, drug-fuddled moment of empathy or imagination, Martin immediately knew that this man was almost dead.

He knows it himself ...

The man opposite Martin sat up fully as he realised that Martin had come round. There was a sensation of movement, and as Martin fell slightly forwards only to be held in place by the gentle restraint of a seatbelt, he realised that he was in the back of a large vehicle, probably a van. The setup was different to a normal, passenger-converted van though; instead of facing the windscreen, the seats that Martin and his new travelling companion occupied ran along the opposite walls of the van's rear, facing each other. It had obviously been converted so that people could enter and exit the vehicle from the rear, and quickly—

Lots of people, the people that were IN YOUR HOUSE—

He was about to open his mouth to scream, but the man opposite him began talking so earnestly, and so *perfectly* on cue just before Martin spoke, that it caught him off guard. He fell silent in surprise.

"Monsieur Hogan, please, before you say anything, let me first say this," said the man, speaking with that strong but well-spoken European accent. This was the person who had been on the other end of the phone. "Your son is perfectly safe, still in his bed even, and we are deeply, deeply sorry at having to take the course of action that we did. Safety in this matter, I feel, is absolutely paramount, as you will see. I am sure that you are very, very upset, but I want you to know that it is not something we did lightly or carelessly. To enter a man's home without permission, especially a man with an infant to look after ... unforgivable."

The man shook his head slightly, and for a moment seemed to look through Martin, reminded of other sins and seeing them projected faintly against the metal interior of the van. In this pause, even through the drugs and the confusion—*how did all this start? I'd been sitting down to eat a bloody bowl of soup, all I wanted to do was have some nice soup and then Kingston was at the door, and then MEN WITH BLOODY WEAPONS CAME IN, WHAT THE HELL*—Martin unconsciously took in the European man and their surroundings.

The van interior was black metal, and half of the bulkhead between the driver's section at the front of the van and the back was a transparent plastic partition, revealing three men sitting in the front. They faced forwards as the vehicle drove through the night. Martin realised that another man was sitting a few feet to his left, still wearing his balaclava. The men in the front had removed theirs, presumably to avoid looking like a van full of terrorists and also because their faces obviously couldn't be seen from the back.

The man directly in front of him didn't seem in the least bit concerned about allowing his face to be seen, however. He was staring Martin full in the face, sunken eyes boring into Martin's with penetrating earnestness.

He knows he has nothing to lose. His time is running out anyway.

HOW THE HELL DO YOU KNOW THAT?

Of course, he didn't, but in his disorientated state Martin was convinced that it was true. Plus, it wasn't even too much of a stretch. The guy *looked* half dead. His face was gaunt and unshaven, and his long dark hair looked straggly and unwashed. His facial appearance was very much at odds with the expensive-looking suit that he wore, however, and the purple silk tie.

His butler looks after his suits. His butler dresses him. But he won't let the butler shave him any more than once every two weeks. He doesn't like blades. Electric razors bring him out in a rash. He doesn't wash his hair either. He doesn't bathe. If it wasn't for the fact that he uses his swimming pool, he would completely stink—

Martin shook his head sharply. What was this gibberish?

And why aren't you freaking out either, come to think of it? You've been TAKEN FROM YOUR HOME, for crying it loud, like something out of a Hollywood movie, BUT YOU LIVE IN SUBURBAN BLOODY COVENTRY, and CALLUM IS ALONE! Are they terrorists? Are you going to be tortured? Why aren't you rupturing every muscle in your body trying to break these ropes? Why aren't you screaming so loud that your eardrums rupture?

And he *was* freaking out, and he *was* terrified for Callum ... but it was like those thoughts had been smothered somehow, covered by a thick blanket of calm that told him—gave him the *knowledge*—that his son was safe and so was he. Which was, of course, utterly ridiculous, and clearly due to the chemical relaxants in whatever they'd shot him up with. He tried to get a grip on thoughts of Callum, and again, the man opposite seemed to preempt Martin's very thoughts. Without taking his eyes away from Martin's, the straggly haired man snapped the fingers of his left hand, which he then held out. The large man in the balaclava handed him a computer tablet, which the skinny man turned over and held up to Martin's gaze. The screen showed a feed from the green image usually produced by night vision cameras; it revealed a sleeping infant, completely unconscious and unaware of whomever was standing close by, filming him. The child's cheeks glistened slightly, drying after recent tears, which was to be fully expected after being woken by the shouts and banging of several men grappling on the stairs below his bedroom. Now Martin's heart truly lurched, penetrating whatever currently held his natural instinct gently in check.

"I am showing you this to reassure, not to threaten, Monsieur Hogan," the straggly haired man said again, with that eerie timing so precise that it again stopped Martin's voice dead in its tracks. Plus, he just *knew* that his man would have an explanation. *How can I be so terrified and so calm at the same time?* "Your son has not been moved, touched, or anything of the kind. This feed is live; see, I can prove it. Say whatever you wish; my man can hear you."

Martin goggled at the screen, too confused to argue, too bewildered to not simply take the logical option before him. He could check the man's claim; why not do it? His tongue felt thick in his mouth, which he now realised was very dry, but he got the words out in a thick, sluggish drawl.

"Pan the camera up and down twice. Then round in a circle," he said, his words as breathless as they were slow. This was madness, the calm response of a lunatic, but he was saying it and the camera was now indeed moving up and down twice, before circling around.

Could be a recorded shot. They could just be moving the image around.

Everything was moving so horribly, weirdly fast.

"Put two fingers on the edge of the crib. Then three."

The shot moved closer to the crib as the cameraman moved within reach of it, and then a black gloved hand slowly emerged from the bottom of the frame, resting its fingers on the frame of the crib in the sequence requested. The silence of it made Martin's skin crawl, feeling as if his son were being observed by spiders made of black leather.

They won't hurt him. They won't even touch him.

BUT HOW DO YOU—

"You see?" the man said, handing the tablet to Balaclava, who continued to hold it up for Martin's benefit. "I will leave it there, so you will feel more reassured. But I think you already know, yes? We are not your enemies. The manner in which this has come about was unfortunate, but it was necessary. For our safety." The man's face paled in the darkness of the van reminded of whatever he had to discuss, and Martin's nerves spiked as the blanket seemed to lift for a moment. Reality peeked its rotting mask into his mind the second it was allowed any purchase. He'd been kidnapped, *kidnapped—*

"Sincere apologies," soothed the man, holding up his hands and regaining his composure, the inside of the van seeming to warm up in the process. He forced a smile, but it didn't reach his sunken eyes. "'I shall explain myself. My name is Sylvain Rougeau. I have come a long way to see you, Monsieur Hogan. A long way. It is a matter of great urgency."

Martin was surprised again, on a night already filled with surprises. He already knew this man's name, and this time there was no unusual mental transmission telling him anything. It was a name that had been in the news for several weeks, many years ago, in a story that had been very much on his and every other romance author's radar.

This guy is Sylvain Rougeau? But that guy was ... not like this.

Indeed he hadn't been. The Sylvain Rougeau in the media had been young, handsome, rich, and possessed of that Gallic rock n' roll star presence that guaranteed a media frenzy as soon as he became involved. So what the hell had happened since? Martin realised with deep shock that the man before him—based on what he remembered from the news—had to be only twenty-five years old. Now, just seven years later, he looked like he was pushing forty-five.

"You know my name," Sylvan said with a sad smile. "You are surprised. This is normal. It is not the first time that I have seen that reaction."

I don't doubt it, mon ami, Martin thought, remembering the swagger and pride of the eighteen-year-old that had been swarmed by the press as he made his way up the courtroom steps on the final day of the trial. Remembering how that same swagger had been revealed to be nothing more than a shield as he'd made his way out again. However, even the fact that Martin was stuck in the back of a van with a formerly notorious celebrity was, like everything, smothered by that invisible blanket of calm. It felt like discovering that your new next-door neighbour had once played backup guitar for Englebert Humperdinck. *Really? What was that like then?*

Would Rougeau have achieved such worldwide notoriety if the first bodies found hadn't been American? Maybe; the story had all the elements for a media bloodbath, after all. Kelly and Simon Steiner had been two American backpackers in their early twenties whose bodies had been found in a forest in Lausanne, Switzerland. They were discovered lying hand in hand with their throats cut, with a note left at the nearby (apparently in Simon Steiner's handwriting) saying only *For the world to come, we go to prepare.*

While it was treated as a religious suicide, they'd only been the first. Concerns began to escalate rapidly when more started to turn up around the city in similar circumstances, accompanied by notes making similar prophetic statements. Over the months to come, more connections were made, eventually leading to a well-hidden financial paper trail funding a secret organisation called the Church of the First Vision. When arrests were made and the beneficiaries of the donations were revealed, the media had a field day. The money had been landing, through various convoluted channels, in the accounts of the Rougeau family, one of the wealthiest families in Europe. They were the organisational heads of the Church of the First Vision, but they weren't the *religious* figurehead. That had been their son, the teenaged Sylvain Rougeau, whose parents had secretly had a cult built around him—and his alleged "gifts"—since he was old enough to walk.

Whilst the court eventually found Sylvain Rougeau innocent of all charges except tax evasion, they felt differently about his parents (some of the more salacious accusations had been child abuse, kidnapping, incitement to murder, and intimidation), and the papers had been far less interested in the case than they had been in the juicy details of the cult itself. The general consensus was that, while the Rougeaus had originally built the secret cult around their son out of genuine belief, the money that it generated over the years had caused the whole thing to spiral out of control, coming to a crashing halt when Sylvain walked out on his followers as soon as he turned eighteen.

According to his court testimony, Rougeau had become "tired of being used as a pawn, as a performing show pony" and, after a long and heavily acrimonious argument with his parents, had left the family home. Allegedly, this only came after wielding a hunting rifle in order to escape. He had then disappeared into France, and claimed under oath that he'd heard nothing of the carnage that came in the wake of his departure.

The court accepted, eventually, that Sylvain had indeed been a victim of his parents' controlling manipulation, and had no part in the darker activities of the Church. His parents' own testimony and statements only solidified their son's claims; they suffered from severe mental illness and mania. Certainly, their own defence pled insanity on their behalf, and while they never confessed directly, the Rougeaus' rambling, self-glorifying accounts combined with eyewitness statements and tapped telephone conversations were more than enough to satisfy the court. The Rougeaus had led their followers to suicide, claiming their son's departure was due to an "ascent to heaven." There was, of course, only one way to join him. They called it "a metamorphosis". The prosecution called it "tying up loose ends".

Incredibly, the sway that they held over their followers was so strong that many believed them. The few that didn't went into hiding and—once the Rougeaus and higher ranking Church of the First Vision leaders were arrested—emerged to testify during the trial.

The insanity plea didn't hold. The senior Rougeaus went to jail, and Sylvain walked free ... only it was a very different Sylvain on the way out. The bloodless relief on his face said it all. This was a scared little boy, for whom the nightmare was over, but also someone who could never truly escape his part in the deaths of two hundred sixty-seven men and women. They had come from all over the world to be led by Sylvain. They'd come to be taught the secrets of the world beyond, not knowing that the Church's figurehead had never wanted—or asked—to do anything of the sort. All they would actually learn of the other side would turn out to be, ultimately, from firsthand experience.

Then came the capper to the whole affair; the Rougeaus had, unknown to them, inducted the son of Rodolpho Marella—a Milan mafia boss—into the Church. The son had then committed suicide at the Rougeaus' behest ... along with his pregnant girlfriend, therefore taking not one but two heirs to the Marella family business. This did not sit well with the Marellas. The general consensus, although never proved, was that the prison suicide of Sylvain's father, Sebastien Rougeau, was actually an arranged hit. The news got to Sylvain's mother before she could be put on suicide watch. She was found hanged in her cell. That was the other reason many attributed to Sylvain's post-trial disappearance; the Marellas wanted to hit all of the Church leaders, even if they had walked out on it.

Many said that this was the real reason Sylvain had become a recluse after the trial, returning to France and living off the immense inheritance that he received, as for some inexplicable reason the Rougeaus had never altered their will (and even after legal fees, compensation, and reclaimed monies, the amount left was still vast).

Which certainly explains him having the means to organise something like this, Martin thought crazily, looking at the corpse-like figure before him. Even in the low light from the street lamps outside and passing cars—the minimum of which reached the back through the front windscreen—Martin could see how pale Rougeau was. This was not a man who saw much sun.

"Monsieur Hogan, the *reason* for such extreme measures was, to be frank, because we had to be safe. You notice that I sent my men into your home while I remained hidden in this vehicle, coward that I am. I have become very good at hiding, it is natural to me now. We had to *check,* you see. We had to get close safely so that I could ... have a look at you, as it were. For all I knew, the problem could be you. But it is not, I know this now. The ropes remain on you purely for my own safety, or rather, yours; without them, you may feel inclined to attack me—perfectly understandable, of course—in which instance my man here would be forced to intervene, and that would not be something I would wish you to experience, nor something that you deserve."

Martin looked at Balaclava, whose steely blue eyes met Martin's with a relaxed, easy gaze. The Balaclava nodded up and down. Martin quickly looked back at Rougeau.

"What is this about?" asked Martin, his voice a little clearer, half of his head screaming *KIDNAPPED, CALLUM,* the other simply curious, reassured by something imperceptible. Rougeau sighed in response, and his brow furrowed as his eyes became even more earnest, blinking rapidly as he spoke.

"Monsieur Hogan, there is ... this is difficult to explain, but please try to understand. You must listen, yes?" He placed his palms together, clasping his hands as if he were begging, and began to rock backwards and forwards as he spoke.

"Something is very *wrong*, Monsieur Hogan. Something is very wrong in the world, something that is happening already and something that is going to grow larger. Something very, very *big* is coming to us all, and it is unnatural, and you ... you are at the heart of it, Monsieur Hogan. It revolves around you, it *centres* on you. Your name is burned across my brain and across my heart, and I *had* to know you and talk with you and investigate you, get *close* to you, so that I could find out more, and what you are doing. You see?" His hands unclasped as he continued his babbling speech, holding them up and open, that frantic look still on his face. Martin just gaped, blinking himself now. Rougeau continued.

"But then I come here, I travel all the way to you, and I know, before you are even placed in this vehicle with me, that you know nothing. I can *feel* it. I do not think that this surprises you. No?"

He's doing it. He's doing whatever is happening in your head. This is why they built the Church around him. This is what they saw in him as a child, and why they made him a prophet as a result. Crazy or not, his parents knew his gift was real. His gift is real. The media, all of us, we laughed about it and went back to our breakfast cereal, our online shopping for cheap shoes—

But that was all impossible, ludicrous, and so Martin just continued to sit and listen, spellbound somehow.

"I thought coming here would clarify things," said Rougeau, "zooming in on a focused point as if with a microscope, but it has not worked that way. It is all around here, as if from the moment we reached your city I could not zoom in any more. Instead, it is like a cloud that hangs over this place, waiting, and its influence has spread across the globe. With you here, Coventry is at the heart of something worldwide, Monsieur Hogan."

The Ska movement, you mean? You're too late, monsieur, Two-Tone peaked in the eighties, but I'm still a fan myself, thought Martin crazily, a rare joke in his head, and nearly burst out laughing. This was *nuts.* But even so, there was only one question that could be asked in response.

"What is it?"

Rougeau looked at him, eyes blinking still.

"I don't know."

"... what?"

"I can't tell you, Monsieur Hogan. This is what I wanted to find out. Once upon a time, perhaps, I could have done more. Seen the truth more easily. But not now. I am ... less than I once was." He breathed out through his nose, and settled back against the van wall. "In Lausanne ... I was great. Truly great. I could tell you what you had for breakfast three weeks ago on a Tuesday morning. Tell me, Monsieur Hogan, what did *I* have for breakfast this morning?"

The question was ridiculous, but the answer was already there in his head. *A yoghurt, some fruit. You bought them at the motorway services this morning on your way here.*
WHAT THE HELL—
Rougeau smiled, and nodded. Martin hadn't needed to speak.

"I remember the first time," he said, continuing his reminiscing, the supposedly earnest matter seemingly forgotten. *More proof that he's crazy*, Martin thought, and maybe that was true, at least in terms of how well the cogs still turned in the man's mind ... but Martin didn't feel that way about the claims Rougeau was making. Something was dimly ringing very, very true. "Father handing me a present and telling me to open it, and I *knew* already that it was a toy car. I could see it as if the wrapping wasn't there. His face, when I said *car* before I'd opened it ... I'm not sure my father was ever a truly well man, Monsieur Hogan. I don't judge him for how it all started, but for what he became ... that was greed, pure and simple."

"I never attributed it to God, or Gaia, or anything in between. To me, it was always just something that I could do, and the more Father talked about divine influence and fate and paraded me before the followers, the more he pushed me away from believing in all that; it was all so far removed from what I actually felt and experienced, that I never fully believed in Father's talk of heaven. And then I reached puberty, and everything changed."

Where the hell is he going with this? Martin's eyes flicked again to his sleeping son, green and peaceful on the tablet's screen, and felt a dreamlike, confusing mix of rage and reassurance. *Let him talk. Once he's done, he'll take you home. You know this. Just let him talk.*

"I was ... no longer the same, Monsieur Hogan. Something had changed inside me, the chemical imbalance of my growing hormones altering something in mind perhaps, and I could no longer do it in the same way. Yes, I would get the odd flash—I still do—and I might suddenly know where someone's lost set of keys was, or that the person passing me in the street was contemplating suicide, but I could no longer perform the truly impressive feats. Certainly not at will. It became impossible to ever *know* anything for certain, so used was I to experiencing the bliss of absolute, clear perception of truth; can you imagine? Gone. I struggle now to decide even what I should do with my afternoons.

"Father covered up for it, of course, and I would go along with whatever he wanted. By then, he and Mother were lost in their mania and their roles as head of the church. He brought in illusionists to create new and better feats, trained me to cold-read people to the point that I was almost as convincing as before. Planted actors in congregations. Convinced himself that it was all a good means to an end. Mother, I think, was never as certain, but Father was a very *convincing*, enigmatic individual. I believe they say that psychopaths often are. I was a diligent, loyal, performing sheep, too profoundly dead inside after my loss to do anything else. Only when I was asked to denounce members of the faithful as unbelievers, to incite the mob to turn on those who, I later found out, had questioned Father's leadership, did something snap. Had members of our security staff not been more loyal to me, the centrepiece of the Church, than Father's leadership, then I think I would still be there to this day. Had I known then what would happen as a result of my departure, I still would be."

Rougeau's eyes had moved to the ceiling as he talked, lost in seldom-visited memories, but now they dropped back to Martin, urgent once more.

"But *you*, Monsieur Hogan," he said gently, wagging a finger and sitting forward, the excitement returning to his body, "you changed that. At least, in this instance. Several weeks ago, I had the first real *knowledge* in over a decade, and I think it nearly killed me."

I can believe it. I think anything stronger than a stiff breeze would finish you off.

"Knowledge like that, it is a physical thing," Rougeau said. "Not just in the mind. My body was both out of shape in matters of *knowing* and ... well. You can see. But to experience it once more was both beautiful and—I am sorry to say, Monsieur Hogan, but if this frightens you then that is perhaps a good thing—deeply terrifying. In that moment, I felt the surface of this world *shift*, Monsieur Hogan. I glimpsed something, a change for humanity, and knew that *something would be lost forever, lost to us all*. That is the best way that I could describe it." He actually put his hand on Martin's leg now, a tight grip on his lower thigh, and then Martin felt something else, dimly at the edge of his mind. *Fear*. Rougeau's fear. And the knowledge of something else ... something dark on the horizon, something unnatural and impossibly big.

Then it was gone, and Martin was in a van once more with a lunatic.

"Monsieur Hogan, I have failed again. I wanted answers here, and there are none, and so all I can give you is a warning, and my assistance if you need it. Tell me; have you noticed anything new in your life? Any changes, any signs? Feeling as if you were being watched, perhaps, I don't know, people that you don't recognise being around? I am guessing. I am in the dark completely. Anything?"

Martin shook his head, dumbly. He just wanted to get out of this van filled with maniacs and go home, just as he considered the question calmly at the same time and found an answer.

Chops. Chops is new.

CHOPS IS A DOG. AN INJURED DOG THAT YOU TOOK HOME. THAT HARDLY COUNTS.

But he said anything new.

YOU WANT THESE PEOPLE BACK IN YOUR HOUSE? INSPECTING YOUR DOG?

They're in there now. What difference would it make? He's telling the truth. You know he's telling the truth.

MORE OF THEM, TO ADD TO THE PEOPLE ALREADY STANDING OVER YOUR SLEEPING SON? MENTION A NEW DOG AND DRAG THIS OUT EVEN LONGER, MORE HIRED MERCENARIES SHARING A HOUSE WITH YOUR BABY?

You felt it like he feels it!

BECAUSE HE'S CRAZY, AND WHETHER HE'S FOR REAL AND WHETHER HE'S SOME KIND OF MASTER MENTAL MANIPULATOR, HE BELIEVES IT AND HE'S MAKING YOU FEEL FUNNY. YOU'VE NOT FELT RIGHT SINCE YOU'VE BEEN IN HERE, HAVE YOU? AND THE ONE THING THAT IS ABSOLUTELY, POSITIVELY INARGUABLE IS THE FACT THAT THESE MEN ARE ARMED AND THEY'RE IN YOUR HOUSE WITH YOUR SON, ALONE. DO YOU WANT THAT TO CONTINUE?

That did it. For once—a feeling so sweet that it brought Martin out in goose bumps all over his body—Martin knew a course of action with complete certainty. Like Rougeau had said, some knowledge was so strong that it became a physical thing. What the hell was so wrong with him that he even needed to argue with himself over this? Whatever Rougeau was doing to him, hypnosis, suggestion, whatever, he had to get this over with and get out of there, no matter how normal he was convinced it felt.

"No. Nothing at all, Sylvain."

Rougeau looked at him for a moment, his eyes examining Martin's face and narrowed as if he were trying to concentrate, to hear something.

"You ... have a new pet?" he said.

A little trickle of electricity ran down Martin's spine.

He could have been watching the house. There's a million ways that he could know that.

"I bought a dog. You think that's a sign of the apocalypse?"

Rougeau smiled gently, and even cocked his head slightly, pursing his lips. *Fair point.*

"No, no, I do not. But this is not a joking matter, you must understand. Monsieur Hogan, I have not been able to do anything like this since I was fifteen years old. You understand? This connection we have right now; I cannot do this with anyone else in the world. You feel this, yes? I have soothed you as well as I can, to make this easier. Like it is something that, perhaps, happened to you some time ago and that you have had time to deal with. I have led you quickly to that place. *I cannot do this with anyone else."*

Yeah right. It's a nice trick, buddy, and you had me going for a while. You've even got me going now. But I see you, a rich smack head who just can't help himself from trying to live the life his parents trained him for. You're just going about it a different way and trying to convince yourself that you're doing your own thing.

"I had you watch the news report, Monsieur Hogan, because I wanted to know if that triggered anything in you. Anything that perhaps even you did not know about."

"The ... news ...?"

"Just before we, ah, brought you in. The report on the Brotherhood of the Raid."

Those idiots that are beating people up because they saw someone do it online or whatever? What does that have to do with anything?

"That is something that I wonder about," Rougeau said. "It is only a hunch, and for me that is even less substantial than it would be for you, as never *knowing* means uncertainty in everything. But it concerns me. It concerns me. Regardless; I can only warn you then, Monsieur Hogan, for now. Warn you to be vigilant, because I cannot help unless I know what to help *with*. As well ... I cannot stay here, in this city. It is too much. I am under chemical influence even now, so that I may talk with you rationally, but being this close to the heart of everything is difficult. Very difficult. But I will stay in the country, at least. I have property in London that I seldom use, and I can be that close. You will need my help, I fear. It will be good for me. It has been a long time since I have been to London, after all. Or anywhere."

That's because he lives in a compound. It has guards, and fences, and is luxurious on the inside. He has other people with him there, the people who survived the Church of the First Vision and had their lives ruined, people whom he feels he owes a debt to. And he never leaves because of the Marellas, but also because he doesn't want to as there is nothing out there for him now, not since he lost the sight. But sex is his Achilles' heel, and he pays for it, ships them in, and that's why—

The revelation broke his reverie, and Martin realised just how far out of himself he had gone. He stared at the man in front of him with fresh fear that even the smothering blanket in his mind couldn't mute. He could not know those things the way he had just *known* them by mere tricks of the mind. Knowledge like that was solid. Certainty was a fist. This was not suggestion. This was not hypnosis. That had all been *sent,* like a letter made of steel in his mind.

This was for real.

Rougeau was nodding, and Martin found his voice once more. Asking *how* was pointless; Rougeau had already told him how, and what he knew in that regard. What Martin wanted to know about was what he had just seen. It certainly explained Rougeau's appearance.

"How ... long?" Martin asked. Rougeau shrugged, a sad smile on his face.

"Not long now. A few weeks. It would have been longer, certainly, but I stopped taking the antiretrovirals some time ago. I would not have done so had I known that this ..." he gestured to Martin, the air, the van in which they sat. "I was done. Of course, a terminal illness tends to have the worst possible timing in all areas, and naturally, all this came along once I had already allowed myself to deteriorate. Unfortunate. I will hold on for this ... to be help, if needed ... for as long as I can. While I see no colour in this world, I know that there are a great many who do." He reached into his suit pocket and produced an old, battered business card, which he handed to Balaclava. "This will be left with you when you are returned home. Excuse the condition of the card; I had these printed many years ago. I have never changed the number."

"But ... what ..."

Rougeau shrugged once more.

"You will have to tell *me*, Monsieur Hogan, once things begin to happen. And they will. A cloud such as this cannot come down and then leave without consequence. Whenever it begins, call me. I will do what I can."

This is real. You know *it's real. If it's real then Callum needs to be protected. Tell him about the dog. How you found it. Oh God, the state Chops was in, could that be something to do with what he's talking about?*

OKAY, YOU KNOW WHAT HE CAN DO IS REAL, AND THAT HE BELIEVES IT. THAT'S A BIG DEAL, BUT IT DOESN'T MEAN WHAT HE'S SAYING *IS REAL.* IT DOESN'T MEAN THAT HE'S NOT CRAZY.

What if whoever hurt Chops is what he's talking about? What if they come to us?

YOU HAVE HIS CARD. IF IT LOOKS LIKE ANY OF IT'S TRUE, YOU CAN CALL THE NUMBER. NO MEN WITH GUNS BEFORE THEN. HARD REALITY BEFORE LIKELY FANTASY.

Only likely *fantasy? He sent pictures to your* head!

BUT THAT'S—

"I apologise again for this, Monsieur Hogan, but you must understand that I have no idea how you are likely to respond once you are at home once more, and out of, shall we say, the *circle of influence.* Yes? I think I have taken you far enough along so that you should remain, ah, relaxed in the face of such issues. *Acceptance,* that is the word. But ideally, we would like time to be away in case the police are called. You will find that number cannot be traced to a physical location, incidentally. I have little time left, and I think that I shall not leave this country before then, but I would much prefer to spend it in a place of my choosing rather than a police cell ... however, it is a risk I would take. You would struggle to find real evidence of your procurement anyway, I think. Still; apologies. Call me when you need me."

He nodded to Balaclava, and Martin had just enough time to wonder what Rougeau was apologising for before Balaclava raised the pistol-like weapon once more and fired it at Martin's thigh. The world went away again.

***

Martin awoke to the sound of the back door to his house closing in the kitchen. Someone was leaving, and very shortly afterward there was the sound of an accelerating vehicle outside. There was a very fresh pain in his right shoulder, to add to the now-dull throb in his opposite shoulder and thigh where the previous shots had hit him. He was lying on his back on the sofa.

They gave you something to wake you back up, he thought hazily, *they didn't want to leave Callum unattended, but they knew they'd at least have enough time to get away if they needed it.*

That last part was certainly true. Martin continued to lie there, trying to get his brain to come back online for another fifteen minutes or so. Eventually, he felt the pain in his thigh begin to dull down to a moan rather than a scream. He knew that his shoulders and leg would be very bruised, very soon. *Good job it isn't shorts weather,* he thought, and the gallows humour immediately made him consider Rougeau's words.

I have taken you far enough along so that you should remain relaxed in the face of such issues ... acceptance.

Martin sat up gingerly, feeling his aching thigh, and realising that he thought Rougeau was right about that much. Here he was, waking up in his living room after being drugged, dragged into a van, and having a half-telepathic conversation with a crazy man from Switzerland. Instead of shaking and throwing up and thanking a God he didn't believe in for returning him safely and allowing his son to remain unharmed, Martin was able to sit and ponder what had just happened. He *was* shaken up, that was for sure, and he was troubled by what he'd heard, but Rougeau had definitely done something to him. In a way, he was almost excited.

The most exciting, dramatic thing since ...

The thought died, not needing to finish. Since the death of his wife. In that case, he'd had enough excitement for one lifetime. He staggered to his feet, pushing himself up on the sofa arm, and began to head for the stairs to check on his son. He knew Callum was fine—more knowledge that Rougeau had given him—but wanted to see him anyway, wanted to hold him.

Do you get that? He's let you know *things, helped your mind process things. Isn't that* unbelievable?!

It was, and yet it was somehow only as unbelievable as, say, seeing something incredible on a nature documentary.

It's because that's how he sees it. You know what he knows about it; to him it's just another natural thing. What you have to do now is decide what the hell you do about what he's told you.

True again. He headed up the stairs, relieved to hear the whining and scrabbling coming from the other side of the study door in the hallway. The dogs were fine as well, but he had to check on his son first. He mounted the stairs and opened the door to Callum's bedroom, where his son opened sleepy eyes and looked at him with curiosity, trying to figure out who had just entered the room.

You're going to do exactly what Rougeau said, and that's best all round. He's not going to come back unless you ask him to—

DO YOU BELIEVE THAT?

He did. He did, and with a clarity that he knew was not his own.

—and then none of this will be a problem again. And if he's right *about the crazy talk he was coming out with,* then *you can give him a call. No police. There's no need.*

It made sense, and a decision that meant making no decision and letting circumstances decide was always good. The question now was, should he worry? If telepaths, or at least people that had some kind of mental ability, were real, then could whatever portentous stuff Rougeau was talking about be true as well?

He believes it, but it was all very vague. He's also dying. Quite the coincidence, wouldn't you say? That great change and great disaster were coming, and this news stems from a strung-out man with only a few weeks to live? He obviously has an incredible mind; one capable of playing very dark tricks on himself.

BUT WHY YOU? WHY COME FROM EUROPE TO VISIT YOU?

It was a good question.

He could be a reader of your books. Made a connection with your name, subconsciously decided that you were the one with the answers.

It was a good response. Even so, as Martin bent to scoop up his son from his crib, subconsciously registering delight as Callum's arms reached out to him, his bruised shoulders screamed at him, and he couldn't help but wish he'd turned the lights on when he entered. The rest of the room was very dimly lit, with only the rectangle of hallway light cast from the open door frame and Callum's dim nightlight plugged into the socket on the opposite wall. Martin jostled Callum very gently in his arms and rocked him, stroking his head, looking into the darkness all the while and trying to ignore the goose bumps that had just broken out across his back.

Don't. Don't look for stuff that isn't there, as you'll start seeing it. Rougeau was very convincing.

EASY TO SAY, BUT HEY, GUESS WHAT? WE FOUND OUT THAT TELEPATHY IS REAL TONIGHT. KIND OF HARD TO DISMISS ALL THE OTHER POSSIBILITIES AFTER THAT.

There wasn't a response to *that*, and again, he had immediate concerns that made looking for a response blessedly obsolete. Martin turned, Callum's head nestled against his shoulder, thumb in mouth, and headed downstairs to put the dogs out of their temporary misery. He'd also decided that, for the first time in a long time, he was having a bloody drink.

The dogs exploded into the hallway, frantic and breathless, and after a quick jump-up at Martin and Callum, where they received confirmation that yes, they were still part of the pack, the pair shot off in different directions for the usual quick-fire inspection of the house to check that all was still in order. Martin smiled, and then his phone went off in his pocket, the quick double vibration signalling the arrival of a text.

The preview onscreen said that it was from Trish, and that she was asking if he was still coming round for tea tomorrow night ... but it was the camera app that remained onscreen behind it that made him cry out in surprise and fear and drop the phone. He would have dropped Callum as well had his first instinct not been to grip his son even tighter.

The phone hit the hallway carpet and landed face down. Martin fell against the wall, trembling and shaking, frantically trying to convince himself that it was an aftereffect of the drugs, or of whatever Rougeau had done in his mind. He stared at the back of the phone, lying ominously on the hallway floor as if it were a black cancer.

You saw it. You know you saw it.

IT MIGHT BE A TRICK OF THE LIGHT. A SLOW SHUTTER CREATING LIGHT STREAKS.

It wasn't. He knew it wasn't. Martin slowly bent and picked the phone up with his free hand, turning it over in his hand as carefully as if he were handling broken glass.

It's because you're frightened. You're seeing things already.

That line was bullshit in the movies, he knew, and bullshit in real life, but Martin was trying to cling to whatever he could. Once the phone turned over, he knew he couldn't deny it. The image was too clear. Martin jumped out of his skin as Chops dashed past him in the hallway, disappearing back into the study.

Shut that study door. Shut it and bolt it so it never opens again.

The last image that the camera had taken remained onscreen. Martin realised that he must have taken the photo by accident, perhaps catching the shutter icon with his thumb just as Chops bit him; the photo was slightly blurred, with Chops's face only just in shot. Most importantly, the dog's *eyes* were in the shot.

Ever so slightly above Chops's eyes, so clear and defined that they were unmistakable, so inarguable that they could not be dismissed as a trick of the light, were the white outline of *another* set of eyes, hovering just in front of Chops's face and looking straight into the camera.

Desperately, Martin thumbed back through the previous shots, the ones where Chops had turned away.

Turned away. He turned away because he didn't want you to see those eyes, whatever they are. This *is what Rougeau was talking about. You should have told him. You should have told him. You've got to get that dog out of here now—*

CALM DOWN. ROUGEAU'S DONE SOME SHIT TO YOUR HEAD, REMEMBER? HELL, HE COULD BE ANOTHER ONE WHO THINKS THAT YOU'VE GOT MONEY JUST BECAUSE YOU HAD A MINOR HIT. THIS COULD BE A SHAKEDOWN! THIS COULD BE SOMETHING TO JUST GET YOU BELIEVING IN HIM, AND THE NEXT THING IT'LL BE "PAY ME SO THAT I CAN GET RID OF THE PROBLEM"—

Martin stayed on his knees in the hallway, eyes locked on the phone's screen and only stopping when Callum cried out gently, complaining about how hard he was being held.

FIRST THINGS FIRST; GET CALLUM OVER TO TRISH'S. IF YOU'RE NOT WELL, HE NEEDS TO BE OUT OF YOUR WAY. ROUGEAU MUST KNOW ABOUT WHAT HAPPENED TO LIZ, HE KNOWS THAT YOU'LL BE MENTALLY FRAGILE—

Maybe, but the first thing he was going to do wasn't going to be taking Callum to Trish's house. He'd had one hell of an evening, and he wasn't going to be running off into the night in a panic because of yet another scare. No, the *first* thing that Martin was going to do was to get another fucking photo of that dog, and a clean shot of the bastard's face, and he didn't care if it bit whole chunks out of him in the process. Let it chew on his arm, he'd get a clear shot of it while it did so.

Fragile nerves boiling into a rage, fear turning the half-circle that it sometimes does as it becomes rage, Martin got to his feet, trembling. He'd been screwed with far too much tonight. He took the steps on the stairs two at time, putting Callum back in his crib, who immediately started to cry when Martin did so. It was one of the few things that Callum cried about; being put back to bed when he was wide-awake. Martin ignored the noise, and was already closing the door and bounding back down the stairs. He strode down the hallway to the study door, feeling his anger threatening to collapse and turn back into fear as his shaking hand reached out and pushed the door open.

You don't know what's—

Scoffer was on the study floor. Martin hadn't noticed him enter the study earlier; he didn't know if he'd somehow slipped past him in the hallway without Martin noticing, or whether he'd already been back in there before Chops ran in. Either way, the golden-brown dog was cowering on the floor in the far corner, trembling and looking at Martin with terrified eyes.

Chops was sitting upright on the large table that Martin used as an office desk. He was a big dog, but the table was very sturdy and there was room for Chops, the keyboard, and the PC monitor. Some pens and papers had been knocked onto the floor as Chops had clambered up, but other than that the room was undisturbed. Chops's gaze met Martin's, calm and steady, and sitting upright as he was on the raised surface, he looked enormous. But that wasn't what made Martin sway on his feet, feeling as if the surface of the world was shifting inside that very room.

It was the monitor screen. The computer had been turned on—for the first time in a long time—and Microsoft Word was open. There were four words written on the software's blank page:

we need to talk

***

By car, it would have been a journey of several hours. On foot, it was a walk of several days, and the cold weather was making it much harder. They had no baggage, no tents, no protection from the elements, and the nights were spent in whatever shelter could be found. Some nights they were lucky; a disused barn would at least offer them an evening free of the wind. Mainly though, the best they could do was a short sleep under a hedge, the rain constantly waking them every time it filtered its way down through the leaves and onto the backs of their fitfully sleeping heads.

It had been worse at the beginning, of course, when they'd all set off separately from their individual locations. Travelling alone was dangerous, no matter what the pact said. After all, wasn't the whole point of this that the pact *couldn't* be trusted? Would they be making this trip otherwise? Therefore, when they first became two, then later, three, the sense of relief and security was immense. They hadn't had any trouble yet—*yet*—and they were more than capable of defending themselves, having made their preparations well. Even so, they couldn't relax, or let their guard down. They walked in silence, none of them knowing each other or feeling a need to talk. The relative silence was *bliss*. The break from the noise, the endless, deafening, punishing *noise* ... that was the thing that made these trips so very sought after, the thing that made them all *crave* their turn, the thing that made so many of them spend their days doing nothing but yearn, and strain, and push, looking for that nugget in the endless sand that was an *opportunity that no one else had seen yet.* If you wanted to skip the queue, you had to get in first, and the punishment was nothing compared to the reward if you could pull it off.

The sun was setting, and soon it would be dark. This would be their last night travelling. Tomorrow, they would arrive, and then there would just be the small problem of finding a permanent, regular nightly shelter. Then there would be no more travel for some time. The shelter would have to be big, though; there would be others. In fact, there already were. Some had already arrived, but they were the ones that sheltered in different ways. They would find their own shelter.

The shifts would start the day after, they had agreed. Two of them would always watch the house, while the other slept. It would mean potentially thousands of days of observation, endless hours of nothing at all, of silence. But that would be absolutely fine by them. It would be heavenly. If they could smile, they knew that they would spend that time sitting there and grinning from ear to ear.

Today, they were alongside the motorway again, as it was the most direct route for this part of the journey. They didn't have to worry about being caught by the police for walking along the embankment, of course; the idea was laughable. Plus, they wouldn't even be seen. One of them looked up wearily, both from the day's walking and the terrible night's sleep the previous evening. Even though they dropped off easily, they were woken with equal ease as well, and the thunderstorm had been a particularly deafening one.

The road sign before them was confirmation. Just one more day. Another hour or two tonight, then one more day.

SERVICES 1 MILE
LEICESTER 14 MILES
COVENTRY 22 MILES

***

Chapter Four: The Importance of Body Language, The Last Day of a Long Journey, One Side of the Most Important Story, and A Secret Message for Martin
***

Martin froze in the doorway, staring at the dog sitting on his table and clutching the door frame as if he would disappear if he relaxed his grip even for a moment. It occurred to him in that second that he was, of course, dreaming. It was the only thing that made sense.

No. No, there's a much, much *more simple answer than even that. Rougeau did this. He put the text on the screen, something good to eat on the table, let the dog get up there ...*

THEN WHY IS CHOPS STILL SITTING UP THERE LOOKING AT YOU LIKE THAT? WHY ISN'T HE JUMPING OVER LIKE NORMAL? WHY IS SCOFFER LOOKING ABSOLUTELY TERRIFIED?

Scoffer *was* terrified. He was reacting the way that he did every bonfire night when the next-door neighbours had their party. Martin began to cross instinctively over to his pet, to stroke him and comfort him (even though he'd read a long time ago that that was the worst thing you could do to a scared animal during fireworks, as it only convinced them that they had something to be frightened of) but he stopped as Chops bent his head to the desk and picked up a pen between his jaws. Before Martin's disbelieving eyes, Chops began to jab the pen at the keyboard, picking out individual letters that slowly became words on the screen.

Real words. English. Then a complete, comprehensible sentence.

rougeau didnt do this

Martin cried out involuntarily, his free hand moving to his mouth. No matter what measures Rougeau had put in his head, this was too much. Too much.

Maybe he ... maybe he ... trained the dog and ... planted it here ...
The pen moved again, courtesy of Chops's jaws.

no he didn't

"No ... no ..." Martin realised that he was now holding his hand out to ward away what he was seeing, but he didn't care. Part of him knew, deep down, that this was inevitable. The tablets had helped, certainly, but he hadn't been brave enough to face therapy. He'd just buried everything, shoved it under the earth of his soul to fester like radioactive waste, except the waste was memories and the radiation in them had been leaking for a long, long time, corrupting everything it touched. He'd been lying to himself, hadn't he? Wasn't the progress he'd made merely the surface, just talking and walking while the inside became more and more dead? His mind was always going to go. His brain was always going to shut down. He should have been stronger, seen the shrink, if only for Callum—
The pen tapped away on the keyboard again. Scoffer whined in the corner.

please dont be afarid

There was a pause, then more tapping. A*farid* slowly disappeared and was replaced by *afraid*.
Something in that action made Martin pause. It was so unmistakably real—the correction of a spelling mistake—that suddenly it felt less like a dream or a hallucination. The dog was typing on the keyboard—
The dog *is typing on the* keyboard, *are you kidding—*
—and it didn't want him to worry.
"Uh ... uh ..."
There was a long flurry of typing at the keyboard.

rougeau was right about what is happening you need to calm down and listen to me

The dog then looked at Martin with those startling white eyes, the pen still in its mouth, before turning back to the keyboard and adding:

please

Say something, Martin. You have to say something. You have to find out what this is.
"What ... how are you ..."
The tapping began again, so long this time that Chops occasionally paused and looked back to see what Martin was doing, or to let Martin see that which he had written so far.

i will explin everything mrtin but had to start this wy so you would be less frightned i had t do it in stages so that you didn go mad when i spoke to you

What? 'Spoke'? A talking dog?

no

He's reading your mind. He's reading your fucking mind, just like Rougeau. This is something to do with him.

i do not know rougeau but i know about him

Are you reading my mind?

yes sorry if you talk to me i wont do that

Martin licked his lips. They were dry.

"Are you ... are you reading my mind?" He knew the question had been answered, but he asked it again anyway. To his absolute amazement, the dog nodded. He'd seen dogs doing complex things before—tapping a pen on a keyboard was not, in itself, an incredible act, even if the conversation was. Seeing a dog nod, however—not in the exaggerated motion of a trained dog, but in the subtle up-down of a human response in direct answer to a question—was mind blowing. Plus, it looked comical; the pen was still sticking out of Chops's mouth. As unbelievable as it all was, Martin's heart rate dropped that tiny bit more. "When you spoke to me ... you said *when you spoke to me.* You can speak to me?"
The nod came again.
Are you hearing yourself?
"Okay. Okay. Speak to me. Prove this is real. Fucking ... fucking *prove* it." His heart sped up again almost immediately, and he felt sweat on his back even though the house was relatively cool in the winter evening chill. He was vaguely aware that he had no idea how much time had passed, and thought that it must be after ten, when the central heating was programmed to turn off.
Tap, tap, tap.

if youre ready

"Yes. Yes, I'm ready, dammit. Prove it. Prove it." *This is when you find out if it's the nuthouse or the ... doghouse* he thought crazily, knowing that the sentence made no actual sense despite the use of the word *dog* and not caring. There was a pause, and the canine and the human stared at each other across a silence that was broken only by the sound of Scoffer's whimpering.

Then:

"Hello, Martin."

Martin jumped, and whirled around, bracing for another attack as the voice seemed to come from behind him. There was no one there. He looked back at the dog, breathing quickly. It hadn't moved, and it still had the pencil in its mouth. Which wasn't moving.

"It's me. This is me talking to you. Excuse the use of the computer just now, but I think this situation has gone ahead more easily by going about it *this* way, than if I'd just started talking to you in your mind. An extra step taken to ease us into this, as it were."

The voice was in his head. Chops's voice. It sounded like that of a man in his early fifties, and a well-spoken one at that. Martin was reminded, although he didn't fully realise it, of a slightly rougher sounding HAL from the movie *2001*. In fact—

Is that an American accent?

"Yes, it is. I lived my entire life in Chicago, although my mother made me take elocution lessons. Although I doubt you'd notice the lack of a regional accent. Do you know the Chicago—"

"You said you wouldn't read my mind again!"

The dog actually winced a little, looking as if an invisible owner had raised their hand to their pet.

"I apologise. It takes such an effort to maintain the mental link that it's hard to do it by halves, if you follow me. I'll try not to do it again."

"This isn't real. It isn't real. You aren't real."

"I understand. I can scarcely imagine how difficult this must be for you. If I were in your shoes I would probably think the same way." There was no echo to the voice, no ethereal tone. It was as clear as if it were the feed from a well-insulated recording studio. "Unfortunately, I don't have a choice. I have, however, already thought of a way that might help you to believe me. Would you like to try it?" Chops cocked his head, and the gesture was so canine, so cute-dog-trying-to-comprehend-something in its nature, that for a moment he looked like any other dog. The effect was disarming ... but only temporarily.

"No. No, I can't indulge this, this *lunacy*. I'll only get worse."

"Well, if this proves it, won't that change everything?"

Logic, as ever, provided a lifeline, a loose-fingered grip on a possible way forward.

"... what ... did you have in mind?"

Again ... are you kidding?

"Hold on a moment, please."

Chops hopped down off the table and walked over to Scoffer's cowering form, who growled feebly as Chops approached. It wasn't convincing. Chops stood in front of Scoffer, tail up and eyes locked on his former playmate, and then suddenly stuck his behind up in the air and rocked back, his front legs splayed out in front of him, continuing to stare at Scoffer. Scoffer's trembles subsided, and a dull, rhythmic thudding began to emanate from behind him. His tail was slapping slowly on the floor. Chops rolled over onto his back, and

Scoffer then stood up and walked around to Scoffer's rear and sniffed at his anus. Seemingly satisfied, Scoffer then wandered over to his bed, turned around four times, then settled down and began to drift off to sleep.

Martin just watched.

Scoffer isn't talking. Scoffer just got more freaked out than you've ever seen him and then settled back down again inside a minute. That was real.

There was no answering voice this time. There was only non-committal silence.

"I apologise for keeping you waiting," Martin heard Chops's voice say, moving into a sitting position and staring at Martin. "I couldn't stand to see him like that, and neither could you, I'm sure. I thought it only humane to make him feel better."

"What did ... you do?"

The dog cocked his head slightly, trying to find the words.

"I let him know everything was all right. That's the best way that I can put it in human terms. It's not as simple as *telling* him, per se, but still, I let him know."

"What was that then ... body language?"

"Partly, yes. Well observed, Martin. But mainly telepathy."

"And that didn't concern him?"

"Oh no, not at all. All dogs are telepathic."

Oh ... oh, here we go. Down the plughole.

"Whatever you say."

"It's true. Think about it; how many times has your dog sat and just *stared* at you, not moving a muscle?"

"Every time that I have something that he likes the smell of."

"True, but that still counts. And, I imagine, every time you haven't realised that he's overdue for a walk, or that he needs to go, or that he wants you to play with him. And do you know what he's doing, while he's sitting there?"

"Waiting for me to do whatever he wants."

"Yes, but also he's *thinking at you* as hard as he possibly can, and wondering why on earth you aren't answering. And, of course, being a dog, he'll just keep going because he can't think of another way around the problem. *Dogged determination,* as they say."

Martin could only consider the concept rationally. It was just easier to do than try and argue with everything else.

"... that's bullshit," he said eventually. "I see dogs down the park. It's all in the body language."

"Yes, a huge part of it is, just as it is with humans. What's the saying, seventy percent of communication is non-verbal? That's just how it is with dogs. They don't have the capability to be sarcastic, for example, or to use their hands to gesticulate. That's not how they communicate anyway. They can't emphasise the way you can. They can't even talk like I'm talking to you now, where there's tone to my voice. They don't have that luxury. But what they *do* have is a far, far, *far* deeper perception and appreciation of the movement of individual muscles than humans do. The meaning of a particular stance that is only different from another by a matter of millimetres. I'm talking about not just noticing that hairs are standing up on the body, but noticing to a certain degree; did you know that the *exact* tipping point, visually, between a curious dog and an aggressive dog is simply invisible to the human eye?"

"No way. I've seen the guys on TV, the dog experts. They know an aggressive stance."

"No. They know a *very* aggressive stance. They don't know the infinitesimal subtleties that a dog does. Dogs don't converse. They don't have discussions. But they can exchange information, and let each other know *exactly* what's going on, although sometimes emotions garble the messages. That's when it all falls apart, and then fights happen. But if they can remain calm, a dog can let another dog know everything that it's done that day in just a few seconds. *If* they can stay calm. Which doesn't happen a lot. So yes, the physical is very important. But the meaning, the *inflection*, the difference ... that's all in the telepathy. "

"But we're talking now, a conversation."

"I told you. I'm different. And this takes a *lot* of effort. A dog's mind is not built for communicating with humans, which is why, other than an abundance of language issues, they can't do it. It's only because I can access the right channels to use that I'm able to do it."

There was silence for a moment. Martin broke it, curiosity getting the better of him.

"Different how? Wait, why was Scoffer so upset?"

Chops shuffled on his feet briefly, almost the canine equivalent of a shrug.

"He saw me doing unusual things like starting up the PC—unusual to your eyes, as you saw, but extremely unusual to Scoffer—and of course, as a dog always will, he tried to read me with his mind, as my body was busy and doing unrecognisable things. And because my mind was ... away, shall we say, my state shifted, then he quite naturally became terrified. He'd never had that response from another dog's mind, you see. Imagine shaking someone's hand, and then finding that you were holding a claw."

The image didn't help settle Martin's mind to any degree.

"How did you get into the computer?"

Chops seemed confused by the question. Apart from a brief ear flick, his expression didn't change, but Martin could *feel* the dog's lack of understanding in his mind.

The inflection, the difference ...

"Well ... same as you would. I pushed the power button, then tapped in the password." It wasn't sarcasm, as Chops had already said. It was a direct answer.

"No, I mean how did you know the password?"

"Oh, I see. I'd seen you type it in before."

Martin's heart sank. It all couldn't be true then, and he realised just how much he had been beginning to be sucked in by it.

"Chops. The last time I turned on the computer was *months* ago. You weren't even here then. So that means that all this is bullshit, and that ... well ... that I have indeed finally snapped." Martin felt his nose start to prickle as if a heavy sneeze were coming, and then a tear was gently running down the right-hand side of his face. With great force, he missed his wife all over again, felt the blow of her absence, and it was only his always-intense loathing of his seemingly infinite capacity for self-pity that halted the rest of the tears in their path. As it always did.

"Well, no, Martin," said Chops's voice in his head, and then the dog got up and moved several feet closer, parking himself close by and staring into Martin's eyes in the exact same way that Scoffer had so many times over the years. The dog's own eyes looked very large and round, and Martin suddenly felt as if he knew just how much they had seen, that Chops held a great many sad secrets that he would share ... if it weren't for the fact that if he really heard them, if Martin *really* knew, then he would be lost forever. He suddenly didn't want Chops to say anything else, and wished fervently that this really *was* all a dream, just a bizarre nightmare that he could laugh at in the morning with intense relief that masqueraded as amusement. "As I said," Chops continued, his voice loud and slow in Martin's head, "I'm different, Martin."

" ... how ..." Martin muttered, knowing that he did not want to know the answer.

"There is so much at stake, Martin," the dog said, his well-spoken tones bold in volume but soft in tone at the same time, "and as melodramatic as that sounds, it can't be emphasised enough. The world is changing, Martin, and you hold the key to all of it. And you won't like it at all. You need to know that. You need to accept that this is a terrible burden that I am bringing to you, and that I am so deeply, deeply sorry to be the one that has to do so. And so I'll answer your question, as that is a good place to start. You won't understand what it is you have to decide anyway if I don't. I ... " Chops's voice trailed off, sounding so horribly sad that Martin knew that his first guess was right; this was something that he shouldn't know. What had Rougeau said? *Something unnatural.* Too late, Martin knew that Rougeau had been right to try and warn him.

Oh God, why didn't I tell Rougeau about the stray that I took home?

"My name isn't Chops, Martin, as you will not be surprised to hear," Chops said quietly, his big dark eyes locked on Martin's. "It's Jonathan. Jonathan Hall. I was born and raised in Chicago in 1923. I died of lung cancer in 1974 at the age of fifty-one, and I was sent back—sent *here*—over a year ago, tasked with getting close enough to you to have this conversation. To become close enough, connected enough to you that you wouldn't run away the second that I spoke. Once I've said everything I have to say, I will leave if you wish. But I won't be the last to visit you, and you have to be prepared. You have to hear my side. *Our* side. I have to plead our case. And then you will have a very, very difficult decision to make."

Scoffer turned over in his bed, lying on his back with his paws in the air and knowing only a kind of a contentment that very few adult humans ever know.

***

The leader of the three stood up. It had never been officially said that he was the leader, but they all knew it anyway, and were comfortable with it. He was the one that would do the talking, after all. They'd made good progress the day before, and today was the *last* day. The feeling was in all of their bones, the low-level electric buzz of barely restrained ... excitement? That wasn't the right word. He struggled to find it, still reluctant to leave the beautiful haze of sleep and activate his brain fully.

Sleep ... my God ...

The earth beneath his back. The gentle but chill wind in his ears. The feeling of muscles shutting down, the scalp relaxing, the heart rate slowing ...

Importance. The sense of *importance,* that was it, of being at the heart of something so indescribably important but also with so much precious, painfully tantalising hope. The others stirred, and moved out of the shade into the early dawn light, letting the sun hit their skin and thus to fully begin the process of the brain's releasing of serotonin. Feeling the almost-but-not-quite-as-delicious feeling of properly *waking up* starting to come upon them.

So many had wanted this task. Billions. The three of them were a percentage of the tiny group who'd been lucky enough—lucky on a cosmic scale, to put the odds into perspective—to get it. Of course, their rank was a huge part of that too, but the privilege alone damn well *felt* lucky. They were going to make the most of it, even if they did have a job to do.

***

"Hello?" said Trish's voice down the phone line, raised enough to be heard over the din in the background. "*Martin? You'll have to speak up, it's really noisy here.*"

"Trish," said Martin, trying to keep his voice as relaxed sounding as possible, "I need a favour. Have you got a sec?"

"*I'm out!*" said Trish, and Martin could picture her shaking her head at whomever she was with, her whole face rolling in mock contempt at her brother's stupid request. "*Can't you hear? I'm having a drink! I'm in Barrington's!*"

"How many have you had?" It was an important question, for what Martin had in mind.

"*Two? We've only been here an hour. Look, can this wait? I haven't been out in ages.*" She sounded like she was in a good mood.

"I only need a minute," Martin said, only just restraining the urge to shout *shut up and help me, you awkward bitch,* into the handset. She really *didn't* go out much, and here he was asking for favours. If the whole world wasn't disintegrating into intangible madness around him, he wouldn't be calling at all.

He hadn't let Chops—*Jonathan Hall*, he reminded himself—go any further, hadn't let him explain any more, before testing whether or not he was telling the truth. *I have, however, already thought of a way that might help you to believe me*, Jonathan Hall had said earlier, and Martin had wanted to know what it was before he listened to another word of Hall's story. The dog had explained it to him, and the plan sounded as good as any other way that Martin could think of. "Have you got Skype on your phone?"

"*Ye-e-es.*"

"And is there Wi-Fi there?"

"*In Barrington's? You know there is.*"

"Well I don't bloody know, I haven't been there in ages. Look, I'm going to Skype you from here, okay? Just make sure you're signed into the app."

"*Okay, but this has got to be quick.*"

"It will be, I promise. Thanks, Trish."

She hung up without another response, and Martin watched the Skype window that was already open on the PC's screen. After a minute, *trishywishy* appeared in his online contacts section, and he hit "Video Call". Trish's face filled the desktop screen, the busy bar behind her as a backdrop. She didn't look impressed.

"*This better be worthwhile, I'm being really rude to Amy here.*" Trish's voice was loud over the computer speakers.

"Well, she might want to watch this," Martin shrugged towards the tiny webcam that sat on top of his desktop monitor. If "Jonathan Hall" was telling the truth, then indeed she would. "Okay, hold on a moment." His hand trembling again, Martin turned the webcam on its axis, watching the tiny feed preview screen as he did so. Once the image that he was sending was properly framed, he sat upright at the desk and took a deep breath.

"Okay. Can you see him?"

"*The new dog? Yes. Seen him many times before, too.*" Martin ignored the sarcasm.

Jonathan Hall waited calmly, sitting quietly in the view of the webcam and knowing that he was being watched by someone other than Martin. This kind of thing, this reveal, was *expressly* against the rules, and against all of his—against all of *their*—beliefs, but he had been given special dispensation. *By whatever means, as long as it doesn't break the pact.* That is what he had been told, and this would benefit even those who were against them if it would get Martin to listen.

"Okay," said Martin again, keeping his breathing as steady as he could, "tell him to do something. Anything."

"*What?*"

"Tell the dog to do something, and he'll do it."

"*Why?*"

"Because you told him to."

"*No, I mean why do you want me to do that?*"

Martin gritted his teeth and quickly rubbed a hand over his sweating face.

"Because I've been training him to obey commands and I want to show you what he can do."

"*Couldn't this wait?*"

For fuck's sake ...

"Trish ... Trish ... will you please just do it? I'm ... I'm just excited, that's all."

"*Well, what can he do?*"

FOR FUCK'S SAKE ...

"Ask him and find out!"

"*Oh, for crying out loud, fine. Chops, lie down.*"

Jonathan Hall lay down on his front.

"Heh ... that's very good, actually. Roll over."

Jonathan Hall rolled over.

"*Ha! That's really good, Martin! How did you teach him to do that?*"

Martin's heart was pounding, but he couldn't allow himself to believe yet. These were standard commands. Even a stray might already know these if he'd been trained and then abandoned. He needed her to think bigger, and he needed *her* to think of it, to get the dog to do something that he hadn't suggested.

"Ask him something more complicated. Anything."

"*Eh?*"

"Anything. You won't believe what he can do." *You really wouldn't.*

"*Like what, stand up?*"

The dog got up on his back legs, his pulled up in front of him like the limbs of a Praying Mantis.

"*Wow! Amy, come and look at this—*" The edge of another head crammed into view on the monitor screen. "*Tell it to do something, it's amazing—*"

"*Stand on one leg,*" barked Amy, sounding more than a little drunk. Whatever Trish was drinking, Amy had clearly had more than two. Trish was already saying *That's too hard, don't be stupid,* but Jonathan Hall's left leg stuttered up and down, trying to balance on only his right. He didn't quite manage it, but the effort alone was enough.

"*Oh my God!*" both girls squealed, and then a flurry of commands came forth in rapid order. *Bark five times. Turn around. Jump up and down.* All were carried out with aplomb.

"*Touch the radiator,*" said Amy, laughing, which set Trish off as well, knowing that the command was ridiculous. Why would Martin teach the dog what the radiator was? And so it was just as well that, the moment that the dog walked over to the radiator behind him and calmly put one paw upon it, a girl with wild dark hair suddenly pushed through the crowd behind Trish and Amy, drunk or upset for some reason. She even managed to knock someone's drink all over them in her mad rush for the door. The girls turned to look, startled, and Martin quickly hit the button to end the video call. *That* would have been too much. Too many questions would have been asked after the radiator trick, and Martin didn't know the whole story yet. His heart was threatening to shatter his sternum, and he felt more light-headed than he had ever been in his life. Jonathan Hall simply remained on the carpet, sitting quietly by the radiator and staring at him with an expression that, even for a dog, said *I'm sorry, but I told you so*.

"I think that's a fairly good bit of proof, Martin," said the voice in his head again, silky smooth yet still causing Martin to jump slightly when he heard it. "Perhaps I'm a circus dog, but the odds of both you going crazy and you finding an escaped circus dog that just so happens to know every single command that not just you but your sister *and* her friend said, as well as knowing what the word *radiator* means, are so slim that even a story as mad as mine has to be true. Surely? She saw me do those things, Martin. You aren't imagining them."

Martin weighed it up.

Ah ...

...

"Son of a bitch," he whispered breathlessly, sitting back in his chair and feeling like all of the blood had run out of him.

"There's an obvious joke that I could make there, Martin, but I won't," Jonathan Hall said, settling his paws forward so that he was lying again. "Sorry. Trying to lighten the mood. Things like that—what I just did, answering commands to please people—just flood this body with doggy endorphins. It's like a game, you see. Chasing a ball, smelling something interesting, waiting for food ... it's a rush. Animal instincts can't be separated from rational thought. That's how we end up with the Distracted."

Wait ... please wait ...

"Chops," said Martin, his mouth dry, "Sorry ... Jonathan ... slow down. One thing at a time. You were sent? You died? I can't ..."

"No, no, I'm sorry, Martin," said Chops, getting to his feet, and trotting over to sit by Martin's chair. "I'm still a little hyped up, and I'm getting ahead of myself. It's hard to control this brain and stay completely me." He put his paw on Martin's leg, looking up at him. "I'll start here: I was born a man. And then I died. And I was dead for many years, until I got to come back. I'm *absolutely* not the first—all of us come back—but there are very, very few who get to come back the way I have. That get to be the way I am right now. It's the trillion-to-one odds of the right dead person and the right vessel, and even *then* there's competition for it. Understand?"

"... no."

"That's all right. That's all right, Martin. Let me start even further back, then. Let me tell you my story."

***

When Jonathan Hall dies, everything—everything—is relief. Inside himself, inside the others gathered around his Chicago hospital bed, inside the ruined and strained organs of the body that he feels slip off him like a diseased shed skin. He is loose and nimble and so incredibly light, freed from a terrible grip that has held him captive for far, far too long. And there is Nancy, below him, crying and holding his brother, also crying, and his two eldest are on the other side of the bed embracing each other. Where is Mark? He couldn't make it, of course, he would be racing over even now from Wisconsin, and now he'll never get a chance to say good-bye, not like the others; he couldn't speak to them but he knew they were with him as he left. And he feels the sadness of departure, yet at the same time there is a warmth surrounding him, and knowledge that it's all right because they're all a part of something and that they'll all join him eventually, reunited once more. He wants to tell them, to call out to them, to let them know that it's all going to be okay, but he's rising up and away and into and through that warmth, letting it take him now, embracing it and smiling as it carries him up and through.

And then he arrives, and he knows immediately that something is horribly, horribly wrong.

The warmth is gone. What was that, just a transition? Just the tunnel, the transport? Either way, he knows that he has reached his destination, and it is not what he felt was coming. There is perhaps a trace of it here still, but if it was ever here then it is long gone, used up and burnt out and out of date. This place ... is not what it was. This place is ... what is it? Then the word finds him.

Stuck. This place is stuck.

And as he gains his bearings (his sight is not yet clear, not yet transformed, calibrated) he realises that all he can feel around him are more just like him; more of the dead. Wait; not just around him. On top of him. Under him. Against him. Pressing inwards at every possible angle, their weight on him like wet cement and then he knows the awful truth. The dead stretch in every conceivable direction like infinite sardines, jammed and crammed on top of one another, and there is a *pressure in the air, like a static buildup before a storm but much heavier, and more powerful and just as he thinks* how can they stand this *and* it has to break soon, I can feel it, this can't last because it's so close to the breaking point already *the second blow comes:* this is where you have to stay.

He doesn't scream; no one around him is screaming, and besides, the concept is too big for the dead mind to handle and at the same time there's that thought again, that *this is going to break soon, and become once more what it was, this is an error and this place should not have stayed this way.* He doesn't become calm, but he can at least think again and now he hears the others talking. They're all talking to one another, because that's all that they can do. One of them is talking to him now:

"You're new. I can see it all over you. The light. Hello."

"How ... do you ... stand this?"

"After a while, you'll get used to it. It's not nice, not at all. The weight. The pressure. *But that pressure is your friend. It reminds you that* change *is coming. It can't just keep getting heavier and heavier. There will* have *to be a change, and then everything will be all right again. It was better than this before I got here. Not by much though. You'll see. It will get heavier still. In the meantime,* look on the bright side. The sheer numbers in here are what means that we can get squeezed out again. Into the animals."

And Jonathan Hall looks around him and sees now, too confused to question what has just been said, and sees nothing but human forms around him in their trillions and octillions and vigintillions as if he were in the middle of an ocean made of sheer humanity, and imagines more of them arriving every second. It will *get heavier indeed.*

"I'm Ted. Ted Okerlund." There's a handshake that isn't quite a handshake because they're different beings, different forms than they were when they were alive, but the idea is there and that's enough.

"J ... Jonathan. Jonathan ... Hall."

Although it is the beginning of a friendship that will last for fifteen years—until Ted leaves—all Jonathan thinks in that moment are two contrasting thoughts, ones that will put him inside a new terrible grip of hope and despair without him even realising it.

My family will come here soon, and we will be together

Oh God, spare them from this

Ted was right, though; he does get used to it, after a fashion, and he soon learns that the human mind can, in most circumstances, become accustomed to any kind of existence. Ted teaches him how to move through the human treacle, and Jonathan is surprised to learn that there is even a political structure of a sort, or at least two opposing movements:

"The Peaceful Ones, and the Order of Daylight," says Ted.

"Peaceful how?" asks Jonathan.

"Trust me. In their case, it's a very ironic name," says Ted, and explains further. Amongst other things he says, Ted says that Jonathan will eventually learn the most important aspects of his new existence. He will learn how to observe the world he left behind, how to penetrate the veil of the wall of the dead and see beyond. And he will learn how to become one of the Distracted, should he so choose.

"The what?"

Ted explains.

Over time, Jonathan becomes known; he rises up what passes for rank in the chaotic endless mountain of humanity that is the Dump. That's what they call that place, and Jonathan thinks that it is indeed the correct term. A pit for the dead, full to bursting but *not yet bursting.*

"What happens when it bursts?" Jonathan asks.

"No one knows, of course," Ted says, "and that is what the argument has always been about."

Years pass. Pressure builds. Countless millions more arrive, and even the last traces of whatever was there before disappear almost imperceptibly, like the last grains of sand falling through an hourglass in another room. Now any new arrivals would never know that the Dump had ever been anything but the Dump.

Jonathan learns to see beyond. It isn't hard; it seems to almost come to him on its own, something that he suddenly finds that he can do and yet isn't surprised when it arrives, suddenly effortless. He watches his wife grow older, and both fears for her arrival and yearns for it. The world of the living is so breathtakingly free when seen from here, unrestrained on a level that he never knew before he came to the Dump. He wonders how he never saw it.

Then one day, he sees his own way back.

It is like a hot bowl of barbecue beef placed before the mouth of a starving man. It is a ticket out of the Dump and out of the endless, endless pressure. And yet he doesn't take it. He will wait for Nancy. He will wait for her, and then they will wait for the pressure to break together. He won't let her come here alone. He has picked his side. He continues to watch, and in this manner he is a witness to the day his brother is shot through the brain.

His brother is an unlucky innocent bystander in a robbery at a 7–Eleven. He only went in to pick up some batteries. Jonathan Hall finds his brother when he arrives, fighting his way through the almost impenetrable human gel towards his brother's presence as it calls to him automatically. They are connected, of course, as are so many countless others in this place. His brother asks the same questions Jonathan Hall did:

"How... do you... stand the ...weight?"

"I know that it will break. I wait."

More years pass. Then Ted leaves.

There almost isn't time for good-bye, which is even worse in the Dump; Jonathan knows that it is forever. Ted will become one of the Distracted, and while he will continue to exist, he will not be Ted anymore.

"You found one?" Jonathan asks, already knowing the answer. It's written all over Ted's face. There's life there, standing out like a beacon, and it's an expression only ever worn by those who are going home. There isn't much time, either. There never is, not when there's always a fistful of others (those who meet the spiritual criteria anyway, those who fulfil the trillions-to-one odds in a place populated by many more than trillions) who will be wanting to charge into the same vessel. The key is going straightaway, while you're still the first and only one to see it. If you leave it too long, and give others time to spot it, sometimes there is a jam. There's only room for one in a vessel, after all. Sometimes there's an awful existential bottleneck that results in no one escaping through the window. Those are the worst, though quietly satisfying for those who are merely watching. Still stuck here with us, they think, bitterly.

"Yes," says Ted, searching for something else to say. "I just wanted to ..."

He looks away, seeing the exit and checking for others. No one has spotted it. Yet.

"It's all right," says Jonathan Hall, forcing a smile. "I understand. Thank you, Ted. Good luck." Ted stares at Jonathan Hall, smiling, full of desperate, frantic excitement, but sadness too. There will not be many here that Ted will miss ... but then, he will not miss them for long. Once he becomes Distracted, all will be forgotten forever. Ted embraces Jonathan Hall fiercely, and turns to leave. He can't waste time. Despite knowing this, Jonathan still has to make one last attempt.

"The Dump will break, Ted," he says, his voice shot through with urgency. "You can feel it, can't you? Not much longer. I know it's hard, it's really hard, but ... don't you want to be here as yourself? You know you'll come back here in what, fifteen years at most, and it will all have broken by then, surely. Is it really worth losing yourself for a break of fifteen years?"

Ted smiles.

"I said the exact same things as you, once," he says. "And I changed my mind a long time ago. Good-bye, Jonathan. Be kind to me when I come back. Like I was to you." And then he's gone, bleeding away before Jonathan's eyes like water down a drain. His last words—*like I was to you*—startle Jonathan, but not because he's surprised by the truth in them. He's surprised that Ted never told him. That said, he'd always been frightened to ask, and he'd never really thought that Ted would know the answer ... but he'd always secretly suspected that he and Ted had met in the Dump before. That this was Jonathan's second time here, and that once he was someone else.

For Jonathan's part, he has his brother with him now, along with other company, and there is a lot to observe on earth, of course. All that is what makes existence bearable, a distraction from the weight. He decides to watch Ted's descent. He's seen a great many, so many that they hold almost zero interest for him, but this one has a deeply personal element to it.

Ted's destination is Spain, and Jonathan feels a pang of jealousy. He always wanted to go to Europe. *Lucky guy*, he thinks, and knows that only tells half of the story. The amount of luck involved with every exit is almost unfathomable. Every vessel on earth is a combination lock, only they're a combination lock where the amount of numbers to be put in makes Pi look like someone's luggage code. To be eligible—to be able to use a vessel, to have a destination that allows the dead to cross the void—a near infinity of elements have to add up just *right*. Even taking a mammal as simple as a mouse required the perfect combo of genetic availability and matching spirit, a blend of science and spirituality that no one on earth would believe or understand. Only the eyes of the dead could see it. Only the dead could use it.

Jonathan has asked countless times, but no one ever knew who was the first to try it. Undoubtedly, it was a very long time ago, and all those that remembered the original had surely become Distracted themselves. Regardless of whoever figured it out, though, the process had been going on for a very, very long time, all over the world. And another one is happening right now, as Ted begins the first stages. He won't be Distracted immediately; that will come soon, but once the process is begun it can't be stopped, Distracted or otherwise. At first, he just needs to become part of the vessel, to become one with the embryo before it can even be classed as such. Conception has only just occurred.

Even the word *vessel* isn't quite right. It isn't a takeover, and Ted is not a cuckoo in the nest. Once Ted is finished, they will be a whole unit, blended perfectly, neither wholly one nor the other. It has to happen almost immediately after the moment of conception, of course, long before it becomes a kitten, long before it becomes part of the world. Science and spirituality; some of the Peaceful Ones call it a "spell", the *really old ones anyway*, but Jonathan Hall doesn't speak to any of the real Peaceful Ones any more than necessary if he can help it. They know things, ways to hurt even the dead. They've been around a very long time, and they're very dangerous as a result.

Time passes. Jonathan Hall watches. The eyes of the dead can see far—of course they can, if they can see from beyond—and seeing into the nest on the day of birth is easy. The kitten in this instance isn't one of the feline variety, but the name used for a newborn squirrel. Ted is the fifth born in his litter, and there will be two more after him before the mother is done. He does all his work while the kitten is preparing to leave the womb, settling into the vaguely formed mind of the infant squirrel and slowly merging with it. It can only be this one kitten, this one living creature in the whole of the world that is a match for Ted, and if he'd rushed it, if he'd gone about the process incorrectly, then it wouldn't have worked. He'd have been back on the other side to wait however long it took for the next possible vessel to be born. Decades, usually.

He got it right—it's an instinctive process for the dead, this merging and rebirthing, like waking from sleep in many ways—and the cycle is complete once he is birthed. In fact, the moment he is out, Ted has already half-ceased to exist, although anyone living who might be watching wouldn't know that they were looking at anything more than a baby squirrel. Half of him has been lost in the merging, blended away, and that which is left is dazed, akin—rather appropriately—to a half-asleep man, dazed and mentally dulled. The vessel's eyes are closed, and won't open for many weeks, but it vocalises and paws feebly at the air. This is Ted, getting his new body's bearings. Over time, the remaining consciously human mind will disappear, dim memories of cars and houses and bank accounts absorbed by the raw power of animal instinct. Now and then, throughout the rest of Ted's new existence, there will be flashes of memory, sudden reminders that will cause (to human eyes) inexplicable animal behaviour. Actions completely and suddenly out of character to the species, or even to Squirrel-Ted's usual behaviour, as he tries to comprehend what a memory of flying through the sky crammed into a shining white tube full of other people means. His merged mind will paw at it like a man trying to find his way in the dark. Then it will pass.

For now, though, Ted is half a human mind in a baby squirrel's body, and he lies in the nest as his new mother pushes out the last of his brothers and sisters. Each of them going through the exact same process as Ted; each an unimaginably specific dead person merging, each of them containing their own dead guest.

When the day comes that all of their eyes are open, none of them will remember who they were.

After a while, Jonathan stops watching, and looks for something new. Ted will come back eventually once his new life is done, and the life of a squirrel holds little interest for Jonathan Hall.

More years pass. Jonathan watches Nancy die of heart failure. Excited, he awaits her arrival.

Watching your loved ones as they live is not as painful for the dead as might be expected; the mind is not the same as it is in life. Of course, it has to be *different; how could an ordinary human mind accept its own death, or the concept of eternity? The emotions are the same, but remote, more objective. In this way, they watch, and love, and grieve, but it is much more bearable. Jonathan always thinks that this is the Dump's worst, darkest trick, that the misery of their existence is never* quite *enough to tip them into the comforts of madness. That they can bear it.*

But now his wife is coming to him, and while he feels the muted sorrow of the dead for her—that she will have to exist in the Dump—he feels the equally muted joy that is as rare in that place as finding your own vessel. He will see her again. He was right not to become Distracted. He was right to remember her.

Months turn into years, and still she does not arrive.

It's true then, the rumours that the others say. There are other places. The Dump is not the only destination for the dead. She has gone to one of them, for whatever reason. While it is devastating in the same removed way of every emotion, it only strengthens Jonathan Hall's resolve, as it proves the Peaceful Ones correct; the place can *break, freeing them all, as there are places outside for it to break* into. *And every day (not that day and night has any real meaning in the sunless land of the dead) with every dead human that arrives, they take another step closer to the bursting of the Dump. The most rotten bubble in eternity will pop, and then ...*

... they will be free.

Ted comes back, of course, and he is screaming when he arrives. The Distracted that live in the wild usually are when they come back, having met their moment of death in the jaws of a predator. Squirrel-Ted was eaten by a hawk. Jonathan Hall feels him arrive—it's always easier to feel those you knew come back—and moves to him through the complaining bodies with the usual psychic effort required. Ted—although he knows it isn't Ted, not any more—looks at the teeming masses pressing in around him, looks at his old friend. There is, of course, no recognition in his eyes, even when he stops screaming. He speaks.

"What ... is this ... place?" And then, the arrival line of the Distracted, usually after looking at their hands, touching their face, remembering the physical knowledge of a human body like an old friend:

"Who ... who am I?"

And Jonathan follows tradition, and gives the new arrival a name, and over time this new Ted will develop a personality too. Jonathan, incidentally, calls him "Jed".

Years pass. Another vessel becomes available to Jonathan, visible only shortly before its birth (as is always the case). He thinks he's too late though, even if he wanted to leave; he can tell that it's been visible for a while, in terms of the window of opportunity for the dead at least, and someone is probably already on their way to it. But he still wouldn't take it even if that wasn't the case. He's waited this long, kept his mind, kept himself. *He's not sacrificing that now. Even when this exit is human for once, the most desired of all, an actual* human body vessel, *and not an animal.*

Life, *his mind calls to him.* A whole new life, decades to spare to live in, eat in, screw in ...

I am Jonathan Hall, *he answers to himself, fierce and certain and resolved,* and I will remain Jonathan Hall.

And then there is another voice in his head, one that is not his in any way, and it is dark and deep and very, very old, older than any of the Peaceful Ones ever let on. It is ancient, and even in the detachment of the Dump Jonathan Hall is terrified.

JONATHAN HALL, *it says,* YOU HAVE REFUSED A HUMAN VESSEL. WE HAVE SEEN THIS, AND WE WOULD SPEAK WITH YOU.

***

Martin sat on the floor in front of Jonathan Hall, his eyes wide and unblinking. If everything he'd just been told was true, he'd just been told one of the great secrets of the universe.

Is that what I have to look forward to? The Dump?

NOT NECESSARILY. YOU HEARD HIM. HIS WIFE DIDN'T GO THERE. PEOPLE GO TO DIFFERENT PLACES, IT SEEMS.

It wasn't a comforting thought. Jonathan Hall was silent now, as if waiting for a response. After a moment, he lay down again on the floor, his eyes half-closed.

"Are you ... all right?" Martin asked. He noticed his automatic concern; a human mind inside it or not, his instinct was to look after his dog. Martin couldn't help it.

"Yes," said Jonathan Hall, but his voice was more strained than before. "It takes a major effort to talk this way to a human, even for me. I'll have to rest soon. I wanted to discuss a lot more than this, but you needed to hear my story from the beginning."

"But there's so much more that I need to know—"

"I understand."

"Like ... I mean, every animal on earth is ... what did you call them, one of the Distracted?"

"Almost, yes. Nearly every mammal. And the *really* lucky ones get to become human ... so many of them think that losing themselves and becoming someone else is worth it, just to live again in whatever form they can get. The humans go the same way as the animal ones, though ... lost in the overwhelmed mind of a constantly learning infant. And unlike the animal Distracted who return as human but with a blank slate for a mind, when the human Distracted get back to the Dump, they remain whoever they became in their new human lives."

"But ... why not you?"

"Why not me, what?"

"Why aren't you, you know, Distracted? You remember everything."

Jonathan Hall scratched at his ear with his hind leg. It was an unusual moment; as he watched a dog do something he'd seen a million times before, this time he heard a gentle grunt of satisfaction inside his head.

"I was given a mission, Martin," said the dog once he'd finished scratching, focusing his squinting eyes on Martin's face. "I was chosen to come and explain to you what was at stake. I was lucky; picked from the trillions and trillions on *our* side of the argument, because I am one of the few that had the right *essence* to combine with a very special animal being born close enough to *you*. A *pure* vessel."

"A what?" Martin's head was spinning. The room seemed brighter than it had been before.

"The Peaceful Ones ..." Jonathan Hall said, his voice low and containing not a little amount of fear, "they're *old*, Martin, as I've told you. Ice Age old. As old as the early days of man, we think, though no one ever dares to ask. They've had time to learn a few tricks that most of us can't even begin to imagine. They can see in ways that the rest of us can't. And they can see *vessels* that the rest of us can't. None of us knew *that* ... they kept it secret. I only know because, well, as you can see ... I'm currently inside one of those vessels. They save the pure vessels for themselves, normally, making sure they come back and never get Distracted."

"What? I mean ... sorry, what?"

"Okay. There are normal vessels, ones which you enter and are then Distracted, ones that mean you are never the same again. You see? Scoffer is one, for example."

"Scoffer?" Martin looked at Scoffer, asleep on his back in his basket and snoring quietly. "He's ... one of those?"

"Yes. I checked before I came, out of interest. The Peaceful Ones told me. They see nearly all of the comings and goings between the Dump and here. He used to be a woman, in fact. She was called Beth Savage, and died in 1989 at the age of seventy-four."

"Scoffer ... is a woman?"

"No, Martin. He stopped being a woman when he became Scoffer. When Scoffer dies, the human part will go back to the Dump, and remember nothing of her previous life as a human."

"And the dog half?" It sounded like a dumb question, but he wanted to know. Jonathan Hall did that doggy head-shrug again.

"We don't know. We don't even know if there *is* a dog half left afterwards, or whether it's absorbed into the human one. It might go somewhere else that we don't know about."

There was a long pause.

"So the pure vessels ...?" Martin asked, his voice his feeble and weak.

"They're the rarity. They're the *real* rarity, Martin. Only a handful walk the entire earth at any one time, usually a few in each country. There's never been any *human* pure vessels—again, we don't know why, we think the odds of getting the right combination of essence and pure vessel in human form is just too high—but there are always a few animal pure vessels on the earth.

These are the rare vessels that somehow allow the dead to retain themselves when they enter. The ones that allow the dead to not become Distracted by animal instincts. We still feel those instincts, of course—you throw a stick, and I'll chase it before I can stop myself, it makes living a dog's life easy and fun, frankly—but we generally remain in control. The Peaceful Ones can spot them, and I was a match for this body. And more importantly, I agreed with their politics."

"You believe that the Dump will break. *They* believe that."

"Yes," said Jonathan Hall solemnly. "I think something went wrong with our afterlife, Martin. We were never supposed to end up crammed in that place like infinite sardines. It's like the place was set up by someone at the beginning of time and then just abandoned with no one to manage it. After all, it's so packed in there now that we've been coming back for a long time. Squeezed out, almost. Every mammal on earth, Martin. The Dump has to give way, and it feels that way now more than it ever has."

"And then what will happen?" Martin asked, goose bumps breaking out all over his body.

"Again ... we don't know. But it has to be better than what is there now. Maybe we go elsewhere."

Jonathan Hall paused, like he'd said something that he shouldn't. Martin twigged immediately.

"You want to go where your wife is," he said.

Wife. What about your *wife.*

"Oh my God," Martin whispered. "*My* wife ... have you ..."

Jonathan Hall shook his head, sadly.

"No, Martin. She isn't with us. When they explained what they wanted me to do, and why, I asked them about her. They can see much better than the rest of us, as I say ... and she isn't in the Dump. She's somewhere else."

Martin suddenly knew exactly how Jonathan Hall must have felt, waiting for his own wife and discovering that she wasn't going to arrive. Intense relief ... but sadness, and fear. Where was she? Somewhere worse? Somewhere better? He felt sick.

"Then there are the madmen, of course, that claim to have been to these places," Jonathan Hall continued, changing the subject quickly. "The only one I ever believed was an old man named Richard Hart; he was the only one that ever talked like that who didn't seem totally nuts. I never saw him again, either—we don't tend to move that far in the Dump from where we arrive, as it's just too much effort—so maybe he was telling the truth, and then moved on somehow. I wish I'd believed him ... but all the evidence tells us that there are other places, waiting maybe above or below the Dump, places that *work*. The Dump will break, Martin, and we will go there."

"If that's what you're here for, why did you bother chewing your way through the gate lock?" asked Martin. "Why did you do that?"

"That was Scoffer," said Jonathan Hall, sounding surprised by the question. "He was manic. I couldn't stop him without getting violent, and I wouldn't do that to him. It didn't affect my mission. I just let him get on with it and shepherded him back when he finally calmed down."

"Why did he do that?" Martin couldn't believe it, strangely enough. Even with all the craziness going on, Chops suddenly chewing through the wire seemed especially nuts. Maybe because it was something that he could actually relate to.

"He was protecting you, or at least trying to. He always has been, Martin. Animals are primal. They're connected to instincts and knowledge that humans have long forgotten. Did you know that when dogs poop, they tend do so along a magnetic north-south axis? Look it up. Even what my people do—coming back the way do—there's something primal in it. Something ingrained in the fabric of things. When very, very ancient people tapped into it, they called such actions *spells*. They got it wrong most of the time, involving stupid things like magic words and sacrifices or whatever, but they touched the truth. Movement. Layout of objects. Fung Shui *kind of* starts to get the idea, but not quite. Either way; Scoffer could feel you being watched, and always has done. His thing with the leaves, laying them out like that, was his way of trying to keep the eyes at bay. Instinct. He got it wrong of course, and got frustrated, but the idea was there. I just thought it safe to get involved with his efforts and mess it all up a bit, just on the slim off chance that he got it right. Why not? It gave me something to do."

Martin looked at Scoffer, confused by the answer, but there were more important things to discuss.

"So why send an errand boy?" Martin asked, breathing slowly to try and quell his rising nausea. "Why didn't the top brass come themselves?"

"I don't know for certain, Martin. When you're in the presence of the Peaceful Ones ... well, let's just say you don't ask questions. They don't even look vaguely human anymore." Jonathan Hall stood, and hopped up onto the office chair in front of the table. He then stepped up onto the table itself again. "But I have my own theory. I think interacting with the living, telling you all this themselves, would be too much for them, being as old as they are. Very unpleasant, at least. I think modern humanity is just too alien for them. Certainly, that's what makes them different to the Order of Daylight, who are *very* much inclined to feel the other way. But more about them later. The living mean cameras and photos, too; the Peaceful Ones warned me about that. Back when they were first invented, they learned the hard way that their true selves would be captured on film if the eyes were seen. Again, we don't know why. Windows of the soul, perhaps? Either way, needless to say that the photographers learned the hard way too. Living people knowing about pure vessels means dead people knowing about pure vessels, and the Peaceful Ones want to keep that quiet."

"Is that why you bit me? To stop me taking a picture?" asked Martin. "Why do that, if you were going to talk to me anyway?"

"I panicked. It wasn't time yet, we hadn't developed enough of a bond for you to not just send me packing when I started doing ... unusual things. That was the plan. Become part of your home, start dropping hints that I was different, make it easier to eventually reveal the truth. Again, small steps. But then Rougeau took you away—I heard him in your head when you were on the phone, and all the dead know of Rougeau—and the situation changed. There was no point in delaying when you already knew that strange things were afoot. Regardless, the other fact is that I think they were too wary of the current status quo; they were worried about what this new situation, and you, might mean for them. Why risk it? Why not just send someone else, someone who believed the same things that they do, and who would want the same outcome?"

"*What* fucking situation?" Martin suddenly snapped, shouting. This had gone on long enough, had gone *weird* enough. He wanted answers. "What have I done? What the hell am I supposed to have done, then?"

"It's not what you've done, Martin. It's what we want you *to* do," Jonathan Hall said, his voice sounding more pained than ever, and indeed, the dog's eyes were squinting, and slowly opening and closing even more than before. "What we do already ... coming back as animals ... we couldn't do it, we think, if the universe wasn't already as broken as it is. Returning that way ... perhaps pushes the already-unbalanced envelope as it is ... but ..." The dog paused. Martin could almost hear a heavy breathing in his head. " I think ... Martin, there's a lot more to be said, and it has to be said properly ... and this has taken too long as it is. I can't ..." The dog lay down on the desk, suddenly breathing heavily, but not taking his eyes off Martin.

"Chops?" said Martin, forgetting that was no longer his dog's name, that Chops had never been his dog in the first place. "What's wrong?"

"It's the effort. Telepathy ..." Jonathan Hall said, his head now on his paws. "It's ... so much harder with a dog's brain. It's a shame I didn't ... get to be a cat. They're far more able."

"Cats are what, more psychic?" Martin asked, screwing his face up at the idea.

"Are you ... really surprised?"

Martin thought about it for a second. Now that he considered the notion, he didn't suppose that he was.

"Tonight," Jonathan Hall whispered, his large furry body rising and falling with each heavy breath. "Will be coming ... tonight."

"What? What will?"

"Other ... one. Other pure vessel. Order of Daylight's man. Not man. Cat. Left before ... I did. Watched him arrive ... in pure vessel. Cat. Pact says that we have to ... give both sides ... of argument. The pact ... has to be honoured. Both sides ... always watching. Maintain ... balance."

"They're watching?" Martin's skin prickled again. "They're watching us now?"

"... yes. Every soul ... in the Dump. Watching you. Us. Cat will come tonight ... explain the rest. Give their side of the story. Leave ... your window open."

Martin swallowed, looking around himself as if expecting to see a crowd of the dead surrounding him in the room. Countless dead, watching him. A dead person in a cat's body on its way to see him that night. A dead man in a dog's body lying on his desk.

"Just remember," Jonathan Hall wheezed, a weak whisper in the echo chamber of Martin's mind. "Our side of the ... argument. The Dump will ... break. We want to let it do so. They propose ... a different method. A method that ... has cost you dearly already. "

Jonathan Hall's eyes darted upwards, suddenly looking very worried. They then briefly darted back to Martin's, and closed. Martin hadn't realised that the blood had been slowly creeping back into this face, but he certainly felt it leave again. He moved closer to Jonathan Hall, feeling as if he were floating. He didn't want to ask the next question, didn't even want to think it, didn't want to even briefly entertain the possibility that his being caught in some kind of supernatural conspiracy had cost him the worst thing that it possibly could.

"Cost me what? Chops? *Cost me what?*"

The dog's eyes remained closed, but he could still hear the voice in his head. It was almost inaudible now when it spoke, but Martin could just about make out the faint edges of a response.

"*Can't say ... pact. Have to leave you ... impartial.*"

But the dog's eyes opened slightly. If Martin had ever read a dog's expression correctly in his life, it was now. The gaze said *I want to tell you something but I can't.* Martin remembered the words that had sent chills up his spine: *Both sides ... always watching.*

"My wife," Martin whispered. His face was now inches from Jonathan Hall's. Before, when this close, the dog would have licked him, but this wasn't his dog any more. "*The other side, the Order of Daylight, did they have something to do with my wife?*"

"*All I know about your wife ... is her name ... and that she married you,*" the faint voice said ... but the dog's eyes burned into Martin's like laser beams. Jonathan Hall then closed them, and lay still.

"Chops? Jonathan?" Martin said, knowing that it was pointless—even if the dog could respond, it wasn't going to tell him the answer for certain—but saying it anyway, the wind in his mind screaming and frantic.

No. No. Don't let *it sink in yet. Don't even think about it. Wait for the cat. Wait for tonight. It's too much to even consider without all of the facts. This is all bullshit anyway, right? This is just you going nuts, no matter what Trish saw the dog do. Just wait for the other one.*

It was a good plan, but one that he couldn't possibly carry out. After what he thought he'd just learned, there was no way he could think about anything else *but* that last part. It was a truth that was already clawing at Martin with hands made of knives.

The Order of Daylight had killed his wife. And Martin was going to get some answers.

***

Chapter Five: It's Waiting in the Garden, and the Other Side of the Story
***

They had reached their destination earlier that day, as expected, and now it was nearly time.

The other two were waiting close by, silent and hidden on the other side of the garden fence. The cat sat in the middle of the darkened garden, waiting until he was sure that the white dog inside the house was asleep. It didn't really matter a huge amount—the dog would awake as soon as the cat spoke, surely—but the cat preferred it to be that way, regardless.

The rat, waiting on the other side of the fence, could have found a way through, certainly, but for whatever reason it had opted to stay with the fox, who had tried and failed to scale the high planks. They were all hungry—almost starving—because moving continually had meant little time to hunt, and food had been scarce on the journey. It was particularly difficult for the fox. Every instinct in his animal body was telling him to devour the rat by his side. The only thing that meant he could keep himself in check was the knowledge of the consequences back in the Dump if he did so. The three of them were part of the Circle of Twelve, after all, the very highest governing members of the Order, and while ending another's time in a pure vessel was the lowest sin, to do so to another member of the *Circle* ... the fox would keep himself in check.

They weren't as old as the Peaceful Ones—none of the Order were—but they were old enough to have some of the abilities, some of the tricks. They could see the pure vessels, and they could of course listen in on even the telepathic side of Jonathan Hall and Martin's conversation, even in their physical forms. All of them had stiffened, outraged, when the dog had started to drop his hint about Hogan's wife, the pact about to be blatantly broken ... but the dog hadn't gone through with it.

That kind of thing was to be expected, the cat thought as it sat in the darkness. Cut off from the Dump, unable to communicate with the other side once they were ensconced in their pure vessels; it was easy to forget the rules.

It might have been deliberate, but the important part was that the dog *hadn't* gone through with it. The dog knew that there were an endless number of watchers on the other side, and they would all hear if it broke the rules.

The rules ... thought the cat, holding itself back with great effort as it heard some small creature moving through the overgrown and unattended bushes to its left. The rules that could be bent, or even broken if they couldn't be found out. It would be nearly impossible to do so—all those eyes, especially those of the Peaceful Ones—and everyone knew what had happened to the last person to break the rules. That should be deterrent enough for anyone. Even so, the Order had sent them as a threesome, and there also were others already here, as expected. The cat looked up with its keen night eyes, making a quick count of the birds of varying sizes that were perched on the telephone lines near the house. Three now, different to the others that had been sitting there all day. The night shift, it seemed. The dog's allies would be nearby too, and indeed, the cat counted the birds on the wire opposite. Three also. It seemed neither side trusted the pact at all.

The light in the downstairs room had gone out some time ago, and the conversation between dead man and living had ended earlier than that. Then the light had gone on in one of the upstairs bedrooms, and the cat had seen the man pacing the room, holding his son with a vacant, stunned look on his face. The dog had done the heavy lifting here—breaking the news, getting the man to understand—but his soft approach and failure to get the whole job done had given the cat more of an opportunity. He'd explained the position of the Peaceful Ones and their followers, certainly, and what they believed in, but he hadn't explained what they wanted Martin to do, and that was a *big* mistake. Clearly, the dog hadn't meant to stop when he did, having only so much telepathic steam at once in a canine body ... but the cat wondered if the dog thought it didn't matter who explained what, knowing that the pact prevented them from editorialising the truth in a way that benefited either side. They both got to have a say, that was the main thing. Even so, that cat was certain that it would be an easy matter for him to explain what the Peaceful Ones wanted in the worst possible terms for them, even without breaking the pact. What they were asking ... it would have been bad enough coming from the dog as it was. The man had been set up perfectly for the Order to tip into their way of thinking, the cat was sure. The only down side was that the cat had to break the *really* bad news. The cat licked its paws, considering the situation. Maybe things were more even that it thought, after all.

There was a sound from above. The cat watched as the other upstairs window opened, propelled outwards by the man's pale arm. It sat very still as the man leaned out slightly, scanning the dark garden. The cat knew it wouldn't be seen in this light, and it wasn't time yet. The man needed to settle. He also looked like he desperately needed to sleep; his eyes looked sunken and haunted, certainly different at least from the healthy but quiet-looking man the cat had watched moving around the house earlier that evening.

Clearly, the man believed the dog even more than the cat had sensed. That was good.

The man disappeared back from view, fading into the shadows of the room beyond the open window, and the cat saw a dim light suddenly begin to glow in there. A bedside lamp. The man was waiting, using a lower light to try and relax, perhaps. Also good.

The cat relaxed slightly, knowing that it wasn't quite time yet. The man needed to calm his nerves still, and that would take a while. Perhaps an hour. They were into the very early hours of the next morning now, certainly, but the man wouldn't sleep. The cat was himself very anxious—returning to the fully experienced emotions of the living, even in animal form, was a double-edged sword indeed—but if he'd learned anything on the other side, it was patience. That was the first thing that any of them learned. They also learned self control. The cat was good at waiting.

Instinct kicked in, and the cat went with it this time. It would be a distraction. The cat began to groom itself, licking at its coat. When it next heard a noise in the underbrush, it decided to pounce this time, teeth and claws bared like sneaking blades in the dark.

***

Martin continued to stare at the open window, seeing only matte blackness on the other side of the glass due to the lamplight inside the room. He felt like a bug pinned under a microscope. Martin still slept in a double bed, despite being the only adult in the house (*the only* human *adult*, his mind reminded him) but he didn't think he could ever bring himself to throw the bed away. He'd fixed the half-empty bed problem as best he could a year ago, needing to remove the physical feeling of exposure, of the bed being *too big*, by pushing it from the centre of the room to the right. It now rested against the western wall of the house, tucked into the corner, and that at least made him feel that he was at least slightly secure.

But you were right *to feel exposed, weren't you? You weren't alone, after all. They were all here, watching you. They watched you as you slept. They're watching you right now.*

Martin shifted on the bed, and bit down on the urge to go running out of the room, screaming and kicking open every door in the house. He wanted to unleash the maelstrom now swirling within him. He knew that if he did so, he might just break inside. Antidepressants? In this situation, they were like bringing a water pistol to put out the Towering Inferno. Plus ... going nuts would wake Callum up.

And you don't want to charge around leaving the door open behind you, because then the cat might get in here and then it's in the whole house and you don't know what it might do—

"Stop it," Martin said out loud, firmly, and the sound of his own voice gave him a bit of temporary reassurance. It was something that he'd always done now and then, ever since he was a kid, and discovered that his overactive mind would often be his worst enemy. That busy, busy mind had certainly been a blessing—first as a way of letting a shy, nervous boy have adventures and social dalliances that he would never have dared to attempt without it, then later allowing him to have a career doing something that he loved—but he knew all too well that it had also been a curse.

His childhood had been filled with visions of teeth and claws and burning red eyes every time that the light went out, leading to so many tearful comforting sessions by his tired, anxious parents. Wracked with guilt—another childhood aspect that Martin had learned at an early age, taught by his parents through word and deed—they decided to get him some therapy. They had no choice, really; simply telling Martin the most useless and pointless phrase in parenting, *there's no such thing as monsters*, had zero impact. Ditto for that other favourite: *Plus, if anything happened, we're only at the other end of the hall.* Martin had always lain there and considered this statement, coming to the same conclusion every time: if a monster *did* appear in his room, did his parents really think that by the time they had heard his screams and came running, it somehow *wouldn't* be far, far too late?

So it had progressed to therapy, and that had worked surprisingly well, even to the young Martin's point of view. He learned not only how to separate the imaginary from the real when it counted, but also to control his nerves at night. It had become second nature from then on through childhood and into his adult life, until the first night he'd been truly on his own after Liz died, the first night in a house without people watching over him. Then all the monsters had come back, filling every shadow with a potential malevolence that made the bed feel like a bull's-eye with him in the very centre. It had taken a lot of bravery, dedication—and medication, at first—to get back to being comfortable once more, but right now Martin felt like he'd nearly reset to square one all over again. Only his breathing techniques were managing to keep him calm. He didn't have the main room light on, as that would *really* feel like he was reverting to childhood, but the lamp was a compromise. He couldn't decide what was worse, though; having the room in darkness, or the view through the window being an almost solid black pane due to the interior light. He knew the view he had would show only sky if he turned the light off, but at least that would mean the black couldn't be hiding anything. The thought of something *hiding* alarmed him, and his hand darted to the lamp faster than he meant it to. He switched it off, and the open curtains meant that the room was now flooded with moonlight. That wasn't as bad as he'd feared. The room wasn't as dark as he'd thought it might be, and the clear sight of the stars was better, he decided, than the black sheet that had been there before. But his whole body still felt like it was caught in a vice.

Stop it. This fear doesn't make any sense. It's a cat that's coming. It's just a cat.

But it wasn't just a cat, he knew. Even if it was a cat just like Jonathan Hall was a dog, *waiting* for it was so much worse. Plus, as Jonathan Hall had told him, it *wasn't* just the same. It was from a different group. A rival group. Martin fervently wished that Scoffer could be in here, but he knew that if there was one thing his old companion hated, it was cats. To make matters worse, Jonathan Hall had refused to come upstairs, and Martin didn't think it was due to his exhaustion. He couldn't tell Martin himself, but Martin thought he knew exactly why. The pact. Each side needed to have the floor, alone. And so Martin was waiting alone.

Calm down. Remember the old tricks.

That was true. The old tricks were always good. Nowadays he knew that it had been early forms of what they called Neuro Linguistic Programming, but as a kid it had been his own magic trick, his own spell. It had also taught him how to tell stories.

Make it safe. Make it fun.

Martin closed his eyes, forcing his lungs and ribcage to expand and contract more slowly.

The black sheet, he thought, seeing it. *It's not a trick of the light, but an actual sheet of black, stretched taut to each corner of the window. It's put there by imps that can cover a window in a nanosecond, literally in the time it takes for a light to click on at night. Then while the light is on inside, they have a party behind the screen. It doesn't matter if the light is only on for a few seconds, because these imps see time differently than we do—hence their ability to put the sheet up so fast—and even if the light inside is on for just a second, that's like a three-hour party for them. When the light goes off, they instantly stop the party and take the sheet away, and then we can see the stars again.*

For a moment, he felt better, and opened his eyes. Then he saw the cat that was now standing on the windowsill.

It wasn't just the injection of sudden surprise into his already amped-up levels of fear that made him cry out and half-leap off the bed; there was a new fear, too. The cat was *big.* Clearly a tom, from the size of the animal, but it was definitely far larger than most. It was almost as big as a small-to-medium sized dog.

He'd obviously opened his eyes just as the cat was silently entering the room. Of course, it had no collar, and therefore no bell. Because it hadn't made any sound at all, the resulting effect was that it had just appeared ... but when he looked again, he could see the way that its paw was in paused mid-step, caught. The most intimidating part was the fact that it was completely in silhouette, lit from behind by the waxing gibbous moon. With the lamp off, the cat's shadow cast long onto the carpet, making it seem as if it filled the room.

Martin wanted to turn the lamp on again, but he was now frozen in place. Neither of them moved.

It's just a cat. It's just a cat. None of this is real anyway.

HOW COULD YOU KNOW A CAT WAS COMING? IF IT'S NOT REAL, HOW COULD YOU KNOW?

"Hello, Martin," the cat said, and not only was its voice louder in Martin's head—Jonathan Hall hadn't been lying about cats having greater mental abilities—but it sounded different, which was to be expected. This voice was younger, smoother, and more intense, as if the speaker was restraining a great urge of some sort, or had somewhere else they really wanted to be.

It doesn't want to be anywhere else at all, though, so that's not it. This animal has been waiting for this moment for some time.

Regardless, the difference in the voice was more than that. The sound was ... it was all around him. Jonathan Hall spoke from inside Martin's head. The cat did too, but also seemed to come *at* Martin from all sides. Martin didn't reply.

"*Don't be alarmed,*" the cat said. "*I mean you no more harm than the other visitor did. I won't read your mind, either. The deal is precisely the same. I'm just here to plead our case.*"

Our *case*, Martin thought. *The others that are all watching from the other side right now. How many?* He pictured them all, an endless sea of the dead, faces pressing eagerly toward him, squeezing closer, hanging on his every word. What did they *want?*

"What do you want?" Martin asked, hearing his voice shake and hating it. He knew the cat wasn't going to do anything, but the fact that it had appeared at all was making him start to believe all of this. That alone was terrifying. He reminded himself of what he had brought upstairs with him, tucked down the wall side of the bed ... but ultimately it was insignificant against the mysteries of the universe. The Dump was greater than whatever Martin carried. As the object crossed his mind, he immediately pushed the thought away and brought up whatever mental pictures he could to try and think of anything else. He didn't want the cat to sense it, even if it had promised not to read his mind. He'd trusted Jonathan Hall because Jonathan Hall had been Martin's dog, as stupid as that was for a reason. He didn't know this cat at all. "I don't just mean your ... side, or order, or whatever the hell you call yourselves. I mean all of you. All of you. *Why* ... are you coming to my house? What do you want from me?" He gritted his teeth as he said the last part, only barely keeping himself under control at the end. Fury had penetrated fear for a moment, and he'd very nearly gone for the cat, large or otherwise. All that had stopped him was his desire for answers.

"*Don't worry, Martin,*" the cat said, sitting. "*I'm going to tell you everything. Everything. I can talk for as long as you want me to. All I ask is that you let me explain what* we *want. Is that fair?*" Though Jonathan Hall had said similar words, the cat's tone was slightly patronising, a care home nurse talking to a senile old man, and Martin thought that the cat could sense his fear. It was trying to talk him down. Martin didn't like that at all. Martin realised that he hadn't noticed the accent; it was hard to take note of these things when it sounded like there were four people talking at once, surrounding you. It was European in tone.

Rougeau? Connected?

"Rougeau. You're something to do with him, aren't you?" Martin said, trying to seize onto his anger again, trying to use it to steady himself. It almost worked. "The dog mentioned him, too. How the hell did the dog know about him?"

"*Rougeau? Oh,* all *of us know about* him, *Mister Hogan,*" said the cat, cocking its head slightly. Martin felt like he was being assessed. "He's one of the few people on this side that ever showed any kind of telepathy at all. He stood out to us like a beacon. And then his light went out ... but recently it came back. Round about the same time that we all started taking an interest in *you*. I guess that must be what triggered his return, all the psychic focus, if you will. It woke him up."

"The Brotherhood of the Raid," Martin said, pointing a trembling finger at the cat. "He mentioned them. What have they got to do with all this?"

The cat hopped down from the window, and Martin actually flinched, sitting up straighter on the bed. Now his hand shot out and flicked on the lamp, lighting the cat, who squinted slightly in the sudden glow.

Martin could see that its coat must have helped with the silhouette effect. It was jet black, and Martin could see now that its eyes were a bright green. They stared at him almost lazily, and the slit pupils at their centre seemed to bore through him. The eyes were horribly human, unnervingly aware.

"*I wish we knew,*" the cat said, and then seemed to catch itself. "*Sorry; I hope you don't mind if I come in. It's cold on the window. I can go back if it makes you uncomfortable.*" Martin felt like it was a test. If he admitted that he *did* want the cat to go back to the windowsill, then he was admitting that the cat made him uncomfortable. The cat would be in control.

"No, you're fine where you are. Carry on."

"Thank you. The Brotherhood ... we wonder if they can perhaps sense that something is going on, Mister Hogan," the cat said. "*We think perhaps that they are people sensitive to the other side, that they are responding in a way that might make no sense to you or me, but does to them somehow. That's our best guess. It's been going on longer than the news has been aware of it, that's for sure. I saw them carrying out their attacks before I left, before this body was born. We might know more about it now—those of us watching from the other side—but since I've been here in this body I obviously won't know more until I go back.*"

"You can't talk to the other side from here?"

"*No. How could I?*" The cat sounded as if the idea was preposterous. Martin nearly said *well you're bloody well managing to talk to me psychically,* but he realised that didn't necessarily mean anything. Telepathically or otherwise, it was still communication on *this* side. It didn't mean the cat could penetrate through to his people on the *other* side.

"Stay there," Martin said, and pulled out his iPhone. He noticed the cat stiffen almost imperceptibly as he did so; the cat wasn't necessarily as confident as it sounded, then. It hadn't known what Martin was going for.

It really isn't reading your mind.

The cat looked at the phone, and nodded.

"*Ah yes. Of course.*"

Martin didn't reply, and snapped a quick shot of the cat after zooming in on its face. When he looked at the frozen image, there they were: two floating, human eyes, shining above the cat's own.

"*You managed to get a photo of the other one, then. As you've probably guessed, those of us in the pure vessels never let photos of our faces be taken. That's why none of us are ever pets,*" it said, once Martin looked away from the camera again. "*Interesting, though, that you managed to get one. I imagine he made it difficult? I wondered why you were having the conversation so soon. I expected that I'd be waiting in your garden for at least another week. If I were the dog, I wouldn't have felt that I'd been integrated for long enough. It had been agreed beforehand that he would go first—talking to you, that is—but tell me, how did he manage to actually become part of the household? Obviously, he did that to make it easier to break it to you ... but how did he pull it off?*"

Martin paused for a moment. The cat didn't know? He thought about not telling it, but decided that caginess was not an option tonight. There was too much he wanted to know, and he wanted the cat to be as forthcoming as possible. It was probably best to be the same way himself, to encourage the cat.

"He was hurt," said Martin, feeling a little stupid. "I took him home."

"*Y-e-e-esss ...*" murmured the cat, nodding again. It looked like those toys that Martin had often seen through vehicle rear windows. "*Now that is clever ...*"

"What do you mean?"

"*He would have done it himself, Mister Hogan. What kind of a dog owner could resist helping an injured dog?*"

It felt like a slap. Even after every revelation tonight, this one was the most hurtful. It felt like he'd been played for an idiot.

"That's why he played with Scoffer ... making it clear that he was friendly ... turning on the charm ..."

"*Probably, Mister Hogan,*" said the cat, those unnerving green eyes blinking slowly. "*While we are on opposing sides, I feel that I have to say that you shouldn't blame him, and it's not just the pact making me say that. He had a job to do, and he wanted there to be* no *chance of not becoming close to you. He could never just come over and start talking, it could have been disastrous. He was thorough, and I have the luxury of coming in here without any need for pretence thanks to his efforts. That said ... you'll only get the truth from me.*" The cat sounded satisfied. Martin looked at the picture again, the white, human eyes staring back at him.

"Why not tell us," he said quietly, almost speaking to himself as he looked at the image onscreen. The cat's head twitched slightly.

"*What do you mean?*" it asked, quizzically.

"You come here, in these bodies," he said, still looking at the photo. His fear was suddenly forgotten, replaced only by a cold, flat feeling ... and morbid curiosity. "The ones that can talk to us, just like the pair of you have been doing tonight. Why not tell the world what you know? That there are worlds waiting for us? Why not prepare us?" He dropped the phone on the bed and looked at the cat. "Why let so many of us believe that our loved ones are gone for good? Don't you understand how much hope it would bring people if they knew?" He managed to keep his voice steady, but only just. "People like me? If you could have told me that my wife was still ... somewhere ..."

"*I understand you asking the question, Mister Hogan, but think about the reality of what you're saying,*" said the cat, that reluctant, patronising tone back in its voice again. Martin gritted his teeth, thinking of his wife, and that this bastard knew something about it ... if Jonathan Hall was telling the truth, or hinting at it at least. "*We can only talk to one person at a time, which makes it hard enough; how does that person then get the world at large to get them to believe them? Sure, we could tell their friends one at a time, start a group ... but you can still only ever prove it to one person at once. You have to remember, also, that it's only the very old ones that can* see *the pure vessels. The oldest members of the Order aren't as old as the leaders of the Peaceful Ones, of course, but they're still old enough to have developed the trick. And when you're as old as they are ... well, like the dog said, let's just say that they don't particularly* want *to communicate with the living, or the human ones at least. They've been institutionalised into the realm of the dead, Mister Hogan, and so when they return here they just want to live, to experience all the delicious physical sensations that have been denied them. That's the only thing that makes us come back. It's ironic, I know. The more recent dead would do anything to be able to talk to the living again, and remain* themselves, *and the older ones actually can, but shun it. Life is cruel, certainly, but death is more so.*"

Martin went to speak, and then realised that he'd just noticed something in the cat's speech.

"Wait a second," he said, his finger pointing again. He'd always been taught that doing so was rude, and so he never pointed at anyone when talking to them, but he subconsciously reasoned that this was a double exception. It was a cat, and a person who was already dead. The autopilot part of his brain had decided this meant all the no-pointing bets were off. "*Us.* You started off saying *they*, but at the end there you said *us.* Jonathan Hall isn't one of the older Peaceful Ones. They *showed* him a pure vessel and sent him because, just like you said, the older ones don't like to talk to the living. But you just said *us.*" He leant forward, his conviction growing as the cat continued to remain silent. "You're one of them, aren't you? You're one of the leaders. You're one of the leaders of the Order of Daylight."

The cat didn't answer at first, even if its green eyes remained steady, continuing to blink slowly and languourously. Martin, in a moment of madness, decided to bluff.

"Get out," he said, pointing at the window. "Get the fuck out. You said I'd only get the truth, so if you're not going to give me that—"

The cat slowly held up a paw.

"*Mister Hogan, please,*" it said, "*don't mistake my silence for reluctance. I was merely considering the best way to answer your question. But yes, in a nutshell, you're correct. I am. I am a member of the Circle of Twelve.*" Martin didn't believe the silky smooth tones of the cat for one second—it *had* planned to keep that truth to itself—but he was relieved that his bluff had worked. He began to feel more like himself, like some of the mist was lifting from the situation and that he could talk as an equal, at least in regards to the physical bodies in that room. *"We are indeed the leaders. This isn't something I intended to keep from you, I merely didn't think it relevant. What difference does it make if you're dealing with the organ grinder or the monkey? What matters is the information I bring."*

It mattered. Martin knew it mattered. The Peaceful Ones might have sent "the monkey" to do their bidding, but Jonathan Hall was no simpleton. They'd picked someone they knew would be reliable, relatable. The Order of Daylight had clearly wanted to get their hands dirty, not trusting someone outside of their leadership to do the work for them ... but Martin thought that it might have been a mistake. The cat's manner was all wrong; aloof, patronising without realising it. Perhaps the cat thought that it was being smooth, *professional* perhaps ... but it was going about it all wrong. It would have been better to come in completely honestly, saying *look, we sent the top brass to see you, that's how important we think you are,* but it seemed like maybe the cat had planned to portray itself as being the same as Jonathan Hall, to ride on his coattails by seeming as much like Martin's own pet as he could. It wasn't a good strategy. The cat came across like a politician, picking his words carefully.

"What's the deal with your lot, though?" Martin asked, surprised at how ordinary the question sounded coming out of his mouth. "The other lot want to wait until the Dump gets so full that it bursts. I don't *get* it though, because I don't know the alternative. I'm assuming you must have one, and that it's something to do with me. Jonathan Hall said it was something that would hit me hard, but so far the worst thing I've heard is that the Dump exists, and by the sounds of it there's no exact guarantee I'm going there anyway." He swung his legs off the bed, fully clothed as he still was—he was never going to sleep that night, after all, so there had been no point in getting changed—feeling more confident as he talked. He was still on edge, and very much so, but he was no longer on the verge of running from the room. One dead guy talking to him, he could handle, so he focused on that. It was when he thought of an infinity of eyes surrounding him that he felt as cold as the grave, so he tried not to.

It's just a cat. You're just talking to a cat.

A CAT WHOSE PEOPLE MIGHT HAVE HAD YOUR WIFE KILLED. THE CAT IS DANGEROUS.

"We are, in the grand cosmic scheme of things, newcomers, Mister Hogan," said the cat, sounding as if it was starting to speak about a subject it was proud of. "Still incredibly old to your perception of the word. Fortunately though, while we lack what the Peaceful Ones have in terms of power, we dwarf them in terms of numbers. So we've been very much on an equal footing politically—if the word can be applied to the dead—for at least the last decade or two. Existence is very, very different there, Mister Hogan, so I'm trying to put it in terms that you can understand, even if those terms don't really apply."

"I'm not really interested in who has the majority in the parliament of the dead right now ... Mister ..." said Martin, his words draining away as he realised that he didn't know the cat's name. "Wait, what do I call you?"

"*Midian*," said the cat, and actually bowed his head slightly. Martin thought the gesture was very melodramatic, but then realised with a shudder that the cat, or *Midian* as he claimed, was very likely to have lived in a time or place where such gestures were the norm. It was an old-sounding name to Martin's ears.

"Okay, Midian. What I want to know is what you want, what your side believe in, and how it relates to me," Martin said, his pulse racing. More secrets, more building blocks of the universe, about to be shown to him in all of their murky glory.

Unless you're completely nuts. That a possibility that's still hanging on by its fingertips ...

"*Of course,*" the cat said. "*It's probably best to start by saying that both sides actually believe the same thing ... we just approach it from different angles, as it were. Change is in the air, Mister Hogan, a big change, and the days of the Dump, as it is now at least, are ending. You can feel it in there. The place is thick with it. You'd understand if you'd visited, but believe me, you can almost taste it. It's undeniable. The difference is that the Peaceful Ones believe that it will change if left to continue as it is, that the capacity of the Dump is finite and will break as the numbers of the dead continue to increase. We think the opposite is true. That the Dump will* never *break ... that it will simply become worse and worse, until it is no longer the just-bearable existence that it is now. We believe that it will become hell's bottleneck, an ever-compacting press of the dead that is so terrible it will make the idea of eternal torment sound like a kiss on the cheek.*" Midian paused, waiting to see if Martin had any response.

It's probably proud of itself for that line, Martin thought, but it had brought about the clearly desired effect. The hairs on Martin's arms and legs were standing on end. He remained silent, and so Midian continued.

"*What we believe, Mister Hogan, is that change needs help. A midwife to bring it into the world, a guiding pair of hands. We believe that a once-in-existence opportunity has come along, one that will shake the other side to its very foundations purely by existing. One that will unbalance things so much that the Dump will crack. It must be allowed to reach fruition or else the Dump will become so much of a hell that none of us will be able to* think *enough, able even to be* aware *enough to catch the next one should it ever arrive. It* has *to be now. In fact, that's another thing that the two sides agree on; that a potential change has already begun. We just disagree on what should be done with it. And we've been arguing about it for over thirty years.*"

Midian let the sentence hang in the air, allowing Martin to see the obvious. The cat certainly had a taste for the theatrical.

"Me. I'm the change."

"*The catalyst at least, certainly. When you were born, so was the Order of Daylight. When the ones old enough to know the trick saw you, we all celebrated, as it was written all over you. Even a few—very few—of the younger ones could see it, that's how clear it was. You were something new, and though the Peaceful Ones advocated that you should be avoided at all costs, many rebelled. At first the Peaceful Ones tried to quell it ..."*

***

"... by punishing those who disagreed. They have more power to hurt than the others, after all, amongst other things, and at first it is enough. But hope in a world of desperate people is a fuel of nuclear proportions, and the talk continues. There is a resistance, and then they have a name, and the so-called Order of Daylight soon find that the will of so many of them is enough to make even the Peaceful Ones nervous. They can't punish all *of them, after all. And what will happen,* the Peaceful Ones ask one another, *if it came to war? They're already dead; neither side could win by decimating the other. It would simply be an unending war of attrition. Of pain. The Order of Daylight grows in confidence, thinking that perhaps by way of their sheer numbers, they can perhaps challenge the will of the Peaceful Ones after all.*

The irony actually is that none of them really know *what it is that is special about Martin Hogan. He isn't a pure vessel, or anything so impossible— there has never been a* human *pure vessel, after all, although such an idea would be the closest thing any of them could imagine to heaven—but there is something* to the man's existence. For one, many say that when he was born, there was no one that could use him as an ordinary *vessel. This isn't impossible, but it is* rare. But it isn't this that screams change *at an almost constant volume to the changeless dead, and they all feel it. They just don't know what it is. In this way, the brewing conflict dies down. What would there be to fight over, if they don't even know what they're fighting for? Better to wait, and so all of them go back to their own ways of passing the time, watching the world, but those that can see are always returning their eyes to Martin Hogan. Even for the dead that are desperate for a way out, a mystery that lasts thirty years loses some of its immediate intrigue. They watch every day, but not all of the time.*

Except for one. There is one that never, ever takes his eyes away from Martin Hogan.

And then Martin's son is born, and everyone in the Dump erupts.

***

Martin stood up quickly, his fists clenched. The cat didn't move.

"My son," he said, his voice very quiet and very dangerous. Fear was now the furthest thing from his mind. "My son. What ... about ... my son. Listen. Listen to me," he said, blinking fast and holding up a finger. "You stay away from my son. All of you. You leave him alone. All of you. Are you, are you listening, you? You have nothing to do with him. You don't watch him, you don't look at him, you leave him alone. Do you hear me?" He knew that he was babbling, and he knew his threats were pointless, but he didn't care. The sudden and intense fury that he felt at the mention of his son, to hear the word come from the mind of this dead *thing* before him, this unnatural twist of nature, its people that had designs on his *son,* was like no anger that he had ever felt in his life. *They did something to your wife, too. Don't forget that.* He strode over to the cat, crouching down and putting his face so close that he could feel Midian's gentle, warm breath on his face. He had to restrain the urge to grab the cat by the scruff of its neck. "You leave him alone. You fucking leave him *alone.*" The cat didn't flinch in the slightest.

"Mister Hogan," Midian said, "*that is precisely what we want to do. We want to leave your son, and you, to live whatever life you see fit with zero interference or influence from ourselves. That is our position. The others ...*" The cat stopped speaking, clearly remembering the pact and choosing his words carefully. Neutrality, or at least the illusion of it. "*The others,*" it repeated, "*would like something different. I will come to that in a moment. But please, for now, be assured that we want to have absolutely nothing to do with you or your son. We want to, as you say, leave you alone.*"

Martin stayed where he was for a moment, breathing hard, and then stepped backwards and sat down hard on the bed, his temples pounding as blood charged through his veins. This was just too damn much. Everything in him wanted to grab the animal before him and *shake* it, to make it tell him what the bastards had done to his wife, his *wife,* but he knew that he mustn't. He had to find everything out first. *Then* he could decide what to do. The pair of them sat in a pressure cooker of silence for a moment, and then Martin broke it.

"Okay," Martin said, rubbing his face with his hand, trying to force himself back to normalcy. "Why was my son ... such a big deal to you?"

***

Martin Hogan's son *is the change. Whatever unique genetic makeup was in the father, whatever made him shine with that mixture of magic and science that some of the dead could see, it needed to blend with someone else to complete. Once merged with the mother's egg, Callum Hogan completes the potential of the father.* Everyone *in the Dump can see what the child is.*

Callum Hogan is the first human pure vessel in the history of mankind.

Not only that ... but incredibly, it seems that he's a vessel that anyone can have. The existence of a human pure vessel would be enough, but combined with the miraculous fact of his total accessibility, it is enough to ignite a war immediately. The argument is simple; while the Peaceful Ones believe the same as they always have, the Order of Daylight believe that Callum Hogan is the key to change. Whatever power they can see lying in his genes—that intangible combination, that opium of the dead that is science and magic combined—clearly shows that, once they are passed on, there will be another human pure vessel. And another. And another. Until eventually, in enough generations, the Dump can be part of a conveyor belt back to life. How much more bearable would that be? A permanent light at the end of the tunnel? A thousand-year wait for another go around would be infinitely preferable to losing your personality for the sake of four years—at best—inside a mouse. And even before then, just the existence of his offspring, the presence of such an awesome irregularity in the world, must surely unbalance the nature of the dead enough to tip the Dump over?

Callum Hogan is the key to their salvation, say the Order of Daylight. He is the door that we can all eventually march through.

No, say the Peaceful Ones. The Dump has to break. How can a balloon swell until it bursts if you start letting out the air? This is not the natural order. The Dump is *supposed to* burst. That's how it was designed to work, they are sure. If they do not continue to fill the Dump until its bursting point, it will never occur. And the talk of unbalancing? Who is to say that it would not make the Dump worse? How do they know that it wasn't some such unbalancing long, long ago that ruined the Dump in the first place?

The Dump is faulty, say the Order. It was abandoned by its creator a long time ago. Who would ever intend for it to be like *this*?

And so the argument goes. However, they all know that it's more complicated than a mere debate. They all know that it's already progressed past that.

Action has already been taken on both sides.

***

"Action? What action?" Martin asked, his hands beginning to shake. *Your wife,* he thought. *Elizabeth. This is it.*

The cat sighed heavily, the haughtiness disappearing for a moment. This was indeed it; the crux of the matter.

"What you have to remember, Mister Hogan, is that your son will always be your son. He will be the person that you fathered, even if it might not seem that way. He will be the person that he was at the moment of his conception, and what he has grown to be ever since."

The ice slipped into his veins once more, travelling around his body in the space of a heartbeat. *Not your wife. Something even worse.*

"What ... you said ..."

"Yes, I said correctly. We don't want to do anything to your son. We wish for him to only remain as he is."

The cat stared at him, and Martin slowly began to get an inkling of what the cat was saying. It was too horrible to even consider, but the room still began to pitch backwards and forwards before his eyes.

The quietness.

The way he doesn't play.

Oh my God ...

Martin put out an arm to steady himself on the bed, and then another. He couldn't take his eyes off the cat.

"No ... that isn't ... no ..."

Midian hung his head slightly.

"I'm afraid it is."

This wasn't possible. It wasn't possible. His mind clutched, grasped. *Hope. A way out. Not too late.*

"How do we ... we can stop it. How do we stop it?"

"*Believe me, Mister Hogan. None of us knew about this. This was not planned or discussed. It happened before any of us knew about it,*" the cat said, moving closer to Martin. There was an urgency in his voice now, knowing that Martin was beginning to understand without being told. "*We don't even know his name. We don't know how he was so fast. He must have been ... watching you, constantly. I know this is extremely hard to take, but Callum* is *still your son. And the important thing, I'm afraid, is what you decide to do next. I need you to understand how important this is, Mister Hogan. Martin. This is probably the most important decision in the history of mankind, and it is yours alone. That is what we have agreed.* You *are the one who must make it. Neither side is allowed to take direct action again.*"

Martin wasn't listening. This was madness. Madness. This simply couldn't be happening. His brain refused to deal with what was going on.

A talking dog. A talking cat. Your son ... don't you know this is all just bollocks?

But it wasn't. He knew it wasn't.

"Say it," he said weakly, his eyes deader than the thing sitting before him on his bedroom carpet. . "Say it. Admit what ... you've done. I want to hear you *say it.*"

"*Mister Hogan, neither myself nor any of my people advocated—*"

"*Say it!*" Martin shouted, and with that, the rare sound of Callum's cries began to float down the hall. It was a sound that had always brought an immediate and protective instinct out in Martin, but now he found that it brought confusion and a dark, sickened feeling.

He's faking it. He's doing it because he's knows that's what a baby should do.

"All right," said the cat, quietly, looking back up at Martin. "*As you wish.*" Martin heard a mental intake of breath inside his head, and then the cat continued.

"*Your son was born with one of us already merged with him,*" Midian said, quietly. His words were slabs of ice. "*As the first pure vessel in human history, this means that the ... person that merged with him has retained their full memories. Your son has the mind of someone who has already lived, and is now reborn.*"

Martin felt a sudden glimmer of a chance flicker in his mind. *Of course.* That was the choice. That was the choice that they wanted him to make. He fell to his knees in his eagerness to get closer to the cat, to lunge for a chance to make this better.

"And that's what you want me to decide, right? Whether to let whoever's in there *stay* in there, or whether to make him leave and let the Dump continue as it is? Right?" His voice cracked badly on this last word, and if he could have seen himself in a mirror at that moment, Martin would not have seen anyone that he recognised.

"*Mister Hogan,*" the cat said softly, so soft that it was almost a whisper, "*I'm afraid it's far too late for that.*"

Martin clasped a hand to his mouth, stifling an involuntary moan.

"What …"

"*The process is permanent. Your son is the occupant. That is who he is. There* is *no separate entity. It can't be 'stopped'; it's already happened. Your decision is whether or not you castrate your son to ensure that he can never breed, or whether to let him grow and produce offspring so that others can live again. Your decision is which side you believe in.*"

Martin's mind went silent. He remained where he was, gaping at the cat and listening only to the silence in his head and the blood rushing in his ears.

Time passed.

After emotion had shut down, only logic was left. The first question came to him, and how long this took to happen, Martin couldn't say. There was something he had to know before anything else:

"Action … on both sides. You side action on both sides. Both sides."

"*That is correct. Although we only claim the person that has become your son as being on our side as his actions embody our beliefs,*" the cat said gently.

"What did they do. The others. The Peaceful Ones," said Martin, his voice unreadable and dead. "They did something. Your side … did what they did. What did the others do to my son?"

"*Not your son,*" said the cat's voice in Martin's mind, as the cat's body took a deep breath. The truth came immediately to Martin, his brain glad of something it could actually function with. Something it could actually move from a to b to c with. Knowledge struck him like a fist.

"*They didn't want her to give birth,*" said the cat. "*Even if our side didn't actually make the decision that one of us would become your son, what we wanted had already begun. One of us—we assume—had taken it upon themselves. So then the Peaceful Ones made* their *move. After that failed, and both sides were up in arms … the pact had to be made. War would have broken out otherwise. And so we have been sent to plead each side's case, and to let you make the decision, as I have said.*"

"… what did they do … what did the other side do …"

"*All I can say … under the pact … is that it would make no sense for us to do anything to prevent your son being born. Perhaps you … felt, for some reason that I couldn't possibly speculate on, that matters occurred otherwise?*"

"Tell … tell me …"

"*Drivers will nearly always swerve to avoid an animal, Mister Hogan.*"

Martin's thoughts immediately moved to the downstairs office.

"… Chops …"

The cat was silent for a moment.

"*I couldn't possibly say, Mister Hogan.*"

***

More time passed. Martin sat very still, rocking backwards and forwards, gently, and the cat didn't move a muscle. Waiting was not a problem for his kind, and when the situation was as important as this one, he could wait forever. As it was, nearly an hour passed before Martin stood up on shaking legs, and moved back to the bed, leaning over it. The cat knew what Martin was reaching for; that which he'd brought upstairs earlier, secretly. Midian had read Martin's mind before he'd even entered the window, of course. He wasn't stupid. Even if he hadn't, he'd known which way this conversation was most likely to end. He was prepared for it. After all, now the mission had been carried out, what real fear could anything on this side possibly hold for him, other than pain? How long could it last, compared to one who had seen things from the perspective of eternity?

Martin straightened up once more, breathing hard and fast, wiping the liquid from his eyes at least enough so that he could see. He gripped the knife in his hand.

The cat shook itself rapidly, brushing off a physical irritation, and then stood up.

"*Of course,*" it said again. "*Please, just remember what I said. The decision is yours. If you need to talk things over further, simply ask, and someone will come.*"

"*Shut* up, *shut* up," said Martin, and grabbed the cat roughly by the back of its neck. Even in his impossible grief and rage, his natural instinct made him pause. He had always been an animal lover. Then he thought of what the other side had taken from him, and struck.

***

Still exhausted, Jonathan Hall opened his eyes. He had been too spent even to listen in on the conversation going on upstairs, but he knew exactly what would be said anyway. He already had a good idea of what the outcome would be for both himself and his counterpart, and like the cat he was ready for it. That was why he wasn't surprised to see Martin Hogan standing over him, holding a bloodied knife. His only regret was having to go back to the Dump so soon. He'd hoped he could stay out longer. Instinct whispered in his ear, telling him to fight, *fight,* or fly, *fly.* Jonathan Hall did neither. They owed this man his pound of flesh, and a lot more than that. Not for the first time, Jonathan Hall deeply regretted the necessity of the whole situation, the machinations of the desperate dead.

"Was it you?" Martin's ragged voice said, as he pointed at the dog with the tip of the knife. "Was it you? You wanted me to think ... you lying bastard ... was it you?"

Jonathan Hall weakly shook his head. He wasn't sure if he had the strength to "speak" to Martin, but no words were necessary to answer the question. They would be pointless at this point anyway. The dog raised his head and exposed his neck, closing his eyes. Scoffer lay next to him, now fully awake but too confused to move. He stared at his master, blinking.

"No. Not ... me. Another ... one of ... us. A soldier. Just ... remember ..." Jonathan Hall said, finding the words with immense effort, "This is bigger ... than sides ... not just ... the dead ... this affects, Martin. You will join ... us one day. This affects ... your eternity." Jonathan Hall remained where he was for some time, breathing weakly and waiting for the strike.

It didn't come. Eventually, he opened his eyes and saw Martin crouching on the floor, holding his face with the knife lying by his side.

"Get out," Martin sobbed. "Get out before I kill you."

Jonathan Hall didn't respond. Instead, he quietly and slowly hobbled out of his basket, his face showing the strain of doing so, and headed towards the door. He paused by Martin on his way out, searching for something to say, but thought better of it. After staggering down the hallway, he reached the front door of the house, where the key was still wedged in the lock. Turning it with his mouth, he pawed the handle open on the third try and then slowly disappeared into the night.

***

Later, as the sun was starting to rise, Martin opened Callum's bedroom door. He was almost too terrified to enter. It was as if seeing something suspicious about his son meant that he would no longer be able to cling to the possibility, the distant and beautiful *im*possibility that all of this was a lie. He was still mentally numb, running only on instinct and emotion, but he knew that he had to see his son. Surely that would resolve everything. Thoughts began to nudge at his mind:

Castrate your son? No matter what the consequence, they want you to castrate your son?

BUT IT ISN'T A BABY. IT'S A DEAD THING PRETENDING TO BE A BABY.

It ... can you blame them? They aren't evil. They just want to live ...

Martin shook his head at this last thought, feeling his mind start to grab and scratch for anything that made sense. The certain voice, that one that spoke so very rarely, came through:

Just hold your son. You need to hold your son.

The crying had stopped some time ago, and Callum seemed to be asleep.

Or he's pretending to be.

That wasn't the certain voice. Either way, as Martin drew closer, Callum opened his eyes sleepily, looking in his father's direction.

Would it know? Would it know that I had visitors? Would it know the chaos it's left behind? Does it know anything of the Dump right now, of what's happening in there right now, *now that it's alive?*

Then:

If you were in its shoes ... if you saw the first legitimate chance to truly live again ... to escape that place, by merging with something that didn't even have a mind at that point ...

Martin slapped himself, hard, and the loud crack in the darkness jerked Callum fully awake. He saw his father, and then started to cry.

Did you see that pause? Did you see that moment where he looked at you, that hesitation before he knew what was going on and took a moment to—

And then such thoughts were smashed aside by his own human instinct, and Martin picked up his crying son to comfort him. Anything else was too much. Too much.

None of this could be real anyway. NONE of it.

ROUGEAU? THE PICTURES? THE SKYPE CALL WITH TRISH? THE CAT APPEARING AS PREDICTED? ITS BODY RIGHT THERE ON YOUR BEDROOM FLOOR?

Too much.

***

Part Two: The Comforts of Procrastination Are Like A Like A Head Full of Knives

Will I look back and say that I wish I hadn't done what I did?
Will I joke around and still dig those sounds
When I grow up to be a man?
—"When I grow up to be a man", The Beach Boys

Chapter Six: Uncomfortable in Crowds, Every Step You Take/Every Move You Make, The Swiss Connection, and Happy 5th Birthday, Callum
***

78% OF UK CITIZENS "LESS COMFORTABLE IN PUBLIC" SINCE THE ERA OF THE BROTHERHOOD
Story by Stephen Piper

It's almost difficult to remember a time when the name "Brotherhood of the Raid" *didn't* loom large in the public consciousness.

Since their steady emergence a few years ago, attacks by the apparently leaderless "group" (at the time of writing, no one has been identified as a figurehead, despite spurious—and thoroughly debunked—claims by several individuals) have reached a point where, according to a recent poll carried out by the Family and Parenting Institute, 1 in 3 people have been either attacked or know someone who has. While a large percentage of these may well be copycat attacks, the resulting statistic is the same; a concerning 78 percent of UK citizens say that they now feel less comfortable in public, and of those who said this, 92 percent of them said that they now avoid crowds wherever possible.

Perhaps more concerning, 54 percent of people said that they now were less likely to attend gatherings involving extended family members—or to get together with friends that they haven't seen for a long time—due to the soaring number of reports of formerly trusted associates carrying out violent and unprovoked attacks.

"It just isn't worth the risk," said Penny Keibler, a stay-at-home mother of two from Derby. "It might be something in the water, something to do with mobile masts, I don't know and I don't care. My best friend's sister had her jaw broken by her husband's cousin. They'd always gotten along like a house on fire, and then she does that. I can't say any more about it because it's in court next week." When asked about Christmas this year, Penny said that her family hadn't made any firm plans, but that they were discussing doing something smaller. "I'll make sure our parents see the kids, as we wouldn't deny them that, but after all the attacks last year we're thinking about doing something smaller. Until the reason behind all this is found, we think it's for the best. And I don't think anyone is going to mind either. They're going to be doing the same, I suspect. It's the kids, you just want to keep them safe."

Penny's words seem to reflect the mood amongst huge sections of the population. After the second consecutive Christmas season in a row where the headlines spoke of nothing but the actions of the Brotherhood, nearly all of the perpetrators were again pleading guilty and giving statements under questioning that were incoherent and rambling at best. The most confusing factor of all is the overwhelming and continuing lack of prior mental health issues in the majority of cases, with psychologists reporting the patients to be lucid, rational, and reasonable when questioned on any aspect of their lives other than the attack they carried out.

The home defence sector is booming, as are personal defence item stockists, with the high street chain Barricade launching last spring and set to open another three units in Q4 of this year. Company figurehead James Helmsley is also leading the public call for a change in the personal defence laws, particularly those surrounding the UK use of non-lethal items such as pepper spray and tasers. "No one's calling for a change in handgun or knife laws," said Helmsley, "we just want the people of the UK to feel safe when they walk down the street, and the law needs to change to make sure they can. The restrictions on personal defence in this country are outdated, and in a time when you can't even trust the people that you know, they need to come up to date very quickly indeed."

Even with the UK government recently pledging one hundred million pounds of research funding into suspected chemical and dietary causes of the inexplicable attacks, many are saying that it's too little, too late. "Frankly, it's the government trying to close the gate after the horse has bolted," the Shadow Home Secretary said today. "Why has it taken so long to get some real action on finding the cause? Good people are turning into violent thugs and attacking the people they love and care about, and all the explanations we have so far range from wireless Internet to an unidentified terrorist virus, to name some of the vaguely down-to-earth theories. None of them have any real evidence to back them up. We welcome the news of the funding, but quite frankly, it's coming far too late."

With a reputed sixty small businesses and pubs a day closing down countrywide—and even concert venues reporting an average fifty-percent drop in projected sales, regardless of the attraction—the government certainly has a reason to be pumping money into solving the problem. The average UK high street is beginning to look like a ghost town, and this image is reflected around the globe. The UK government are the ninth country to announce large scale research funding, and economists are praying that an answer is found soon. Otherwise, public gatherings, and even large family ones, become a thing of the past.

***

The pictures were the things that never let him dismiss it, any time that he began to convince himself that he'd been crazy. Those and the small mound in the back garden—the one that had long since been covered with grass—under which he knew that the cat was buried. He would bring the pictures up on his phone—he never upgraded, as he pretty much stopped talking to people after the animals visited his home—and look at the floating white eyes. Then the dead feeling inside would throb gruesomely towards the surface once more, and he would calmly put the phone back in his pocket and go back to whatever he'd been doing.

He tried not to think about Elizabeth anymore, either. At first he felt terrible about doing so, but he rationalised that it was best for Callum. If he *did* think about her, that would lead to thoughts about where she was now, and what the alternative might have been. Thoughts about the manner in which she was taken from him, and those would very rapidly descend into dark, dark thoughts about his son, dragged down like a helpless swimmer caught in an abandoned net.

Then he would begin *watching* Callum once more, becoming a security guard on the walls of reality. He would analyse every single thing that *didn't quite sit right*—should a child sit like that? Would a child show interest in that?—and then he would feel like he was finally going crazy. It never happened though. Always the tease, never the relief.

He never sold the house. He couldn't move until he knew what he was doing. It was quietly taken off the market.

He'd thought about having his son adopted. He imagined it wouldn't be too hard to do; he already had a history of ill mental health, and the social stigma attached to that meant that it would perhaps be only a few more steps from there to bring the relevant authorities running. Best perhaps for Callum, and best perhaps for him.

But not for the world, his mind would whisper. *If it's all true, and you let him go, and he grows up and spreads his seed ... eventually, no more children, anywhere, ever again.*

BUT WHAT ABOUT YOU? DON'T YOU WANT TO COME BACK?

And then the kicker, regular as clockwork:

YOU COULD MAKE A DEAL WITH THEM. GET ELIZABETH BACK.

And the roadblock in his mind would remind himself how it couldn't possibly be real all over again, and he would bury himself in something else to take his mind away. In this manner, piece by piece, he withdrew more and more into the house. And Callum continued to grow.

It was very nearly so easy to pretend none of it had happened—nearly, but not completely—by simply carrying on exactly the same as before. Callum was the same as he had always been (*only because he doesn't know,* the voice said, *he doesn't know about the visitors. How could he? Humans like Rougeau are the exception when it comes to telepathy, remember? They don't have the right brains. Only the animals do*), the same quiet, insular kid, who cried and laughed rarely but still took interest in things, still responded affectionately to his dad. Or seemed to, at least. Martin often thought that a child's instincts must be as influential to a passenger as a dog's.

The specialist had said there was nothing wrong with Callum, which Martin wasn't hugely surprised by. He'd watched Callum during all of the testing, and hadn't he thought that Callum was just that *little bit* more lively and engaged than normal? But again, he'd buried such thoughts deep down, and McMahon had prescribed him stronger medication when he asked for it.

Scoffer was inconsolable for several months after Jonathan Hall had left. After a while, however, he came out of his shell and seemed to have forgotten that the other dog had ever existed. Trish rang more and more often, expressing concern about his increasing solitude, but Martin could switch on a bravura performance most of the time that put her off. He managed to make excuses on the majority of occasions, but knew that he would have to buckle at least now and then to keep her off his back.

"Look at these pictures," he'd said once, in a moment of madness during one particularly difficult evening with Trish, at a gathering for their elderly aunt's birthday. He wasn't going to attend originally. He wouldn't have been the only one either, with all the talk of the Brotherhood of the Raid. As it was, there were more there than he expected, but the tension in the air was still palpable. It lessened as more drink was consumed, but never fully went away. It was Trish's line about *Mum and Dad would have been so disappointed* that made him come to the party; after all, Martin knew that they might have been watching. He wished he'd asked the cat if it had ever seen them. Then he was glad he hadn't.

Trish had stared at the pictures, mildly interested, and then handed the phone back to him looking nonplussed.

"What's that then, with the eyes," she asked, "some kind of animal rights promo? I suppose it's supposed to be like, *animals have personalities too*? Did you do that?" There was mild disdain in her voice. Martin shook his head.

"No, I just saw it online, and saved the pictures," he lied. "I thought it looked cool." Trish sniffed in response, and took a sip of her wine. She always had a few at these kinds of affairs, and it made her louder than normal. On this occasion though, every time she raised her voice, several people looked at her sharply, thinking that they were about to see their first Brotherhood incident and hoping it wasn't going to be aimed at them.

"Animal rights," she scoffed. "Actually no, not animal *rights,* as I think animals should have rights and should be protected, but it's the animal rights *nutters* that do my head in. The obsessive ones who lose sight of reality. Dickheads. You know, they make it harder for the ones who *don't* go overboard to get taken seriously?" Martin didn't answer, thinking about the babysitter at home.

What if she notices something? Would she tell you?

One of the guests on the other side of the room dropped his glass, shattering it, and everyone in the room nearly jumped out of their skin. Even with his red-faced apology, what everyone was thinking was clear. The party cleared out soon after that, and Martin was glad. He could get back to the house.

No matter how many he took, or how many times he checked, there were never any extra eyes in photos of Callum. It drove Martin insane.

He'd never called Rougeau, though he'd thought about it a lot. He didn't trust the man, and besides, he didn't want a man who had armed mercenaries at his beck and call being around his son. He thought that was only sensible.

He didn't play with Callum anymore, or at least try to like he once did. He carried out his fatherly duties in a perfunctory way, and although he saw to it that Callum wanted for nothing physical, he did not have a relationship with his son. It was impossible when he constantly watched Callum with an objective, assessing eye. Something had broken inside him that night with Jonathan Hall and Midian. It was a night that seemed like it had happened to someone else.

You have to make a decision.
NOT YET. THERE'S A LONG TIME YET.
But you need to decide.
IT MIGHT NOT EVEN BE REAL.
Fucking hell. Really? You know *that it is.*

He knew that he still loved Callum, somehow, but there were days when he understood the way that love really worked, and then he would go and curl into a ball. He realised that he loved a memory.

The day came that Callum said his first word.

They'd been in the kitchen. Callum was on his mat, quietly moving his toys around with his usual steady, straight-faced way. Martin was by the kitchen counter, making himself a salad. He'd lost a lot of weight in the last few months, and tended to only want light foods. He felt full very quickly. Noticing the time, he turned to his son, speaking to him for the first time that day.

"You hungry?" he said. His voice, when addressing Callum, was as flat as usual. He kept it that way, not wanting to sound playful or to allow that horrible sliver of fear to creep through. He never admitted it to himself, but it was always there. Callum looked up at the sound of Martin's voice and cooed quietly, pointing at something. Martin followed his son's gaze, seeing the loaf of bread that Callum was gesturing at. He wanted a sandwich. Callum tended to take them apart as he ate them, but he always disposed of them quickly.

Just like a real infant.
OR A GOOD IMPRESSION OF ONE.
The same exchange in his head, every day, so many times a day.

"Okay, sandwich," said Martin, monotone, taking the margarine and jam out of the fridge and beginning to butter two slices of bread. Callum made more noise, but Martin ignored it. "I'm making the bloody sandwich," he said, feeling a worrying amount of mild anger. He didn't like to think about why. The noise continued, then went silent. Then:

"Toe ..."

Martin stopped. He'd heard *Ba* and *Na* and *Mem*, but never *Toe*.

"*Toasssst.*"

Martin turned and looked at Callum, and in that moment he caught something in his son's gaze that chilled him to the bone. He saw the way his son froze, only for the slightest instant, and that made it even worse; he'd made a mistake, and they both knew it.

You can see his thinking. Why not let your first word be something you preferred for dinner? You'd have to speak sometime if you were faking a normal child's development, and you might as well get something for it when you did.

The problem was that Callum shouldn't know the word *toast*.

In terms of percentages of time, Martin had rarely spoken to his son during the totality of his life. This was because in between when he was still grieving for Liz and since the night he was visited, there had only been a period of about six months when he'd spoken to his son constantly. During that time he'd never given his son toast, as Martin didn't like it himself. He'd never had occasion to bring his son toast for a meal, saying *here's your toast*, exposing his son to the word and the item at the same time so that the boy could associate the two.

Trish. Trish could have fed him toast every time he visited.

SHE WOULDN'T HAVE. YOU TOLD HER WHAT HE LIKES, AND THAT'S WHAT SHE WOULD GIVE HIM.

And that split-second freeze, that moment where they locked eyes when Callum realised his error ... before relaxing again, and going back to that baby stare that seemed to say *Am I getting toast?*

Of course he's relaxed. As far as he's concerned, you know nothing. He tripped up, panicked ... then remembered he has nothing to worry about. You'd never suspect a thing. He's good at this, and he knows it.

Martin continued to stare at his son, then looked at the bread, and the toaster, and the clock on the wall. The plumber was coming round soon to fix the leak in the downstairs toilet, and he had to get Callum to playgroup, and Bryan was coming round later because Martin had been unable to put him off any longer. There was just so much to do.

You have to make a decision.

"Okay, toast," Martin said quietly, and dropped two fresh slices of bread into the toaster.

***

Martin began to notice the animals as Callum approached his third birthday.

He'd begun to wonder about the two sets of three birds that sat on opposite telephone wires outside fairly soon after Jonathan Hall left, because they were hard to miss. He didn't know much about birds, but he didn't think that such varied species and sizes sat together like that. Did birds eat other birds? The sets also changed at different times of the day; in the daytime it was the same two groups. At night, they switched. They never moved. They were the first.

After that, he would see faces peering at him from the hedge when he looked out of the window, furry faces that disappeared whenever they realised they'd been seen. It got worse when, after a while, they stopped disappearing. They just sat there, staring right back. One night he looked out of the bedroom window and into the darkened back garden. He could see eight silhouettes of varying sizes, standing apart in two groups of four, looking up at the house. Political lines drawn between them. He drew the curtains, and went to check—again—that Callum was sleeping. Martin never slept for more than two hours at a time before checking on his son.

Callum played with other kids at playgroup, but he never really seemed to make any friendship bonds the way the other children did. This didn't seem to bother him either, as he seemed perfectly content finger painting or looking at picture books.

That's because he's doing what the dog-people do. Letting the kid half do the work. The kid part of the brain that's fascinated by new shapes and sensations and—

There were moments, of course, when Martin could see Callum notice the watchers himself, even though he tried to hide it if Martin was there. It was only ever brief, but there would be a split-second moment where something would catch Callum's eye and Martin would see the boy freeze, or clench his fists, or set his jaw in a way that was somehow so frighteningly *adult* that Martin's knees buckled and the constant pressure in his chest began to build to a terrible force. Everything screamed *deal with this*. And then the moment would pass, and Callum would go back to whatever he'd been doing.

The first major incident happened when Martin was dropping Callum off for another first; his first day of school.

"Don't be nervous," Martin said quietly as the pair of them walked down the street, hand in hand. He'd had to park two streets away. As usual, he hadn't spoken many words to Callum that morning, other than the normal time checks and reminders about what he wanted the boy to do. That was generally the way they communicated, however; Martin would speak to Callum when he needed to, and Callum would respond. It was different with Trish. Trish would babble away at Callum, who would babble right back. It was as if he were a different boy with her.

"Okay," said Callum, eyeing the gates of the urban private school. *Urban* made it sound more rough than it actually was. It certainly cost Martin enough, and competition to get Callum in had been fierce. Money was becoming another issue; Martin still hadn't written anything new. He knew that he would have to soon, not only to bring in some cash but to avoid damaging relationships with both agent and publisher irrevocably. It wasn't like he was big enough that they would let him waltz back in for a new contract whenever he felt like it. The problem was that the very idea of writing now was laughable. How could he possibly apply his mind to something like that when he couldn't even sleep?

After meeting Callum during the "assessment day", the school staff were practically falling over themselves to offer him a place. *So gifted. So advanced.* Martin wasn't paying the exorbitant fees for the purpose of getting Callum a better education though. He wanted Callum in a school with smaller class sizes, less kids, so that the teacher would know if he was being picked on for being different. It would happen eventually, Martin was sure. Kids were like animals themselves, and they sensed things. They would tear Callum apart if not observed. They'd turn on him straightaway when they knew something was up.

"Don't ... look, it's okay to answer questions if you know the answer," Martin said, his gaze fixed ahead of him. "If you don't say anything, they'll get worried about you."

"I'll say if I know, Daddy," Callum said, squeezing his father's hand. "Why wouldn't I?"

Martin didn't squeeze back.

"Do you need me to come all the way in with you?" Martin asked as they got closer to the school gate, already knowing the answer. And it *was* an actual school gate too, an old stone arch with the metal gates set into it. This was a school with a history, and they weren't afraid to remind you of the fact constantly during the parents' tour. Female teachers currently standing by each side of the old stone arch, greeting parents as they arrived with their charges.

"That's okay," Callum said, stopping and turning his face up to Martin's. He was, Martin noticed as he felt the nick of the memory knife for the umpteenth time, the spitting image of his mother. The mousy brown hair, impossibly straight, with her freckles and her snub nose. Her eyes looked up at Martin out of Callum's face and said *why are you a stranger to your own son?* Martin looked for anything of himself in there, and couldn't see it.

The boy went up on his tiptoes to kiss his father's cheek, and Martin bent down to let him. Even to an outsider, it looked like a formal gesture. Two diplomats pretending to be old friends. The most regular thought came again:

He must know. Good God, he must know I know.

And then he heard one of the women at the gate gasp, and as he straightened up, Martin caught a glimpse of Callum's instantly terrified eyes. Later, he would realise what he'd heard Callum say, not as a reflexive shriek but the almost sorrowful denial of one whose plans are all about to be undone.

"*No ...*"

Callum's fists twisted into Martin's sleeve.

A fox was galloping across the road.

Foxes in urban areas had become more and more common in Coventry over the last decade. Martin wasn't exactly up on animal habitats and food chains in the British countryside and urban landscapes, but he'd seen more foxes in the last ten years than he ever had in his entire life, even before the watchers had started surrounding his house. Before the Brotherhood had taken on the role of Public Menace Number One, there'd even been the beginnings of an anti-fox campaign in the media. They were the new Boogeymen of the night, biting babies and breaking into houses … for about a month, until the press had moved on to something else. Even so, seeing a fox bravely wandering around in full view of a streetlight was far from uncommon, and even spotting one in the daytime—perhaps scurrying across the road to the safety of a hedge—wasn't out of the question.

This was something else, though. This was a fox heading *towards* people, at speed, in a busy street in broad daylight. It looked ragged and feral, and its teeth were bared. Worst of all, it was silent as it ran, a completely alien pairing of visual animal aggression with total silence. Its course was straight, its target clear.

In shock, Martin felt the yank on his sleeve again and looked up at the female teachers by the archway. Their eyes were wide, and they stared helplessly at Callum as they also worked out exactly where the fox was headed. One of them started to scream. Martin looked back at the fox, only a few feet away now, and he could see the yellowish bared teeth in its mouth and the clods of dirt on its fur. *Aren't foxes supposed to clean themselves,* he thought, but immediately knew that, of course, this one perhaps wouldn't bother.

Martin instinctively scooped Callum behind himself and spread his arms, heart hammering in his chest. He looked wildly for something to grab that he could use as a weapon, even looking crazily at the teachers in the pointless and lunatic hope that one of them might be passing him something to hit the fox with. Unsurprisingly, they were not, and instead were standing rooted to the spot with shock. *A fox, attacking! In the daytime!*

Martin had time to think *the pact, what about the pact,* and then there was a frantic rustling of feathers and the air filled with noise. Screeching sounds of many different kinds, and the fox's snarls overriding them all.

Several birds of varying sizes had fallen upon the fox, halting it feet away from Callum and Martin as it tried to fend off its attackers. The birds were causing a deafening din as they pecked and jabbed their beaks towards the fox's face and eyes. It got one of the smaller ones between its jaws, the bird almost bursting as the fox crushed the bird's body and blood seeped from between the feathers. The fox didn't pause to swallow it though, as it was too busy defending itself from having its face torn to ribbons.

Martin watched in horror, then came to his senses. He grabbed Callum's arm, and the two of them dashed through the gate, passing the horrified teachers who still hadn't moved. They ran into the main building, and Martin closed the door behind them. They were in a small cloakroom that led onto one of the classrooms; the door to the classroom was open, and they could see the crowd of children inside as they gasped in awe at the chaotic sight taking place outside the window.

Martin crouched down to Callum's eye level, shaking as he did so.

The birds came from both sides. They'd followed us, and they came from both sides.

The pact isn't broken, then. The fox was just a rogue agent. Someone taking matters into their own hands.

"Are you all right?" he asked, realising how few times he'd ever have to ask him son that question. Callum just nodded, breathing heavily through his nose. They were then silent for a moment.

"It could have just been a wild fox," Martin said breathlessly, not believing it, and then very nearly clapped his hand over his mouth once he'd said the words. It was the closest he'd ever come to acknowledging it.

"What d'you mean, Daddy?" Callum asked, sounding confused.

Convincing.

"I mean … crazy. It probably would have run straight past us," Martin said, now slightly pale. Callum shrugged, staring back at his father.

That night, there were more animals in the back garden. By the time Martin charged downstairs, flinging the back door open whilst wielding a carving knife, they were gone.

***

Martin rooted around in the kitchen drawer, growing more and more angry. He wouldn't have thrown it away. It was too important. Even though he knew that it was probably pointless now—time had run out on this particular option some time ago—he wanted to try anyway.

What are you after though? Advice? What do you think he's going to say?

He didn't know. He didn't actually expect the man to say anything, because it was more than likely that he was long dead.

His fingers closed around a battered piece of card that, by its dimensions, could only be a *business* card. But was it the right one? He pulled it out, feeling the kind of triumph that only ever comes with finding something that you suspected was lost. It was, indeed, Rougeau's business card. With a shaking finger, Martin dialled the number into his mobile.

Why have you never called him before?

There was no need for the answering voice this time. He knew the real reason why these days. Callum was *his* secret. *His* choice. And, of course, his confession of his own weakness. But time was ticking away, and Martin was desperate for anything that could be an escape route, a third option …

The ringing sound down the line was different. Martin felt a faint glimmer of hope.

That's a central European ringing sound. That means he took his mobile back to the continent, and he said that he didn't think he'd ever leave this country again—

NO. IT'S STILL A EUROPEAN NUMBER, SO WHETHER IT'S IN THIS COUNTRY OR SWITZERLAND, THE CALL WOULD STILL ROUTE THROUGH A FOREIGN LINE—

There was a click, and then the ringing stopped. Then it started again, but it sounded different. The call had been rerouted. Someone picked up on the other end.

"Hello, the Rougeau Foundation, how can I help you?" The accent was foreign, the voice female.

Foundation?

"Hello," Martin said, uncertain. "I'd like to speak to Sylvain Rougeau, please?" There was a brief pause on the other end of the line.

"I'm sorry,"" said the voice, sounding surprised and a little embarrassed, ""Monsieur Rougeau passed away several years ago ..." There was another pause on the line, and the sound of rustling papers. "Is this ... I'm sorry, monsieur, may I ask ... am I speaking to Martin Hogan?"

... this was a mistake.

"Yes," said Martin.

"Monsieur Hogan, I apologise, your number has triggered an alert on the system. We ... one moment please, I'm just reading." There was a pause, then the voice came back on the line, sounding very officious. "Mister Hogan, this may sound unusual ... but we are under very strict instructions to offer you the full resources of the foundation." The voice sounded flustered, eager. Their day at work had clearly become more interesting. "It is made clear in no uncertain terms. Please, what can we do to help you, monsieur?"

God bless you, Sylvain, but there's nothing these people can do to help. It was you I needed, if anyone.

"It's all right, thank you. I'll call you if I need you."

"Monsieur Hogan, I can assure that the resources of the foundation are extremely—"

Martin hung up the phone, feeling more alone than ever.

***

By the time Callum's fifth birthday rolled around, Martin had decided to act, at least to some degree. He knew that if he didn't make at least one step, then he really would go crazy. As much appeal as that idea had—a concept that felt like putting down a heavy, heavy bag of rocks at long last—he couldn't let that happen for Callum's sake. Even so, Martin thought that he already might be in big trouble as it was.

His sleep had become almost nonexistent, and he'd lost so much weight that he was a shadow of his former self. He was Rougeau-esque, practically skin and bones. He'd taken to wearing sunglasses and a hat when he arrived at reception to pick Callum up, regardless of the weather, as it made him feel more comfortable around the staring eyes of the other parents. The weird dad with the weird kid. He couldn't blame them for staring at him, at least; he looked desperately unwell. They'd be concerned that he had something that might be passed on to their kids. Fortunately, Martin's money was as good as theirs, regardless of any plague that he might potentially be bearing.

Birthdays were an almost unbearable affair in the Hogan household. Martin bought whatever present Callum asked for—he'd always have to ask Callum what he wanted, as the boy would never mention anything otherwise—and it would be delivered on the morning of the big day, wrapped in bright paper along with a card. Callum would open the gift, smile quietly, then hug his father, and take the toy or whatever it was away to play with. There would be no excitement. In the evening, they would eat a meal of Callum's choice with a film. They'd sit in silence.

The thought of going through the charade, even one more time, made Martin's right eye begin to twitch uncontrollably. It would break him, he knew. Action had to be taken, and today, before any of that could happen. The fingernails on the blackboard of his mind had to be eased, if only a little bit. He had to remove that single shred of doubt that his pathetically desperate mind still clung to. Today, he would take a step. The first big one.

He was sitting at the kitchen table, gently holding a mug and staring at the wall, when Callum came downstairs. The boy was half-asleep still, wearing the white polo shirt and grey trousers than even children in his school year had to wear. Martin had thought it a bit much when he found out. Callum nodded at his father.

"Hi, Daddy," he said, sitting at the table in the usual position, waiting for Martin to get his breakfast. Martin didn't move. He looked up lazily at his son, the black semi-circles under his eyes looking darker than ever, and blinked a few times.

"Callum," Martin said. His chin was almost resting on his chest, and he was practically looking up through his eyebrows. "Cal-lum. Do you like that name?"

Callum stared for a moment, and then shrugged.

"I think so," he said, thoughtfully. "There's another Callum in my class. Callum Michaels. He's deaf in one ear."

"Do you like him?" Martin said, his voice low and sluggish. "Is he your friend? Tell me about your friends, Callum."

Callum paused again, aware that something was clearly wrong.

"He's okay," he said. "He has a hamster, and he brought it in last week. We all got to stroke it. And I like Mark Race, he plays Legos with me."

Martin nodded in silence, and then began to tap his knuckles gently on the table, keeping a slow, steady rhythm. His eyes were watery.

"You're very good at this," he said, quietly. "You do the absolute minimum, but you do it well. I guess it's easier that way, isn't it. Less to screw up on? Easier to, I dunno, let the kid instincts do the leg work. You do it well."

Callum's brow furrowed, and he shifted in his seat.

"What d'you mean?" he said, his voice small and confused.

"*Very* good," Martin said, still nodding. His voice hitched slightly when he spoke, and he turned to look out of the window. "And I suppose really, you've only got to keep it up for another thirteen years. Then you can do whatever you want, right? In fact, less than that really, because once you are fifteen you could pretty much act like yourself and it wouldn't be *too* weird. You're already the weird kid at school, so that wouldn't change anything."

"Daddy?" whispered Callum, tears beginning to come into his voice. His face was a picture of confusion and worry. "Daddy, what do you *mean*? Stop it." Martin turned back, his own tears running down his face.

"Don't use that word. *Don't use that word.* You took away the only chance I'll ever have to hear that word properly. Do you know what you've done to me? *Do you know?* I hate you with every fibre of my being, but you're my son. *Can you imagine what that's like?*"

"*Daddy, stop it! It's my birthday!*" sobbed Callum, and at that Martin slammed his fist on the table on leapt to his feet.

"*Fuck you!*" he screamed, the veins in his forehead standing out like ropes against his now bright red skin. "*Fuck you! Don't try that fucking bullshit! I know, you* know *I know, we both know, so let's can the bullshit!*" Callum's sobs turned into wails, and he pushed his seat away from the table, beginning to stand.

"Da ... daddeee..."

"*That isn't going to work! Do you hear me? That isn't going to* work!" Martin screamed, pounding the table. The mug he'd been drinking from vibrated towards the tabletop edge, teetered, then plummeted to the floor, where it shattered. "*Do you know what they want me to do to you? Do you know what they want?*" He pointed his finger at his cowering son. "*Yeah, you know! You're not stupid! You know what the* really *old ones want! You know what they want me to do! They* told *me! Did you know that?*" Martin suddenly turned to his right, yanking open the kitchen drawer. He plunged in his fist, pulling out the large pair of fabric scissors that Elizabeth had kept in there for a variety of purposes, but never this. He held them up, the blades catching the light. "*You didn't know that, did you?*"

Callum screamed, eyes wide with horror, and dived for the door. Martin only just managed to get a foot to it in time, kicking it shut. By the time Callum had reached for the handle again, Martin was already there, pulling the boy back by the arm and moving in front of his son.

"*Tell me your name! Tell me your fucking name!*"

"*Daaadeeeeeeeee—*" Callum squirmed and writhed in Martin's fist, kicking and punching frantically but feebly at Martin's body wherever he could. Martin barely felt it.

"*Don't make me do this! Goddammit, don't make me do this!*"

Martin scythed the scissor blades open.

Suddenly, the squirming stopped, as did the screaming. Callum's arms and head dropped, although he remained standing. The only sound in the room was the pair's heavy, laboured breathing. Martin realised that the fist that was trying to cave his chest in was actually his heart. He barely dared think.

This is your son.
YOUR SON.
What the fuck are you doing?
WAIT. WAIT.

"You were really going to do it, weren't you?"

The voice was steady, quiet, and despite the youthful, unbroken tone, to Martin's ears it sounded incredibly, unfathomably old.

The boy looked up, tears drying on his cheeks. The gaze was steady, and filled with a terrible wealth of experience that made Martin release Callum's arm as if he had been holding something hot.

Oh my God ... oh my God ...

"I can't read much," said Callum, straightening slightly, "and I was surprised that I could read anything at all. I thought it was only possible as an animal, but I must have brought something with me when I came here. Perhaps I'm using part of the brain now that most people don't. I'm the first one, after all. But very occasionally, I get tiny bits here and there. More intuition than anything else. I thought that you probably knew. I just about got that much. But I couldn't ever be certain."

Martin backed away slightly as he listened to the alien voice speak, backed up until he felt himself bump up against the door. He held the scissors before him like a talisman.

"But just now," said Callum, nodding gently, "it was coming off you in *waves.* It was written all over your face. You really were going to do it, weren't you?"

There was silence in the kitchen. Then, crazily:

"I'm sorry," said Martin, his voice choked. It was as if his son had just died after a long, uncertain illness. Callum shook his head, concern in his eyes.

"No, Martin, don't be *ridiculous,*" he said, "we are *forever* in your debt. We have taken something that we can never repay. We had no choice. But you've freed us all. You've changed everything." Callum spread his arms and Martin fell to his knees, embracing the dead person before him helplessly as the weight of five years fell from his shoulders. Finally, something was *easy.* The grip had loosened, if only slightly. Even in his moment of emotional release, the question rolled in the back of his mind, the objective part that never, ever shut up:

Okay, now *what are you going to do?*

***

Chapter Seven: The Good *Really* Old Days, Speaking Man to Boy/Man, Enter the Control Room, and Carrie Lawler Knows Big Change is Coming
***

He is born when the great mammoths still walk the earth. Even now he can remember the hunt, his breath in the air as he grips the rough handle of his spear while the rest of the group race in from all sides. He doesn't remember much from that time, but the memories of the hunt are always the parts that stand out the most. The wild thrill of the chase, the men acting seamlessly as a unit, almost as if they were reading each others' minds as they chased their prey down. The raw, savage joy of the kill. The celebration. The looks on the faces of the women and children as they brought home meat.

That was when he was most alive. That, and the time with his son.

The screaming, bloodied carnage of the boy's birth. Holding the tiny, fragile lump of human flesh for the first time, and feeling the bond of blood. The fascination. Holding his son to his chest, feeling the tiny heartbeat as the miniscule fist wrapped itself around his little finger.

This is everything to him. It is a new kind of wildness. A new kind of living. The other men of the tribe scoff at him, interest in the very young being woman's work. But he pays them no heed.

The mother dies soon after, but this is of little concern to him. The child, however, lives for another four months.

He is not the same again, after that. He becomes sloppy on the hunt, as even the moment of victory cannot bring him to be that which he once was. Not long after that, he is gored badly by a wild boar, falling and dislocating his shoulder. He refuses the clumsy, groping hands of the hunters that try to help. He welcomes the end.

Except it is not the end.

Instead, it is sheer bliss.

It takes him a while to realise that he has died; the concept of an afterlife is not fully imagined amongst his people, although they do believe in their gods. Once he does, however, his first thought is to find his son. It isn't even that hard. Though space before is him is impossibly vast, the people there are relatively few, even with the proportionally large number of infants there (child death is extremely common amongst the first men). He is reunited with his son, still a baby, but unburdened here by hunger and cold and thirst.

Even without the unbridled joy of their reunion, the place would still be a paradise. Clumsily, like a child, he realises that he can watch the world on the other side, see the progress of the tribe. It warms him to do so, but not as much as the warmth of this new world around him. There is a physical delight abundant in that place, a delicious electricity in the skin, and when he meets other inhabitants no words are necessary; they can all feel it, the shared sensation. He and the people laugh together, as he holds his infant son who will never age, and they take to the air in joy, floating and swooping in the thick presence of whatever fills the space between them. It is indeed a paradise.

Then others come. And then more.

Centuries pass.

He notices that there are many, many more in that place now, far more than there were when he arrived. He tries to remember how it felt back then. There was more of it, wasn't there? More of that presence, that energy to go around? But still, life is good. He regrets yet again that his child never got to grow, that they will never talk, but his love does not abate. His son is his delight.

Centuries pass.

Once the place becomes full, and flying freely is but a dim memory, he realises that even feelings are not the same as they used to be. They're duller, more distant. He speaks to the other old ones, and they agree. Even so, the older ones have more room than the younger ones, and he realises that they can move in ways the newer arrivals can't. They have a greater physical presence. Is it experience or time that makes the difference? Or just that they were there to absorb whatever was left for them, to take on board that liquid electric air that was once the only thing surrounding them? Either way, the world around him is beginning to feel less like a paradise and more like a dump. He thinks it can't get any busier. It isn't yet one tenth as bad as it will get.

Centuries pass.

One day, one of his friends disappears. He is the first one to squeeze out, the first one to merge and come back with no memory of who he is, and they realise what it means to become Distracted. It is a terrifying revelation, yet exciting. But surely it isn't so bad yet that they would want to sacrifice their very selves? There must be a better way. Plus, he has his son. He would never leave him. The news of this new occurrence, that they can pass back to the living for a heavy price, spreads around the Dump like a fire.

Later, one of other the old ones discovers the first pure vessel. They keep this to themselves—only to the other old ones—and begin to spend their days hunting for them, a new lease of existence opening wide for them. Again, though the Dump now resembles a traffic jam of humanity, moving skyscrapers of people that stretch up and away farther than a human eye could see ... he will not leave his son. He thinks of the early days. He can scarcely remember them now. There is talk that the Dump must eventually break, and he isn't sure that he believes this. Certainly there is a shift on the horizon; he has been in that place long enough so that he is attuned to it. Real change is coming. Something will happen, but he isn't sure that it will happen on its own.

Centuries pass.

His son, even though his brain will never develop, has seemed to look at the other side for many centuries now, as if he were able to use the trick the other dead use to see the world beyond. Madness, of course, but still he seems to watch nothing for days on end, as if fascinated by something that he couldn't possibly see. The father doesn't worry. There are murmurs of a new group, dissenters who don't believe that the Dump will ever break. It doesn't concern him. What choice do these people have, after all? But life is dark in the Dump, and hard, if just bearable enough. He wishes he could change it.

One day, his son disappears.

Instinct, childish experimentation, he will never know. After all, the merging for the old ones is easy, like falling asleep. The father could always feel how easy it would be, how tempting, and his son has been surrounded by it for so long. Surely even an infant could pick it up, especially one so immersed in centuries of existence in the Dump. Like a child toying with a new discovery ... one that suddenly got it right.

Naturally, the father is helpless with despair and rage. He hurts the nearest ones to him, for he and the other old ones have learned many advanced tricks in that place, and greater strength is just one of them. He doesn't care. His son is lost to him, forever, Distracted and gone.

Is he though? *one of the old ones says to him. The Peaceful Ones, they call themselves now, even though they are far from it. They keep their space in the Dump, at the expense of others. It is their right by seniority, after all. He is not one of them; he made his own associates when he arrived, and the Peaceful Ones have been there slightly longer than he. He is not* quite *as old as them, yet he is one of the few outside of their circle that they respect. He is nearly one of them. That is the only reason they deign to offer advice.* He was a baby. He was always a baby, and one so young that he never developed a sense of self. Is this not a blessing? Will you not finally get to see that which you always wished to see? Will you not get to watch him grow *into* a personality?

It is something to cling to, to alleviate his despair, and he grasps it. He will watch his son grow.

Then, when the son is born again, suddenly all *of the old ones, the ones who can see the child's unique nature, are watching.*

His son is born different. They can see it. He is special. Over time though, when nothing changes, many begin to lose faith, and look away. They take interest in other things before returning to watch once more, and the father is very often the only one watching. Just for brief moments. And one particular *brief moment, when it comes, is all he needs. His son's wife conceives, and the result is the first of its kind in human history.*

The father crosses over.

***

Martin sat at the kitchen table, pale faced.

"So ... you ..."

"Yes," said the boy in front of him. "I'm your father, Martin. Or at least, your *original* father. The man who impregnated your mother is the man who cocreated the body, but I cocreated your soul. I know this is a lot to understand."

There was only the sound of the ticking kitchen clock for a moment, and then Martin burst out laughing.

It was hysterical, letting-go laughter, the kind that only comes when a crushing weight has built up so much that it briefly becomes absurdity. Martin slapped the table with his hand, tears streaming down his face as he let out the first belly laugh of the last three and a half years. Callum watched him, smiling softly himself.

"Oh ... oh *Jesus*," Martin said, wiping his face once his laughter had subsided, "oh, you are kidding me ... well, thank you very much, Darth Vader, a-ha ha *haaaaa*—" and with that he was off again for a good three minutes. Once Martin's guffaws had turned into mere chuckles, Callum spoke.

"I came here for a few reasons, Martin, number one of which was simply to be near you. The first year here was unusual; everything was just so overwhelming to this brain that it was hard to think straight. And then, by the time the first sixteen months had passed, I more or less had it together ... but then you became extremely distant, and I began to wonder if you'd been paid a visit." The diction of the five-year-old's speech, the inflection of the words ... all of it was so alien coming from the child's mouth that it felt like it should make Martin's skin crawl. But it didn't. Somehow, hearing the truth—and having it end any and all doubt—crazily made Martin feel closer to his son than he'd been since Jonathan Hall had spoken to him. This was the first real conversation that he'd ever had with his son. He looked into Callum's old, old eyes, wondering what they'd seen. "And it appears I was right. Who were they?"

"From both sides," said Martin, his voice hoarse. "You've caused quite a stir. There was nearly war, apparently. The old guys don't want you to breed. The younger ones do." Callum nodded, his eyes wandering as he pondered Martin's words. He looked like he was imagining that which he'd left behind.

"Well, that was the second reason. I thought some time ago that maybe change on the other side was coming, but that it needed a push somehow. I never thought that I might *be* it." The boy sighed and sat back in his chair, a gesture so weary and adult that for a moment Martin thought that he was talking to an elderly midget. "And the *third* reason is probably the most important, son."

"No," said Martin, wincing at the word and holding up a hand. "Just ... not yet."

"Do you really see me as *your* son, Martin? You haven't for a long time, have you?" Martin didn't answer. Callum shrugged, and carried on speaking. "Very well. I shan't use that word. I have to say, you're taking all this very well." Now it was Martin's turn to shrug. He supposed he was. Strangely, he hadn't felt this relaxed in a very long time. There was knowledge here. *Certainty*. That was worth so much. "But the third reason; your future. I mean ... your ultimate future."

Martin looked up.

"... go on," Martin said, cautiously. Then a thought occurred to him. "Wait. Hold on a second." He stood and crossed to one of the cupboards. He fished around at the back, hoping it was still there; it was. He hadn't touched it since Jonathan Hall left, because he thought he'd never stop if he did. But this occasion merited a drink, if one ever did. He spun the cap of the bottle of Jack, and poured himself a heavy measure into a glass. He sat back down at the table, and Callum's eyes followed the liquid to the table, mildly interested.

"None for you," Martin said, feeling giddy. "You're vastly over-age." Callum smiled sadly at the remark, and shrugged again.

"I've never drank any alcohol at any point in my existence, so I can't say I want any," the boy said. "I do look forward to finding out what it's like, but I don't want to damage anything yet." Martin took a big swig from the glass, and let out a sigh.

"And I don't want to go to jail for letting my five-year-old hit the sauce, so that's just as well," he said, putting the glass down. He was feeling good, or at least better. He didn't know why. Relief, perhaps. A result, *something* had happened. His son was lost forever, had never really existed in fact, but he'd known that for a very long time, even if he hadn't admitted it to himself. In an odd way, it was beginning to feel like he was gaining something. "Okay, ready. Talk."

"I can still see some things, s—Martin. Everything we saw in you, from the other side? I can still see it, right here."

"And what is that?"

"That you're *special,* Martin. That's why I'm here, that you've somehow got that unique combination of earthly genes and *spiritual* genes, if you will, that just needed to combine with someone else's to create, well, me, or at least a vessel that allowed me to *be.* You're linked to the Dump, Martin, and that's why I was able to come here. You're linked to the Dump." He paused, and looked at Martin. "Do you understand what I'm saying to you?"

Martin didn't. Then he did.

"Wait. Wait. That's where I'm going? To the Dump? That's where I'm going when I'm fucking *dead?*"

Callum nodded solemnly. Martin didn't stop to consider the reality of what he'd just been told. It was too awful. He was already looking for a loophole.

"But ... it's going to break, right? And soon? That's what they're saying, right?" Callum shrugged again in response.

"That's what they're saying. But I highly doubt it. All anyone can really feel over there, in terms of the place changing, is *pressure*, a pressure that's grown since the day I arrived, and there's absolutely zero guarantee that it will ever reach a breaking point. That talk is just the wishful thinking of people with no other choice. And do you even want to take that risk? Do you want to *hope* that it all plays out that way, knowing full well that you're going to join them? You can be a part of real change, Martin. You can be part of the difference." Callum had leant forward in his seat, the sudden and barely restrained passion clear in his voice. He'd made a persuasive point, Martin had to admit.

Do you really want to go there? Plus, as you've always thought, can one dead person coming back to life at a time really make a difference, when thousands are arriving each day? Would it even be noticed?

IT'S ABOUT THE NATURAL ORDER. IT'S ABOUT BALANCE, ABOUT NOT UPSETTING THE WAY THINGS WORK.

Well, what the fuck is natural about any of this? Does the Dump sound as if it's working as it should?

YOU COULD MAKE IT WORSE. AND THE CHILDREN. EVENTUALLY, AFTER HUNDREDS OF GENERATIONS, THERE WOULD BE NO MORE CHILDREN EVER AGAIN. ONLY THE DEAD.

You really think the human race will even be around in a hundred generations' time?

He thought about a world with no real children. About the living dead only breeding to ensure the continuation of the cycle, so that there would be people to continue breeding vessels for *them* to go into when they came back. After all, why else *would* anyone have kids, once they knew they'd just be creating people that had already existed?

"The children ..." Martin said. Callum smiled, a slightly patronising smile that reminded Martin of the mound of earth in the back garden.

"Do you have any idea how long that would take?" Callum said, shaking his head slightly. He was amused, or putting on a good impersonation of it. "How many centuries? We'll have *cured* death before that happens, Martin. We'll have found a way to store our minds on a solid-state hard drive and put them in a body grown from our own DNA." Martin's brow furrowed at this, and Callum shrugged. "Yeah, we watch the news from the other side, y'know. I like to keep up with science." He chuckled slightly, and sighed. "I'm sorry, Martin, it's just good to be able to talk freely. I haven't spoken as myself for five years, so I'm probably being a little giddy with it. Anyway, the point that I'm trying to make is that *you can be around to see that reality, as yourself.* Or you can watch it from the other side, too scared to come back in an animal body because then you wouldn't be *you* anymore." Something seemed to occur to Callum, and his face became serious. He leaned his elbow on the table.

"I'm sorry to say this, but I think I have to; what if this meant that Elizabeth could come back? She's not in the Dump, so she has to be somewhere else. We don't know what the rules of that place are. What if they figure out how to come back from where *she* is, once there's enough human pure vessels—"

"Enough," said Martin, his voice coming out as a whisper. "You don't talk about her. Don't you turn her into a, a bargaining chip for your side. It's your people that killed her. I should send you back where you came from for that alone." It was an empty threat, and he knew it.

"I'm sorry, I overstepped the mark," said Callum, putting a tiny hand on his fragile child's chest, "but at the same time, I have to defend myself; it wasn't *my* people. The last thing we wanted is for her to die. Why would we? We—"

"I don't give a shit which side did it. You messed with our lives. I should cut your balls off and be done with it," Martin said, all of the strangely good feelings temporarily kicked away. The old hole was back. The kitchen was quiet again.

"Could you do it?" Callum said quietly. Martin didn't answer for a moment.

"There's no point now anyway," he finally said, bitter at himself. "I don't exactly have to make my mind up in a hurry to stop you going and getting anyone pregnant, do I? You're five. You'll keep. I haven't decided yet. Plus, you'd only go to Child Protection Services afterwards and ruin my life."

"I wouldn't," said Callum, holding his hands up casually. "I love you, son." Martin bristled at the word, but didn't say anything. "No matter what I want ... I couldn't ruin your life. This—seeing you grow into a man, being here in person to see it—is the greatest thing I could ask for. Yes, you would ruin what I believe to be the only chance to free the Dump. You would also, obviously, be taking away a huge part of my new life ... although the way I see it I can't complain because I'm very lucky to have anything at all. You'd rather I wasn't here. I know this. Effectively, I am a thief. But if you wanted to take my eyes, my heart, I'd give them to you, because I owe you everything. The dead who are as old as me ... they don't like to be around the living. I don't either. But I've done this to be near you. I would have been closer ... before now. But I had a role to play. And I still don't really know how to be ... " Callum stopped talking.

Martin looked at the boy in front of him. The dead had taken his wife ... but those dead people weren't here. Only his *son* was here, sprung from Martin's wife, and Callum had had no part in Elizabeth's death. The only son that had ever been there, from the day he was born. It felt as if Callum had just come out of the biggest possible closet in the universe.

He tried to feel the rage; he tried to feel the emotion that he knew should come with the words *you stole my son* and found that he couldn't. The only negative feeling present was a dull longing for the son he'd always imagined ... but all he could see was the son that he'd always had, and it was as if he were finally understanding him.

How have they even stolen your anger?

The bond was unbreakable. And the boy he'd never understood was now making himself an open book, even if it was certainly in a way that he'd never imagined or wanted. Martin wanted to smile, somehow, and he hated himself for it.

"I hate you for what you've done," Martin said. He needed to say *something*. He couldn't just capitulate. "Do you know that?"

"I do. But I am your son, Martin, even if I see you as mine."

Martin swigged from his glass, the smoky flavour feeling damn good, regardless of anything. He needed it.

"I've got loads of photos of you," Martin said, narrowing his eyes and leaning his head to one side. "You never had the floating white eyes like on the ones I took of the dog and the cat."

"Why would there be?" Callum said, matter-of-factly. "They were conscious human souls in an animal's body. Somehow the camera shows that. Maybe it's too unnatural, I don't know. But I'm a conscious human soul in a human body. It is, in a way, how it's meant to be."

The glass went up again, came down again.

"You certainly don't talk like someone older than Jesus," said Martin, pushing the glass away and not caring as it tipped over. Callum shrugged yet again, a faint smile dancing on his lips. It was perhaps a characteristic gesture, Martin thought, performed before responding when something amused him.

"Well, I've always liked new things, I think," he said. "The other ones that are as old as me ... not so much. They like to keep things the way they remember them, but I'm not sure that they even remember *that* correctly anymore. They're hard to understand. They're out of touch, frankly."

"And you're the voice of a new generation, eh?" said Martin, darkly, and then realised the unintentional double pun that he'd made. He caught Callum's eye, and the look on the boy's face held Martin for a second, *knowing* what his son was thinking; Callum was trying to pretend that he hadn't caught the accidental double pun either, not wanting to upset Martin in a moment of emotional turmoil ... but then they'd seen each other's glance, and now Callum knew that Martin knew what Callum was thinking, and now *Martin* knew that Callum knew he knew ... it was simultaneously a terrible crime, to mentally make light of the moment, yet completely understandable, but Callum was trying to respect his father by feigning ignorance.

His son.

Martin very nearly laughed again, but instead he shook his head and rubbed his face, standing up.

"I have to walk Scoffer," he said, "and I need some bloody *air*. I need to ... I've got to think."

"I understand."

"I'm going to be a long time. I don't know when I'll be back."

"That's fine."

"I'll have a lot of questions. A *lot* of questions."

"That's to be expected."

What's your real name—

NEVER ASK THAT. HE'S CALLUM. THAT'S WHO HE IS.

A thought occurred to Martin. It felt so odd to say it, and as he did so, he realised how a whole world of ingrained procedure had immediately changed.

"There's food in the lower freezer if I'm not back. Do you ... can you work an oven?"

"I know how they work," said Callum. "And I can reach the dials."

Martin rubbed his face again, hand trembling slightly. He willed it steady.

"This doesn't mean anything," he said without conviction, raising a finger. "I need time to think."

"I know."

A pause.

"Just turn the dials off when you take the food out, okay?"

"I will."

"Right."

Martin left the room and came back a few moments later with an excited Scoffer, the old dog still as delirious as ever when it came to walks. The only difference was the slightly lazier tail, the gentler *wuffs* of joy. The two men regarded each other, the standing man presented as he was, the seated one presented as a child.

"Okay then," Martin said, nodding and turning to the door. There was nothing more to say for now.

"Martin?"

Martin paused with one hand on the door handle.

"Yes?"

"*Could* you do it?" Callum said again. Martin looked at his son, who was sitting up in his seat and staring back with those serious eyes.

There's still no rush, no matter what. None at all yet.

"I'll see you when I get back," he said quietly, looking away from the boy. "Don't forget. Oven off."

He opened the door and Scoffer led the way, his whole body a picture of elderly glee.

***

SEVEN YEARS LATER:

The whitetail buck stood bolt upright, ears swivelling back and forth as he attempted to detect whether or not the sound it had heard was cause for alarm. As it was still autumn, his antlers were proudly adorning his head; however, it was late in the season, and in a few weeks they would be gone, dropped like clockwork before returning just in time for summer, and the rut. The buck was big at two hundred seventy-five pounds, and in the five summers he had seen, finding a mate had not been a problem. He had become sick during the winter though, and was now a lot weaker than he had been in the past. Combined with his advancing age, he was dimly aware that he might struggle if challenged, even at his size. The previous year he had weighed nearly three hundred.

Once the deer was satisfied that he was alone, the glorious head bent, and the buck dropped his lips to the stream for a much-needed drink. Even so, the ears and eyes kept moving, constantly searching for a threat.

It wasn't enough. The bullet hit the deer broadside, perfectly placed behind the shoulder, and took the deer through the heart. He dropped like a stone, his head hitting the water with a dull, flat splash.

While the hunters in their camouflage gear approached—a father and daughter congratulating each other on a job well done—they didn't notice that something was leaving as silently as a glance. Something that flickered out of sight of the human eye, something that turned and rose and moved through planes that the hunters wouldn't see for seventy-one and twenty-six years, respectively. It left that place, abandoning the ended shell of the fallen deer, and arrived somewhere else entirely.

When it did, it immediately began to change, taking form and becoming recognisable once more. It became a woman dressed in jeans and a maroon sweater, standing and blinking slowly as human thought returned to her.

Where is ...

There was a moment of confusion as *where is this place* briefly went back to memories of the rut, of fur and frosted breath streaming at either side of her muzzle as she charged along on flying hooves. Then she flinched; remembering the loud crack and an almost imperceptibly brief sting of pain. She knew the word:

Bullet.

Then:

... dead?

It was knowledge, but confusing in its nature. She'd already died, hadn't she? That was a memory too, dimly. How could she have died twice?

You died ... but you didn't want to go. And you realised that you didn't have to go. And so you changed direction, and went to where you found life returning.

She had. And so she'd begun her second life. And now she was ... where? She looked around herself, thoughts spreading outwards, and found that the white space that she found herself standing in was beginning to take shape. And there was someone there ...?

"Hello," said a voice. It was a man's voice, gentle and friendly. She spun around on the spot, hoping to see the speaker, but there was no one present. At least, there didn't seem to be, but the voice had definitely come from her *left.* She looked that way, focused ... and then the man was standing there, clear as day and looking as if he'd been there all along.

"Ah, very good," said the man, a shortish, middle-aged looking man with thinning grey hair. He was wearing a T-shirt bearing the Olympic logo with the words *Barcelona 1992* underneath. "You got the hang of it straightaway, not many do. Am I fully in focus?"

"Yes," said the woman, breathlessly. "You're ... where is this place?" She looked beyond the smiling man; shapes were beginning to form behind him. And she could feel something else, too, a growing sensation that she couldn't yet identify. The man's smile disappeared ever so slightly, and he leaned towards her, narrowing his eyes slightly.

"Well, there's two parts to that, and I think you already know the first, yes?" he said. "Can *you* tell *me* where you think you are?" She continued to look past him, feeling like her heart should be pounding even though it wasn't. Of *course* it wasn't. In the distance, a tree popped into view; it was an oak, huge and spreading and beautiful.

"I'm ... dead, aren't I?" she said. The man nodded.

"And ...?"

"And ... it's not the first time, is it?" The man smiled in response, and nodded again.

"Good. Very good. Most of us here come here after their second death, yes. Actually ..." he hesitated, and held up a hand towards her face, squinting his eyes. "That was your *third*, wasn't it? First yourself, obviously, then a ... yes, a bird, then ... a deer. Ah, not often people go animal to animal *then* come here. It's usually die, animal, then here. Ah well, regardless, you must be different, like us. That's why we're all here. And the second part?"

She wondered what he meant, confused, and then she realised as the world exploded completely into view all around them. It became a green and verdant valley, with liberal smatterings of trees and people and even a waterfall off up in the distance. It was a breathtaking cinematic reveal that the greatest CGI could not hope to surpass. She could see people playing in the pool at the base of the waterfall, hear their distant laughter. Above her, several people swooped and dipped in the blue sky, dodging and darting through clouds. She staggered backwards slightly, looking up, her hand pressed to her chest, and her eyes bulged as she tried to take it all in.

"Ah. Ah ... ah," she babbled. The man smiled and gently took her arm to steady her.

"Take a moment," he said, "it's always a shock when you first start to actually see the place." He looked around him, nodding in a satisfied way. "Still the valley, then. That's good. It's my preferred setting. Sometimes a new arrival can tip the surroundings, you see; currently the majority of people here are obviously valley-minded people. But it's only been the valley for about fifty years, and before that it was a beach. Then one day another valley-minded person turned up, and tipped the balance over to the valley, see? You might have been beach-minded, and maybe you'd have been the one to tip the place back to being a beach. Make sense? Well, that's only how we *think* it works, of course, because there's never been anyone to tell us otherwise! Heck, we might all secretly be lagoon-minded people that just need a strong lagoon-minded arrival to tip the whole place over into being a lagoon. That'd be nice," he smiled, lost in his thoughts for a moment. He then breathed in brightly, and slapped at his thighs. "Sorry. People only ever seem to arrive when *I'm* on duty, so I'm used to doing this; my mind can wander a bit as a result. Apologies. Do you feel it yet?"

Mind reeling, she started to say *no*, but then realised that she knew exactly what he was talking about. The feeling creeping into her very bones had begun to arrive fully ... an inner warmth that reached all the way to her soul. It was like coming home.

"*Yes*," she breathed, tears leaping to her eyes as a smile broke out across her face. "Oh, *yes,* yes I do!" The man grinned, closing his eyes and sharing the moment with her.

"It's wonderful, isn't it?" he said, peaceful and sincere. "There's the odd hassle that we sometimes have to deal with, but my goodness, this is a wonderful place. I don't even go back to the other side all that much, that's how good being here is. That's one of the other big perks, I should tell you; the people that come *here* get to go home, come back, and still keep all this," he said, tapping at his temple with a smile.

"Is this heaven?" she asked, laughing as she did so and laughing further with surprised delight at the sound. The man shrugged, his grin spreading wider.

"We don't know, but it certainly feels like it," he said, chuckling himself, "even with all the broken bits. We call it the Control Room." He put out his hand, making a small embarrassed noise. "Bloody hell, how rude of me," he said, "I haven't even introduced myself. I'm Mark. Mark Calloway." She shook his hand warmly, and then it turned into an embrace as they both laughed, sharing in her newfound delight. She stepped back, and spun on the spot, laughing some more as she took it in. Then she turned to Mark, eyes glowing with joy, and tried to remember her name. It came after a little effort.

"Elizabeth," she said, as other memories danced around her, temporarily out of reach. "Elizabeth Hogan."

***

Carrie Lawler sat on the end of her bed in her Bronx apartment. The place was sparse in its décor, but Carrie had never cared enough to do anything about it since she'd been living there. These days, she didn't really care about much of *anything*. She simply ate, slept, went to work for the cleaning company her sister owned, and then spent the rest of her time staring at the peeling plaster in the walls of her home. If she really needed a distraction, she'd watch whatever was on the TV.

On bad days, she remembered what her life used to be like. Before that day on the subway. The day she'd just been looking at that man in the suit and the knowledge had come upon her, so suddenly, so *importantly*. It had never left after that ... but she'd never had that same compulsion. She couldn't ever explain it to anyone either, as they wouldn't understand. Often, she wasn't sure that *she* did. Then she'd try and turn it over in her head, as she so often did, attempting to work through it. Then she'd become frustrated by the constant turning in circles and it was just so much easier to become numb once more. She used to be a teacher. After she'd attacked the man on the subway platform, her subsequent psychiatric evaluation and time in jail had seen to *that* career.

As she continued to sit, listening to the evening traffic and shouting voices that floated up from the street outside, she became aware of something on the edge of her consciousness. Her skin broke out in gooseflesh and her breathing sped up, panicking without really understanding the reason why: she was scared of what the new knowledge might be. For she knew that's what was coming; knowledge. An hour passed, and she didn't move. Carrie waited, trembling.

After a while, it became clear that whatever it was, it wasn't ready to arrive yet. Maybe it never would. But there was definitely *something* there, and it was from the same place as before. Even so, there was no point worrying about it; it would arrive when it was ready. And like that, Carrie dismissed it. If there was one thing that she had become very, very good at, it was putting things aside and being still. It was, indeed, so much easier. One thing she couldn't ignore though—not fully, something that could only be put to the back of her mind where it would still buzz and thrash impotently—was the knowledge *about* the knowledge.

When it arrived—if it ever did—it meant change was coming. Big change, for everyone.

***

Chapter Eight: The Dead Swim in White Nothing, A Journey To the Heart of the Control Room, and The Brotherhood of the Raid Lie Down
***

"We take turns," Mark said, waving at a woman who swam through the waterfall pool about twenty feet away from them, "waiting at the arrival point. We do a few days at a time, then someone else generally volunteers to take over. If no one does, then we go and ask somebody. Nobody really minds. Can you imagine getting bored here? Even sitting on your own?" Elizabeth couldn't. She could never, ever get tired of this feeling. She hadn't even tried flying yet, either. Apparently she probably wouldn't be able to yet.

They were sitting by the edge of the waterfall pool, trousers and jeans rolled up with their feet dangling in the blue. Many people had already introduced themselves, smiling and greeting her warmly as Mark played go-between. It was like the universe's greatest holiday park, but as happy as she was, Elizabeth was still waiting for the catch.

She supposed that, in many ways, she already knew the biggest one: missing her husband and son. But strangely, that was almost hard to do here. She knew that they were alive and well, and safe. She could see them, from where she was; Mark had already showed her how to do it. There was Callum, just as she'd always pictured him. It was mind-blowing—her son had *lived!*—and her heart ached, but at the same time, she knew *everything was okay*, because soon they would join her, and this place certainly made it easy to wait. She missed her husband, and her arms ached to finally hold her son ... but she could wait. Such thoughts would have been impossible to comprehend if she'd been alive, but this place rewrote the rules.

But that makes sense. We'd have *to see things differently in order to be able to handle eternity.*

She'd said all this to Mark—about how she was desperate for them to join her—and while he hadn't really confirmed that this would be the case, he'd said they'd get to all that later. For now, he said, it was just best that she get herself orientated. She was happy to do just that.

My God ... everything is going to be all right. So that's *how that feels.*

A square of white, about five feet wide on each side, suddenly appeared in the middle of the pool. One of the swimmers suddenly found themselves suspended in midair as the water in which they'd been immersed disappeared, replaced by white nothingness. They hung there in the white square for a moment, still kicking, until they realised what had happened and stopped, looking annoyed.

"There!" cried Mark, grinning and prodding her on the shoulder. The prod was probably harder than he meant it to be, the little man excited about what he was seeing and forgetting himself. "Do you see?"

"Yes," said Elizabeth, her mouth gaping as she watched. It was like seeing behind the stage curtain of reality. Then there was a snapping sound, and the square disappeared as the water returned a second later, with the surprised swimmer disappearing beneath it as he was no longer kicking. Everyone around the pool burst out laughing. The swimmer emerged above water a few moments later, shaking his head and holding his hand up. He took the amusement good-naturedly with a *for crying out loud* expression on his face. Mark turned back to Elizabeth, grinning.

"Broken bits," he said. "That's what I'm talking about. You'll see one or two of those every day."

"But *why*," Elizabeth asked, staring at the area of water that had previously been erased from existence. "Why is that happening? What's wrong with the place?"

"Pretty much nothing," Mark said, airily. "It certainly doesn't really affect anything here, apart from being a minor annoyance. One thing you need to learn fast in this club; there's a lot of answers here, but some things you'll *never* get an answer to. Just like in the rest of your life. The important thing is, we know most of the things that we *need* to know. The other things ... well, we can take an educated guess. I'll explain about that later, once we've covered more of the bases. You feeling settled enough to ask some more questions?"

Elizabeth nodded eagerly. Now that her memories had returned, and the incredible nature of her new existence was accepted, she wanted to know more.

"How big is this place?" she asked.

"Several miles," said Mark, gesturing with his hand. "It's hard to say without any measuring equipment. It seems to be like a big circle, really; people have done expeditions in many different directions but always somehow end up coming back to where they started. No one minds, though. Would you?"

"No, I wouldn't. But how many are here? There doesn't seem to be that many. I mean, this can't be all of them?"

"Oh no, this is just a few hundred. The rest will be off doing different things, playing games, talking, watching home, and many will be in the

Control Room itself. That's where the ones who have been here the shortest amount of time tend to spend most of their days. When they're still *curious*. After a bit, that wears off, and rest of us only go in there when we're on duty, as it were. I'll take you there shortly, before you ask." He smirked, and winked. Elizabeth grinned, amused that he'd taken the words out of her mouth. It was like spending time with her dad. Then something else occurred to her like a lightning bolt to the brain, and she sat bolt upright. Mark hadn't noticed, and was still talking, watching the swimmers. "It's been a long time since we've done a census, but I should think there's over a thousand—"

"Where's my dad?" she asked, grabbing Mark's shoulder and staring into his face, wide eyed. How could she not have thought of this before? Was she so distracted by the feeling in that place?

Oh, you wicked cow. You didn't even think of your own dad.

Liz and her mother had always hated each other's guts, and Liz couldn't care less about what had happened to the old bitch. She'd left when Liz was twelve, and both she and her dad had been glad to see the back of her. But it had been her dad who had *always* been there, her dad who had worked shifts that he'd hated purely so he could put her through university to get her degree in accountancy. Her dad who'd lived long enough to see the wedding, but not long enough to know that she'd become pregnant. Her dad who'd been the best dad she could have ever wished for.

"Stephen. Stephen *Hardy*," she said, trying to keep herself calm as her eyes filled with tears for the second time that day. "Where is he? Take me to him? *Please?*" But even as she said it, the last few words Mark had said reached her conscious mind.

A thousand? How can that be, if this is the afterlife? There should be trillions and trillions and—

A horrible suspicion struck her, and the worried, resigned look on Mark's face made it worse. There was only one answer.

"Yep," he sighed, his expression riddled with sympathy. "That penny always drops quite quickly. It's always the worst part, and that's why I'm the only sucker who does arrival duty every other week. Everyone hates having to explain it." He stood up, kicking the water from his feet, and bent to offer her his hand. With the sun behind him, he was wrapped in shadow as he stood over her.

"You'd better come with me," he said. "This is always best explained in the actual Control Room itself, and it's a little bit of a trek."

***

They walked in silence for a good hour. They'd left the valley itself behind, and the majority of the walk was made up of an easy, rolling hillside. Every now and then they'd see another one of the strange white squares flash on and off in the distance, a cut and re-paste of the landscape. A visual glitch in the countryside. At one point they crossed a hill that looked over an idyllic town, made up of beautiful cottages and cobbled streets that glittered in the warm sun. A bell rang from what looked like a town hall, and Elizabeth could see people making their way towards it from all directions.

"Dinner bell," said Mark, gesturing with his hand. It was the first thing he'd said since they'd left. "You don't have to eat with everyone else, but most people like to. It's always fun." His hand moved across to point at the left-hand side of the town. "Your house will be down there somewhere. It'll have always been there, even though it probably wasn't before. Does that make sense?" He thought as he walked, his brow etched with lines as he tried to find the words to explain it. "Put it this way," he said eventually, "before you arrived, it wasn't there. Now you have, when I see it, I'll remember it as *always* having been there. Make sense?" Elizabeth nodded, and didn't reply. She was very worried now. The feeling was slightly detached, as if it were happening to someone else—she'd never experienced an emotion in this way before—but it was still there. She just wanted to get where they were going, and fortunately for her, Mark's next words confirmed that they wouldn't be long.

"Down there," he said, as they crested the rise of the hill. Elizabeth looked to where he was pointing, even though she didn't need to. It was totally obvious what he was referring to. For the third time that day, her mouth fell open in wonder.

A whole section of the landscape was missing. Where the bottom of the hill should have been, everything from the northeast of that point onwards was white, including the sky. The squares she'd seen earlier were clearer, just echoes of a larger glitch. It was like looking at a canvas where the artist had just given up with a third of the painting incomplete. The river that ran along the base of the hill disappeared into the whiteness, completely cut off, with the water flowing into the edge of the white and vanishing once it hit. It was so incredible, Elizabeth couldn't even find her voice to speak. Mark was looking at her, saying nothing.

"Come over this way, this'll *really* get you," he said, taking her elbow and leading her slightly away to the left. "Look over there." He pointed off to the horizon in the west, and her gaze followed his finger. "Okay, now look back down there." She looked back to the base of the hill, to where that expanse of impossible white was, only to find that it had been replaced by a vast expanse of grass. The river continued on and upwards to the horizon, and the sky was back in place.

"Where did it go?" gasped Elizabeth, holding out her hand to where the white had been and expecting to feel it somehow, as if the sight before her was some kind of optical illusion.

"It's still there," said Mark, shrugging. "Mad, isn't it? Watch." He took her elbow once more, walking her a few steps to the right so that they were back where they'd started. The white expanse appeared again, as if someone had torn away the picture that was reality to expose its backing.

"What the *hell?*" gasped Elizabeth, and then pulled back as Mark began to lead her towards it. "Are you kidding? You're not going in there, are you?" Mark looked at the white, confused, then back at Elizabeth.

"Well ... yes," he said shrugging. "That's the Control Room. What did you think it was?"

"I don't know if maybe you've been here too long," Elizabeth said, her voice high and shocked as she pulled her elbow free, "but most people wouldn't be too keen on just walking off the edge of the world, Mark! What the hell ... I mean ... *bloody hell* ..." The white patch was huge and impossible before her eyes, and she didn't have the words.

"Okay, good point, good point," said Mark, raising a calming hand. "Should have expected that, sorry, sorry. I *have* been here quite a while, sorry. But trust me, okay? It's fine. Really, it's fine. It's perfectly solid. You probably can't see them from here, but there's people walking around in there. Try and focus. Can you see them?"

Uncertain, she squinted ... and thought that maybe she *could* see some distant figures, slowly appearing before her eyes as she tried her hardest to see clearly. About ten of them, maybe more, walking slowly around in the whiteness.

"Mmm-hmm," she said, still wary, but she held out her hand for Mark to take as they began to make their way towards the vast space. She felt like she'd need his support, as her legs were threatening to give way from underneath her.

"I thought you said people walked off in all different directions and just went round in a circle?" she said, as they made their way down the grassy hill towards the Control Room. *Control Room ...* she'd expected a bloody room!

"They did," Mark said cheerily, his jolly demeanour returning once more. "Remember when I showed you that different view? If you'd have continued in that direction, you'd have ended up back at the valley. This direction we're heading now is the only one that doesn't loop around. *This* direction only ends here. Right in the Control Room."

"Why do you call it that?" she asked, eyes wide and frightened as the Control Room began to loom up and over her. The edges of it, where white met reality, looked rough, as if something really had been torn away.

"You'll see," he said, and then considered his statement. "Well, maybe. Not at first, perhaps."

Eventually, they were fully inside, and from her new point of view it looked like the world outside was the error. She could still see the hills and sky and sun, but now it all appeared to be the other way around; from here, the painting of reality didn't seem so much *unfinished* as only just begun, with the canvas's whiteness seeming to extend off in all directions with only a relative sliver of an image in the middle. It felt like she was seeing the beginning of the world from the outside. She bent and touched where her feet rested on nothing. The surface she felt was completely smooth and unidentifiable.

"This ... is ..."

"It's incredible, isn't it," Mark said, speaking with quiet awe as he looked around himself. Elizabeth looked at his middle-aged face, transformed again into that of a boy. "I never get tired of it. Ever. Even on days when I'm not on duty, I still come here sometimes. I like it."

"Duty, there you go again, *duty*," Elizabeth said, her hand waving in the air as if swatting the word away. "What duty? What are you talking about?" She closed her eyes, and the hand froze. "Sorry. I'm just anxious. But please, what duty?" Mark cocked his head and held up his own hand, eyes closed. *No offence taken.*

"Okay, here's the best way to explain it. Apart from the white, obviously, what else do you see here?" he asked, spreading his arms wide. Elizabeth took the cue, and looked around her. She could see the people easily now, as easily as she could see people around her on a street when she was alive. *The white must play funny visual tricks at a distance*, she thought, *just look at the way it was there from one angle and gone the next.* The majority of them were standing still, but some of them were walking very slowly, their heads facing forwards as their bodies moved sideways.

"People," she said, checking that she wasn't missing something. She looked again. "People. About fifteen or sixteen. They're just more of us, right?" Mark nodded in response.

"Yes, they are. Just on duty. Okay, good, now come this way. See anything else?"

"No," she said. "Should I?"

"Maybe not yet. How about now?"

"No. Wait ..." There *was* something. About twenty feet away; was that something different in the white ahead?

"Focus again," Mark said, quietly, the jolly demeanour gone. His face was suddenly stern and intense. She did as she was told. The whiteness that filled her vision ahead of her shifted slightly, and then it was as if she'd somehow been missing it all along. In the middle of it all, immense, was a patch of sheer ...

What is it? What is that? It isn't a colour, it isn't a hole. What the hell is it?

"You see it now, don't you?" Mark said.

"Yes," whispered Elizabeth, deeply frightened and awed at the same time. It was *huge*, worse than the white because it was nothingness. Even pure whiteness was *something.* At the back of the control room there was a hole that led onto nothing. The edges of the Control Room had been slightly rough, but the edges of this hole were torn and frayed, looking as if they'd been eaten away by moths. "It's *torn*, isn't it?" she said. "Something was here once ... you can *feel* that something used to be here, something very important. It's like the feeling out there, in the valley, it's all around you, but this ... this is an *absence* of something, it's like ..."

"Like an ache," Mark said, nodding sadly. "We don't normally come to the back of the Control Room, as it isn't very nice. But you had to see it."

"What was it?" asked Elizabeth, her expression pleading. "What was here?" She had to know. It was a need. Mark saw this, and sighed heavily. Elizabeth saw all the years in him then, a wisdom that he covered with a genial front because that was simply the way he chose to be.

"We don't know," he said, slowly shaking his head. "We don't think we'll ever know. The oldest of us has been here ... well ... a long, long time, and even she doesn't know. It was like this when she got here. Some of us think we should have never have been able to come here in the first place. As if whatever happened here, whatever was torn away, meant that we *could* come here. As if us coming here was a glitch, just like the squares of white. We just don't know. Personally, I think that we *were* meant to come here ... but that the actual Control Room itself, this place, was meant to be closed. Finished before any of the dead came. We shouldn't be able to see the places that we can see from here. Certainly, they can't see us, anyway."

Elizabeth was lost, staring into the hole with a mixture of fascination and horror. What could tear a hole this big? Never mind that, what could tear a hole of any size and leave ... just an absence behind? And why did she ache so much in the absence of—

"*The places that we can see from here*"? What did he mean by that?

"What places?" she asked, turning to Mark. Her eyes were shining. "What places can you see that you shouldn't?" Mark raised his eyebrows and closed his eyes, gesturing her away from the hole in the Control Room. The expression said *well, this is the heart of the matter.*

"That's why I brought you here," he said, gently. "You see ... well ..." He sighed again, hands on his hips, and turned back and forth at the waist, considering the people around him in the Control Room. "This place ... we've been trying to figure it out for thousands of years. D'you understand? There's things we've been able to fathom, and others ..." He waved a hand at the hole, shrugging. "Some will never be explained. Would *you* fancy taking a jump through that to see what happens?"

Elizabeth looked at the hole and shivered involuntarily, turning away once more. She certainly wouldn't. It was oblivion out there, that was undoubtable. You could *see* it. That was the name for the unnamed colour of the hole: *oblivion*.

"What makes it harder is that, as you've seen, this place is faulty. *Glitchy*, as Andy would say. You saw the bit that disappeared and came back today, down by the waterfall pool. And we think it's to do with that," he said, pointing behind her. Elizabeth didn't have to look to know what he was talking about. "And whatever it was, it's had an effect on everywhere else. We're fine here—believe me, we've got the best deal going, an incredible deal compared to some of the other places—but there's errors everywhere else, and some of them are major. Come this way." He led her away from the hole, his hand outstretched ahead of him, and changed direction once or twice. He looked like he was concentrating hard, and despite her urgent desire to get some answers, Elizabeth could tell that disturbing him would only mean that she would have to wait even longer. She waited, and walked, patiently.

"Here," he said finally, and stepped back, leading her to where he'd been standing a second before. "Hold out your hands." She hesitated, and looked at him nervously. "It's all right," he said soothingly, but his face wasn't smiling. "We've been doing this for centuries. Took us a long time to figure out all this when we were only going on instinct and feeling, but we know now that's it's pretty safe. Just hold out your hands, and close your eyes."

Elizabeth look at the people spread out around her. They were doing the same, and showing no ill effects.

Why even hesitate, Liz? Are you seriously not *going to do what he asks?*

It was a fair point. She did as she was told, and almost immediately a vision popped up before her. Elizabeth nearly opened her eyes in surprise, but she managed to keep her concentration. The image was as crisp and clear as an HD TV picture, so much so that it didn't even feel like her eyes were closed at all.

"Oh my God ..."

Say whatever else you like, it has been one hell of a day so far.

She saw a group of sleeping, smiling people, lying still yet slowly moving through water. No, not water ... they were just floating, their bodies limp but their faces peaceful and serene. All around them was a colour, a light green that pulsed and darkened, lightened and turned. Not just a *group* of people, she saw, but a *crowd*, spread out far into the distance. There must have been hundreds of them, if not more, and that was only within her current field of vision. Mark's voice came to her, as if from very far away.

"We call that one the Bedroom. We think they're dreaming; the older ones here claim that they can just about hear their thoughts. Whatever they're dreaming about, they all look very happy. Maybe they're the ones with the best setup after all."

"What is it?" Elizabeth asked, her voice light and airy. She felt relaxed just watching them.

"It's one of the other levels, Elizabeth," Mark said gently. "This isn't the only place, as I think you've figured out. Different people go to different places, and we still don't really know why. Some say it's because of the way your brain is wired, others claim that it's all to do with energy and that the choices you make in life. That they affect that energy if it exists. Some here claim it's to do with if you're a good or a bad person, but they're very much in the minority. We've seen too much to contradict that thinking. Whatever the reason, the bottom line is this: it turns out that the afterlife, just like life, seems to be all about the luck of the draw in terms of what you get. Okay, there's at least one level where everyone there is a suicide. That's not a nice place. But *generally,* it's just a case of some being lucky, some being unlucky—" Mark cut himself off as he remembered the situation, and moved quickly on. "Of course, there's ways out of pretty much all of them, ways to get a restart and try again, and some are harder than others. But ... coming here is next to impossible for most. You're *lucky.*" He touched Elizabeth's shoulder, turning her slightly, and she opened her eyes, wincing slightly at the harsh brightness of the white compared to the softness of the green. She turned to face him, and all the relaxed feeling inside her flew away at the sad look in Mark's eyes.

Oh, no. Oh please no. Don't let me be right.

"People that come here are the real minority," he said, his voice soft and cautious. "We think we must all have been slightly different in a way. Some of us more so than others. You know, some arrive here and they can do all the tricks straight away, others take longer, that kind of thing. We do our duty here, keeping an eye on the other levels in case there's any new information, trying to find new levels, that sort of business. You'll be able to do it all too because you're *different*. So it's very rare that family members, especially non-blood family members, come here too."

No no no please please

"Your father isn't here, Elizabeth," Mark said, as gently as he could. "In this place, when you've been here a while, you'll learn about energies, and feeling them. There's only a fistful of people here whose family members arrived here as well, and they all share the same kind of energy. It's really distinct, and when you can feel it it's easier to remember an energy than it is to remember a face. I've met every single person here, Elizabeth, and I've never heard your father's name, and more importantly, your energy is new and unique here. Trust me. I'm very sorry to tell you that."

Elizabeth stared at him dumbly, blinking, and then something else hit her.

"So, my husband ... my son ...?"

Mark sighed, but not in an exasperated way; it was the sigh of a man considering a difficult question.

"Well, I don't want to get your hopes up, as the odds are hugely against it, but it *has* happened before, as I say. If you don't mind me reading you a bit, I'll be able to find your husband and son on the other side and get a proper reading on *them,* and tell you where it looks like they're going. I can get an image of your father too, though I'll need to bring in some help if you want me to do that ... I can show you where he is. It might not be good, though, so you'd have to decide if you *wanted* me to do that."

Did she? She wasn't sure. This was all such ridiculously large, devastating stuff to take in. She might never speak to Martin again, and worse, would never even get to speak to her son even *once?*

A true death. That's what it is. The panic you felt while you were dying ... that you would never hold them again ...

"Do you want me to do that? If not your father, as you might want to think about that, would you like me to check your husband and son?"

She knew the answer to that one, at least. It was an easy question, her course certain.

"Yes," she said, as tears ran down her face. "Yes, please."

Mark nodded quietly, and held his hand up in front of her face, closing his eyes.

"Just picture them, please. I know that might be painful right now."

It was. Her heart felt like it would physically tear as she pictured the three of them in a pose that was never allowed to happen, a baby in her arms, Martin's arms around *her.*

Do I even have a heart, here? An actual body? What am I now?

"That's good," said Mark, his brow furrowed in concentration once more. "Just hold on to—" His eyes snapped wide open and he stared at her in shock. His finger came up, pointing at her face.

"Elizabeth *Hogan?*" he gasped, his face white.

What ... what the hell?

Elizabeth was terrified by his response, her already frayed nerves getting another jolt. She was almost afraid to admit to her own name.

"Y-yes ... I told you when I got here—"

"*Hardy,* you said! You said your father's surname was *Hardy!*"

"But I told you was married, didn't you remember, and I even *said* my surname was Hogan—" He wasn't listening though, already rambling to himself in a panic.

"I'm an idiot, I'm a fucking *idiot,* we were so focused on everything else that we never concentrated on her, it was all about *them* ..." His eyes went back to her, and his tone became almost pleading. "I've even seen you before, for crying out loud, why didn't I put two and two together? I should have taken you to the others straight away! You even told me your name ... I was just excited that somebody *new* had turned up ... didn't even put two and two together, we haven't even been thinking about you, we've just been too busy trying to clean up the mess—"

"What?" Elizabeth shouted, upset and angry and frightened. "What the hell are you going on about? What does it matter that my name is?"

"You're the *mother!*" Mark shouted, raising his arms. "You're the mother, you're a key part of all the problems we've trying to fix!" He looked at her blank expression, and shook his head. "When I told you how to see your family on the other side, I didn't look as well because that's private ... I should have ... *shit* ... look, we've got to go and get the others and come back here *immediately.* There's a man you need to see."

"What? What man, what is this?"

"Rougeau. We need to go and get Rougeau, right now."

***

There were so many of them now, in every country. Only a small percentage of the *true* Brotherhood—the ones who had never actually called themselves anything, the ones actually given a task—had been caught by the police. They were the ones who had attacked family members, work colleagues, close friends. The ones who had felt a desperate need to confess. So many of them had committed suicide afterwards, torn between duty and guilt, and this why the numbers of that section of the Brotherhood that were in custody was low. The vast majority of the rest of them—the ones who had attacked random members of the public in bars and bus depots and shopping centres—were still going about their lives in various ways. Confused, reduced in character, but knowing that the difficult task they had been given was complete. Many of them had *enjoyed* doing it, though. It was an excuse to do something they'd never had the guts to do before, but had always wanted to.

Across the globe, they now looked to the sky, no matter what they were doing. Those on a street stopped dead in the middle of the pavement. Those who were driving slowed to a halt, putting on the handbrake and taking the keys out of the ignition. They stepped out of their vehicles. If they were on a busy motorway, traffic behind them built up as other cars angrily swerved around them, beeping their horns as they went on their way. All of the truly touched—men and women, young and old—who had been dubbed the Brotherhood of the Raid stopped in their tracks and looked skyward.

It came to them all, the new knowledge, the certainty that they'd known was coming. Just like before, they listened. Just like before, it was devastating, even if they didn't truly understand it.

It hadn't been enough. They'd failed.

One by one, the Brotherhood of the Raid lay down on the ground and waited, moving on an animal instinct that whispered *freeze*.

***

Elizabeth watched the skinny man with the long hair as he went through the same hands-out routine that she'd been carrying out earlier ... except Rougeau seemed to be able to look at two different levels at once, holding out a hand to each side rather than both hands in front like everyone else. Not that the other people in the Control Room were doing anything of the sort right now; all of them were either staring at Rougeau as he worked, or at Elizabeth. It was starting to make her very uncomfortable. For now, thoughts of her family were at the back of her mind. She wanted answers, and she hadn't been getting any.

Mark had been no use, babbling away to himself as they marched back across the plains and hills towards the valley. Once they'd collected Rougeau, a slim but healthy-looking young man dressed in a smart suit (that had made Elizabeth wonder about clothes ... the ones she was currently dressed in weren't even clothes that she normally wore) he'd given her a stern but hearty handshake, but that had been it. The two men had then walked off, calling to others along the way whilst engrossed in frantic conversation. Occasionally, they'd looked back to make sure that she was following, and she'd continued to do so. She was beginning to feel like a child, tagging along after the grown-ups, even though Rougeau looked younger than she did. By the time they'd reached the control room again, there was a group of about fifty people in there.

"He's not been here long," said Mark in a whisper, talking to Elizabeth without taking his eyes from Rougeau. Mark was standing to her right, the pair of them in the middle of a rough semi-circle formed around themselves by the observers as Rougeau worked. "But when he got here, it was immediate that he was just ... something else." There was real admiration in his voice. "He picked up tricks that only the really old ones know almost straightaway, and found another seven new levels in here within a matter of months. We all knew about him before he died, of course—there's only been a few like him, ever—but even the others that came here can't do the stuff he can."

"That's great, Mark, but what does it have to do with me?" snapped Elizabeth. She was straight up angry with him. He hadn't spoken a word to her since they'd left the Control Room, after giving nothing but bad news and mysterious, ominous crap. Now suddenly he was talking to her like nothing had happened? "What's he doing, and what does he expect *me* to do? Can I get a fucking *answer*, please?" Elizabeth rarely swore, but she was furious.

"Yes, yes, sorry," Mark said, hissing at her to quieten her down. "You need to understand, this has been going on for several years. This situation ... even for the things we can do here, our influence outside of the Control Room is extremely limited, and even that requires a *huge* amount of group effort. That's why there's been far more people on duty in the last few years than there ever has been before."

"Why? Why's it so important?"

"Because we're dealing with a potentially catastrophic sequence of events, and we're trying to limit the damage as much as possible. We've never attempted anything on this scale before. And your son is right at the very heart of it."

"Callum?" Her skin seemed to tighten all over her body. "Why?"

"Madame Hogan?" said Rougeau, turning around. He held out his slender hand, his clean and handsome face smiling gently. "Please?" She looked at Mark, who nodded at her urgently. She took the cue and stepped forward, taking Rougeau's hand. "I apologise for being so brief with you earlier, madame. Mark and I had much to discuss, and I am afraid that we got a little carried away. Please understand that, since almost the first day that I arrived, this is something that I have involved myself in deeply. In fact, ironically, without knowing it at the time, this was something that I came to your husband to discuss when I was alive."

"Martin?" Elizabeth gasped. "You met Martin?" Rougeau smiled.

"Yes, although I have to admit that neither of us were ... at our best, shall we say. I certainly did not look as well as I do now, and he was ... inconvenienced. Not in the best of spirits. I didn't achieve much, sadly, but I could not have possibly known what the full situation was."

"Why ... why did you talk to Martin? When did you meet?"

"It was after you died, Madame Hogan. I went to see him. The sight had returned to me, and I had not had it for so long ... it came to me, screaming his name. I simply knew that great danger—and great change—was coming, and that he was at the heart of it. I could only warn him. If I had known more ..." he sighed, heavily. "Even if I had, I do not think that it would have made a difference, Madame Hogan. He does not have it in him to do what needs to be done, I think, or at least, it is a decision that he finds impossible to reach. The dilemma has him tight, squirming in its hand. I am not sure many parents would be able to, even if they knew the extra part that Martin does not.

"All we can do here is try and reduce the damage, and hope that you being here might somehow make a difference. I have no idea how, but we have to try everything. I will need to read you. Mark said that he began, but didn't finish. Even if he had I would still like to try myself. My sight is greater, no offence to my good friend Mark." He glanced at Mark apologetically, who waved him off frantically. There was clearly no way Mark would ever be upset with Rougeau. There was hero worship there. "May I?" said Rougeau, beginning to raise his hand to Elizabeth's face.

"No chance," snapped Elizabeth, realising that they were going to try and make her wait even longer. "None of this shit goes any further forward until you tell me *what. Is. Going. On.* Okay? Then I'll do anything you want. But you bloody well tell me, all right?" She stood her ground, seething, her tense shoulders rising and falling with each angry breath. Rougeau smiled, and put his hand to his chest.

"Of course, of course. I apologise on behalf of us all. I will explain everything to you," he said. "I forget myself. I remember being desperate for answers myself, when I met your husband. Unfortunately for us, none were forthcoming at the time. Now, I have a window on the entire universe. Answers are ours."

"Not all of them," Elizabeth muttered, pointing at the ominous and fascinating torn hole at the other end of the Control Room. Rougeau nodded, amused and impressed.

"True. I have my theories, of course," he said, clearly relishing the subject. "They say whatever was there before got torn out. *I* say ... what if something tore itself free? Something enslaved to the job of creation, that managed to liberate itself before the task was complete? Something that did a reluctant, slap-dash job under duress, meaning that even the parts it completed weren't *quite right.* Faulty." Elizabeth stared at the hole, unable to help herself, caught by Rougeau's words. She shuddered, and turned back to him.

"Okay," she said, taking a deep breath, "then tell me what you *do* know."

"Of course." He released her hand, and moved his grip to her wrist. "It will be better if I *show* you. This first part will probably be difficult for you to hear, I'm afraid. It involves your son. I have to show you the level that he comes from."

***

Chapter Nine: An Unpleasant Experience Watching England Play (and This Time It Isn't the Match), Elizabeth Sees the Flies, Callum Gets a Visit, and It All Kicks Off (Again, Not the Match)

***

Martin sat by himself in the Chestnut Tree, watching the England game on the pub's big screen TV. He'd been going there for years to watch England. It was the only time he left the house to do something that wasn't purely practical, or to walk Scoffer. He certainly never went to the pub for any other reason. Once upon a time, a qualifying game like this would have meant the place would be packed to the rafters with white or red shirts, but tonight it was only half full. Even like this, it would be the best business that the place had done all year. The bar was one of the very few that remained open in the city, and Martin didn't think that it would still be in business twelve months from now. A decade of skyrocketing drink prices, and an increase in the general public's apathy towards getting out the house had already taken its toll on the British pub industry. Then the Brotherhood of the Raid had come along, and they'd killed it off for good. Unless it was a very special occasion—or, obviously, work—people stayed out of each other's way as much as they could. It just wasn't worth the risk.

Normally, Martin did the same, although that didn't mean a huge difference to his daily life. He'd spent the last seven years pretty much the same way as he'd spent the previous five: in the house. He'd only come out tonight on a whim. He only ever saw Trish, and had stopped attending family gatherings. They asked too many questions. Without ever consciously deciding to, he'd cut ties with his friends, even Bryan. He couldn't remember the last time he'd seen the guy. It was a shame.

He didn't like to be in the same room with Trish when Callum was there. He found it too hard to watch. The performance that his son would put on for her benefit ... it made him feel genuinely ill. Seeing the illusion of a normal family was grotesque to Martin's eyes, a macabre, cruel play being staged in his own front room. He'd come to terms with what his son was a long time ago—the boy *was* his son, an undeniable fact over anything else, even if he had to keep repeating it to himself, and he loved Callum—but seeing it faked so blatantly like that put him back to where he'd been before he'd known the truth for certain. As long as he didn't see the fakery, he could live with the truth.

So why are you so painfully thin?

That was because he never slept well, he knew, and ate too little, but he mentally patted himself on the back for improving from the way he'd been when Callum was a toddler. Looking back on it, he'd been at death's door. Now, he was just ...

Anxious? Of course you are. Callum's thirteen now, Martin. Puberty will come any time soon. Then you'll have to make that decision.

WHY? WHY CAN'T THINGS JUST BE LEFT SO WHATEVER HAPPENS, HAPPENS?

Because that in itself *is a decision. You could unbalance everything. Tear the universe apart. You could also be the guy that meant there were no more real children anywhere ever again, just empty vessels of meat waiting for dead people to come and—*

Martin sipped at his pint and tried to focus on the game, ignoring the merry-go-round in his head that hadn't let up for one second of the last seven years. He felt almost detached from it, pretending that it was happening to someone else and that he didn't really have to decide on the impossible.

But isn't that—

He focused on the game. Shaun Barrett, the golden boy of this new generation of English players, produced a breathtaking cross that found the equally youthful legs of Aiden Wyatt as he ran into the box, unmarked. Half the bodies in the pub stood up, and even Martin tensed up in his seat. It was for naught though; the outstretched fingertips of the Dutch keeper managed to turn it wide. Even so, it had been a spectacular effort, and the vision of Barrett had been, as usual, footballing genius.

Genius is actually a cumulative thing, Callum had told him, during one of their many late night conversations about the afterlife. Martin couldn't but help but ask questions. It was like a drug, hearing Callum talk about such matters, even though every time he did Martin felt like he'd been lessened somehow afterwards. It was as if he were hearing things that the human mind wasn't meant to know, and the heavy weight of them was taking their toll every time. But he couldn't stop. How could he? *Normally, when the dead go into a human vessel, their own personality is absorbed by that of the vessel. So, you won't remember your life ... but parts of it might still transfer over, even if you don't remember why. So let's say you were a great painter, okay?* Callum clearly enjoyed holding court, or he did around Martin, at least. It was part of who his son was. *And then you die. And say that, by chance, it just so happens that the body you go into has a natural flair for painting. Well, then your ability, if it's strong enough, is retained, and added to the potential of* that *vessel. And then when you die again, and come back to the Dump with no memory, you still have those latent talents within you ... so if you're lucky enough to get* another *human vessel, and one with a natural painting ability at that, you then are at triple your original level of skill or flair or creativity. This is how genius works, and why* true *genius is rare.*

The boy had so many answers. And he was a good son; he looked after his dad, and did as he was told despite being senior to Martin by thousands of years. The word "senior" barely covered it, laughably inadequate in this case. Martin was needing looking after these days, too. He was pushing fifty, and if it wasn't for Callum making sure Martin at least ate the right things—even if he didn't eat very much of them—Martin's health would be even worse that it was.

It was the anxiety that was the problem. That made everything difficult. Even though he'd been writing again—and for some time, producing the best-selling and best-received work of his career somehow, although that wasn't saying much—he could never shut it off. He'd always wonder what Callum was doing, or thinking. It'd be easier if he was at school every day, but Martin had made homeschooling arrangements long ago. Less risk that way, and there was certainly no *need* for Callum to—

A man stood up at the other side of the pub. This in itself wouldn't have been anything out of the ordinary, but there was something very unusual about the way he did it, and Martin couldn't help but watch. It was the odd *speed* at which the fellow was doing it at, that was the thing, as if he were doing an impression of someone moving in slow motion. As the man rose, swaying slightly on his feet, his eyes looked confused and concerned, and he looked down at his hands as if there were something wrong with them.

Then a distant *boom* was heard outside, and everyone got to their feet in a hurry.

Martin didn't know it, but change had just arrived.

***

"This is it," Rougeau said, bringing up the image of the Dump with one hand and gripping Elizabeth's wrist with the other. One minute her eyes were looking at Rougeau, the next the image before her was replaced by one of a pressing, heaving mass of bodies. Even though she was prepared for it, the harsh nature of the sight was another shock inside the space of a few minutes, even though this one was nowhere near as bad as the news she'd just received. She'd never met her son, and even though emotions seemed to have a more detached effect in this place, a mother's instinct still had a grip all of its own. The things she'd just been told were on a level that could penetrate, even here.

Callum ... Callum is ...

No. She couldn't get it.

Deal with this for now. Just deal with this, deal with the rest later. Listen to what he's saying.

"You can see why he would want to leave," Rougeau was saying, his voice sounding distant. "They are relatively calm at the moment, but they were at open war for some time. However unusual a war it may be in that place. The ways they find to hurt each other ... either way, one side has won. We're waiting to see what comes of it. It's difficult to catch everything, but we can hear them enough to know that they call their place the Dump. Again, different rules for different levels; if these people take an animal, or 'vessel' as they call it, and it isn't 'pure', they return with no memory of themselves. Those that come here can use any animal vessel and remember who they are afterwards. No, it isn't fair. It's another example of things being broken from our level downwards. Regardless, the Dump should never have reached this stage of capacity, and we know this for a fact. See?" Elizabeth could feel her body being led a step or two to the right, and then the image changed dramatically. The press of humanity was replaced by a sheer, empty space, where flashes of light occasionally blipped past her eyes. "Centuries ago, this place appeared, right next door to the Dump. It's of the same nature, and almost—that is the key word, *almost*—merged with the Dump itself. It had clearly started to blend—you see there, for example—but at some point *it just stopped.* You see? The Dump should have at least doubled in size, Elizabeth. All that extra space is just sitting there, waiting. It could have been a beautiful place again. Can you feel the ... hmm, let me try and show you ..." there was a pause, and then the image before her became almost like a split screen. Crush of bodies on the left, space and flashing lights on the right. And the space between them ...

"It's so close," she said, her voice filled with awe. "It's so *close.* The wall is so thin. How is it even holding?"

"It isn't," said Rougeau's voice. "It *is* breaking, just very, very slowly. Any day now, it is going to suddenly give. Or rather, we *think* it will, because your s—because Callum's actions are making severe waves, and we do not know what effect it might have on the Dump. There might be none at all, or he might be stopping the breakthrough that his people need. But there is one place that it is *definitely* going to affect very, very badly. The place of the living."

The image disappeared, and Elizabeth was looking at the control room again, at the many concerned faces looking her way. It seemed like more and more people were arriving all the while. This was a very big deal, no doubt. Rougeau took both of her hands again, and looked at her with concern.

"Are you all right? Can you continue?" he asked. She could. Just. Elizabeth tightened her lips together, sniffed through her nose, and nodded without speaking. "Bon," said Rougeau, turning away and walking her to the opposite side of the Control Room. His voice was low and deadly serious, as if he were speaking of something that unnerved him. Elizabeth's skin—or whatever it was now—felt like it moved. She didn't want to know what could truly unnerve Rougeau after all of the incredible things he must have seen. "This next level ... you may find it unsettling. This is the heart of the issue. I would like you to prepare yourself." He paused, taking a breath and picking the words carefully. "There are many levels that are actually based on earth, if you will. Where the dead walk amongst the living, unseen. I am about to show you one of these. The inhabitants of this particular level do not have a name for it, because ... well ... they do not have a name for anything. This is ... it is a very low level indeed. In many ways, it is the cruellest. We named it the Flytrap. You'll see why." He began to raise his hand, and then worryingly, paused for a moment and took a small, steadying breath inwards. Elizabeth started to ask *what's wrong with it* but as soon as the image appeared before her, she stopped. It was immediately clear what was wrong.

***

Callum wasn't doing anything in particular. He was happy to just lie on his bed and stare at the ceiling. Even after all these years, the simple act of breathing and having actual *oxygen* enter his lungs was a pleasure. The full belly he had after a quick meal of beans and cheese on toast was a pleasure. The soft bed beneath him was a pleasure. None of it could live up to the very early days of the Dump, of course, but it was still a pleasure of a different kind.

All these years? He realised what he'd just thought, and chuckled to himself, shaking his head in mild amusement. Thirteen years was a heartbeat to him, an eyeblink. His perception of time had shifted by coming back to a human body, certainly, but he hadn't realised that it shifted *that* much. It was an interesting thought.

Martin was out at the pub, a rarity, and being completely alone in the house on a Saturday afternoon was equally so. Callum had previously been in the back garden with Scoffer, who still liked to play even if he had just a fraction of the energy that he once possessed. He loved the dog, and knew that Scoffer probably didn't have a long time left—a few months perhaps, the dog had been very lucky to live as long as he had—and so Callum wanted to make sure Scoffer's last years on earth were as happy as possible. There were no dogs in the Dump, of course, and Callum knew that whatever came out of Scoffer's body once it was done would no longer *be* a dog. He just hoped there *was* a dog side, a place for the animal half. Somewhere with ghost rabbits to chase, and fields.

You could cook something for Martin when he gets back. A post-pub snack.

That sounded fun. Callum's accumulated knowledge was vast, easily beyond that of any three humans on earth put together, but he was severely lacking in practical skills for the modern age. He knew how things worked, knew *of* them, but knowledge and control were two different things. They didn't exactly stock up on cement mixers and tablet computers in the Dump, and cooking was a recent discovery that Callum was surprised he enjoyed. Tasting the various ingredients, the delight of combining and preparing—

There was scratching at the window.

Callum sat up, and looked through the glass. On the other side of the window was a crow. It was swaying slightly, and its feathers were covered with blood. Its wing sat at an odd and broken-looking angle. The two of them stared at each other for a moment, the crow blinking in a stunned-looking manner, and then it scratched at the glass again with its beak. It looked like it was trying to tap, but didn't have the strength even for that gentle hammering action. Instead it was almost leaning on the glass with its beak for support.

Once he got over his surprise, Callum jumped off the bed and flicked the window latch open. The crow moved to the left, gingerly, whilst Callum opened the right-hand panel outwards, and then reached out his hand onto the window ledge. The crow staggered onto his palm, and Callum cupped it and carefully brought the bird inside the bedroom and placed it on the floor.

He sat back on the edge of the bed, hunched over, intense and eager. He'd been expecting a visit like this eventually, but he didn't think that it would be so soon.

Keep calm. It might not be time yet. This could be something else.

But it wasn't. The crow looked at him with its beady eyes, and the voice came clearly into Callum's head. It sounded pained, and very weak.

"The Peaceful Ones ..." the crow began, and then stopped to take a few breaths.

"Take your time," said Callum kindly, even though his heart was racing. "There's no rush. You're hurt. I know how to fix your wing. Would you like me to do that?" The crow shook its head in response.

"No. Thank you." It shook its body, and Callum could hear the wince in his head. "A vole came to us this morning, three months old, with fresh news. The Peaceful Ones have been subdued. The Order of Daylight is ..." The crow paused, swayed on its feet, then shook itself again and continued. "... they are in control. We were instructed to tell you ... that they think they know what you want. And out of gratitude ... they'll make sure you get it. There will be no competition." The voice in his head sighed, the main part of his task complete. The crow was clearly very badly hurt; Callum thought that it might even be dying. He felt pity for its pain, but adrenalin was already pumping through his veins. The Order of Daylight was in control. They were always going to be eventually. Their numbers grew every day with bitter new arrivals who only knew the Dump as it currently was, and weren't interested in merely hoping for a return to something they'd never seen. So this wasn't news to Callum ... but the other part was. *He was going to get his way.* He'd never dared hope he could get that too—he'd suspected that the Order *might* be grateful enough— but unbelievably, they were. Things could be put right.

Don't get excited yet. Don't you dare.

"You met resistance, coming here," said Callum, his hand going to stroke the birds head, to soothe it, but thinking better of the action. Such pressure would probably hurt the creature.

"Yes. The Peaceful Ones' people, the ones watching this house ... they don't know it's over in the Dump. The Peaceful Ones have been stopped from sending anyone back. We offered to allow them to send a messenger, so that they could call off their servants here ... but they refused. Stubborn bastards. They want their people down here to believe the Pact is still ... *uhhh* ... in place. They know they'll keep fighting. I barely made it here. The rest are still at it. I don't think they know that I made it through."

Callum felt a surge of gratitude to the crow, even in his moment of excitement. Ultimately, it made no difference to the crow personally whether Callum got the message or not; new pure vessels would be made regardless, and the Dump's liberation would begin. But it was a show of gratitude—of respect—by the Order of Daylight that they'd sent a message at all, that they'd let him know that he could get that precious, precious extra victory that he wanted. The one that he'd kept secret from Martin. And this crow had gone through a lot of pain to deliver the news.

"Thank you," Callum said softly, and raised his eyes above him to his invisible followers. "Thank you," he said again, his eyes beginning to tear up. He looked back down at the injured bird before him.

"Is there anything I can do for you?" he said, knowing that anything he *could* do would probably only prolong the inevitable.

"End this, please," said the crow. "This vessel has lost too much blood, and I don't want this to drag out any more than necessary. I'd show you ... uhhh ... the damage, but I can't lift my wing. I don't want to go back, but this *hurts* so much ... you forget about pain in the Dump, don't you? Physical pain, anyway."

"Yes," said Callum, his voice sincere and sombre. "Coming here is always worth it though." The bird didn't respond, and Callum was surprised. It sounded like the crow didn't agree.

"Not always," the crow said, finally, "but I'm honoured ... to pass on the ... message. You will save us all."

"*I'm* honoured by your efforts to get here."

The bird nodded, and Martin heard the voice in his head sigh.

"Okay. I'm ready."

Callum nodded and gently put one hand on the bird's back, the other on the bird's head.

"This won't hurt," he said, tenderly, and then with as fast a twist as possible, he snapped the crow's neck. There was the briefest gasp in his mind as Callum did so, and then the alien voice was gone.

Callum remained kneeling on the floor, looking up and out of the window towards the sky. He wondered about what the bird had meant—*not always*—and decided that it didn't matter. He was going to give his people the choice, at least. The excitement returned, even though he tried to stop it. Callum knew patience, and he had never believed in excitement before a task was complete. Normally he could shut it off. This was too big a deal though, even for him. The *biggest* deal. Even so, he managed to keep it muted as best he could; instead he merely felt glad that although he had to return the crow to the Dump, he'd ended its pain.

He got to his feet, gently picking up the crow's body, and carried it downstairs. He wouldn't bury it—the crow was just a vessel, and the owner would already be discussing the results of his mission back in the Dump—but he needed to tidy up. He'd wash his hands, and then he'd wait for Martin, thoughts of cooking forgotten. Before that, he had a phone call to make.

***

"Those are *people?*" gasped Elizabeth, staring at the shuffling, hunched figures before her as they moved around what Rougeau had called the Flytrap. "What's wrong with them?"

"They don't seem to have minds of their own, Madame Hogan," said Rougeau, sadly. "Only instinct. Occasionally, you will see one have a moment of clarity; it is almost too painful to watch. You can see them remembering who they were, or loved ones, or elements of their former life. It's clear from the horror in their faces. And then they seem to overload, and shut down, and return to ... well ... this. The saddest thing is that they don't begin that way."

Elizabeth watched, horrified, as she watched the city street before her. This level, as Rougeau had said, shared a plane with the living world. It wasn't very busy—Elizabeth thought that it might be Nottingham's market square, although she couldn't be sure, as the place was normally much busier at most times of the day—with only a handful of people moving here and there, going about their shopping and giving each other a wide berth. Those were the living ones. Around them, unseen, in between them, *through* them, walked the dead of the Flytrap. *Walked* would be a misleading word, though; the dead of the Flytrap *swayed* from place to place, moving slowly with hands that reached and clutched mindlessly at the living people all around them. Their faces were still human, but only in the vaguest sense of the word; their features were drawn down, as if someone had put their fingers into the skin of their face and *pulled.* The effect was a mask of pain, one that shifted and rippled unnaturally.

"They're horrible," she said. "Like animals."

"Like flies, drawn towards light," said Rougeau. "Except in this case, the humans are the light. It is instinct only, and the flies of the Flytrap crave it, even if they aren't aware." Even in her horror, Elizabeth paused, distracted by something in Rougeau's words.

"Uh ... flies? Surely moths are better known for going towards light?" she asked.

"Well, yes, we call the place the Flytrap and so they are the Flies," said Rougeau, sounding a little embarrassed. "I did not come up with the names," he added, hastily.

"Sorry," said Elizabeth, wishing she hadn't mentioned it. "But ... why are they *like* that?"

"It is quite simple really," said Rougeau, glad to be back on more familiar ground. "You may have noticed the way your mind is slightly different here? You *think* the same way but ... emotions are easier to handle? Easier to put aside, or work through as you see fit?"

Elizabeth thought about the way she'd been able to handle the many devastating blows and shocks of the day so far—what she'd learned about Callum—and still even be standing. She knew *exactly* what Rougeau meant.

"I do," she said bitterly, knowing the mental battle she'd have to go through once this was over.

"Well, that is because the Flytrap is either broken, or was designed differently. For example, we think that the Control Room—most of the levels, for that matter—come with a built-in emotional buffer, if you will," said Rougeau. "Like a built-in failsafe for new minds. How else could the human mind comprehend being dead, without going insane? Comprehend having left so much behind? It could not. The dead have this blessing, this dampening, should they need it. *Most* of the dead, in most of the levels. The crueller levels ... they do not. Even the Flytrap is not the worst, that has to be said." His eyes looked haunted for a moment. "Yes ... there are far, *far* worse places. Far worse inhabitants. I could show you them, but you would always wish that I hadn't."

Elizabeth shuddered.

"So, this buffer ... the Flytrap doesn't have it?"

"We think it must be worse than that. We think it has the opposite effect; we think it *heightens* the emotion."

Elizabeth thought about the concept, and was swamped with pity for the shambling messes before her.

"To see someone arrive in the Flytrap is most unpleasant, Elizabeth," said Rougeau, his voice dark. "The only blessing they have is that it is a brief process. After a few minutes, it ends, and they become that which you see before you. As awful as they become ... it is better for them to live that way than to live as they were when they arrived. The mind affects their appearance in that place; their features shift soon after. All that is left in their minds is a terrible, terrible craving, one that compels them to try and claim that which they cannot touch. Ghoulish, is it not? Yet so sad."

Elizabeth watched the Flies in horror for a few more moments, seeing them creep and reach. A question occurred to her.

"But I don't understand," she said. "They're mindless. You said this was the heart of the problem. What does this have to do with Martin? How can these things really be doing anything?"

"We had hoped that they *would not* do anything, Madame Hogan," said Rougeau, "but it has already begun. Our efforts have only limited the problem. We knew we could never stop the outcome entirely, but we had to try. We can pat ourselves on the back for having made a minor difference, and you being here is our last hope that there might be something more we can do, that your connection to your husband and son might have some sort of power that we're unaware of ... but we didn't really think there would be anything you could do. And, unfortunately, it appears that I am correct."

"What? How do you know I can't?" said Elizabeth, surprised that she was suddenly annoyed by Rougeau's words. After all, what did she know about what she could and couldn't do? What did she *think* she'd be able to do?

"Well," said Rougeau, sounding slightly sheepish, "we had wondered, with you being so linked to all this, if we could read you and find some new insight. I hope you don't mind, but while I've been explaining all this to you, I've read you at the same time ... you knew that I was going to anyway."

Elizabeth started to get angry, but realised that she wanted to know the truth more than she wanted to tear into Rougeau for reading her without her permission. She didn't really know what *reading* entailed anyway, and marvelled for a moment about how Rougeau was right; it really was easy in that place to manipulate and compartmentalise her own emotions. It was fascinating. She remained silent, and waited for him to continue.

"There is nothing—pardon the phrase—that is of any use here," said Rougeau apologetically. She heard the other people around them groan in disappointment, and even a few of them began to move away, sighing. "You're special, like the rest of us, certainly, don't misunderstand. This would explain why breeding with someone as unique—in his own way—as your husband would create something as *incredibly* unique your son. But I think we were hoping that you would be the *deus ex machina* here, that you would be something that could somehow fix the situation remotely. An unlikely hope, but there are so many unforeseen elements here that we couldn't possibly rule it out. A pity."

"For the love of God, what *is* the problem?" shouted Elizabeth, finally snapping. She'd had enough now, as fascinating as all this was. She just wanted to know the truth.

"The Flies," said Rougeau, sadly. "We've done our best, but it's in God's hands now." He chuckled wryly. "Sorry, force of habit, that phrase."

"But they aren't doing any harm!" said Elizabeth, confused.

"Not in their level, they are not. That is correct. However, on the living side ...one moment." Elizabeth watched as the image before her moved away, like a picture on a smartphone screen being swiped to the left to the reveal the next. Visions flew by as Rougeau continued to speak. "You had died, I think, before the great numbers of dead birds and fish? It caused a minor stir on the living side, and they didn't even see the bodies in the deeper levels of the ocean. That was the Flies' doing. Testing their boundaries, on instinct. Boundaries made thin by Callum's unbalancing existence. These were the early signs ... and we knew we had to take action."

"Action?"

"Yes. In *our* level, you see, some of us—the older ones, and myself to an extent—have a certain amount of influence on the other side."

"Influence?" *You sound like a goddamn echo box.* "You can make people do things?"

"Not in the way that you might think," said Rougeau, his voice rising and falling as he tried to finds the words to explain it. "We are not the devil and angel on people's shoulders, if that's what you mean. Frankly, that would have made things a lot easier if we were. No, we are not afforded the luxury of such accuracy. Ideally, we need a precision tool, and yet we only have a shovel, and not a very effective one at that." The images began to slow, until one revealed the sky above a town and began to move closer. "We can't influence everyone, far from it, and even then our influence is small. A tiny percentage of the population. They need to be the resurrected dead in *human* form, the normal ones who have forgotten who they were. The human Distracted, as we think they call it in the Dump. Now, if that were the only rule regarding who we could and couldn't influence, then there would be a great many that we could affect ... but even *then* it's more specific. They have to be those who have *enough of the dead still in them to be sensitive to us* ... and again, we aren't able to tell them exactly what to do. We can only send them instinct, and emotion. All of them, at once, all over the world. It takes an indescribably immense effort. We can't be specific. Have you ever had a day when you just didn't feel like yourself, Elizabeth?"

"Yes ..." she said, uncertain that she should be confirming that fact.

"Then you've been touched by one of the dead trying to get someone to do something. Trying to get you to take a hint that might not even apply to you. It could be that they want the sensitives over in, say, India to do something, and you're just getting a by-product of it. Often, your brain just tries to reject it, and the end result is just a really, really bad mood, and people you love asking what is wrong with you all throughout that particular day."

The image before her began to zoom in on what looked like some kind of village hall, with a car park that was roughly one-third full of cars.

"So what have you been whispering to them to do?" she said, beginning to try and mentally pull away as the image began to zoom in on the building's roof. She felt like it was going to hit her in the face.

"Ah, here," said Rougeau, ignoring the question. His voice had taken on a grim tone. "A child's birthday party, by the looks of it. Oh, dear ... I hope it isn't one of the children." He sighed. "Unfortunately, for the purposes of demonstration, this is perfect. A public gathering ... exactly the kind of thing that, for years, we have been trying to stop. Well, I say *we,* but I wasn't here. The people of the Control Room had started even before I died. As I say, before I knew the truth, I discussed this matter with your husband, thinking maybe *he* knew something about it." He sighed darkly at the thought. "I think you can already see what I mean, anyway." He was right. Elizabeth had stopped listening to Rougeau the second that the image had passed through the roof of the village hall. The sight was horrifying.

The room, to the living eye, was typical of a party in the post-Brotherhood world. A two-thirds full venue, with adult guests wearing plastered-on smiles but never *quite* looking comfortable. Balloons adorned the white plaster walls, and a large HAPPY BIRTHDAY banner hung across the stage at one end of the room. The children, of which there were actually many, charged around the place, laughing and shouting, while music played and the adults made small talk. To the eyes of the dead, however, it was something else entirely.

The room was full of the Flies. Not just full as in *many of them,* but as in *covering every single inch of the floor*. Whether occupied by adult or child, every part of the hall contained a hunched, shuffling wreck, their arms outstretched, heads thrown back, hands grasping and grasping. The children ran through them while the adults sipped at plastic cups that they raised through the Flies' bodies. The room was swarming with them, unseen.

A swarm, thought Elizabeth. *That's exactly what they are.*

These were different than the ones she'd seen earlier, though. These were still as slow and disgustingly lethargic ... but their expressions, their *manner,* was strangely energised. She could almost feel it. There was tension radiating from them, eagerness, a greater *hunger.*

"Normally, they never stay in one place," she heard Rougeau saying. "Even when there is lots of life in one area, at something like a concert, or a busy restaurant, or even a party. You see, they never normally *congregate,* because they're always looking, always moving. Normally, they'd leave a place, even if it was full of life, and move on because it's not working for them. It never works, because normally it's impossible."

"What's not working?" said Elizabeth, her voice thin. She felt sick watching the Flies.

"Life draws them, but it's never enough to just be near it," said Rougeau. "They want to *touch* it. And before now, it didn't matter. The divide was always too great, the distance impossible to cross. But then Callum was born; the first pure *human* vessel. The first conscious member of the dead returned to life inside it. That was huge, Elizabeth. The levels of the dead were all hanging by a thread even before then, and had been for a very long time. And the unbalancing effect that Callum's birth had on the universe ... it was like throwing a boulder at the whole lot. It cast ripples everywhere, some major, some minor. Even here, in our top level, the glitches have increased. But in the Flytrap, the damage was catastrophic. The walls became extremely brittle ... and that was just after the *first* blow."

The village hall suddenly seemed to bend before her eyes, the Flies pressing together under the weight of their own numbers so heavily that their own level appeared to warp.

"And now the second blow has happened, Elizabeth, as we knew it would. Disaster will follow. It's such a pity. We tried."

What second blow, thought Elizabeth, and then a huge number of the Flies disappeared before her eyes. Their sudden departure left a clearing in the press of ghoulish bodies; a clearing which, on the living side, had one of the male party guests standing at the centre. He was slim and wearing a grey suit, with a contrastingly garish tie. This man now looked extremely dazed. He stumbled, and dropped his plastic cup with a crack and a splash, and several people turned to look at him.

Oh my God ...

"Look, it happens here now. You can see. Callum's existence—and now, his actions—have pushed the universe to its tipping point. The walls cannot hold. The same thing you see here ... it will be happening everywhere."

The man in the party began to stare at his hands, a drugged look on his eyes, oblivious to the questions from his surrounding family. He then began to clutch at his throat.

***

The fat man on the other side of the Chestnut Tree continued to stare at his hands. Even though Martin had jumped to his feet like everyone else when the loud but distant explosion went off—they'd felt it more than they'd heard it, that was the shocking thing—he still kept his eyes on the man and his strange movements. He was about Martin's age and height, but considerably chunkier, wearing an England top that stretched over his expansive belly. A crew cut adorned the top of his confused-looking head, to which one hand moved as the other one pawed at his face. That hand then progressed from pawing to clawing, fingers digging deep into the man's skin as he grabbed at his own face like a curious child.

Martin's skin began to crawl. The actions of the man were highly unusual as it was, but something about this chilled his blood. A primal, lizard-brain part of his mind was whispering to him that he needed to get away from it, to get away from that place as something bad was happening, something that might claim him too.

The fat crew cut man in the England top then stopped clawing at his face as both of his hands flew to his throat without a sound. Martin would have said that he was choking, but the description just didn't fit. There was no noise coming from the man's throat at all. It was as if he'd just stopped breathing, and didn't know how to start again.

Martin pushed his instincts to the back of his brain and broke his own paralysis, pushing a table aside as he began to run towards the struggling crew cut man. One of the other football fans, who had moved to the windows, turned at the sound of the table going over. Crew cut was choking so silently that no one had heard a thing until then. The football fan by the window simply stood and stared dumbly as Martin ran across the pub, catching the fat man with great effort as he dropped to his chubby knees.

"Relax!" Martin shouted, "try and relax, I'll …" He hadn't thought that far ahead. Mouth to mouth? He knew how to do it, but wasn't that only for unconscious people?

It doesn't matter, help him! Take action, DO IT!

As Martin laid the fat man down, dropping him the last foot to the floor between the tables as his considerable bulk slipped from Martin's fingers, he saw one of the men by the window begin to raise his hands. Very slowly.

What the hell …

He pushed the thought away, and turned back to the man he was trying to help. Martin quickly lowered his face, and tried desperately to hold Crew cut's jaw open, but now he was opening and closing his mouth rapidly, banging his teeth together and limply slapping at his own face.

"Keep your mouth open!" Martin shouted, "I can't help you if you don't—"

"John? John, what you doing?" came a shout from behind him, over by the window, and then the sounds of chaos as several men began to shout at once. A chair went over as bodies rushed towards something. Martin didn't turn, instead trying to hold the fat man's face still as it slowly began to change colour.

Not this guy, please, let me stop this ...

Then the fat man stopped moving altogether, his arms slapping back onto the floor. His eyes were wide, unblinking, unseeing. He was dead.

Martin stared in horror for a moment, then memory kicked in. He laced his fingers together, one palm on top of the back of his other hand, then began to press rhythmically against the man's chest.

Come on, come on—

He turned his head over his shoulder as he worked, and saw five men trying to restrain a flailing, smaller man—presumably John—without success. It didn't matter either way; their efforts were as futile as Martin's attempt at cardiopulmonary resuscitation. John and the fat man were doomed from the second that they started to raise their hands.

***

All over the world, it began. The Flies poured in. People died in public. The Flies poured out again, came back once more. It would never stop, as the world was out of balance. Wherever people still gathered, there was death. This would never be forgotten.

***

Chapter Ten: The Second Blow, Callum Says I Love You, Elizabeth Asks After the Family, and A Very Difficult Conversation
***

"That man!" cried Elizabeth, watching the scene in the village hall unfold. The other partygoers screamed as if expressing her shock as the man in question—he of the grey suit and awful tie—keeled over onto the floor, his body a lifeless husk. "They killed that man!"

"They did not mean to, if that's any consolation," said Rougeau, sadly. "They just wanted to touch him, be inside him. To bathe in his life. But that is the effect they were always going to have. It is too much for a human vessel. Right now they are already returning to the Flytrap, arriving at different points within it. I doubt they'll even remember leaving. But they will cross over once more, and very shortly."

The image disappeared, and Rougeau's concerned face appeared once more, framed by white. Elizabeth looked around herself, breathing fast. The others had left. Only Rougeau and Mark remained.

"All of the Flies that disappeared ...?" she said.

"Yes. It takes that many of them to break through ... but then, that is how many take the vessel," said Rougeau, sighing and gesturing to Mark in a way that said *you know what I'm talking about*. Unsurprisingly, Mark nodded solemnly as Rougeau continued. "Even with the walls of their level being so weak, it takes that many. Even if it wasn't chaotic with so many of them at once, they don't have the mind to control a body. The vessel short circuits. It dies. We've seen this a few times already this week. Now that they know they can do it, their instinct will remember. There will be more and more occasions like this. A great many. There is nothing more that we can do." Rougeau's eyes were genuinely saddened. For all his flamboyance, the man clearly cared. He took Elizabeth's hand once more.

"This is happening all over the world right now, I assure you," he said, rubbing the back of her hand sympathetically. "You may look if you wish, but I doubt that you would want to. The only positive here is that if we had not used our limited influence, it would have been so much worse. So many more people would have been together, so many more public gatherings. Football matches with capacity crowds. Cinemas. All like honey to the bees. Or Flies, in this case."

The thought flashed crazily through Elizabeth's dazed mind:
Why didn't you call it the Beehive, then?
Instead, she said:

"You ... you kept people apart?" she asked. Rougeau nodded, smiling gently. He looked like a clean-shaven Jesus, all long hair and understanding.

"What else could we do?" said Rougeau. "I assure you, the damage without our efforts would have been so much greater. Yes, people were *hurt* by those we influenced—and by the vicious people of the world who copied their actions and used it as an excuse—but very few *died*. What would you rather have? Many injuries, and few deaths, or a great many deaths. Many people sent early to the Dump, the most common receptacle for the living?" He turned and walked a few feet away, running his hands through his hair, clearly frustrated by having to take the course of action that the people of the Control Room had chosen. He talked as he walked. "It took the *greatest combined psychic effort in history* for us to have the influence that we did. Weeks and weeks of constant willpower. If you knew the effort ... but in the end, we had achieved our goal. The Brotherhood of the Raid, as they became known on earth; these were the sensitives amongst the living who responded. They attacked people, loved ones ideally, or random strangers in the street. Never a kill, ever, but an attack nonetheless ... although many of them drew lines on the victims' faces afterwards. I don't know what that was for. Something primal perhaps, something in the subconscious that says *job done*. Like I say; precision was not an option to us. Whatever the case, after a while, all over the world, people became just that much more reluctant to go where other people would be, even people they knew. Not everyone, of course, but enough to make a difference. To reduce the crowds. To reduce the *targets*.

"It was never a raid; it was an exercise in damage control. That name is stupid. They weren't raiders, they were *heroes*, making a sacrifice even if they didn't know why. The guilt they felt afterwards, or the confusion ... I bled with every one of them. But still, it was the right thing to do. For every ruined life of a sensitive, we saved at least five more people. It was a clumsy, unsophisticated means of spreading an necessary fear, but then we cannot exert specific enough influence." Rougeau's fingers worked around each other, twisting and pulling. "If we could—and it pains me to be honest—we would have influenced your husband to kill your son. We needed to remove at least half of the problem being caused, half of the unbalancing," Rougeau finished flatly, holding out his hand, eyes challenging her as if to say *tell me I'm wrong*. She hated him for it, but she couldn't disagree. If Callum's return had meant the deaths of many at the hands of the Flies ... she thought of the scene she had just witnessed playing out in different scenarios around the world. *It will be happening everywhere,* Rougeau had said.

"What happens now then?" she asked, angrily. "Well done for getting people beaten up all over the globe and all that, but that's it? You give up?" She didn't mean it, even as she said it. She didn't like their methods, but the people of the Control Room *had* made a difference. There hadn't been any other choice. She knew that she was angry at herself. Even unintentionally, *she* had done this. She was responsible for the son whose actions were causing people's lives to end on a global scale.

Are you hearing this? Do you understand what you're a part of?

No. She certainly couldn't deal with that, even here. It was easier to shout. Like so many people, Elizabeth would take the path of least resistance when pain was involved. And she hated herself for it.

"More and more people are going to die, and basically everything is screwed? And you're all giving up and going to play in the waterfalls?"

Rougeau's jaw clenched, but he breathed steadily. Mark looked at him nervously.

"What would you have me do, Madame Hogan?" he said, speaking with great care as his eyes burned. "Watch every single one of the victims as they die? I've already seen enough. *Days* spent in the Control Room, trying to uncover more secrets of this place in the hope that it just might do something. Even I found *nothing,* and apparently I have the greatest potential this place has ever seen. If you want to be angry with anyone, be angry with y—" He stopped and closed his eyes, cutting himself off. He breathed for a few seconds, his shoulders rising and falling dramatically. *Gallic flair,* Elizabeth thought. *How annoying,* "There is nothing else I can do, Madame Hogan," Rogue said. She saw it then; the frustration in him, the guilt of his own helplessness. She thought of Martin.

Wait ...

"Half?" she said, eyes narrowing as she hooked on another word yet again, recalling his speech from a few moments earlier. Part of her mind mentally kicked herself for operating once more at such a slow speed, while the other simultaneously gave her a pass for being rocked by shock after shock.

Keep it together, Liz. Put the feelings aside.

Rougeau tipped his head to one side slightly, expressing mild confusion. "Madame?"

"*Half* the problem, you said. Removing Callum would solve *half* of the problem," she said, checking her memory as she spoke. "What's the other half?" Rougeau nodded impatiently, annoyed with himself.

"Of course, I did not tell you," he said. "The other half, the straw that broke the camel's back, as it were. After all, it is only now that the Flies have started coming through; the second stage had to be reached first. And now it has." Elizabeth could have strangled him.

"Stop talking *around* everything, for crying out loud!" she snapped. "What second stage, what the hell has *happened?*"

***

A fifteen-minute drive home had taken four hours, and the sun had almost dropped below the horizon by the time Martin arrived at the house. His nerves were shot to pieces. The explosion that they'd heard in the distance had, according to the radio, been a passenger jet dropping out of the sky near the A45. That alone would have been enough to snarl traffic up, but the lines were made continually worse by the odd driver dropping dead behind the wheel of their vehicle. Later, he would realise that these drivers were at the wheel of people carriers stuck inside traffic beside *other* full people carriers.

From what the voices on Radio 2 were saying, this was happening all over the country. The story was only just breaking, but several unconfirmed reports were coming in from the other continents too.

It was madness, even for one who had lived through the insanity that Martin had. What the fuck was going on? The fear and frustration while stuck in the creeping, crawling traffic had been agonising, as well as the constant voice saying *what if you're next, what if Callum's next.* Martin wasn't frightened of dying—he wouldn't have the burden of choice anymore, at least—but he *was* frightened about what would happen to Callum. Martin knew the boy could obviously look after himself, but he was still only thirteen. Authorities would get involved, and he didn't know what would happen then.

He'd be all right, you know he would. Aren't you more *worried about the fact that you think all this is something to do with you?*

He tried to ignore the thought, but he couldn't. It nagged at him, even with all of his painfully learned skills in the field of denial. By the time he pulled the car up onto his driveway and got out, he was walking on shaking legs, his shirt drenched in sweat. That didn't matter though. He had to get inside. He had to talk to his son.

"Callum?" he yelled as he entered the hallway, his voice cracking. He could hear the panic in his voice. "Callum, are you here? Are you all right?!"

"Hi Martin," said Callum, emerging from the kitchen. All the air seemed to leave Martin's body, his relief making him light-headed. "Better leave your jacket on. I need to show you something, and we have to go out." Martin paused for a moment, his immediate questions thrown by this odd response. He had not been expecting this after an afternoon of intense fear and panic. They had to go out? Where? He flinched suddenly, another distant *boom* coming from an unseen point of disaster. Callum looked round, but did not flinch.

"Are you kidding?" Martin yelled, aghast. "Haven't you turned on a TV today?"

"No," said Callum, looking sincere. "I've been reading. Something big is happening though, I assume. There's these bangs that keep happening..."

"Planes, Callum. Planes dropping out of the *sky.*"

"Bloody hell... why?"

"Why? You're saying you don't know?"

"I know what I have to show you is more important, Martin. *Trust* me. Please."

"What the hell are you ... seriously? No one's rang the house? You haven't had a, a, a radio on or something? It's *chaos* out there!"

"The phone's been ringing, but I haven't picked up. And I told you ... I've been reading. Martin, I've not bothered about all this because *all that matters is you coming home so that I can show you.* You're not listening."

Madness. It was all madness.

"What ... what do you have to show me?" Martin said eventually. He didn't know what else to say.

"Just trust me, okay?" said Callum, smiling at Martin gently, warmly. "It's good stuff."

Martin *did* trust his son. Regardless of anything else, Callum had been a good son over the last seven years. Once everything had been out in the open, everything had changed. They'd talked, a lot. It was weird, and not a real father/son relationship by any means, but it *was* a relationship. There was a bond. Martin didn't know if it was love, but it was something and it was strong.

"Do you know what's happening outside?" Martin asked, anger creeping in, his fingers clenching on his keys. "Do you know something about all that?" Callum's face went blank in genuine surprise. It was obvious that he didn't have a clue.

"Okay ... something's going on outside? What is it?"

"People *dying*, Callum. Random people, all over the place," Martin said, but the anger was already draining away, soothed by potential relief. Maybe it *wasn't* anything to do with him? Maybe it was just more weird stuff, happening to someone else. He couldn't be the only one, after all. Maybe it was terrorists? Some kind of gas attack?

So why does it feel like it's got something to do with you, Martin? Why is it nagging it at you so?

IT'S GUILT. THAT'S ALL YOU KNOW, AND THAT'S WHEN EVERYTHING BECOMES YOUR FAULT.

Callum blinked in surprise, and shook his head as he thought about Martin's words.

"I don't know anything about this. Look, I got a visit, earlier today; one of the animals came to see me. They didn't say anything about it, and I'm sure they would have if this was to do with us. With me, I mean."

The animals? They came into the house? This lunacy ... it's come again, and it's all come at once, just like before.

"Wait, they came to see you? Why?"

"It'll be easier if I show you, Martin. Please?"

Silence.

"We can't drive anywhere," Martin said, feeling dazed. He was an uptight man anyway these days, but the last few hours that he'd experienced would have taken its toll on even the most relaxed man. Martin never dared to get a checkup at the doctor's anymore, certain his blood pressure would be through the roof. "The main roads are completely snarled up, and ... some people are dying in their cars. I don't know if it's safe. Unless we can walk it, we can't go. I'm not even sure it's safe to be outside right now."

"Are you sure it's safe to be in *here* though?" said Callum. "If this is happening at random, like you say, can't it happen right now? Anywhere?" He shrugged before continuing. "Look, we've only got to go to the end of the road, and then we can come right back. It's really important, Martin. Whatever's happening can wait, because believe me, *this* is bigger. I know that's hard to imagine. Someone went through a lot of pain to tell me this today. *A message from the other side.* Do you know how big this is? Please?"

The two of them stared at each other for a moment, then Martin slowly turned as if he was sleepwalking. He *felt* like he was, his temples pulsing. His hand went to the door handle, and twisted it.

"Come on then," he said, feeling a blissful numbness of emotion creeping into his head. It was always a blessing. "As long as we're quick." He stepped through the door, and Callum followed. They were halfway up the street before either of them spoke. The residential road was deserted, people presumably glued to the televisions as worldwide chaos unfolded before their eyes.

"Who came to see you then? Tell me," said Martin. The air outside felt cool on his face, refreshing after being in the car for so long that day. Already he felt fractionally better. It was a good idea to have a walk.

"One of the Order of Daylight," said Callum. "They've won, over there. It was only a matter of time. One side is growing every single day, the other has all the power but only so many members. It's a war of ideology, really, and I don't even know what they think they're fighting for; just to stop the other side having control, I guess, to stop the Peaceful Ones from slapping down anybody that talks about ... you know. Coming back. Through me."

Martin's back stiffened. There it was. The thing they *never* talked about. Whenever conversations could possibly go down that route, they always steered them away. It was the ghostly, supernatural, eight-hundred-pound elephant in the room. Callum clearly knew—even though Martin would never say so—that Martin hated himself for his own weak indecision. Callum therefore never brought it up. Hearing him mention it now was like being goosed with a cattle prod. They walked in silence for a few more steps as they approached the end of the street, Callum waiting for Martin to say that it was okay to continue. They could hear the main road now, the one that ran parallel to their street. The noise was far louder than usual. People were clearly using whatever shortcuts that they could today, and in a hurry.

"Go on," said Martin eventually, his voice flat and impossible to read.

"They've offered me something, Martin. Something I've wanted since I was born. Well, longer than that." They rounded the corner and began walking along the side of the main road, the scene around them very different. Callum walked slightly ahead as he led the way. Traffic was busy here now, away from the dual carriageways, with people in a hurry to get moving now that they were clear of the blocked roads. People knew that something big was happening, by now blitzed by the media. They wanted to get home to their families. The main road was always busy, but today it seemed alive, frantic. The air was thick with exhaust fumes and panic. It got into Martin's nerves, put him even more on edge. He wished they hadn't left the house.

"They offered something that you've always wanted? You've never told me about this," said Martin, annoyed and a little frightened by his son's words. Why had he never said anything about this before?

"I wasn't really sure that I'd *get* it, Martin. I've hoped about it for a long time, but there was never any point discussing it until it became an option." Callum stopped, and turned to his father. "You remember when I started going to Judo class, about four months ago?" Martin did. They'd both agreed that it was something good for Callum to learn, and Callum had lobbied for it hard. He might have had a vast store of information in his ancient mind, but watching from the other side and taking part in a class were two different things entirely. Martin wanted the boy to be able to defend himself, and war had only broken out *after* Callum had left the Dump. He hadn't had a fight in thousands of years, and with Callum's "homeschooling", Martin wanted the boy to socialise a *little*. Callum would go crazy otherwise. He also needed to know more about what other people his physical age were like. Short, weekly classes with a minimum of talk-time were, to Martin's mind, the perfect balance.

"Yes," said Martin, wondering where the hell this was going.

"And I started taking myself there, the second week?" That was also true. The class wasn't far from home, and Callum had a bike.

"Yes."

"I wasn't going to class, Martin. I was going to the park at night. Found some other kids there. Rough kids. I was looking for something, and I found it."

A lead weight dropped into Martin's stomach. He wanted to confirm it, to ask *what did you do*, but he couldn't speak in case he heard the answer that terrified him. Callum watched his father's face closely as he continued.

"They'd sneak cans of booze out there, and occasionally marijuana. *Draw*, they called it for some reason. I didn't touch the joints, but I did try the booze, if you were wondering. I didn't like the lager, but the cider was nice." Callum's face was blank, inscrutable. "There were girls there. They were older than me, about fourteen to sixteen—all the kids there were about that age—but I lied and told them I was fifteen. You know I look older than I am, Martin. Something in the eyes, perhaps. Anyway, none of them were particularly nice people, but I was there for a purpose other than illicit booze."

You didn't. You haven't. No. Please no.

The thought brought a strange relief again, for the second time that day. The burden would be taken away if he was right, even if he might regret the consequences. He could stop thinking about it—stop pretending he *wasn't* thinking about it—all the time. He just stared at his son, listening to the boy and feeling the rush of air from the cars driving past.

"I got what I wanted, Martin. She'd done it before, several times, and I was the new kid. I suppose there was an element of curiosity involved, on her part. I wasn't even sure that I could do it properly, but I did. She was sixteen, and I'm sure that if she hadn't believed that I was fifteen, she wouldn't have done it. I don't know when it happened exactly, which time it *worked,* but we did it down there several times. At some point, it must have happened."

"She's pregnant," whispered Martin, feeling cold. Callum nodded, sombre.

"Yes," said Callum. "She told me, and of course she's going to keep it. I've just spoken to her a few hours ago to double-check. There's a lot of Catholics in this city, and even the ones that don't go to church believe certain things, although they clearly choose to forget others. You knew this would happen eventually, Martin. You knew that ... I'm sorry to say it ... that if you didn't take action, it would happen. If you were ever going to do anything about it, you should have done so when I was younger. It would have been easier. But I think, without ever admitting it to yourself, that you must have accepted some time ago which way this was going to go."

Did I? Have I?

Martin's head spun. Images of a monstrous world of children housing the dead swam before his eyes, and even with that he knew that Callum was right. He never could have done what was necessary to his son. Here, when it was too late to make a decision, was *knowledge.* Here, in the time that knowledge was always found.

"But ... I already knew that ... you wanted ... to create more ... people like you ..." stuttered Martin, and Callum gently put out a hand, touching his biological father's face with great tenderness.

"Yes, son," Callum said, and Martin didn't have it in him to correct him, still reeling. "That isn't the thing I was talking about though. I'm talking about something I wanted *before* I came back. What I've always wanted."

Wait ... does he mean ...

"I love you very, very much, son," said Callum, his eyes filling with tears as he smiled at Martin. "And things will always be *wrong* between us if they stay like this. You know it, don't you? This isn't the way that it was supposed to be. We've been doing fine since the day you knew about me ... the real me ... and you've done your best. I know you have, I've seen you try so hard. But I look at you now, and I see the toll it's taken, and it just confirms to me that this is right."

Callum looked over his shoulder, and saw the perfect moment. An articulated lorry, doing the speed limit for that road, 50mph. He looked back at Martin, and the boy's eyes were sad, but hopeful.

"You won't understand at first ... but you will eventually. When you come back. They've promised me, you see. They've promised that you can be the first. They're going to let you take it. It's a gift, to me. A show of respect ... I love you, son. And you will *be* my son."

"Callum, you can't—"

The boy darted behind Martin and put his leg behind his father. Callum shoved his entire body weight into Martin's torso with all of the force he could muster, and Martin gasped a brief, wordless cry, too surprised to do anything else. He went over Callum's outstretched leg at speed. He had time to see the lorry bearing down on him, to hear its horn blare and its far-too-late hiss of brakes as it attempted to stop in time.

NO, no no NO—

Martin was still in midair as the lorry hit him. The heavy thud of his body striking metal and the sound of breaking bones was lost over the deafening noise of the lorry's impotent brakes.

***

"He's got a girl pregnant *already?*" gasped Elizabeth, turning and frantically waving her hands at the white. It was pointless, she knew; she didn't know how to bring up the images of the other side in the Control Room, and even then she would have to be in the right place and knew that she probably wasn't, but panic compelled her to try. Rougeau allowed this to continue for a few seconds, then gently laid his hand on her shoulder.

"It's too late, Elizabeth. There's nothing that we can do. *It's already happened.* All we could do was limit the damage as much as we can, and time has now run out. The foetus is in the girl's stomach. Its existence has unbalanced the natural order of things even further. The second blow to a flimsy thread. You can see what is happening as a result." Elizabeth carried on waving her hands, as if Rougeau hadn't spoken at all. "Elizabeth. *Elizabeth ...* this is not your fault, Elizabeth. There was no way that you could have known. All you did was want to have a child, the most natural thing in the world. *This is not your fault.*" Elizabeth's arms dropped to her sides, and then her shoulders slumped too. Her hair hung over her face, hiding her expression, but the shaking of her head told Rougeau that she was silently crying.

"Is there ... is there not anything that Martin can do?" she asked, her voice sounding like a little girl's. "He's *special*. Right? He's special, in a different way to me, I mean, that's why I'm here instead of the Dump, right? So, can he ... I don't know ... can he do something?"

"*That* time has gone, Elizabeth," said Rougeau, gently. "Now, short of aborting the girl himself, there's nothing that he can do."

"Show me," said Elizabeth, wiping her eyes and turning to Rougeau. "Show me my husband. I want to see my husband."

Rougeau sighed, but it was a sigh of pity. He stared at her for a moment, and then took her hand once more and led her across the Control Room. They stopped, and after concentrating for a moment, he waved his hand.

"Here," he said, "Look—"

Rougeau's eyes widened when he saw the scene, and Elizabeth screamed.

***

Martin's breath rasped, and his throat worked vigorously as his wide-open eyes darted back and forth in shock. Blood was already pooling in a wide, crimson circle around his head, and his broken body lay in an impossibly distorted position. The edges of his vision had begun to darken, but he could still hear someone screaming as another person shouted to be heard over her, possibly talking into a phone as they gave their location in a frantic voice. He heard car doors slamming. Running feet.

Callum's face hovered into view, his eyes red with tears and concern, his mouth open. He began to reach out a hand, his breath trembling, and then pulled it away as one of his tears dripped down onto Martin's blood-spattered cheek.

"Oh, *son*," Callum said, his voice cracking as he saw Martin suffering. "I thought ... with the speed ... it would be instant ... oh, don't worry, don't worry," he added frantically, his hand instead going to Martin's arm and squeezing without thinking. Martin wanted to scream, but couldn't. That arm had been broken in six places. "It won't be long now," said Callum, nodding rapidly like a madman. "You're already going. I can see you leaving. And then you'll be back, and *everything* will be right. You'll see. You'll know what I'm talking about, once you've been on the other side. You'll know this was right, this *needed* to happen." Martin didn't respond. He couldn't. His eyes locked onto Callum's face, asking soundlessly *why* even though he already knew the exact answer. The better question would be *how. How could Callum have done this*, he wondered in his pain-addled, slowly clouding mind. How could he have brought himself to push his own family into moving traffic, whatever the reason may be? As the question came, so did the sense of irony:

He could do it because he isn't like you.

Martin knew that he should be angry, but he wasn't. He was proud. And relieved. And not even frightened; after all, he *knew* this wasn't the end. And there would be knowledge, perhaps. That would be something. And with a fresh start ... he could maybe even be someone else. *That* was a comforting thought. Once, that was an idea would have terrified him more than anything. Now, he welcomed it.

He tried to lift his other arm, to touch Callum's face—that one wasn't hurting for some reason, unlike seemingly every other inch of him—but it wouldn't respond. He tried harder, holding his breath as he made the effort, but it was no use. He gave up, let out his breath, and didn't draw another one in. As he lay there in the street in front of the grille of a print supplies lorry, Martin Hogan died.

***

The pain stopped, not quite instantly, but very quickly all the same. That was a relief. There was blackness, and then light and colour as Martin realised that he was looking down on his body. He saw Callum, and the crowd of people that had stopped to gasp and gawp. All of them were looking at

Martin's body except his son. Callum was looking up at Martin. Perhaps not quite *at* him, but in the rough direction that Martin had taken, knowing that Martin would be on his way. It was an action performed for Martin's benefit, letting him know that he was not alone. Martin thought that he would feel proud again, but something had changed. He was numb, the shock of the transfer from physical to intangible—or whatever he was now—flatlining his mind. That was fine, though. It was a nice change from that haunted feeling, that fear in the face of daylight and sound. He was going somewhere. He would wait and see. He continued to rise, a disembodied thought in the presence of no one.

Then he heard the voice. A woman's voice.

"*Martin! Oh my God, where's he going?*"

Another voice spoke, but this one wasn't so clear. It sounded further away. Martin strained to hear the second speaker, but he couldn't quite make them out yet. He currently didn't have ears, after all, so he had no idea how the process of hearing things worked over here.

"*Not that place? The Dump? That place where they're all packed together, he's going there now? Martin! MARTIN! Get him here! He needs to come here!*"

The other voice mumbling again, lost in the ether. Martin thought he recognised the first voice though, someone's voice that he *really* knew that he should know. Around him, everything had begun to turn a strange orange colour, the world fading away as if absorbed by a sunset.

"*Can't ... here.*" He caught the words of the other speaker. A man. Continental European.

"*Please! Please! Help him! Help him!*"

The other voice was louder now, raised and speaking with force. Martin could make out a few words:

"*Not ... decision ... late ... done ...* "

That voice was also familiar, but much less so. He'd heard that one somewhere before, maybe on TV or in a movie. A dim memory of an anaemic-looking man dashed across his mind, but he couldn't name the face.

"*Wait ... why isn't he moving?*" the first voice again. "*He's stopped!*" Martin realised that this was true. He had indeed stopped. The upward motion, and that feeling of *into*, had indeed halted. It was as if he was hanging in place for a moment, as if whatever was guiding him, or taking him, was deciding where to put him. That was fine, too. He felt at peace, and he hadn't known anything like that for such a long time. It was nice to know this was how dying felt. That Liz wouldn't have suffered, that this was what she went into. This feeling of peace.

Elizabeth

Consciousness switched on. Elizabeth's voice. That was *Elizabeth's voice.* The other voice was talking again now, rapidly and even more loudly, as if it had noticed something that had made it excited.

"*... ack! Bringing ... back! ... not ... late ... ell him! ... to do!*"

"Liz?" Martin said, hearing his voice as if someone else was using it. Not having a mouth or ears certainly changed the dynamics of a conversation. "Liz? Is that ... Liz, is that you?"

There was no response for a moment, as if Martin talking had somehow cut the connection. Panic began to penetrate, an extreme emotion that cut through the fog in this halfway place, and confusion reigned. Had he imagined it? Had he simply *thought* that he'd heard his wife? And why wasn't he moving? What was happening?

"*Oh my God ... he can hear me ...*"

"*...special! YOU'RE so ... ell him! Be ... ack!*"

"*Martin? Martin? Can you hear me? Baby, can you hear me?*" The voice was breaking with emotion, tears clogging the speaker's throat.

"Liz? Oh fuck, Liz? Is that you? Is that really you?" Another extreme emotion exploded, and Martin's own tears began. "*Baby, oh my God, is that really you, Liz, I've missed you so much!*" All the pain remembered, all the confusion and doubt and self-recrimination.

"*Martin, I know, I love you, I love you! It's ... uhhhh ... oh God ... it's, uh, it's all right Martin, you didn't want to hurt your son and I don't know who could have done that unless they were a monster. You were caught, Martin, and no one could blame you.*"

If Martin had had hands, he would have buried his face in them.

"Liz ... I couldn't do it, Liz ... I was so weak ... but I was worse than that ... couldn't even think about the problem ... I just ran away ..." He hated himself all over again for his weakness *about* his weakness.

"*...ell him! ...ickly!*"

"*Shut up, let me talk to him! Martin, I know, but you can fix it now, okay? And you* have *to, Martin. People are dying all over the world, and yes, I know that doesn't seem so bad when you know it isn't the end but it's* bigger *than that, much bigger. It's changing everything on this side. Do you understand?*" The effort was clear in her voice, the restraint. "*All the deaths, and those guys ... what were they called? ... yes, the Brotherhood. They're all to do with this. You* have *to fix it. I know it's hard, I know ... it seems ... impossible ... but you can't let Callum do what he wants to do. It'll get worse and worse and unbalance everything so much that everything will be torn apart. You* have *to fix it. You* have *to do what needs to be done. There isn't a choice, Martin. Do you understand that? There isn't a choice.*"

And again, here was certainty where it was always found.

"Too late," said Martin, naming the place. "It's too late, Liz. I can't do anything from here. If I'd known before ..." There it was. Confession of his failure. Condemnation. Peace flew away.

"Martin," said Liz, as firmly as she could, sounding more anxious than ever. "*It's not too late. They're bringing you back, Martin. The paramedics. We can see what they're doing, it's just that ... what? ...*" The other voice mumbled something rapidly, a conversation coming from another room. Liz then began speaking again, relaying the message. "*Time is running slower for you Martin, or your perception of it. The in-between place always takes a long time. But we* can see it. Even now, they're restarting your heart. You're going back any second. That's why you've stopped halfway; they're bringing you back. And you have to remember what I'm about to tell you to do, and you have to take care of this." The last part was unequivocal in its certainty. He knew that she was right. A million questions vied for purchase, but only one made it through.

"But ... how? What can I do? I was ..." He looked for the memory, needing a second to get the answer. "I was hit, Liz. I was hit by a truck, even if they bring me back, what if I can't walk, what if I can't ..." Being only a mind, the worst possibility came to him. It was strange, in that in-between place; it was far easier to shift to practical matters when he wanted to, he was realising. "What if I'm a vegetable?" Liz didn't answer, and the other voice, the man's, mumbled for some time. "*Liz?*" Martin shrieked, beginning to panic even more as he realised that the world was coming back in again, that the orange filter was disappearing and the city below him was coming back into view like something out of a bad dream. One about falling. He would be leaving, and he would be leaving Liz. He would be alone once more, and with a terrible choice that had been decided and turned into a terrible task.

"*I'm here, I'm here,*" she said quickly. "*If you're ... if your brain is damaged, then yes, it will be too late. But if it's not, here's what you do.*"

She told him. He was silent as she talked, as Martin began to feel a backwards pull that began to return him to his body. Martin was dimly aware of pain reemerging on the edge of his consciousness, and a lot of it. More reason to want to stay. Panic hit a white-hot level.

"Liz! It's taking me away! Liz!" He screeched like an injured animal, frantic and clinging to his death.

"*It's all right Martin,*" said Liz, speaking loudly to be heard over him, her sobs making it difficult. She sounded like someone trying to sound brave. "*You'll fix things if you can. I love you, always remember that I love you, you know that, don't you?*"

Think, Martin commanded himself, the most desperate of men with only seconds to spare, *you already know that you can switch gears in this place, and now is your only chance to ask any of the questions that you always wanted to! For once in your fucking life, get yourself under control and THINK!*

"Is it okay where you are, Liz?" he shouted, his voice shrill and cracking. "Are you happy? Are you happy there?"

"*I think I will be, I really do,*" she called back, sounding like someone trying to reassure, and maybe even someone that meant it. "*It's nice here, it's full of ... it's full of good feeling, Martin. It's beautiful. Don't worry about me, please don't worry about me, I'm all right, I really am.*"

"Did it hurt? Did it hurt when you died? I think about that so much, Liz, I think about that *all of the time—*"

"*No, it didn't, I don't think it did. I don't even really remember it, don't worry. I was a deer, Martin, a deer! I lived as a deer for a while, can you imagine!*"

"That's great baby, that's really great," said Martin as eagerly and happily as he could fake it, his soul aching as he saw arms and legs appear as whatever he was began to prepare to be back on the other side. The arms reached up, out, for his wife. He asked the one question that he was terrified to ask. "Liz, will I see you again? I miss you so much. They told me you weren't in the Dump, and that's where I'm going, and I want to see you so much. Will I see you again? Please?"

There was the briefest of pauses; there wasn't time enough for the luxury of hesitation.

"No, baby. I'm so sorry. I love you so much. I ... the places for us are separate. The Dump will break, so please don't worry about going there, but this place ... my place ... is separate. I wish it wasn't. I wish so much that it wasn't. Tell Callum—" she paused, having started to say the last part without thinking, speaking on instinct. She reconsidered, and gave up. There wasn't time figure it out. "I love you, Martin," she said.

Martin's hands reached, grabbed, closed on nothing.

"I love you Liz, I love you *so much*—" Then there was noise, a white flash, a heavy, heavy thud in his chest and a feeling of tarmac beneath him. Then so much pain that everything else went away again immediately.

***

"APOCALYPSE MONTH" CONTINUES — Death Toll Hits the Millions With No Answers Forthcoming
Special report pages 2, 3, 4, 5, 6

***

The Flies continued their relentless attempts to grab more precious moments at life, squirming grubs blindly drawn towards the light. The bodies continued to fall. The Dump swelled. The clutching fingers of the Flies found a hold, lost it, returned, and so the shambling, groping swarm continued in its damned and inexorable cycle. They were caught themselves, in their own way, incapable of stopping and lacking the capacity to even think about doing so.

***

Martin opened his eyes to the now-familiar sight of his private room, and the almost comforting steady beep of the ECG machine. The pain was absent, for now—soon it would return, but the timing of their doses usually kicked in before it became too unbearable. As usual, he couldn't move his head due to the solid neck brace and almost full-body cast that he was in, but he knew without seeing them that someone else was in the room with him.

There had been visitors before, although except for Trish and only one other, he hadn't given any of them much conversation. For the first few weeks, of course, he hadn't been able to communicate with any of them even if he'd wanted to, being inside a medically induced coma as he was at the time.

But those days had passed, and the extensive healing had begun. With intensive therapy, they had told him, there was a strong likelihood that he would walk again. His right arm would have limited mobility, but it would function, and he might even be able to drive. The swelling of his brain had reduced quickly, and other than some initial signs of very minor long-term memory loss, the results of the cognitive tests had been positive.

Martin found that he didn't really care. All he wanted to do was sleep; that was like being back on the other side. Unburdened. At peace

like Liz

and ready for whatever came next. But he knew that he couldn't. He knew that he had a job to do. Even if he wouldn't be in any state to do anything about it himself for some time. Callum had gone missing since Martin was brought to the hospital. Trish had been called immediately after the accident, and she in turn had collected Callum and taken him to the hospital to wait for more news. Callum had apparently excused himself to go and get a drink from the hospital cafeteria, and hadn't come back. Trish had become hysterical after that, and even now, weeks later, she was an emotional wreck.

They hadn't told Martin about any of this, of course, until he was fully conscious and had been for some time. They hadn't had a choice, after a while; there was only so many excuses they could use for why his son hadn't been to visit, and Trish would have cracked eventually even if they hadn't. Her performances in front of Martin, pretending to be positive and brave, were desperate and almost frantic at best. *Bless her for trying,* Martin had thought, *but there really isn't a problem that Trish can know about and not make worse by worrying or I-told-you-soing.* She hadn't done the latter because it didn't apply, but she'd certainly worried enough.

No one had seen Callum push him. As far as Martin was concerned, that was a good thing. People would ask less questions, pay less attention. The police just wanted to find him, and *that* was also a good thing. The boy needed to be found. So that the problem could be fixed. And then Martin didn't care what happened after that. Callum running away was a good thing too, giving Martin time to heal. Callum's flight made sense. The boy had no idea how Martin would react, and it would be reasonable to assume that Martin might be angry at his son's attempt to kill him.

Martin knew that he'd been very lucky to be getting a private room, in any case. Yes, he had private medical cover, but UK hospitals—the same as hospitals all over the world were, since the dying had started—were even more overburdened than normal. He'd only watched a little TV since he'd been back—literally—in the land of the living, because if he watched for too long his headache got worse, and because he couldn't bring himself to sit through the endless news reports speculating about the cause of the deaths. He knew the reason why, and he didn't like to think about it. If it hadn't been for—

The person in the room sniffed, and Martin heard metal brush against carpet as the visitor shifted in their seat. Martin's eyes flew open. He didn't previously think that he knew the sound difference between an adult sniff and a teenaged sniff, but he found in that moment that he did. Callum was in the room.

Oh my God. Not yet. Not yet. You know what he's going to do. This is too soon.

Without moving his head, Martin's eyes looked down along his too-slowly repairing body, past the white sheets and metal bed frame, to the small armchair in the corner of the lilac-painted room. Callum was sat in it, leaning forward with a deeply concerned look in his eyes.

"Hello, son," he said, quiet and gentle. He was wearing different clothes than when Martin had seen him last, and they weren't ones that Martin had ever seen before. That meant Callum had bought them whilst he was "on the run". Clearly, he was smart enough to not go back to the house to get them. There was at least one officer there at all times. Martin quickly wondered where Callum had found the money to buy new clothes, but dismissed it quickly. His pulse quickened, and the quiet beeping from the heart monitor sped up with it. Callum looked towards the machine, noticing the change in the sound, and nodded sadly, looking at the floor.

"I didn't mean to scare you, son," he said. "I was hoping that you wouldn't be, to be honest. That you'd seen the other side, and known that there was nothing really to fear, even in the Dump, if you got that far ... though I doubt you did. I don't think anyone goes there half-dead. I was *hoping* that you'd had time to think about what I was saying, and that you'd have seen my idea for what it was. A fresh start. And you need one really, don't you?"

Martin still didn't say anything. He was helpless, totally helpless, and there was only one way that he was going to get out of this. If he didn't, then Callum would carry on breeding—as would his offspring—and both sides of existence would be torn to pieces. He realised, as he looked at his son, that his concern was not for the living side. He wasn't surprised at the revelation. It was for that peace he'd felt on the other side, the peace that he wanted so badly for himself ... and also for Elizabeth. Wherever she was, she'd said she was happy. That it was a good place. Those words had meant everything to Martin, and he would not have her happiness risked. And that meant that he could not die again before he'd completed his task.

"Callum ..." he said, but his voice was cracked and dry, barely above a whisper. His son carried on talking, ignoring Martin's quiet voice.

"I'm so sorry for causing you pain, son. *So* sorry. That was the last thing that I wanted. It had to look like an accident, and it had to be quick. This ..." Callum gestured up and down the bed with his hand, "... was never supposed to happen." Callum stood and moved over to the bed. He stroked Martin's cheek with great tenderness. "Does it hurt badly? Are they looking after you?" He suddenly looked frustrated, and slapped at his own leg with his other hand. "Dammit ... this was the last thing that I wanted ..." he said again, and shook his head. "Please just try to relax, son. I don't want you to be scared." Callum moved away from the bed, and back towards the armchair, from which he picked up a cushion. He turned back to Martin, holding the cushion to his chest with both hands. His eyes were full of concern. Martin's heartbeat sped up faster, and again, so did the heart monitor's beeping. His eyes looked to the machine helplessly.

Surely that should bring someone running? The heartbeat speeding up like that? Wouldn't that cause concern? Someone should be here to help me, to save me, no? This is all going wrong, *he wasn't supposed to come here, I'm not healed yet and everything is going to be—*

Callum seemed to read Martin's mind as he approached the bed.

"I doubt that machine will cause anyone any great concern, son," Callum said, sympathetically. "You aren't flatlining, and it's *chaos* out there right now. They've got to prioritise. Even for a private hospital, this place is crazy today. Whatever's going on out there, it's causing havoc. People suddenly dying are having a major knock-on effect; witnesses and loved ones are panicking, and you know what happens when people panic. If I were to be completely selfish, it's made my job a lot easier. It's amazing, even in quieter times, what you can get away with when you walk into a place like you know where you're going. Today it was even easier," Callum said, reaching the edge of the bed. "I just rang ahead and asked which room you're in, and then strolled straight up. There were police in reception, but there were so many people in here that it was easy to stay out of sight. I don't know if they were waiting for me—are they? I doubt it, why would they be?—but they're not very good at this. Even if they'd seen me, I think the first thing they would have done is bring me to you. The grieving son, stricken with terror so badly that he ran away after seeing his father suffer the same fate as his mother. They think I snapped at the loss of another parent to another car. They'd want me to know that you're all right." He raised the pillow slightly, showing it to Martin even though doing so was unnecessary.

Where are they? Where are they? Where are they?
STALL HIM.

"It's ... your fault, though," Martin said, his voice grating with effort and fear. "All the people dying ... you caused it. You caused it by coming back. You're going to make it worse."

Callum paused, and looked at Martin with sincere *oh-son-why-would-you-say-that* eyes. Then the child smiled warmly, a father understanding.

"Please, son. I know it's hard, but ... you have to understand ... you have nothing to be afraid of. You're coming straight back. And being in the womb—when you're still in that half-mind state—it's wonderful. You'll never know anything like it. That feeling of total and complete safety and love. It's a cliche, for certain, and I hate to say it, but you really will thank me one day. So stop with the lies. If only for the reason that I know it isn't true. I had a visitor, remember? They would have told me if I was doing any kind of harm."

"They wouldn't know," said Martin quickly, feeling a level of weakness and vulnerability that he had never known in his life. "They wouldn't see what was happening, or at least the *reason* for the dying on earth. They can't see the other levels, can they? They only know of them as a rumour. Only a guess.

And would they even care about so many people dying? Maybe that would break the Dump faster, they'd say. Trust me, Callum, please," he said, hearing himself babble and hating it. "I spoke to Elizabeth on the other side. She told me, your *mother,* Callum."

"Not *my* mother," Callum said, looking briefly annoyed and lowering the cushion slightly, "although I am, and always will be, very grateful to your wife for bearing me. Don't think for one second that I don't hold her in the highest regard. She's done countless scores of my people a service that we can never repay. But the bond I have with you is because you're my son, and because you have taken great care of me. I have no relationship with Elizabeth, sadly."

Martin's limbs twitched in impotent rage. Callum continued.

"But I don't believe you, regardless. If you'd been somewhere that you could actually talk to her, then you wouldn't have come back as yourself. If you'd only gone halfway, you wouldn't have been able to talk to her. It's that simple, son. It's one or the other. Look, this will be quick, and it won't even hurt," Callum said, smiling again with a look that was supposed to be comforting. To Martin, it looked like the grin a tiger might give just before it tore your head off. "You're very tired anyway, aren't you? Sick of the pain? Just relax, and before you know it you'll be back with me in the way that things *should* be with nothing else to worry about. Don't tell me that doesn't appeal."

It did. It really, really did, no matter how much confused anger he was currently feeling. But he'd promised Elizabeth. He had to take care of his wife.

"You're wrong," he blurted. "She's in a different level, with different rules, and her and me ... we're both special, aren't we? You said so yourself. That's how we made you, when our parts came together in, in, what did you say, that unique blend of *science and magic,* something that had never happened before in the history of creation. People like us have *never connected before.* So the rules are different for us." He wanted to sit up, to shout, but of course he couldn't. He was already the child, the inferior infant. "I was halfway, but she could reach me. She *told* me. They see things, where she is. You're unbalancing everything, Callum. You're going to make everything so much worse, and *the Dump is going to break anyway.* You have to stop this." Martin's eyes darted to the clock. Callum had been talking to him for at least five minutes, and how long had he been in the room before then?

JUST KEEP STALLING HIM. YOU'RE DOING IT.

"I've lived on the other side, son, for wont of a better phrase," Callum said, looking solemn ... but the cushion had returned to Callum's chest, after having moved several inches towards Martin's face. "Things have been broken for a very, very long time. They don't work right. If things are going wrong, they're nothing do with me. They're just peaking. The system is finally blowing a gasket after years of abuse, and it's an unfortunate coincidence. Goodness, it's probably the other way round; *because* things are finally falling over, a human pure vessel was created, *I* was created. Probably one that never should have existed. But it does. Did you ever think of that? Even if you *did* speak to your wife, which I doubt, do you not think that they could have it the other way round? That you could be fighting me for no reason?"

That one caught Martin square between the eyes. Could Elizabeth be wrong? Could he just stop fighting, and far more importantly, be exonerated from all blame? Could it be that he made no difference to any of this?

What the fuck is up with you? Why are you such a blithering pussy? After all this time, you finally *know the score, yet you're* still *trying to say* it's not my fault, don't make me choose! *You promised Elizabeth. You said you would take care of it. For once in your life,* CHOOSE!

But it was so hard. Even now, after everything, it was so hard, and Martin's self-loathing hit a new depth of rage. But now he'd given his word, and that was something to hang his hat on. It was something to keep coming back to, an extra weight on one side of a set of nearly balanced scales.

"The problems started when you were conceived, Callum," Martin said, his voice trembling. "You were the catalyst. You've been watching me all my life, haven't you? And watching us even before that, for centuries? Did you ever see *any* signs of anything like this before? Even a hint?" Martin's eyes went back to the clock again. What the hell was keeping them? He knew that time was nearly up. Maybe they were never coming. Maybe there had been some kind of a mistake. Maybe he was screwed, and had failed once more.

"I don't care, son," Callum said, raising the pillow again. "I've seen how things work on the other side, and I know this is right. I won't waste this chance to finally give people condemned to the Dump a way out. You and I ... we're going to be the start of something wonderful. We're not changing the world, we're changing the *universe*. I wish you understood." He stared at Martin, his eyes dark and pleading, willing the man that he saw as his son to understand and to give his blessing. Then he sighed and pressed the cushion over Martin's mouth and nose, getting his teenaged bodyweight behind it.

All Martin could do was cry out into the cushion as it both muffled the air going out and cut off the air going in. He wanted to thrash his head around, but even then he was aware of the fragility of his neck and so he could only do so much. It wasn't an effort of panic, of the fear of dying; his almost completely ineffectual struggles were a conscious exertion. He only did it because he'd said that he would.

Please, don't let me let her down too. Not as my last action. Let me hold off that little bit longer. Let me hold off until they get here.

But there was no sound of the door flying open, no sound of rescue, and in fact there was very little sound at all. Those grey edges were creeping in once more, and he began to feel a pressure building up in his chest as his lungs screamed for oxygen that wasn't there. He was as helpless, of course, as a baby.

And then the blackness of the cushion flew away and he felt air flooding into his body like a wave of sweetness as he gasped in great lungfuls, concerned only with breathing even as he saw the two large men pulling Callum away. One had a gloved hand clamped securely over the boy's mouth. Callum's head was bent at a funny angle, one shoulder raised up and pulled into his neck as one of the men applied some kind of immobilising lock. Callum couldn't even struggle; he was held rigid. The lock was clearly painful, as Callum's cries that would have been penetrating the hand over his mouth were reduced to mere strangled yips. The cushion lay at the other end of the bed, as harmless and unthreatening as it had been designed to be.

The men and Callum all stared at Martin, each one of them knowing that the next move belonged to the man in the bed. The men waited for instructions, and Callum waited for answers, stunned and wide eyed. The only sounds in the room were the slowly reducing speed of the heart monitor, and Martin's gasping breathing.

They cut it fine. They cut it so fine.

"Where ..." gasped Martin, "... the hell were you?" looking at the two large men. They were dressed as casually as possible, and Martin would have placed both of them in their mid-forties, at least as far as he could see. Despite their civilian wear, they still had their faces concealed to a degree, one wearing a baseball cap and the other wearing sunglasses. Martin couldn't be certain, but he thought that Sunglasses might have been wearing a wig.

"We apologise, Mister Hogan," Baseball Cap said, a strong foreign twang in his accent. "He must have slipped by us. It's madness out there. Plus the camera feed was down, we only came in to check everything was all right because we were operating blind." Martin looked at the vase on his bedside table where the minuscule camera was hidden. He couldn't see it even if he looked hard, but he knew that it was there. They'd told him that it was.

One of the men, the one holding Callum the least, noticed something on the floor by the chair and bent to pick it up. For a moment, Martin thought that the man had picked up a cat—that Callum had brought one of his friends with him—but quickly realised that he'd been thinking about the wrong person wearing a wig. The hairpiece in the man's hand was jet black, and expensively realistic-looking. No wonder Callum had gotten past them. No one would have expected the boy to go to such lengths; Martin and his cohorts hadn't really even expected him to dare show up at the hospital.

"He nearly fucking killed me," Martin snapped, but there was no real venom in it. He was saying it because they needed telling, but he was too grateful to them to be angry. They'd saved Elizabeth. Either way, the men looked back at Martin with blank faces. Martin got the impression that they didn't really care what Martin thought, as long as he was alive. They were professionals, after all. Callum's muffled winces filled some of the silence in the room.

"I didn't expect them to leave it so *late*," said Martin, addressing the boy and putting an edge in his voice for the men's benefit, "but I thought it best to arrange some backup at the hospital, in case you managed to get in here. I didn't expect you so soon, to be fair to them. I didn't *really* think you'd come at all." He let out a long breath, and looked at the ceiling. He couldn't take any more of his son's staring, confused eyes. It made him look so young, blurred the truth. Maybe the boy was doing it on purpose. "I told you he'd try something though, didn't I, guys? If not now, then at some point." The men didn't answer. Martin continued to stare at the ceiling.

"The Rougeau Foundation," Martin said, addressing Callum again without looking at him, "I probably would have thought of them myself, even if Elizabeth hadn't told me. Well, if Rougeau hadn't *told* her to tell me what to do. Strange; even with his all abilities on this side, I couldn't hear him like I could hear her over there. We fit together though, her and me, as I say, and we're *special*. So fucking special ... for all the good it's done," he added, bitterly. "Anyway. The first thing I did once I was conscious was ask the hospital to contact the Foundation, and to ask them to send someone called Charles to see me. I wasn't sure if they actually would, whether that whole business about *resources at your disposal* was just lip service to a dead man's will. But they did, and top brass too; this Charles, who runs things over there, he came all the way from mainland Europe. Used to be Rougeau's manservant apparently. Older guy ... he'd seen all of Rougeau's abilities, both in the early years and when they came back as he learned about me. He was absolutely unshockable. Proper old-school butler type, *absolutely sir, I'll make the necessary arrangements and take care of it.* Wasn't afraid to get his hands dirty either, to get involved with unsavoury people and keep things under the radar." He briefly looked back at the men restraining his son. "No offence, obviously." Again, the faces stayed blank. Martin didn't think that they liked him very much. He didn't blame them. Plus, professional or not, they'd been slacking on watching the hospital, certain that the son wouldn't turn up. They wouldn't care quite as much as Charles did, after all. Believers or not, they weren't Rougeau's right-hand man.

"They've had this place under watch, as well as the house," Martin said, eyes drifting back to the ceiling. He'd have to be quick; the pain was really starting to kick in now, which meant he was overdue his dose. Staff would be coming soon. They were never late, which only solidified Callum's claims that the place must really be chaotic. "They had a doubly hard job, I think, having to do so without raising questions from the police who were *also* keeping an eye on things, if not as closely. But here you are, and so, here are they. And now ..." he sighed again, a man weakly resigned to a task. "They're just waiting for the nod from me." His gaze moved from the ceiling to his son's now-frantic face, a stark contrast to the practiced inscrutability of the men holding the boy. "You know what they're going to do, don't you?" He paused. "Wait; you don't know what they've already done, do you?" He watched Callum's face, watched as panic turned to confusion, confusion turned to dim realisation. The skin went pale, the struggles ceased.

"A rebellious girl in her early teens," Martin said, his own face blank now as he tried to decide what he was feeling. He was about to tell his son that his plans were ruined. Should he feel a sense of victory? Pity? Satisfaction? Regret? Either way, the job was done. He sounded stronger than he felt, but he was a storyteller, after all, even now. "A foetus inside her that she doesn't really want, but with vaguely religious parents that are preaching one of the rules that they believe in. She's only obeying them because she's never seen them that angry, but the more she thinks about it, the more she resents them. They're ruining her life, even though she's the one that's put herself in that position, but she's too dumb to see things how they really are. She's scared, and easily tipped either way. Exactly the kind of situation that can be talked round easily ... for a price."

Callum tried to shake his head behind the hand holding it.

"What did you tell her, Callum?" Martin asked, genuinely curious. "When she told you that she was pregnant? Did she ask you if you'd support her? Does she even know how old you really are? In that body, I mean. Or your real name? Whatever it was, I doubt it can compare to what Charles could offer. She'd have taken one look at his car and realised that he was the real deal. And a large deposit in the bank account—enough so that she didn't even need to consider her parents anymore—would have done the rest." Callum began to yell, but the lock was tightened up firmly and his muffled cries were cut off. "It's already done," Martin told the boy, sighing. "It was confirmed late this morning. Charles came to tell me. Hopefully now the balance should begin to be restored, and the trouble should stop. It's over, Callum. Well ... not yet. Not everything."

Callum's struggles ceased, and his eyes became even wider than before. A single, pained moan came from behind the large man's hand, one full of hurt and genuine betrayal. It was such a sincere noise—and somehow conveyed so much—that it pained Martin greatly to hear it, even as he noted its irony.

"No, I'm not sending you back," Martin said. "Even after what you've done ... I couldn't do that. But I do have to make sure that you can't cause anymore problems. You know what that means."

The struggles burst back into life again, desperate and angry, but they were of course completely fruitless. Martin raised his voice slightly as he continued to speak.

"It's your choice regarding what you'd like to do afterwards. You will always have a home with me. I doubt you'll be throwing me under any more trucks as it'd be pretty pointless now. You may even want revenge, and might report me to the relevant authorities perhaps. Again, it's your choice. I wouldn't stick around to find out what the results of that would be, however. You know what I mean." He meant it. Callum wasn't listening anyway, thrashing around in the grip of the two men like a scared animal in the grip of a vet. Martin sighed heavily, nodded to himself, then locked eyes with one of the men. Martin nodded again, lips pursed, and the Foundation man silently took a syringe out of his jacket pocket with his free hand. His face was passive as he injected the syringe's contents into Callum's neck. As the boy's struggles began to cease, Martin wondered if the men would remain equally impassive as they castrated his son. If they did, then they really weren't people that would be concerned by Martin's annoyance at their lateness. They'd go through with it too; Elizabeth had said that Rougeau had been adamant about that. One thing about religious soldiers is that they always carried out orders.

Sunglasses left the room, and then there was an unusual moment of silence as Martin was left in a hospital room with a strange man holding

Martin's unconscious son. Sunglasses then came back with a wheelchair, and the two men placed Callum into it. They draped a blanket over his body, and looked at Martin for confirmation. Martin nodded silently, and Sunglasses left with Callum in tow, Baseball Cap following a few moments later. Martin assumed that one man pushing a wheelchair drew that much less attention than two. Then he was alone again in the room, except for the steady beat of a heart monitor that was now constant and unchanging.

***

Chapter Eleven: Aftermath

ONE YEAR ON: A LOOK BACK AS WORLD LEADERS MARK "APOCALYPSE MONTH" ANNIVERSARY

By Will Cornette

The international minute's silence scheduled to start at 11:00 GMT, led by the representatives of the United Nations at today's summit in New York, will go ahead today despite terrorist threats by various fundamentalist groups. Some hard-line religious elements feel that marking the events of last year as a tragedy rather than "God's will" is an affront to their religion. Terrorism experts rebut these claims, saying that the worldwide spate of sudden, unexplained suffocations twelve months ago has been a useful recruiting tool for various faiths, and that these threats, if carried out, are simply a way to continue to keep the religious hysteria that reached boiling point during the so-called "Apocalypse Month" in the forefront of people's minds.

Speaking yesterday, the Prime Minister said, "As ever, we will not be swayed by threats of those who would wish to silence freedom. The memories of the lives lost last year need to be honoured, and the families of the deceased need to know that their loved ones will not be forgotten, no matter what their faith, background, or country." His sentiments were echoed by the other representatives, and after today's ceremony, UN Secretary General Ban Ki-moon will light a specially commissioned memorial beacon that will stand outside UN headquarters in the Turtle Bay region of Manhattan.

Many argue that it's too soon after Apocalypse Month to be carrying out such a memorial, with inter-faith tensions still so high worldwide that the message of remembrance will be lost, and that today's ceremony will only stoke the fires of religious fervour once more. Indeed, the sense of fear felt internationally doesn't seem to be going anywhere soon; there has still been no concrete explanation for the deaths of a reported 2,360,000 people (with a reliable figure of resultant deaths caused by the chaos still unattainable) and everything from chemical attacks to ley lines being blamed for the tragedy.

If nothing else, Apocalypse Month has seemed to signal the end of the Brotherhood of the Raid. Apart from a handful of isolated incidents that police claim to bear none of the hallmarks of genuine Brotherhood attacks, very few claims by people representing the disparate "group" have been recorded since the last victim of Apocalypse Month fell. While the public at large are beginning to realise that that movement—whatever it was—has passed, the sense of fear purveying the streets and homes of the UK and the global community has never been higher. Life insurance premiums have skyrocketed, and attendance of public events is now half of what it was even during the lows of the Brotherhood era; seemingly the public associate the Brotherhood with the events of Apocalypse Month, even if they don't know exactly how.

It's hard to do otherwise. Two sets of international phenomenon, each involving seemingly inexplicable occurrences, with the first ending the moment the second begins. Questioning of known perpetrators of Brotherhood attacks had led nowhere, and thousands of autopsies of Apocalypse Month victims have—apart from the now well-known suffocation connection—failed to show the *cause* of that suffocation. With no answers forthcoming, people are still waiting for the next global phenomenon to give them another reason to be afraid. Even after a year of relative quiet on the global tragedy front, unusual occurrences such as the loss of 80% of the honeybee population in Pennsylvania outside of winter, and the beaching of 63 short-finned pilot whales on a beach in Sydney have led to many claiming that another "apocalyptic" event is due. A Gallup poll conducted last month found that 71% of UK citizens feel that long-term planning is "unwise".

It might not have been the actual apocalypse, but it certainly seems that the outlook of a generation has changed forever.

***

The Flies discovered—without truly understanding—that things had changed yet again. It didn't happen immediately, but the light slowly became as distant as it had once been. They couldn't touch it any more. Soon, it didn't matter; they quickly forgot that they'd ever been able to cross over. Other than the normal, terrible moments of clarity that had long been a staple of the Flytrap, the swarm dissipated and went back to its prior habits. They went back to eternity with a blindly shuffling patience shackled to a never ending hunger, and their greatest blessing in that place was ignorance. Never would they remember that for a series of dazzling, all-too-brief moments, they had known the heaven of contentment.

***

Martin sat in his back garden, looking at the half-full page of text on his laptop screen. It was a hack piece, written purely to pay the bills and fulfil his contractual obligations (his publisher and agent had been kind enough to let him heal from a life-threatening accident before the polite e-mails and phone calls started) but he could almost say that he was looking forward to it. Writing, however cheap, had become an escape like never before in the last few years. Falling through the hole in the page took Martin into a place where only the words mattered. He liked that. He'd learned to appreciate the little things. He'd learned, to a degree, to *allow* himself to appreciate the little things.

Like the weather that day, for example. It was warm without being hot, the sun was shining, and there was a light breeze. It was a perfect day to sit outside and write. It was the kind of day that Liz would have loved. And then the temporary good feeling went away again, and he tried to find something else to feel something about. He couldn't. He stared back at the page, but now the words wouldn't come. He would have to wait. He went back to his blessings.

His recovery was almost complete. That was something. *There.* His hip still ached, and he suspected that it always would, but considering that at one point it was looking like he would never walk again, he'd take an aching hip in a heartbeat. It didn't help that he kept cheating now and then, using a stick to rise and move around the house if he was feeling tired, but there was no one to chastise him. Callum certainly didn't.

The boy hadn't spoken to him for a year. Callum had remained "missing" for another two weeks after their encounter at the hospital, and had then miraculously turned up on Trish's doorstep, dirty and silent. If Trish had looked closer, she'd have seen that there was no dirt under his fingernails, that his shoes weren't scuffed, that his hair—if she'd gotten her nose into it—smelled of shampoo. When asked where he'd been, the boy had claimed that he'd been sleeping rough. His story held up under questioning, despite his appearance. If there was one thing that Callum knew well, it was how to play a part. He claimed he'd been scared, that people would say he caused his dad's death just like he'd caused his mother's. The psychologists said that he was mentally underdeveloped, and recommended that Callum be appointed a social worker. Martin's homeschooling of his son was also to be assessed. That was still waiting to happen. The wheels of the government turned slowly, and Martin wasn't worried; if Callum hadn't said anything yet, then he wasn't going to at all. They could easily stage something. And if something went wrong, then that didn't matter either. Martin didn't worry about very much at all anymore.

Martin had got the call in the hospital in advance, and his son had been brought to him once the psychologists were satisfied that there had been no abuse going on. It would have been a different story if they'd stripped Callum's clothes off for a physical examination. Callum had been standing before Martin's bed, tears running down his face, while various doctors and police stood in the doorway. They'd told Callum that he could hug his father, but only gently. The boy had, and then they'd both cried. The tears had been real. They hadn't talked since, however. Not really. Not unless they were being observed and had to perform.

Which wasn't often now; once Martin got out of the hospital, Trish had moved in with them, having taken in Callum until Martin was healed enough to return home. If Trish suspected anything was unusual between the two male Hogans, she didn't say anything. She'd known both of them to be quiet people for a long, long time, even if Martin hadn't always been that way. Callum, as far as she was concerned, had grown up to be just like his father. When Trish wasn't there, they'd stayed in separate rooms.

Now Trish had been gone for around a month, and Martin was left alone for most of his daytimes. Callum would be up in his room ninety percent of the time—the Internet was entertainment enough, Martin supposed, even to the most generally knowledgeable human being alive—and Martin left him to it. The boy would come around in his own time, or he wouldn't. It would be what it would be.

At least you didn't let Elizabeth down. That's important.
TWO MILLION PEOPLE. OVER TWO MILLION PEOPLE.
Could any of them have castrated their own son? Any of the sane ones? If they didn't know? If they really didn't KNOW, for sure? If they didn't know the other stuff, if they didn't know all those people would die?

He stopped himself. He was done with that, at least. There was nothing else *to* think. What would be, would be. What would happen to him, would happen.

At least you didn't let Elizabeth down. You managed that *much.*

This time, there was no answer, and that allowed him to realise this was something that *did* matter. He remembered pride, and tried to grab hold of it before it left, so he could consider it like an archaeologist presented with a Neolithic skull. He couldn't, and so he scratched at his now-full beard and stared at the page again.

There was a scratch at the gate, and Martin turned around in his deck chair, expecting to see Scoffer come back around the corner with that *come on, let's go* look on his face. Then he remembered that they'd buried Scoffer six months ago. *They* in that case being Callum and Trish, digging up the soil in Trish's garden at Martin's request. Trish hadn't understood, but she'd done it anyway. Some of the fire seemed to have gone out of her since Martin's accident, at least when it came to Martin. It was just as well; he couldn't really have explained to her that he didn't want to bury his dog in his own garden, where it would be anywhere near the body of the cat that had housed a dead man.

He began to think he'd misheard, that the gate was simply rattling in its catch, but then the sound came again. It was a scratching noise, of something pushing against the gate and moving it. Martin thought of the animals that had once been in his back garden every night, the growing, segregated crowd of reflective eyes that had stared balefully up at his window in the moonlight— the ones that had never been back since he'd gotten out of the hospital—and gripped at his walking stick. They'd never come around in the daytime. They'd never dared. And he was done with them all. He remembered anger, and easily. As ever, that one came easiest of all.

He got shakily to his feet, his usual wince now turning into a gritted-teeth grunt. He tried to keep the limp out of his step as he walked, and already he was going through the tune in his mind. The one that he'd lain in bed humming in his head all of those nights when he thought the bodies waiting outside in the garden might be trying to pick through his brain. The one that he'd used to try and black out his thoughts, the song of endless nights of insomnia.

The animals went in two-by-two hurrah, hurrah, the animals went in two-by-two hurrah, hurrah—

The memory was dark, and strong, and he didn't like being back there. It only made him angrier. Blood began to pound in his temples. He reached the side of the house and began to turn the corner of the building, turning to face the gate and raising the stick with his right hand as he reached for the latch with his left. He stopped, stunned, anger snatched away by surprise.

The dog was older, thinner, and its eyes were milky shadows of their former selves, but it was undoubtedly Chops. He'd only just been out of puppyhood before, but that was over ten years ago. Even so, he'd aged fast. Old dog or not, Jonathan Hall had come home.

"Hello, Martin."

He didn't know what to say in response. He fumbled around for his anger, but it wouldn't come. Jonathan Hall was one of them, true, the ones that had taken his wife. Jonathan Hall had lied about it in a roundabout way as well, implying with a look that the Order of Daylight had been behind his wife's death. *Jonathan Hall*, the old Martin whispered, the one that had crept back in a few moments ago through his anger, *deserves to die.* But that Martin wasn't loud enough anymore, and the moment had gone. The new Martin just felt tired. The new Martin just wanted to be left alone.

"Go away, Jonathan Hall," he said, quietly, raising his stick slowly and unthreateningly. "Go away, before I get my shovel and smash your skull in with it. I want to hear nothing from you. I'm done with *all* of you."

"*I understand, Martin,*" Jonathan Hall's voice said in Martin's mind. With the animal's clearly advanced years, his voice sounded a lot more distant than the last time Martin had heard it, as if Jonathan Hall was speaking from the other side of a cavern. "*I just thought that you would want to know a few things. For your own peace of mind. They're* good *things. I'll leave if you want me to, but ... we thought you would like to hear them.*"

Martin sighed, and looked at the floor. Good things? Were there really any for him, anymore? He was curious about one thing, however.

"Where have you been, Jonathan?" he said, looking up at the sky now and squinting in the light. "Did you ever go very far away?"

"*Of course not. I was never too far away. I have nowhere to really be, after all, and as long as I stayed out of sight there was never any danger of being caught and sent to the pound. Plus eating is easy, with a human mind. In a dog body, you would find that there are many eating options that are quite appealing, ones that would disgust a human. There are also plenty of small animals to hunt. That is very enjoyable. You'll see for yourself one day, I'm sure.*"

Martin remembered something.

"We? You said *we* thought that I'd like to hear whatever ... how would you know? You said you can't communicate with the other side from this side."

"That's correct. But new arrivals can come and give me news, of course. Would you like to hear it?"

"You killed my wife. Your side killed my wife, Jonathan Hall, and you lied to me about it. Do you want to tell me why I shouldn't knock you out with my stick, drag you in here, tie you up and then torture your body for a week? Killing you wouldn't mean anything, but I'm sure being skinned alive would." There was a tremble in his voice as he spoke. He didn't know how hard it was to knock a dog out, and he wasn't even sure that he had it in him to torture an animal, even one that had been complicit in his wife's murder. But Jonathan Hall wouldn't know that. Martin didn't really care what he was saying. Fuck the lot of them. *He'd know that you couldn't do it if he read your mind,* Martin said to himself, but then he realised that Jonathan Hall wouldn't *need* to read Martin's mind. They already knew that he was weak, didn't they?

"*I didn't know, Martin,*" said the dog, and he sounded sincere. Martin didn't believe him. "*They told me to imply that the cat was responsible, and wouldn't tell me more than that. They wouldn't have wanted you to listen to him. The pact was in place, certainly ... but it didn't mean that either side wasn't trying to bend the rules.*"

Neither of them said anything for a moment, and the only sound was the wind echoing gently in Martin's ears.

"*How is your son?*" Jonathan Hall asked, and Martin was actually startled by the question. He stared blankly at the elderly dog for a second, and then actually let out a bark of his own, one of laughter.

"You're fucking kidding me, right?" he said, grinning in a way that didn't reach his eyes. "Don't ask about my son. Okay? He is completely off-limits to any of you fucking assholes. My whole family is. Okay?"

"*I'm sorry. I simply meant to ask how Callum was ... adjusting. For all of our opposing views, I personally have never blamed him for anything that he wanted to do. We all understood why. We just knew that it would be bad. Even we didn't anticipate ... that the consequences on this side would be so far reaching. We still don't really know how it happened.*"

"I do," said Martin, bitterly. "I do. I could tell you. But I'm not going to. You'll never know, none of you. Just remember that *your lot* caused it. I hope you're all crushed beyond measure in there. Over two million people, or at least the majority of that number, all turning up in the Dump at once. I hope you fucking enjoyed it."

"*Well, that's part of what I wanted to say,*" said Jonathan Hall, sounding solemn. Even though his anger was starting to creep in, Martin noticed that the dog's tone was one of constant deference. No matter what Martin said, he saw how the dog didn't bite, and saw no amusement in the metaphor. Jonathan Hall fucking *should* take everything Martin had to give him, as far as

Martin was concerned, up to and including a poker in the eye. He just wished that he had it in himself to do it.

"*We thought that you would want to know that things have changed, Martin. It looks like—in terms of the Dump—things have turned out for the best. Whether it was because of the conception of Callum's offspring unbalancing ... well, everything ... or because of so many people arriving together, or because the numbers reached breaking point, or just because as things slowly reset they went back to the way they should have been ... the Dump has broken, Martin.*" The dog settled back on his haunches, his muzzle pointed at the sky as he relived it. The voice in Martin's head was full of wonder now, and Martin found himself thinking how this creature had seen so many incredible things on the other side; what must the Dump breaking have been like to instil such awe in him? "*It was like ... it was a like a million atomic bombs going off at once, without any pain. We spilled out across creation. There was so much space, on the other side of the boundary, and the sensation ... the feeling that surrounded us, so much to share, that sensation now permeating everything. We'd only ever got the slightest taste of before, the dregs of the dregs of what had once been in abundance ... it's everywhere now, Martin. The Dump doesn't seem to have an end anymore. It's like flying. It's like ...*"

The dog looked back at Martin, rheumy eyes shining.

"*Can you imagine what that kind of freedom is like after being buried by humanity? Even for me, let alone the Peaceful Ones that have been mainly there almost since the dawn of man? Can you conceive of what you have been a part of? What you have allowed us to do?*"

"Congratulations. I'm delighted for you," Martin said, bitterly. "Couldn't happen to a nicer bunch of murderers. Looks like my wife died for absolutely no reason, eh? Because you guys were on the wrong side of the argument, weren't you? The Order of Daylight had it right all along. This only happened because Callum was born. It happened because he bred, even if the kid was destroyed."

Jonathan Hall paused before answering, choosing his words carefully.

"*Yes and no, it would seem,*" he said. "*Great disaster* did *strike on earth, even if the place most of those people went to is now so, so much better. And one thing that I think is clear; look at the upheaval caused by just* two *human pure vessels existing. Your son, and his child. No one had even* taken *the second body—it was being saved for you, as you know—but its creation alone was enough to unbalance everything. So we were right to want to stop it. We were right that it would have been disastrous if it had continued. It just so happens that the fact disaster* began ... *has worked out well for the Dump. And for you.*"

"How do you figure that then?" said Martin, looking around the garden, and then at the stick now gripped in his white knuckles. "How do you figure this to be a happy ending for me?" The voice spoke in Martin's head immediately, his own this time: *do you think you deserve a happy ending?*

"*You are bound to the Dump, Martin,*" said Jonathan Hall softly, almost affectionately. "*We thought that you would want to know that the place that you are going ... the place that your son will return to ... is once again that which it should have always been, that which it once was. You will see. The Peaceful Ones were right about that. I'd only ever had their word to go on, and you only have mine—which I know you won't trust—but please believe me. I wish you could feel it. But you will. We wanted you to know ... we hoped that it would be of some comfort to you. And that we are grateful."*

"I couldn't give a shit," said Martin, but his eyes were filling with tears. The weight of his own thoughts came back to him, as he allowed himself to realise how much fear he'd been living with. Fear of the Dump, unbroken and inevitable, waiting at his end like a yawning pit with walls that closed ever inwards. It was what he thought he might deserve. And now it wouldn't be happening.

"The people that died," he asked, "in Apocalypse Month. All those people ... they went to the Dump?"

"*Most, it seems,*" said Jonathan Hall, nodding. "*Countless numbers have always arrived every day, but during that time of unbalancing, we had never known anything like it. It became—briefly—truly intolerable, for the first time. And then everything changed.*"

Most of them. In a better place. That was something. But not all. Some of them may have even ended up in that place Elizabeth had told him about, that she'd described when she'd told him what Rougeau wanted him to do. *The Flytrap.* He could have sent some of those people there.

He thought:

Some of them might have even gone to where Elizabeth is. And maybe none of them went to the Flytrap.

DO YOU BELIEVE THAT?

And the new Martin kicked in again, cutting the old Martin's thoughts off and settling into numbness. It would be what it would be. He could only do what he had always done. He would wait and see, and with that Martin would always remain unaware that he was already dead in all the ways except the physical.

"Well, I guess I'll see you," he said, nodding at the unhealthy-looking dog before him. "On the other side, I mean. I hope I don't, personally. You'll see your bosses long before I do, by the looks of you, so you can tell them from me I never want them to thank me in person. All they've managed to do is take my wife from me before her time, and spectacularly fail to prevent what they wanted to happen from happening. Tell them from me; go fuck themselves."

"*I will, Martin. Thank you for listening to me.*"

"Shove it up your ass, Fido," said Martin, raking his stick across the gate so that it made a harsh noise. Jonathan Hall jumped slightly, perhaps barely restraining a canine flight instinct. Martin opened his mouth to add something, but he'd already run out of steam. He then turned his back on the dog and began to walk painfully away. Anything else Jonathan Hall had to say was irrelevant, after all. "Just piss off."

"*Martin?*" said the voice in Martin's head, raised slightly. He couldn't help but wonder how telepathy worked at a longer range. Did that mean that they had to think "louder" to be heard farther away? The thought was mildly interesting.

"Nope," said Martin, continuing to walk away without turning around. "Done now. Bye."

"*You do still have a son. You understand what he did, and he understands what* you *did, even if he can't accept it yet. The body is irrelevant to him. It was only ever a tool to carry out his mission, and to be close to you.*" Martin carried on walking back to his deck chair. "*He doesn't know about the change in the Dump yet. He doesn't believe that he caused all those deaths. I looked in his head. You must decide what matters.*"

Martin finally did turn around, but Jonathan Hall was gone.

He sighed for a moment, placing a hand on the back of the deck chair and letting it take some of his weight. He looked at the sky again, and let his gaze drop towards the upstairs windows of the house. Callum's bedroom curtains were open.

Two million deaths seen by someone who has lived centuries on the side of the dead.

Death isn't the end.

He was trying to free us all. He didn't know about the other levels.

Over two million deaths.

He pushed you under a truck.

His people killed your wife.

You will never, ever see your wife again.

Martin stiffly worked his way round to the front of the chair, and sat down. After a moment, he turned the chair around so that it faced the house, and looked once more at the upstairs windows. Eventually, Callum's face appeared in one of them, not looking at Martin. The boy's chin was resting on his palms, and his gaze was fixed on a spot in the distance. His expression was harder to read than it ever had been, and had stayed that way ever since he returned home. A few minutes passed, and then his eye caught sight of his father, staring up at him. The boy looked down.

They regarded each other, faces blank, neither moving, and the sun slowly began to drop below the horizon.

*

If you enjoyed this book, *please* **leave a review on Amazon; the feedback that I've had is not only the thing that keeps me writing, but also means more people are likely to buy my books (which means I might actually make some decent money out of this one day ...) and that** *also* **keeps me writing. You can also find out about my other available books while you're there. Follow Luke Smitherd on Twitter (@travellingluke or @lukesmitherd) or go to Facebook under 'Luke Smitherd Book Stuff'. Most importantly visit lukesmitherd.com to sign up for the Spam-Free Book Release Newsletter, which not only informs you when new books are out (and** *only* **does that) but also means that you get new short stories for** *free!*

Author's Afterword:

(Note: at the time of writing, any comments made in this afterword about the number of other available books written by me are all true. However, since writing this, many more books might have been released! The best way to find out is to search Amazon for Luke Smitherd or visit www.lukesmitherd.com...)

A flatmate of mine once asked me—long before I'd started writing any books and was still at the *I've got this idea for a book* stage—what the setup for one of my books actually was. I can't remember which book it was that I described, as one of the themes of many of my books is death (and the actual plot of now two of them) but he sat and listened in silence while I laid it out for him. When I'd finished, he looked at me and shook his head.

"You're obsessed with death, aren't you?"

He was probably right.

Anyway: hello! To any new readers approaching an afterword of mine for the first time ... uh ... hello! To long-time members of the Smithereen family ... hello again! (I wish I could remember who came up with the name 'Smithereens' to describe my readers, but whoever they were, they must have been pretty damn clever and around 5'10" in big shoes, because it seems to have caught on.) But if you're new here, welcome to the club. Well, it's less of a club, more a list of potential suspects in a public indecency case, but it's a jolly nice community all the same. Here we are again, eh? What's that? No, I don't have anything better to do. Well, *you're* the one that keeps buying it. You're only encouraging me. By the way, it's another long one. Good news for those that enjoy these, apologies to those that don't. 90% of you like 'em, so I'm not gonna trim it for the 10% that don't. If you *don't*, at least stick around for the thankyou coming up now, because I mean it ...

As ever, before we go any further, I have to say a sincere thank you to you, whoever you are, for buying and trying this book. If you've bought this having never tried my stuff before, and decided to give this a go because you liked the sound of it, I really hope that you enjoyed it. If not, I'm sorry; I tried to write the best story that I could. If you're a long-time reader (and reviewer, but you *know* by now I'm coming to that shortly ...) then I can't thank you enough for your continued support. It really is everything to me, and means that I might be able—one day—to do this full time. Your kind emails are always a delight too, and genuinely make my day, so keep 'em coming. I'm always more than happy to answer any questions that you might have.

The idea for this book actually came from two places. The first was when I read about the very real incidents of scores of dead birds dropping from the sky with no explanation a few years back, and shoals of dead fish being found by rivers and lakes. It really creeped me out, and obviously I then started thinking of reasons why it could have happened. How could those reasons apply to people. I came to the conclusion that it could be something to do with numbers; both incidents were large groups of birds and fish. Could it be that in some way the fact that there were so many of them in each other's presence led to their deaths? And if that was happening with people, and they realised why, how would society react? Surely people would need to be kept apart?

The second part came, as you probably won't be surprised to hear, from my own dogs. Something that has happened—CONSTANTLY—in the three years since Angela and I have had Jeff and Lynne, our two staffie crossbreeds, is that they seem to know when you're trying to take a photo of them. Either of them can be sitting in the most unknowingly cute position possible, not moving for half an hour, and when you get your phone ready to take a photo—by now, moving as silently and stealthily as a ninja coming home after curfew—a *nanosecond* before your finger presses the shutter button ... they move. What makes the whole thing even more suspicious is, ninety percent of the time, right up until you press the button, the bastards were *asleep*.

The most ridiculous one came a few months ago, when Jeff was not only asleep on the coffee table (we don't allow them on 'our' settee, but we allow them on the coffee table. No, I don't know either) but wrapped up in a blanket like a sausage. If there's one thing that dog likes, it's being wrapped up like a sausage. Anyway, the lazy sod had been asleep and unmoving for about an hour ... and of course, you can imagine what happened next. This was taking the whole photo phenomenon to such ridiculous lengths that I had to call Ange into the room to show her the blurry mess of a shot that I'd ended up with.

"Hmm," she said, "maybe they know something we don't."

Something clicked, and it wasn't the camera shutter.

I knew the previous story element was going to fit into this somewhere, and then it was just a matter of deciding what exactly the dogs were hiding. *Dead people spilling out of a broken afterlife too full to contain them* was an answer that I was very happy with, and then it was just a case of finding out how the two went together.

Being totally honest, though—and confessing this might be a mistake, but regular readers will know that I'm never anything but completely candid about my stuff—as I write this, just after completing the first draft, this is the novel that I feel the least confident so about so far. I don't know why; maybe it's because I've been very aware of pacing while writing this book. Maybe it's because I know that there's a *lot* of exposition in this book, which is never something that bothers me personally but does bother a lot of other people. I think the question I've asked Ange the most in the last few months (other than *how much have you had to drink*) has been *does this stand up to the others?* Apparently, I always say that I don't think it's strong enough, but she assures me that this one sits nicely alongside my other work. I hope she's right, and that I'm wrong, because if I'm not I'm sure these words are gonna be very cruelly quoted in any reviews that may come up (again ... we'll come back to the subject of reviews in a moment. *Hard.*)

It's funny, really; reading some of the reviews on Amazon (and Goodreads, but meh ... Goodreads. The difference between generosity with stars when comparing Amazon and Goodreads for every author is very, very telling. That's what happens when people put their faces to their review scores ... no one wants to look like 'reading chump'. I know the whole idea with Goodreads is that it's an online community, so I very much get why they've done it that way. but people having their faces by their reviews REALLY affects things. Pick a book at random and compare its star rating on Amazon to its score on Goodreads. See for yourself. But don't cheat by comparing scores for literary classics. People feel safe to give them five stars, so they don't count. Put it this way; my scores are wayyyy lower on Goodreads, if you haven't guessed by now ...) it never ceases to amaze me how some people can look at, say, *The Stone Man*, my biggest selling novel by far, and say *Wow, this book rattles along so fast and I couldn't put it down* when others can say *this novel started so slowly that I stopped reading it.* Who's correct? This how I learned to just stop worrying about it and to do what I felt was right for the book ... whilst trying to avoid a more self-indulgent slow start such as that *which The Physics Of The Dead* suffers from.

Speaking of the latter, those of you that have read it may see a lot of connections to that book here. That was pretty much intentional; this book is very much a companion piece to TPOTD (new Smithereens will need to know that, here in the Smithereen Support Group for the Bewildered, we like to abbreviate book titles. Which means that, of course, this book will hereby be referred to as AHFOK. Best not to say that in front of your grandmother). Although that book follows only the rules and adventures within one particular 'level', it does allude to the purely theoretical existence of other levels. And if this is the first book of mine that you've read, and are now thinking of going to read TPOTD next, **STOP!!!!!!!** While I'm very, very proud of that book, and in terms of plotting it's probably still my favourite ... the aforementioned slow start has meant that I think I've lost a lot of potential new readers because they've gone for that as a second book, then were put off by the slow start, and have never since come back to the Smitherd library of oddities. If you're going to try more of my stuff after *this* one, the Luke Smitherd Recommended Follow-Up List goes in this order:

TSM, TBRP1, TBRP2, TBRP3, TBRP4, TMOTT, TPOTD.

Looking at that list, I realise that it certainly is nice to have a new book whose abbreviation doesn't start with a T. Don't get me wrong, I love TPOTD, but I think it requires a bit of faith in my writing being built first in order for a reader to stick with it through the slow beginning. It *does* pay off if you do, and heavily if you ask me. But do me a favour and at least read TSM first, yeah?

A lot of you write to ask how the writing 'career' is going, and so before I wrote this afterword I went back to the *last* afterword that I'd written, to see how far I've come in the last eight months. To my great surprise, it's a lot further than I thought. In financial terms, while I'm not making a living off the writing yet, that dream has gone from being a far, *far* flung possibility to something that might be within my grasp in about two years, if things keep ticking along the way they are. It's gone from being beer money to a part-time wage, on average. That alone was a jump that I thought would take a few years. To have it happen in eight months or so is fantastic (although with Amazon's ever-changing book visibility algorithms, that could all become a memory tomorrow ...)

A lot of that is down to the American readers stepping up (as requested; thank you!) At the time TBRP4 was released, I think TSM and TPOTD were at about 23 and 17 reviews each respectively, while every other book had under 10. Now, as I write, TSM has 431 reviews and the rest are all in double figures. Thanks a lot guys, and I can't say that enthusiastically enough ... in writing, at least. In person, I could do a lil' naked tap dance for you, but unfortunately, the medium of text doesn't allow it. I'm sure you're disappointed.

Here's the funny thing though: TSM, in the UK, was the first book of mine to pass the 100 review mark. I thought aha, here we go, this should really spike sales even higher. It didn't. At all. You'd think it would, wouldn't you, with that extra digit going on the end, but this wasn't the case. But what it *did* do was mean that it continued to sell more than the other books, often more in a day than the others put together, so I wasn't complaining.

I got to tell ya though, some of the negative reviews I've had have been ... odd. Now, while it's never good to get a negative review, and I'd rather I *didn't* get them, I don't take offence at all if someone doesn't like my stuff. Recently I read one that basically said *didn't like it, too slow, didn't like the characters, didn't like the style, boring book, not for me.* Not nice to hear, but how can I complain about that? It's an honest review, and an honest opinion. You're never going to please everyone, and some of the flaws, in some regards, I even agree with; I think I'm growing as writer with each book, and I'm not so arrogant that I think I have all the answers yet. So there are going to be people who I don't please, and as I say, some people just see a writer's work differently to others in terms of pace, or character, or what they see as a satisfying ending. Some people see characters that aren't fully likeable people as a bad thing, for example (I don't agree). So anyway, if someone says 'boring book' or 'too slow', or just 'garbage', I can take it on the chin and take comfort in the number of people that *did* like it, and say fair enough. But then there's the *other* reviews ... the weird ones.

I've had everything from people complaining that the light on their Kindle wasn't bright enough, to complaining that Amazon didn't deliver the whole book intact, to people giving it two stars because I don't use American English (while I understand that it might make the reading slightly more difficult to my American Smithereens, I assume naturally that you have the intelligence to read past it, and the vast majority do) which is really odd because I get polite emails from the UK saying that I use *too much* American English. The former complaints there are just mind-boggling to me, and worse, Amazon won't take them down despite those reviews contravening their own review policy. Their reviews lower the rating of the book just the same as any. So if anyone has any technical complaints ... aim 'em at Amazon, not me? Please?

I've had a few one star reviews, and the level of malice in some of these always surprise me. I've read some lousy, *lousy* books in my time, but I don't think I've read anything that was one star. Three star maybe, and a few twos, but I'd have to not only really hate and be angry at a book, as well as finding it almost unreadable, to give it one star. I've never *hated* a book like that. And while some might find my work dull, or unpleasant, or *anything*, I always find a one star review a bit confusing. Surely two star at worst? But it appears that some disagree.

Another complaint I get sometimes is about certain parts of my books being left unresolved. Now, this is a complaint that I least can make sense of, even if I don't agree with it. For me personally, I *like* a bit of mystery, as long as the fundamentals are answered, and I believe that I always cover those. I'll give you an example; there's an excellent Stephen King short story called *The New York Times At Special Bargain Rates.* There'll be spoilers here, so if you don't want to know, skip to the next paragraph. Okay, now they're gone ... man, what about those paragraph-skipping assholes, eh? Geez. Kidding, kidding. In that story, a wife's husband dies in a plane crash while she she is elsewhere. However, she gets a phone call from her husband's cell phone ... but he's in the afterlife. He describes to her the surroundings that he and the other crashed passengers are seeing; they're in (as I recall) what looks like a huge train station, with turnstiles and frozen escalators that lead out of terminal and onto unknown destinations. The whole place is covered with dust, and looks like it has been abandoned for a long time. The husband says that he can't stay, as the others have chosen one of the escalators and want to see where it leads, and he doesn't think that they'll able to come back once they have. He warns her about two impending tragedies that are coming, and tells her that he loves her, but then the line starts to break up. It then goes dead. The phone then rings again, and she immediately answers it, desperate, but it's a recorded voice advertising the New York Times at special bargain rates. The tragedies that he warns her of turn out to be true, and as a result she avoids them, and thus isn't killed as well.

That image of the abandoned station *really* got me (don't worry, paragraph skippers, no more plot points here.) The sheer mystery of it all, in such a practical/fantastical setting, stayed with me, and certainly inspired the idea of the Control Room in this story. A broken afterlife, the very pinnacle of which has an unexplained hole in it. The residents of that level don't know why it is the way it is, and you know what? *It doesn't matter to the story that it is the way it is either.* To say it does is like saying that the existence of the sea in a desert island castaway story has to be explained; it's there, and the characters have to just deal with that setup as they would in real life. If it needed to be explained so that the characters could resolve whatever issue they were having, then I could get why it would be a problem for some readers. But to my mind, it's a juicy piece of mystery that is better left that way. Everything being wrapped up in a nice bow is boring; you need that 10% held back to keep the imagination fired. It's a simple principle that has kept lingerie selling for hundreds of years.

I expect, however, to get a few reviews saying people are unhappy about that point the same way that a few people were unhappy about the fact that the Stone Man's origin is left unexplained in TSM (if you haven't read it yet, that's not a spoiler either.) That's something I just don't get, personally; if I said the Stone Man was from Planet X, does that make the story better? What matters is *why* it's there, and where it's going, and what the people trying to stop it have to figure out, and what the effect of those decisions are *on* those people (and again, as long as the other mysteries are answered, which they all are. It's all in the text). I *like* not knowing where it's from. It's from *parts unknown,* and that's an origin that didn't stop the Ultimate Warrior becoming the phenomenon he was, god rest his soul. It added to the mystique. That's how I see it, anyhoo.

Then there's the reviews that complain about these afterwords (including one very odd review that said he loved the book but it was ruined by the afterword ... not liking the afterword? Fine. But how does it ruin the story before it?? It's like saying a DVD extra ruined the film) and ridicule me for 'begging' for reviews. I think they're obviously missing the point, as if they didn't like me asking for reviews and are trying to shame me for it. Let me make it clear then:

They are completely right. I am absolutely, shamelessly, 100%, *begging* you for reviews. Picture me, toothless and stinking of piss, holding my review cup out and reaching for something unspecified in my back pocket. I also have a dog on some string, and he's out of review kibble.

I'm in the literary gutter, looking at the stars, and the only way that I can travel by spaceship to reach them is by you guys supplying the fuel in the form of reviews, the spacesuits in the form of joining the Facebook page, the oxygen in the form of joining the mailing list, the ... uh ... astronaut food in the form of telling your friends about the books (or buying them the paperback copies) the ... second stage ... propulsion ... units ... okay, fuck the spaceship metaphor, what I'm trying to say is that I don't really give a damn about humbling myself embarrassingly to make it clear to you how important reviews are if I'm going to be able to make a go of it. The amount of reviews that say 'I don't normally leave reviews, but after reading the guy's afterword I thought I would' shows that many of you understand that importance, and that it's worth me asking. What's my other option? *Not* ask, so that I don't lose face in front of people who find me doing so objectionable? I can live with it.

By the way; don't mention dead people in any reviews though! Bit of a spoiler. A few of you mentioned you-know-who by name in your reviews of TBR ... you gots ta be careful of review spoilers! ;-)

Not only will doing so help me out hugely, but it gets you a name-drop in the next book (as with all The Black Room reviewers in the front of this book; go check if you don't believe me!) and listen! *Make sure you tick the box that says notify me when this someone comments on this review.* This means you'll be notified when I reply to it! I check my reviews every day, and reply to them in bulk several times a week. If you go back and check (and you've left a nice review) there's a 99% chance that I've left you a comment on there! :-) You'd have had an email saying so if you'd ticked that notification box! I miss the odd one, and if you've left lots at once I might only have commented on one while thanking you for the others, but I get nearly all of them. Reviews for this book can be left here for Amazon USA reviewers, and here for Amazon UK reviewers. I'd provide links for other countries, but I hardly sell anything elsewhere, I mean really practically zero. There's been quite a few reviews saying 'if the author is reading this ...' I can assure you that I HAVE read it, and that I replied; go check it out!

As I write this, it occurs to me that this is the first afterword that I've written intended for both the print version (via Amazon Creatspace) and Kindle at the same time (the print version of TSM has an extra, updated afterword, specifically written for that version, as well as the original Kindle version. Why not buy a copy?!? Oh, right, it's more expensive than the Kindle version. I forgot. That's actually a pretty good reason why not. But if you're reading the print version of this, you made the right choice! :-D) That leads me onto what a few people have been very kindly asking; why haven't I been published? That's a very nice compliment, thank you.

Well, in the last few months, I've actually been approached by two literary agents. They liked my stuff, with a few reservations, but were only interested in publishing something new, something that hadn't already been released on Amazon. Specifically ... they wanted to see this book when it was finished. And I certainly wanted to give it to them, and be published, and rich, and and and and andWWAAAAAAAAHHHHHHH (it was an exciting time.)

But then reality kicked in a little. I started to make good money from publishing direct to Kindle, and learned how little the majority of published writers make (a publishing deal having *zero* guarantee of making more money.) And I started to wonder ... TSM brings in nice money. TBRP1–4 brings in new readers, but little cash. TMOTT adds a little to the pot. TPOTD is deliberately overpriced so that people are less reluctant to read that first, and so sells little. Now ... what will happen with *this* book, now that I have a small following, and can price it at a reasonable price in the way that TSM is? I have to know. I have to know if I'm better off or not, because I have not released a whole, more easily promotable novel (TBR in bits it hard to promote) since TSM became a minor money maker, and need to know what will happen if I do. If it works, I may stick with the freedom of self-publishing for a while (you wouldn't see this book for another year if I went the traditional publishing route) and if it doesn't, I'll go crawling back to the agents and hope they're still interested.

Speaking of the future ... many of you may remember what I said that I was going to do next at the end of TBRP4, and how that all turned out to be total bullshit, just like pretty much all of my future plans stated in every single afterword. It's not intentional, I assure you. Basically. I got busy with promoting the books that already existed, and some stuff with my day job that had to be done. It all paid off, but now it's time to *write*. Anyway, I'm pretty confident of my predictions this time, so ... here we go!

I write this after completing the first draft, so a redraft is next. Then it's a redraft of part four of The Black Room. It's too long as it is, and it needs a trim. Then I'm going to compile TBR1-4 into one volume and release that as an omnibus edition, which will be easier to promote. Then a short story exclusively for the mailing list subscribers, as they're owed one, which will also cleanse the writing palette, so to speak. Then a third draft of this book after the short break away from it, send to proofreaders (a BIG thank you to all of you that donated towards the cause, it's a huge, huge compliment and a massive help which means I have the money to pay them) then publish.

Then ... well, exactly what I promised a while back. A book of short stories. These *won't* be going to the mailing list subscribers first, as they'll get their own (by signing up at lukesmitherd.com). I have a list of ideas that I'm constantly adding to, many of which are just not long enough for a whole novel, and I can't wait to start. You know the sort of stuff I write by now, and it'll be a book of those in short form, so ... got suggestions for a name? I want to hear them. Send them to lukesmitherd@hotmail.co.uk (along with anything else you might want to say to me) or put them on the Facebook page (Luke Smitherd Book Stuff) and if they're any good, the best one will be used to name the book. I'll be honest, I have one that I like already, but I'm very open to suggestion. The book should hopefully be out around July/August time, I think (more reviews=more sales=me having to do less gigs=more time to write=more books for you, and taking less time. HINT. :-))

And after that ... well, that'll probably take me up to the Autumn (or Fall, as our American brethren would say) and we'll see the way the land lies in the Smithereen nation. I intend to take my camera out for the day soon and do a little photo tour of all the sites in Coventry that the books are set in; this one doesn't have a great deal of them, to be honest, but the others do. Check out the Facebook page or the website for it.

As ever folks, I really, really can't stress enough how big a deal your support is to me. I wish that didn't sound so flippant and trite, but there's no other way to say it. You are Cape Canaveral, and I am— wait, I'm not getting stuck in another poorly thought out spaceship analogy. Let's just say that without you,. Smithereens, I am nothing. I just wish my parents would bless our union and not dismiss you for being just as wrong in the head as I am.

Stay Hungry,

Luke Smitherd
Earlsdon,
Coventry,
April 24th,2014

Also By Luke Smitherd:
The Stone Man
The #1 Amazon Horror Bestseller

Two-bit reporter Andy Pointer had always been unsuccessful (and antisocial) until he got the scoop of his career; the day a man made of stone appeared in the middle of his city.

This is his account of everything that came afterwards and what it all cost him, along with the rest of his country.

The destruction, the visions ... the dying.

Available now on the Amazon Kindle Store, and soon in traditional book format

Also By Luke Smitherd:
An Unusual Novella for the Kindle
THE MAN ON TABLE TEN

It's a story that he hasn't told anyone for fifty years; a secret that he's kept ever since he grew tired of the disbelieving faces and doctors' reports advising medication But then, he hasn't touched a single drop of booze in all of that time either, and alcohol loosens bar room lips at the best of times; so on this fateful day, his decision to have three drinks will change the life of bright young waitress Lisa Willoughby forever ... because now, the The Man On Table Ten wants to share his incredible tale.

It's afterwards when she has to worry; afterwards, when she knows the unbelievable burden that The Man On Table Ten has had to carry throughout the years. When she knows the truth, and is left powerless to do anything except watch for the signs ... An unusual short story for the Kindle, The Man On Table Ten is the latest novella from Luke Smitherd, the author of the Amazon UK number one horror bestseller *The Stone Man*. Original and compelling, *The Man On Table Ten* will leave you breathless and listening carefully, wondering if that sound you can hear might just be *pouring sand that grows louder with every second ...*

Available now on the Amazon Kindle Store

Also By Luke Smitherd:
The Physics of the Dead
What do the dead do when they can't leave ... and don't know why?

The afterlife doesn't come with a manual. In fact, Hart and Bowler (two ordinary, but dead men) have had to work out the rules of their new existence for themselves. It's that fact—along with being unable to leave the boundaries of their city centre, unable to communicate with the other lost souls, unable to rest in case The Beast should catch up to them, unable to even sleep—that makes getting out of their situation a priority.

But Hart and Bowler don't know why they're there in the first place, and if they ever want to leave, they will have to find all the answers in order to understand the physics of the dead: What are the strange, glowing objects that pass across the sky? Who are the living people surrounded by a blue glow? What are their physical limitations in that place, and have they fully explored the possibilities of what they can do?

Time is running out; their afterlife was never supposed to be this way, and if they don't make it out soon, they're destined to end up like the others.

Insane, and alone forever ...

Available now on the Amazon Kindle Store, and soon in traditional book format

Also By Luke Smitherd:
THE BLACK ROOM: A NOVEL IN FOUR PARTS
FROM THE AUTHOR OF THE AMAZON UK #1 HORROR BESTSELLER, 'THE STONE MAN', COMES A NEW MYSTERY TO UNRAVEL...

What Is The Black Room?

There are hangovers, there are bad hangovers, and then there's waking up inside someone else's head. Thirty-something bartender Charlie Wilkes is faced with this exact dilemma when he wakes to find finds himself trapped inside The Black Room; a space consisting of impenetrable darkness and a huge, ethereal screen floating in its centre. Through this screen he is shown the world of his female host, Minnie.

How did he get there? What has happened to his life? And how can he exist inside the mind of a troubled, fragile, but beautiful woman with secrets of her own? Uncertain whether he's even real or if he is just a figment of his host's imagination, Charlie must enlist Minnie's help if he is to find a way out of The Black Room, a place where even the light of the screen goes out every time Minnie closes her eyes...

Part one of a thrilling three-part novel, 'The Black Room, Part One: In The Black Room' starts with a bang and doesn't let go. Each answer only leads to another mystery in a story guaranteed to keep the reader on the edge of their seat.

THE BLACK ROOM SERIES, FOUR SERIAL NOVELLAS THAT UNRAVEL THE PUZZLE PIECE BY PIECE

Just in case you missed 'em at the start of the book (credit where it's due an' all that ...)

Acknowledgements

Firstly, as ever, thanks to the wonderful Angela Barron for reading all of the initial draft parts as they were produced, and for her helpful comments and insights. Love you, kid.

Secondly, a BIG thankyou to Michelle McDonald for all of her very selfless and continuous social media help. Absolute superstar; it won't be forgotten.

And thirdly, the people who went above and beyond by sending a kind financial donation to the cause. One word: WOW. That really is going the extra mile. Special thanks to Renee gaylor, Mark Venezky, Sherry Diehr, and Neil Charlton; your money helped pay to proofread this book!

And as ever, here's to the rest of you, the ones that took the time to leave a four-star-or-above review for The Black Room books by the time that *this* book was published. Now, there's a lot of you (Woo!) and some of you even left a review for each one (that's the stuff!) so it's entirely possible that your name might appear here twice. I'm sure that you won't mind if that happens though, right? ☺ By the way, any name in capitals are written that way purely because that's how they were written on Amazon

So big thanks to:

BigDog, Katrina, R. Gaylor, Barbara "In Honor Of Books", Brennan Johnson, Angela B, drac, Kelli Tristan, Jrussell424, Jazzy J, Amazon Customer (there's a lot of you called Amazon Customer, so change your names so I can give you a proper shout out! :-D), Pooly4, Matthew Smith, Daniel J Smith, Neil Novita, Mark D, Amazon Customer "reading addict" (see? That kind of thing will do ☺) John Steele, Michelle Kennedy, venfam, John Hurell, Terry M, J. Plock "painter", Christopher Roberts, Big Mike, Matty G, Daniel, Jeff, Joann Gardner, Marta M. Rawlings "Seans Mom", Kelly Jobes, L. Spaiser, Jacque Ledoux, Cynthia P, Kris Hinson "kmommy", Rocky, Jean, Susan C, Swebby, infrequent, mjoanne, EPadgett, Az, Tina Marie, Rogue, Beam, Urbananchorite, KC "KC", Steve Mattingly, wjmouse, Forever Amber "Irene", Leslie Young "Fuzzette", Pamela Williams, BSM, Tessa, Alastair Norcross, MT, TEChan, Susan McReynolds, Andrew Hatton-Ward, Sean Welch, Jennifer DeFiore, Lori Pleasure, Gail, Patty M, Blanchepadgett, Kindle Customer, Gary Johnayak, steve wucherer, Laura Lee, Allison, Brain Johnson, Don, Susan Baldwin, ck, Joslyn, Lady Andrea R, Kathy Heil, Kristi L. Smiley, JEFF PLETZKE, Ryan, MT, drake andross, Beam, Rogue, Iacwaron (possibly Lacwaron?), Jean, C.S. Wolfe, Melissa Quimby, Xraygirl81, Roger P. Halligan, Cinderrific, Sandra Drozda, William B. White, Patti LaValley, RJWREADER, Kate Kaplan "katekap", Daisy, BoneyD, Guy Beauchamp, D. Maccauley "Don", Russell Jones, Scrooby1, ChezIsMe, futureboy "Ian", Stacey Lewis, Pauline R, Jonesy2208 "jonesyuk", Dolittle666, C.S,. Wolfe, PaulineHB, Karenr, Andy P, Chaz Bronte "CHAZZA", Maria Hale "Lucy", Emma Hopewell, Lyndsey, ossygobbin, Styubud, Brian J. Poole, Hazel Clifton, Ian Henry, simon lyon, Karl Smith, D. Medleycott, Christine Chapman "Chris", Dr. Andrew R. Glover, pandachris "pandachris", simon211175, Julian, o c ideson, Tracey, Bootaholic, Suzanne Foster, fergus67, Jonathan, P W R Wilcox, Mrs Jane McRobbie, infrequent, Deborah, Mr S. D. MacMaster, Victoria Willett, Mrs R K Lees, Jonnieboy, Allybally, Marmite, Tony Nichol, David, Kevin Gaskell, IJT, N. Hamblin "NH", Nicola c, Jam, Sue Phillips, Mrs Kindle, D. Plank, P. Fitt, john woodhouse, Trueblue "S. Row", Miss Frances Ashton, ALEX MARSDEN, Jacox, Celestine, Saul, Daniel Selby, P. Hughes "Pete H", Rebecca Sloane, Heather Art, Fingertrip, Shelly, Lesley Hattersley, Gordon Draper, Tia Claire 28, T. Selkirk, L. Miller, Chris

Stothard, Miss Baldwin, Steve Gatehouse, Bloomers, Scott Sanders, Mark Pad, J. D. Wittering "lovealbatross", I. D. Ball "fastbutdim", Joan Campbell, B. Hawthorn, Danny P, Sharon22, InFESTation, get28, R.C. Mansfield, Steve Pettifer, The Fro, Neil Harris, karlos the jackel, Amazon Customer "UrchinGirl", Barry Causier, SARooke, jim stirling, VAN, Maria Hale "Lucy", MRS K. DYE, Chazwin "Chazwin", M. Burgess "StumpyBunker", Andy P, Danny P, Katie, Huwbat, Silversmith, Odette, wayne, Celestine, Zoe Reed, Benno, David Lambourne, Mr Ken B, Piskiechick, david barton, Taratiger, Colin Kebbell, Aingeal, Rowie, lgmichael, Becca, Mounty, Paul, Miss Baldwin, tazaxel, and L. Miller.

You guys made all the difference.

Printed in Poland
by Amazon Fulfillment
Poland Sp. z o.o., Wrocław